KENNETH JOUL

LEGACY OF THE ANCIENTS

Published by

MELROSE BOOKS

An Imprint of Melrose Press Limited
St Thomas Place, Ely
Cambridgeshire
CB7 4GG, UK
www.melrosebooks.com

FIRST EDITION

Copyright © Kenneth Joul 2009

The Author asserts his moral right to
be identified as the author of this work

Cover designed by Jeremy Kay

ISBN: 978-1-906561-72-7

All rights reserved. No part of this publication may be reproduced,
stored in a retrieval system, or transmitted, in any form or by any means
electronic, mechanical, photocopying, recording or otherwise,
without the prior permission of the publishers.

This book is sold subject to the condition that it shall not,
by way of trade or otherwise, be lent, re-sold, hired out or
otherwise circulated without the publisher's prior consent
in any form of binding or cover other than that in which
it is published and without a similar condition including this
condition being imposed on the subsequent purchaser.

Printed and bound in Great Britain by:
CPI Antony Rowe, Chippenham, Wiltshire

CONTENTS

	PROLOGUE	V
CHAPTER 1	ICECAPADE	1
CHAPTER 2	HIJACK	25
CHAPTER 3	A NEW YORK MINUTE	39
CHAPTER 4	THE CAVE	56
CHAPTER 5	A MAN UNDER PRESSURE	73
CHAPTER 6	DEBRIEFING	84
CHAPTER 7	A WAITING GAME	98
CHAPTER 8	OLD ENEMIES	110
CHAPTER 9	AGAINST THE ODDS	128
CHAPTER 10	SURPRISES GALORE	144
CHAPTER 11	TRIBULATIONS AND PROBLEMS	160
CHAPTER 12	ESCAPE	176
CHAPTER 13	A CATCHING OF BREATH	190
CHAPTER 14	PARTY TIME	208
CHAPTER 15	RETURN TO THE LAIR	227
CHAPTER 16	WINNER TAKES ALL	243
CHAPTER 17	TERMINATION OF CONTRACT	261
CHAPTER 18	OVER SEA AND LAND	277
CHAPTER 19	ENDGAME	294
	EPILOGUE	309

PROLOGUE

IT WAS A TIME before the Ice Age when the Earth was still forming itself and the Ozone Layer had not been formed. That allowed the Sun to beat down unmercifully but it seemed to have no effect on the figure that made its way across the ground. The Being seemed to float over the ground, not bobbing around as a walker does. Its strange garb consisted of a smock from head to toe and the hood had a front piece that hid any features it might have had. When it stood tripods appeared instead of feet.

The strange creature carried what appeared to be an egg-shaped container but where the hands would have been were continuations of the arms of the smock. On its back there was a staff, the bottom of which was a large crystal. This was one of a number of such Beings who were there to prepare the Earth for its future. Each one had a specific sector of the Earth to work in.

Similar containers had already been deposited around the Earth's surface. Each one contained the seed of life and those already deposited had now exploded and showered the Earth with the makings of life as we have come to know it. The containers which were now being carried were to be buried, only to be released in the event of a cataclysm affecting the Earth, thereby allowing creation to begin all over again.

The Being studied the terrain and then moved to the side of a rocky escarpment. Setting the sphere safely on the ground, it took the staff from its back and stood with it, the crystal now uppermost, collecting the rays from the Sun. As it was charging, it changed colour from pink to deep red and eventually a pure white light. When this happened, the Being aimed it at the rock face and a vivid burst of energy issued from it, vaporising the rock. The staff was then recharged and time and time again the rock was pulverised into nothing. First a tunnel was created and then a cavern was made at the end of the tunnel. Satisfied that it sufficed, the Being then carried the container inside and set it on a pedestal of rock which had not been destroyed. This was the last cave that this Being was to prepare, and it knew it was the last of the line; the others had already concluded their parts and were now expiring gradually.

By the light of the staff, the Being inspected the work it had done. Knowing that its own end was approaching it went outside and once again recharged the staff. This time, at a point just before the tunnel became the cave, the pulse of energy was directed at the tunnel wall, which gave way and allowed molten lava to flow into the tunnel. The Earth was still forming itself from the molten core and the lava flowed down the tunnel and out. Eventually it stopped flowing and over the years hardened into a hillside. Inside the cave the power of the staff kept the lava from flowing that way and even solidified it. The cave now was sealed and would only be opened up should volcanic activity make it happen, but the Being had chosen well and it would take a massive eruption for the walls of that cave to be breached and allow the contents of the container to be released.

The Being then sat back against the pedestal with the staff leaning against it as well. Eventually the light from the staff was extinguished and, as the Being was an air breather, the oxygen over time became used up. The Being did not move at all throughout the entire period and remained in the same position throughout time as though ready to resurrect itself if need demanded.

Other Beings had created vast caverns that would eventually take up the water which would appear on Earth and try to destroy it. These were the Superiors and once that work was complete, they erected a building in which to live for the rest of their lives. They were there when dinosaurs roamed and all through the Ice Age, continuing into a time when civilisation started to form. Seeing their work was complete, they sealed themselves in part of their dwelling and over time became mummified.

The buildings, which were scattered all over the Earth, were pyramidal in shape, as that gave them a sturdiness for when the Earth vented its natural power against them. Over time, as civilisations formed, they saw these as structures of the Gods and as these civilisations spread, they took the design with them to create their own temples in similar style.

Fast forward now through the millennia to the late Twentieth Century, when the race to find new deposits of oil was at a frenzy. Vast tracts of the sea had been licensed by various countries to drilling companies following an appraisal by geologists and geophysicists. Some of their reports had not been well prepared or the necessary follow-through data collected and in these instances the licence fee was not as great as others.

One such questionable field was off the coast of South America where a few small-time businessmen from that particular area had clubbed together to get the licence and necessary equipment. These men were actually working on the rig itself to keep the costs down. All were hoping to make a large profit when the time came. However, the survey had shown an anomaly, the like of which could indicate a large reservoir of oil. One of those who had put money up front was Miguel Gonzales, although he had been a last-minute addition and only brought in because he had a helicopter. Early in his life, Miguel had sailed close to the wind with many of his money-making schemes. Some had worked but others had failed, losing other people money. A change of name and a change in appearance, as well as a move elsewhere, had kept him from having reprisals taken against him. His fall-back each time had been to implement his training as a motor mechanic. Eventually, by various means, he had made enough money to buy the old helicopter and, after learning how to fly, he had put it to good use ferrying anyone and everything to anywhere, no questions asked.

Miguel lifted the chopper off the platform and corkscrewed away to gain height. Middle-aged with bushy hair and a Zapata moustache, he always had a smile on his face that made his eyes twinkle. Being the owner of the helicopter he was flying, and in view of the impending tropical storm, he wanted to be on dry land when it hit the rig. His spare money, although earned a little on the shady side, was invested in the drilling rig from which he had just taken off.

The Westland Whirlwind helicopter had seen plenty of years' service but was still a workhorse all over the world. Miguel had rebuilt it when he had first got it and had adapted it for his own purpose. It had been the only way he could afford to get one but his mechanical aptitude had allowed it to happen.

The interior had been changed and it would now only take three passengers; four at a squeeze if three sat on the rear seat. The rear area had been left for cargo space, although on a couple of occasions, people had been carried there. Because of a need at times to carry long and sometimes bulky items, the braces above the wheels had been made into little platforms, which meant that when used in this mode, it had to be loaded and then unloaded with him already inside the cabin.

The paunch showed that he lived well, even though his wife had died a few years earlier. He lived on his own as his two children, for whom he had paid for a good education, were now earning their own way in the City and doing well. Just wait until the drilling rig delivered the goods and he could then think about retiring and really enjoying life. Ten percent of the rig was his and a further 10 percent was held by the people of his village; everyone would be in for the good time. Although the drill had now hit something really hard and had burnt out two bits, he still had a good feeling about it; after all, the Earth does not give up its valuables without a fight.

Just then his reverie was cut short as the headphones crackled into life and Jesus on the rig started shouting and praying. 'Miguel – oh holy mother of God –' and through the headphones Miguel could hear all sorts of creaking noises. 'Come back and get us, oh Jesus, the rig is collapsing. Quickly ...' and then all went quiet.

In his mind's eye he could visualise Jesus, always making the worst of any situation, dancing from foot to foot as he was wont to do in times of stress. All rigs tended to move at times and, although something must have caused him to worry, Miguel was in no doubt that he was over-dramatising as usual. The thought brought a smile to his face. Miguel turned the helicopter so he could see where he had taken off from and was just in time to see the rig disappear into the sea. It appeared as though a hole had surrounded it; one minute it was there and the next it had gone, just as though someone had pulled it through. He just stared, the smile wiped instantly from his face as his jaw dropped. Shock and then reaction to what a catastrophe to which he had been a spectator. Nothing remained, not even flotsam to mark its passing.

Quickly he radioed to shore, advising of the problem, and said he would wait until help arrived on the scene, but the authorities could not guarantee anything in view of the storm which was heading that way and other duties from the stretched Navy they had. He realised it was all futile anyway but felt, for the sake of his comrades on the rig, that he should persevere. Eventually, presumably to get him off the airwaves, he was told that orders had been given for a corvette to proceed to the scene but it would be hours before it could be there. No other ship acknowledged itself as being in the vicinity or available to help.

Twenty miles away a Russian submarine was lurking. A brand new model out on secret sea trials with the captain being a newly demoted lieutenant, following a debacle in which he had not, whilst in the secret service of his country, come up with the goods. The fact that he had barely escaped with his life counted for nothing. And here he was, cursing because the crew he had been given were all misfits; probably on the basis that if anything went wrong, none of them would be missed.

Hearing the distress call, Lieutenant Vassilev ordered the sub to make for the scene; not out of any sense of being the Good Samaritan but more because his curiosity, which had been an asset during his previous work, had been aroused. Things don't just disappear without any trace in the sea, there is always a reason and some telltale mark left if you only knew where to look, and this sub could all but see on the sea-bed.

The submarine was a different shape to normal. About half as wide again as a standard submarine, it was also slightly deeper and had extra length. No superstructure on top, but seated in a well at the back was a mini-sub capable of taking ten people and reaching a depth of 500 feet. To see above the sea it sent up a probe on an umbilical; this was like a five-foot long cylinder that floated upright and the electronics it contained made it possible to see all round and skywards. It could even send a microwave charge through the water to agitate the molecules. This acted like a drape over the submarine and distorted any sonar contact.

Miguel kept circling the area hoping to see either rescue or some sign that not all had perished on the rig, and eventually saw something moving under the water, something large and sleek and just about where the rig had been. He took the helicopter lower and was just in time to see a massive disturbance rising from the sea-bed where the rig had been and the sleek form started dancing all over the water and then the strange-shaped tail of a submarine came into view before there was a mighty suck and it disappeared. The waters parted as they cascaded into some unseen chasm and at the same time the surrounding air was also sucked down. Fighting the yawing helicopter as best he could, Miguel could save neither it nor himself from being drawn into the gaping hole and sucked down into oblivion. Even the massive horsepower of the engine was no match for the suction created by the parting of the waves.

On the submarine, it had been the same: one minute normal and then as the waters took control it became a maelstrom. As it went deeper there was an ominous scraping, but she held together, although losing the mini-sub that was mounted on the back. Eventually, when all inside felt they could not take any more punishment from being rolled around as if inside a tumble dryer, all became still, but where were they?

The professionalism of the crew soon had the submarine stabilised. Misfits they might have been but they knew their stuff. Most of the crew had been seated at their respective controls but the Captain had been standing and taken tumble after tumble, been knocked out and only came to when everything was under control.

Lieutenant Piotr Vassilev stood up shakily. His six-foot frame meant he had to stoop as he moved about the submarine. His colouring hinted at his Homeland, which was one of the southern states of the Russian Confederation. Physically fit, he had a temper that could suddenly come to the fore and some of the men had felt his fist when something had gone wrong and the culprit was found, even if it had been a genuine mistake. Clean-shaven but his hair hung down to his collar. This had been deliberately grown that long for camouflage for his previous activities as, in his youth, a fight in a temper had resulted in the loss of part of his ear; something which would have made identification easier for his opponents.

On the coastal marshes some hundred miles away, a father and son were out hunting; just as their forebears had done. Although they did not need to hunt food as there was plenty in the shops, it was always better caught by yourself and so they concentrated on their prey. Guns at the ready and not bows and arrows, but so hard was their concentration that neither heard the ominous rumbling sounds behind them until it was too late. A ten-foot square of marsh on a platform blew into the air at such an angle that the mud and debris on top slipped straight onto the hunters, covering them. The platform crashed back down and created a tidal wave of more mud that further overwhelmed them as they tried to recover from the first onslaught. When it had all subsided there was no sight of either of the two hunters or their quarry. Even the slab had disappeared under the mud. All that had been green was now a dirty brown.

Three hours after the incident the promised corvette arrived on the scene but could find no telltale signs. After circling a couple of times, it headed back for quieter waters to ride out the storm which could be seen on the horizon with the naked eye from the bridge. It took three days before the storm blew itself out. Then all priority work had to be taken with clearing up the aftermath on the coast and giving help to those in need who had lost everything. This had been the one-in-a-hundred-years storm and it had wreaked havoc along 500 miles of coastline. When anyone eventually started to ask about the rig and its crew, their families were told, in the absence of any other information and the Mayday forgotten about, that they had been lost in the storm. The coastal marshes also took the brunt of the storm and the family of the hunters thought that was what had taken them. All the water deposited by the storm had obliterated any evidence of the incident there.

If the authorities had only gone back to look and observed the seabed, they would have seen that for a mile around it had been cleared of everything, and all sea life for a further two miles had been disturbed.

They might even have caught sight of a dark shape slinking away. Whilst the storm had raged above them, the crew had made things shipshape and taken a decision. Not knowing where they were, divers had been sent out to assess the damage, which was negligible, and find the way out. In doing so they had found some other surprising information.

At the end of that year there was an unaccountable scientific blip. Scientists measuring the rate of glacier melt were adamant that the annual rate was as for previous years, but sea levels did not rise. In fact there was an overall drop of one millimetre.

It was the age-old problem of scientists in different fields not talking to each other. When the rig disappeared, a couple of seismic recording stations registered an insignificant tremor but, because it was from an area of known oil exploration, it was dismissed as of no particular value.

Because of the storm, the insurers of the rig and helicopter did not examine things further and paid out without a murmur. If all the relative agencies had collaborated with their information, things might have been different in the future.

CHAPTER 1
ICECAPADE

MATT WESTON WOKE WITH a start at hearing his name; was it part of his dream or was someone calling him?

'Westie, Westie …' and as he put on the light he could see Ray's face peering round the door. A face that looked upside down, as it was round with a full set of whiskers but no hair on top.

'Sorry to wake you but your Boss has been on the comlink wanting to speak with you urgently. I told him you had been on the ice and under the snow for 36 hours but all he said was that he did not care if you were still encased in a block of ice, you had to call him back post haste.'

'OK Ray. If he is that het up it means the shit has really hit the fan somewhere. I'll get back to him as soon as I come round.' As he did so he wondered how the door came to be open. Had he not secured it last night?

Sitting up in bed he recalled the dream – or was it a nightmare? No, it was reliving the happening of years before when, as a Marine, he had been sent to meet an informer in one of the Arab States. Just before the man had arrived, someone else had appeared on the scene. This was a Russian – oh what was his name? – who had come on the same mission. A man had walked into the room and as both had been expecting someone, the actions of the man caught both unawares. It should not have; the sight of each other should have given the clue to a set-up. Instinct took over as the man unbuttoned his coat and revealed he was a human bomb. Matt had dived backwards, catching sight of the Russian leaping to one side when the man blew himself up. Matt had come to at the sound of voices calling his name as his colleagues came to get him; of the Russian there was no sign. Matt had to be carried out, and back at the field hospital it had been necessary to remove his leg from just above the knee.

As he slid out of bed he reached for his prosthetic but it was not where he had left it. It should have been leant up at the side of the bed but it was lying on the floor. Had he been so restless in his sleep and knocked it? Balancing himself on the bed with one arm, he reached with the other and picked it up. Once sat up again, he fitted the false leg as naturally as anyone; after a little over 10 years he had got used to it and it was now just a part of him, becoming part of his daily ritual, just like cleaning his teeth.

The loss of a leg, of course, meant his career as a Marine was ended but as one door closed, another opened. Recuperating back in England and whilst having his first prosthetic made to fit, he had met Wilberforce. Sexton Wilberforce was his full name but he only ever answered to his surname. He had been visiting a friend at the same establishment where Matt was recuperating. Two days after the fitting of his prosthetic, Matt was a little too adventurous and went on rough ground where he fell. Unable to move as the false leg had come away from him, he was seen by Wilberforce who came to his rescue.

A former Major in the Army he had been made a staff officer and then, on his retirement, put in charge of a new organisation, the B-GEE. This was the British Government Exploration Executive, which coordinated the various explorations being undertaken by the British and their friends, whether Government money was involved or not. It had started out to ensure that there was no overlap by explorers or scientists, especially where Government funds were involved, but had expanded its remit as necessary over the years. Now somewhat overseen by the EU, Wilberforce had managed to retain a fair amount of autonomy; sometimes even hiring out Matt to other countries.

This was where Matt had come in. Wilberforce and he had talked about their respective military careers and Wilberforce had recognised his potential. As a non-active serviceman he had been able to go to places that service personnel would not be able to access. The prosthetic always acted as an indicator that he was non-combatant until the opposition realised their mistake too late.

Something inexplicable had happened on one jungle expedition and there was no-one on the staff with any expertise. As a one-off Matt had been invited to go on a fee basis. Success in that had meant him being on call for other problems and within a year he was on the books as a trouble-shooter. Trained in many aspects as a Marine and able to look after himself, he had proved invaluable, especially where expeditions were undertaken in areas of some instability. If he went at the beginning because problems were expected it had been as an administrator but if problems had been encountered after the expedition had begun, it was as a trouble-shooter that he had been sent, although he was still classed as an administrator.

Refreshed after a wash but still feeling tired, he went to the communications bay and contacted HQ. 'Hi Boss, what's the problem?' was his opening comment as Wilberforce came on. 'You know I have not finished here yet.'

'If you have not found them by now, I think we can consider that they are dead. No-one could stay out in that cold for so long and still be alive. Remember they went missing three days before you were sent out there. Anyway we have got problems on the Greenland scientific site. I'll brief you when you arrive here but in the meantime a plane is being diverted to pick you up mid-afternoon. That is your time.'

'No doubt the pilot will be in touch before he arrives, and remember light fails here about teatime at present.'

'Just get your things and be ready. What I will add is that I feel your old skills may really be required this time.'

A frisson of anticipation ran through Matt at that statement as Wilberforce's predictions were usually spot on. 'Looking forward to meeting you again and I will pick up my equipment when I get there.'

For this current job there had been no need to come prepared for action. Two members of the expedition had gone missing whilst out on a scientific trip, going to check on equipment they had set up some days earlier that had malfunctioned. At that time they had said that they had seen a submarine go under the ice shelf but everyone knew that the ice was only about 200 feet wide from the cliffs that went down into the sea and their sightings had been ridiculed. His brief had been to find them or at least rule out foul play.

Their equipment had been still in place and made to work again by others from the base who had gone out searching. There had been no sight of the two men anywhere in the area following the initial search, nor had Matt found any trace of them when he had subsequently gone investigating. The way was straightforward and there was no bad weather to cause them a problem, but they had disappeared without trace. Finding no evidence of foul play, he had then been informed that a snow storm was heading his way and he should return as quickly as possible. On the way he had been trapped in an avalanche. No-one could understand why it had happened when he told them on his return. There had not been recent heavy snow and it was not the thawing season.

His reflexes had saved him from being buried too deep, as he had tried to surf it when it hit him. When all became still he could feel himself suffocating but it had been an easy job to create a hole to the surface. Unfortunately, by the time he had started to dig himself out, the snow storm had hit and he was forced to stay holed up for a good 24 hours.

The snow around him kept him warm although occasionally he had to uncover his breath hole. Sucking on the snow to make sure he did not dehydrate, and with a couple of Mars Bars that he had taken along, he kept quite alright and when it blew out he was able to make his own way back to the Centre just as they were sending out a search party.

Antarctica, the British Survey Station; less than three days here and he was now being sent to another cold area. Was it his destiny to be doomed to be working in cold climates for the rest of his days? The last four had been and this was the second he had been pulled from before the conclusion of his investigations. He pulled up short from his reverie as he remembered that the previous dozen or so had been more affable. One had to take the rough with the smooth but it was still, nevertheless, annoying not to be able to clear matters up before being given another job.

How long was it now since he had been in England for any length of time? Four, no five months. He must surely be due some R&R now. A good job he had no permanent accommodation there. All his worldly goods were in storage at HQ, and when in England, he lived out of hotels, usually the remote quiet ones after a few days in London and using a hire car. He really could be classed as being of no fixed abode with only distant but unknown cousins as his living relatives. As an only child with mother and father killed in a car crash whilst he had been on active service, he had come home to find them cremated and only their ashes to deal with.

His parents had been pacifists, and on his joining the Armed Forces had distanced themselves from him, never really welcoming him back home. Maybe if they had he would not have been so polarised into becoming a Marine; a killing machine. That had estranged them even more.

The Service had always been like a family and he had fitted in from the first day there. It was there to welcome him back from home leave and eventually he had not bothered to go back home. Instead he had immersed himself in the work and had become insular. He had reached the rank of Lieutenant and, because of his ability to work alone, had been utilised for covert operations. He found he could work better alone, not having to worry about others and responsible only for his own actions.

Towards the end, though, his parents had been in touch by letter and eventually they had spoken over the phone but their untimely death had curtailed the rapprochement. His one regret was that he had not been able to get together with them before the accident.

He had eaten well on his return but was feeling hungry again and went to the canteen to see if breakfast was still on offer. He was too late but he found a burger meal and warmed it up in the microwave. Lunches were always on the basis of grab what you can. McPherson, one of the missing men, had been the cook but could be used as a helper elsewhere in his free time and that had been what he had been doing when he disappeared. Now the job was shared. One of the scientists came from a catering family and had taken responsibility for the evening meal. Another had assumed responsibility for making sure everyone started the day with a good breakfast.

The hall was L-shaped with entry being into the dining area from the accommodation corridor. At the far end was the kitchen; fully equipped for what was such a remote outpost although they had to remember to order gas for every drop. The leg off was the lounge, separated by bookcases and other storage cupboards. Opposite the Mess Hall was the entrance, comprising inner door, vestibule and outer door. On either side of the vestibule, but with access from the accommodation corridor, were the staff cabins. On the other side of the corridor, to the left of the Mess Hall, were the storerooms, both personal and for equipment. On the right were the offices and laboratories as well as the communication centre. All in all it was one complete blockhouse.

He was alone; everyone must be out on their respective duties, so he went back to his room to pack. Entering he could swear someone had been in but no-one was there. Nothing tangible but there was a sense of someone. He had to unlock it to get in but, in his haste to contact his Boss, he knew he had left it unlocked. Had someone just been checking then closed it or had there been an intruder? Was he just jumping at shadows?

The anticipation of action, even though it was still some time in the future, had heightened his senses. Why would anyone want to go into his room when he was not there? A question to keep in mind for the near future at least. Was he jumping at shadows or had his brain become attuned to something more sinister?

Everyone arrived back for lunch except Ray Fielder, the one who had woken him and who had been out checking the equipment left by the two men who had disappeared. As he had been in all morning and was packed, Matt set off to check and found him lying just off the track where his footprints led, an arm twisted horribly under him. The pain of the dislocation must have sent him unconscious and the cold was now starting to eat into his body. The days here were getting shorter but 24-hour darkness had not yet arrived. It had been unseasonably colder than usual, so the snow storm which Matt had been caught in had been unusual for the time of year. Anyone venturing outside needed to wear their true winter layering of clothes.

Matt had arrived just before hypothermia had got to him. He had a sense of something being wrong but could not see what it was, being too preoccupied with getting him back. Carried back, still out cold, it was easy to set the dislocated shoulder, as that was all it was, before he came round. He still needed proper treatment though, not available at the Centre, and before he came round it had been decided that he would take Matt's place on the plane out.

The communications system went down that afternoon; atmospherics surrounding the Centre were thought to make that happen regularly at this time of day and so no-one was bothered if communication was lost as nightfall would bring it back up again. Matt had come in via the American Base 50 miles away and knew the way back there, following the clearly defined coast path. He was also aware that every other day they had a plane come in and he decided to get there using one of the snowmobiles, but by the time he was ready to set off the plane arrived.

The adapted Hercules, wearing the insignia of the New Zealand Air Force, landed on its skids on the compacted snow runway, with billowing clouds of snow behind it blown into the air by the propellers. Its ability to operate on short runways made it ideal for this purpose but it had been given extra fuel capacity so that it could make the round trip from its base on South Island to the Antarctic and back.

Antarctica only had two resources for anyone staying there: fish and ice for water. Everything else had to be brought in: fuel, food and equipment. Although some of the larger equipment had to be brought in by sea when conditions allowed, the rest had to be airlifted in and twice a week the plane did the run, but to different establishments each time.

It gave the New Zealand Air Force a nice little earner and the Hercules had been specifically adapted for this particular job. The front of its hold had been converted into a cabin for passengers; not very salubrious but sufficient for its purpose and comfortable enough for the long journey. The rear, still with ramp, was for cargo.

Carstairs, tall and lanky, and Fairfax, short and rotund, were pilots of equal seniority but Carstairs, who flew the plane more often, took it upon himself to be in charge. The two rarely flew together as they were always bickering; today's subject was the various merits of differing New Zealand Rugby Teams. They were barred from flying operational duties together as the other crew members at such times all complained about the arguing and felt that neither was in charge of the situation.

Today's was a standard non-operational flight and circumstances had brought them together again, as happened probably once every three months. This was an unscheduled stop, the British Base not being part of today's run, and was putting extra miles and time on the journey. They wanted to be on their way fast and so accepted the replacement passenger without demur and hurriedly left in another cloud of snow.

Twenty minutes later they landed again for their last scheduled stop of the day. Three quarters of an hour to unload stores and load waste and empties and they were on their way again.

As it was a non-operational flight, a lot of the technical gadgetry was not in use. If it had been, when they were 50 miles out over the sea, there would have been a warning of an incoming missile. As it was, a passenger first saw it approaching, but the shock just froze the warning in his throat. When eventually he did scream, it was too late and the missile smashed into the port engine nearest the fuselage.

The explosion caused the wing to sheer off and debris to smash into the side of the fuselage, opening it up to wind and freezing temperatures. Some passengers died instantly, others were wounded and miraculously some were unscathed. Not that it mattered as the wind and freezing air rendered them unconscious. At least none were aware of their demise.

In the cockpit the bickering stopped with the explosion. If they had not been otherwise occupied, they might have seen the missile early enough to take evasive action. As it was, pieces of the shattered engine came forward and took out Carstairs, who was in the pilot's seat at that side. Fairfax, on the other side, could not see what had happened but knew something serious had occurred as the plane dipped to starboard and literally fell out of the sky. With no great altitude under its wings, there was no time to send out a Mayday call before it hit the water. With gaping holes it filled almost immediately with water and sank.

There were no survivors to witness the sudden appearance of a long cylinder on the surface. If there had been they would not have been able to see the electronics inside scan the area for life. Satisfied that no-one had survived, the cylinder then disappeared beneath the waves. All that remained was a little flotsam from the crashed plane.

Having seen the plane depart, and with another meal under his belt, Matt set off in the dark for the American Base. He left it for those remaining at Base to notify the change of arrangements when communications came back on. Travelling light without his gear as it was more comfortable on the snowmobile, he took things rather leisurely. His gear would be sent out by the next plane and he would be able to pick up more of his stuff at HQ. Just to make sure he did not stray was the reason for his slow pace. His travel to the British Base had been in daylight but now it was night and he was doing it in reverse.

The moon was nearly full now and over the sea, reflecting in ever changing patterns from the waves. A few clouds were floating and these made darker patches on the sea. Bathed as it was in moonlight, the landscape Matt was travelling through took on an ethereal look, although his way was clearly visible.

About half-way there, passing along the side of a cliff about 500 feet above the level of the sea, he caught sight of something different out at sea. Just another dark shape that seemed solid. As he turned to look more closely there was a quick flash from the shadow. His mind went back years; training and instinct took over. He had seen the flash of a rocket launched in the dark before and threw himself off backwards, letting the snowmobile continue. Landing on his feet but having to roll onto his back because the false leg would not allow him to get his balance meant that he was on the ground when the rocket struck the snowmobile.

Kenneth Joul

He wasn't ready for the blast, and the shockwave propelled him over the edge of the track and he started sliding down a gully head-first. A rough ride, and try as he might with his good leg to brake his momentum it was futile as lumps in the ice just bounced his leg into the air. His body was jarred from side to side but luckily he did not hit his head on anything. Eventually the slope levelled out somewhat, enabling him to slow his momentum and at the same time turn so that he was moving sideways.

His intention was to get himself travelling feet-first but there was not enough space or time and he shot off the edge sideways. He had no time to think about what to do as the drop was only about seven feet, so he landed on his back with a thump and the wind was knocked out of him. Five minutes to get his breath back and gather his senses and he was on all fours, ready to stand, when he heard voices in a language he had heard before but had to take his mind back before he realised it was Russian. What in hell were the Russians doing shooting at him, as he was sure they had something to do with the attack, or otherwise why were they there?

Peering over the top of the gully he could see there were three of them having come in an inflatable – and there out to sea he could see the silhouette of a strange-looking craft low in the water. All three were armed and two left to climb up to the mangled remains of the snowmobile. That could only mean they were going to ensure he was dead. Time to go on the offensive, but what with? The weather clothing meant that he could not get at the only weapon he had – the knife in his prosthetic.

The lie of the land was such that the way up was at the far side of the little inlet in which they had arrived, so the one left was watching his comrades as they climbed, with his back to Matt. Making two snowballs, Matt crept quietly forward, although the other man was whistling tunelessly to himself and he would not have heard anything. He was going to hurl the snowballs at the man if he turned but got close up without him turning. Just to keep his attention in front, Matt quickly threw the two snowballs so that they fell in the direction the man was watching and as his attention was drawn to the sound of them landing, he pounced.

Both went down but Matt had the upper hand that surprise gave, and with an arm around the man's neck he kept pulling tighter and tighter. If the others had looked back they would have seen nothing as the edge of the inlet hid them from sight. Eventually, after Matt had exerted all the pressure he could, the other man went limp but Matt continued his stranglehold until he was sure the man was dead. Before standing up he frisked the body, hoping to find an armoury but the only armament was the rifle, which he took before dragging the man to the water's edge and pushing him in.

When the other two returned in an agitated state, jabbering in their own language, Matt was tunelessly whistling and appearing to tend to the inflatable ready for departure. Looking out of the corner of his eye, Matt waited until they were in striking distance and whirled, straightening his body as he did so, with the rifle outstretched. The leading man took the full force at the side of his head and dropped like a log. It showed that neither were combat personnel as the other just stood there, allowing Matt to alter his stance to hit him in the stomach with the rifle butt and lay him out cold with the cracking head blow that followed.

Looking out to sea he could barely see the top of the vessel that was waiting, and he hoped that no-one there had seen the recent altercation. Sitting the two recumbent figures in the inflatable he pushed off and jumped in himself. He had no idea of what he was going to do but a cold anger was coursing through him. Someone was going to pay for the attack, which had obviously emanated from whatever lay out there, whether he was able to get any answers to his myriad of questions; all of which were centred on the word 'why?'. He knew not but was going to try.

Gunning the engine so that it was impossible for anyone on the vessel to communicate with him, he was able to get close to and see it was a submarine, the like of which he had never seen before. Long and wide but with no sail, and at the back of the deck was a recess which looked as though something should be housed there. Half a dozen people were scattered about the deck, and when he was sure his ruse should be detected, he raised the rifle and let loose an automatic volley, but deliberately hitting nobody. There were no raised hatches visible and he wanted to see where they were. Two of those on deck dived one way, three others went another and the last man went different again, and that was the one nearest to him. Gunning the engine, he was at the side when it started to dive but he jumped out on deck and saw the hatch nearly closing hydraulically from the side. Jamming the rifle he was holding into the gap, he just had time to dive back into the inflatable before the sub disappeared under the water.

His hope had been that the act of keeping the hatch open would cause the sub to stay on the surface, even if he did not know what he was going to do if it had. However, it kept on going down, and thinking that there must be some secondary safety device that stopped water entering, he turned the boat shorewards but was stopped short.

When jumping onto the sub, he had held onto the rope from the inflatable whilst jamming the hatch open but as he jumped back it wrapped round something on the sub's deck. Matt was not aware as the inflatable started to pull away, having dropped the lanyard in the bottom. He soon realised something was wrong when the little boat was whipped round; one second he had been facing away and the next he was nose-on to the sub as it started to sink below the surface.

Panic – and then he saw the taut rope and tried to waggle it free; to no avail. He pulled on the rope and moved nearer the sub, which was getting lower in the water every second and waggled it again. A sudden swish by the sub took it out of his hand but must have released it from the tangle as the nose of the inflatable, which had been almost under the water, bounced up, throwing him off balance.

Recovering and revving the engine, he moved quickly away from the frothing water and at a safe distance stopped to heave the two still-recumbent figures over the side along with one of the other rifles he had accumulated. The other he retained along with the magazine from the one he had thrown. He had no way of knowing if they were dead or alive but did not care. It was like the old days; an injured man could cause problems and he did not want to be leaving evidence around of his recent activity.

As he started to leave the scene, the sea behind him suddenly gave a heave and like a geyser spouted into the air. When it settled there was a patch of oil and some bits of debris to mark the submarine's watery grave. 'Whoops,' he thought aloud, and shaking his head at what he had seen, turned away from the inlet and sailed along the coast, coming ashore just short of the British Base, from which a well-worn path came down to where he jumped out of the inflatable and sent it back out to sea with the motor running.

On the walk up his mind was reeling and the conclusion he came to was that someone there had set him up or at least told others where to find him. Carrying the rifle he had taken at the ready, he walked into the Centre and straight to the Mess Hall where he knew everyone would be, in the lounge part. They all turned to stare as he entered and he really got their attention when he fired a burst from the gun into the floor.

'Some bastard here has just tried to get me killed and when I find out who, they are dead too.'

'But …' someone tried to say but Matt was having none of it as he was wound up and angry.

'I have just killed three people out there,' he continued, 'and committed God knows how many others to a watery grave. So one more will make no difference.'

'Hang on,' someone said as Matt caught his breath, 'all contact was lost with the plane you were supposed to be on as well.'

That really stopped Matt short in his tirade. 'You mean to say this could have been a second attempt on my life? If so, and that plane is lost with all those on board, then it is all part and parcel of some conspiracy against me. For what reason I know not but it makes me feel better about those who have recently departed this world at my hand.'

'It could have been an accident.'

'I somehow don't think so. Someone appears to be out to get me by hook or by crook.'

'We have all been here since you left, apart from when some of us were in the com centre advising what had gone on. No-one was ever there alone. Maybe they have been monitoring the calls.' This from Bill

Morgan, the Senior Scientist at the Base.

'Possible, I will admit, but I still have a gut feeling that someone on the inside here has been telling the opposition, whoever they are, about my movements.' He deliberately did not mention anything about the Russians. 'I intend to go through here with a fine tooth comb before I leave and prove my point.'

'You can't go through our private stuff just on a whim,' came from the room.

'Can't I? Just watch; this gun gives me all the authority I want. And, if I find out I am right, I will be judge, jury and executioner. However, just to show how much I understand your feelings, I will take Ray's room first as he is not here to object.'

'I feel I should object on his behalf,' countered Bill.

'Objection overruled,' and Matt waved the gun around.

With that Matt left the room but went first to his own quarters, where he took off his weatherproofs and left the gun after removing the magazine, emptying it and putting it back in place. He wanted to see if anyone still here was against him, even though he still had no knowledge of who or why. On then to Ray's room where Bill was waiting for him.

A thorough search revealed nothing and Bill had to comment; something on the lines of 'I told you so'. Going back out, something troubled him, something he had just seen that was not quite right but he could not put his finger on it. Pausing at the door he looked back in but the point of disquiet remained intangible.

Going back in he carried out the search again but more methodically; again with the same result. This room, like all the other cabins, contained a bed, a wardrobe, and a chest of drawers, the top of which had a slide-out section to form a writing desk. Each room had a secure storage locker elsewhere and he knew he would have to force that open next. However, the locker room was open to all, and anyone making a surreptitious call might have been compromised. 'Now what's bugging you?' asked Bill but got no response.

He could feel it in his water that the answer lay in this room. Something that Ray had said or done, but what? Matt sat on the chair, staring about the room, hoping for inspiration, and when it came it was from a different quarter altogether. One of the other scientists popped his head around the door and said, 'I don't know what you are looking for but I know you are interested in strange things. We are getting some interference on the com link. Sounds like a tick-tick, but in the same way as a telephone ring. Tick-tick, pause, tick-tick.' A light suddenly went on in Matt's head and he reached for the bedside clock. He knew then what it was that had eluded him. There had been the tick-tock but the time had stayed the same. There was the sound tick-tick, pause, tick-tick. Examining it he realised it was a transmitter and opened it up to listen. A voice shouted in his ear: 'What is happening up there, do you know?' Although spoken in English, the intonation of the voice was the same as he had heard earlier that night. Russian.

'This is Pegleg.' A joking name that had been attached to him following the fitting of his prosthetic and had stuck as his call sign. The spluttering at the other end told him he was known, and then quite casually he added, 'I think one of your submarines is missing. How careless of me.' But the person at the other end did not hear the last part as a torrent of abuse in Russian ensued. 'If you are going to shout at me like that I refuse to talk to you any longer, but you should be aware your man on the inside went down with the plane,' and with that he switched off the receiver.

Suddenly a number of points fell into place. Ray must have had a key to his room and that was why his head had been round the door. Was it only that morning? What a lot had happened in the intervening period. When he had found him in the snow the tracks had been away from Base but they should have been on the way back from the equipment he was supposed to be checking. If he had fallen at the time he was going to the equipment, he would have been dead from hypothermia by the time Matt had found him. He must therefore have been leaving Base later. Matt knew then that his feeling of someone having been in his room earlier had been correct. He also realised that Ray had been interrogating him after he had returned from being entombed in the avalanche and talking with him afterwards He seemed to know more about Matt than he should have. Because Matt had still been recovering from his ordeal, he had not picked up on it at that time.

Matt just sat there. In his own mind he had no doubt that the plane on which he was supposed to be leaving had somehow been downed, no doubt by the submarine. That meant that they had killed their own mole on the station.

Bill could do nothing but stare at Matt, allowing the words he had just overheard, and the Russian rant he had also been able to hear, to sink in before asking, 'Why?'

'That is something I have been asking myself for some time now. No answers though. I know my job has caused problems for people in the past but I was not aware that I had left any loose ends to catch up with me, especially Russian.'

'Do you think Ray knew there would be attempts on your life?'

'Not really. If he had, why did he go out on the plane with no fuss? If he had an inkling, he must have thought that only I would be targeted and not that they would take out a whole plane.'

Back in the canteen with the rest of the people from the Base, Bill put them in the picture before Matt asked, 'Has anyone any idea why the Russians would be poking their noses into our affairs?'

Puzzled looks all round and then a voice said, 'Why? We work very closely with the scientists at the Russian Base here in Antarctica. Often we visit each other and have never encountered any animosity or the like.'

Matt did not see who had spoken. It was as though he was in two places at the same time: one taking in the immediate conversations and the other thinking on events from his past that could have led him to being a target.

'Mmm …' from Matt and then after a pause he commented, 'We know that two men have disappeared; maybe they saw something they should not have,' and then continued: 'Before I came, had there been any other mishaps? Anything, however small, that might have seemed inconsequential at the time.'

'Well, our equipment out there has been upset a couple of times without any apparent reason.' From the person who had spoken before.

'And you encountered a strange avalanche.' From another.

'That's all in the northwest sector isn't it?' And receiving confirmation he continued: 'Any strange readings from the equipment in that area?'

'Funny you should ask. On a couple of occasions the telemetry went off the mark,' commented Bob.

'So something could be taking place under the ice.' Matt was thinking out loud. 'Something that someone did not want anyone to find out about.'

'I can follow your line of thought but the ice here is only 100 feet thick and then it becomes rock. There is only about 200 foot of ice stretching out into the sea now. A lot of the ice shelf has gone. That is why this Base is set inland a little as previous ones have had to be abandoned to float away and never be seen again.'

More conundrums, he thought as he walked off to the com link to contact his Boss, adding as he left, not really having heard the last statement: 'Is that why the communications system goes out at the same time each day? Work time, let's say, when any activity might have been picked up on the equipment. Have to see if it continues now there is a different game plan in play.' As he went along, a few lines from a song by Status Quo came to mind:

> The water's getting deep and I can't swim
>
> For its dirty, dirty water.

The water, or at least the happenings, was getting murky and some people were starting to act real dirty. Also he felt as though he was getting in deep or possibly out of his depth as he had no idea of what was going on.

Immediate contact once he got to the communications room, and Matt opened with, 'Hi Boss. Glad I have been able to catch you.' He must have been in the office as there were no clicks as the communication was re-routed.

Before making contact he had wondered what the time was in London, not that it mattered to Wilberforce. He had his own bachelor quarters behind the office and could be contacted at all times. He always went out to lunch at the same place and his evening meal was at another, but the communication system could be put through to his mobile.

'Why are you still at the Base? You should be with the Americans right now; they are ready to send out a search party.'

'Cancel that. All they will find are the remains of the snowmobile scattered no doubt over a wide area.'

'What are you on about?'

'About someone attempting to kill me with an RPG …'

'What are you talking about?' came the interruption. 'Rocket Propelled Grenades?'

'That's right. Launched from a Russian submarine out at sea,' Matt continued before he could be interrupted. 'They are now regretting it as I have sunk it and killed three of their men who came to check I was dead.'

'What the bloody hell is going on down there? You are aware we lost the plane on which you were supposed to be coming out.'

'Oh yes. Looks as though two attempts were made on my life and I am not a happy bunny as I don't know why. Have you any ideas?'

'If we had known anything we would have warned you. Russian you say?'

'That's what they were speaking and likewise when I spoke to them on the phone.'

'You what? This is getting crazier by the minute. We need to get you out fast and have a proper debriefing before anything else happens.'

'Think I am safe for the moment anyway. I don't think they have any more resources to throw at me, although I am on my guard.'

'Anything else I should know about?'

'Only that Ray Fielder was their mole on the inside, but as he was obliterated with the plane we have no way of getting any answers there.'

'Leave it with me to arrange something. Just stay by the com link ready for me coming back to you.'

The line went dead and Matt turned, knowing someone was there, to find Bill Morgan with the discarded rifle held purposefully in his hand.

Long grey hair hung down the side of a round face on which there was a full set of whiskers. It was difficult to tell where moustache, beard or hair either began or ended and with his size, around six foot and nearly the same around his chest, he looked like a great cuddly bear. Someone had said that when he went home he shaved it all off but let it grow back again straight away so that he was hirsute again when he got back to Base. Rimless spectacles sat on a large nose which, because of the moustache, did not look as big as it really was.

'You really should be more careful with your equipment, especially if there is a chance that someone is out to get you as you said.' And with that he tossed the gun to him.

Matt smiled and relaxed, as he had tensed, ready to go on the offensive, saying nothing about the empty magazine but commenting, 'I have no idea what is going on, but I have been having a dream of late that must be linked to it. I know that sounds crazy but this thing is getting crazier by the minute anyhow.'

'I wish I could help but I am as confused as you. None of the pieces of the puzzle seem to fit together. Some element is missing. Do you recall anything else happening that might seem insignificant or untoward?'

'No. I agree it is the small things, the detail, that can give answers but nothing comes to mind at present.'

'What put you onto Ray?'

'Nothing originally but when I got into his room I seemed to start concentrating on him and certain inconsistencies started to come together.'

'Is that why you had to go back in after finding nothing the first time?'

'Yep. The more I started thinking about him, the more I realised he had been watching and questioning me.'

'Well at least that is one part of the puzzle. However, you must be tired after all you have done today and not getting enough sleep after your sojourn under the snow. Perhaps when you are rested your brain might be better able to cope with it.'

'Tired and bruised, I will agree, and on a heightened state of alert which can push other points into the background. Something might come to me when I have slept.'

Bill had nothing to add, so left him to await the call, which was not long.

Still wondering about the difference in time zones, for no better reason than thinking of something else, he wondered if anyone else was in the office. Wilberforce had a full-time secretary and two part-time administrators. The latter would increase their hours to cover each other's holidays and any absence by the secretary. Originally there had been seven full-timers, including himself, but with the EU takeover the staffing needs had been reduced.

When the Boss came back on line he said, 'I have managed to pull a few strings with the Americans, although for once they acquiesced rather easily. Something up there as well, I would say. Anyway a chopper will be calling for you mid-morning tomorrow. It is coming in from an aircraft carrier they have in the area and will take you back there to get a plane for your onward journey, but that for now has not been sorted.'

'OK. Should be seeing you within a couple of days then. Over and out.'

After the bouncing he had received in the fall and the strenuous activity of the last few hours, Matt went off to have a hot shower to ease his aches and pains, but the speed of the comeback by the Boss with answers worried him: less than ten minutes and things were in place. What was Wilberforce up to? Working hand in hand with the Americans? Unusual if that was the case as he tended to prefer them at arm's length. Another disjointed piece of the puzzle.

At five foot eight he looked stocky but that was all muscle as he kept reasonably fit, exercising whenever he could. There were a number of scars on his body, reminders of various actions he had been involved in; some were more hideous than others but all could be hidden under normal clothing. In his late forties, he had the start of a paunch but that was not surprising as the prosthetic meant he could not exercise as thoroughly as he might have wished.

For at least two years he had been promised an all-singing, all-dancing new prosthetic but there had never been the time to go and have it made up and fixed. This one happened to be the second and gave him a certain amount of movement. The leg bent at the knee but had a stop at a certain point when it could spring him back upright. The ankle was partly articulated, which allowed him to move reasonably fast, if somewhat ungainly. The unusual aspect of the leg was the knife moulded into the leg itself, which could be sprung out by a button on the knee joint.

No tattoos, as that was one thing he had resisted as a Marine. Since leaving the Service he had allowed his hair, which was turning grey in places, to grow, but only to his ears. He had grown it longer and trendy at one time but had missed a noise that had nearly been the end of him, which made him get it cut. The face was round and there appeared to be a smile on it but the eyes were hard, and more so now he was in action again.

After the shower he had a large rum and a good night's sleep, but by morning still no answers would come to him. Russians after him; Americans being helpful; what did it all mean?

The next morning, before the helicopter arrived and after having a shave, another shower and breakfast, Matt disappeared, telling everyone on the Base to carry on as normal and not report his absence. He was not taking any chances and wanted to be on the ground of his choosing if anything else was going to happen. As the helicopter with full American markings, which looked like those used by the US Coastguard that he had seen on films, came in to land, Matt sprinted from his hiding place and before the skids had really touched down he had the rear compartment door open and was inside with the rifle, now holding a full magazine, pointing at the pilot and co-pilot.

'Fly!' he commanded, and when there was a delay the muzzle of the gun appeared between them. 'Just get this thing off the ground!' which they did.

'What the goddamn hell is going on?' asked the co-pilot. 'We were supposed to pick up someone called Pegleg.'

'That's me. You have the right passenger. Just make sure you get me safely to the carrier.' But he wondered why there had been the use of his callsign and not his proper name.

'You British sure have a way of welcoming people.'

'So would you if two attempts had already been made on your life and no reason known.'

The inflexion in his voice ensured the pilot and co-pilot stayed silent for the rest of the way. Throughout the journey of about an hour and half, Matt remained alert for anything untoward and only started to relax when he saw the carrier in the distance. The happenings of the past couple of days kept turning round and round in his head, but even looking further back into his past there was nothing that made sense. The dream had to be a clue, but what?

He had never been on an aircraft carrier before and was amazed at the size. It could be seen long before the helicopter made its approach for landing. Floating there like an island. Not knowing what to expect, he was overawed by the way the helicopter was dwarfed by it. When it landed he could see either way along the flight deck and both seemed to stretch into the distance.

On landing, Matt slid open the door and threw the rifle to the seaman waiting to escort him and to the heli crew shouted back as he alighted, 'Thanks lads for the ride; sorry if I was not good company.'

The seaman who had dexterously caught the rifle said, 'The Commander is waiting to see you in the Wardroom. Right this way,' and set off leaving Matt to follow. They did not however go to the Wardroom and instead Matt was ushered into a large office where three people were sat and the seaman disappeared.

'Sit down Mr Weston.' It was a command to which Matt acquiesced, taking the only vacant chair which faced them. 'I am Commander McShane and these are Lieutenants Barrew and Da Silva.' Each man acknowledged his name in turn. 'Sorry to delay your onward journey, and I have been instructed to make haste, but we need to know what information you have on mystery submarines and the Russians.'

Matt outlined the events of the previous day but did not go into too much detail. He did not know how much Wilberforce had let on or was consulting them on. What did they know from their own sources? 'You keep referring to the Russians, Mr Weston, but what proof do you have?'

'All I can tell you is that Russian was the language used, but there were no markings on the sub. Why?'

'I find myself in a difficulty here,' responded the Commander and after a pause to collect his thoughts, continued, 'We are not merely here on an exercise, which you might have guessed. Because various ships have reported underwater activity commensurate with a sub in these waters but no country is acknowledging that they are carrying out any underwater manoeuvres, we were sent to do a little snooping. We even have our own sub in the area carrying out covert surveillance.'

'Don't think you'll be getting any more contacts. Whatever was going on, and I have no idea what, will by now have stopped. The culprit is now full fathom five or more down and the one person who could have given some answers went down with the missing plane.'

'Additionally,' continued the Commander, 'there have been short bursts of energy from various parts of the Southern Ocean. The powers that be think they are encoded short messages which are then bounced off a passing satellite and beamed down to a place in the middle of the Central American Rainforest, as daft as it might seem.'

'That does seem strange but I have a feeling, and that is all it is, that something was going on under the ice because the British Base instruments kept going off line.'

'Why would anyone want to work clandestinely under the ice cap?' The question came from one of the lieutenants but he did not know which one. Both looked as though they had been cloned; same short cut blonde hair, round faces and later, when they stood up, of the same height and athletic build. They even walked with the same rolling gait, although that might have been with too many years at sea, and appeared to be in their late twenties.

'Search me. I was sent down to try find out what happened to two of the Base scientists that went missing but I had hardly started before trouble stalked me.'

'You are definitely sure that they were speaking Russian?' the other lieutenant asked.

'Positive, I have come across that language before and, although I cannot understand a word, I can tell that it was their native tongue.'

All three looked at each other, puzzled, and it was obvious that Matt was not going to get any answers there, although something told him that they had not come totally clean with him. Just as he had been a little judicious with the truth about his escapade, they were also working on a need to know basis.

'Mr Weston,' the Commander composed himself again. 'Thank you for your cooperation. Your report adds to the little we already know, but activity under the sea or even the ice must be out of the question or we would have come across it by now. We need to get you back on your journey but first I hope you will join me for lunch and a well-earned drink.'

'That is the sort of hospitality I cannot refuse. Food sounds good whatever it is.'

CHAPTER 2
HIJACK

LUNCH WAS PLENTIFUL BUT Matt did not gorge himself nor imbibe too much of the wine that was also available. He had no way of knowing what the flight out was going to be like and had no wish to be sick on the journey.

Over lunch the Commander said, 'When I was instructed to pick up someone from the British Base as a matter of a priority, I thought the Top Brass had lost their collective marbles.'

'I know you have your instructions not to divulge too much to me,' said Matt, 'and you may already have exceeded that, but I think you have not been as fully briefed as you might have either.'

'I am sure you are right but having now heard of your recent exploits and been made privy to your past, I realise you are not just someone.'

'Whoever they might be.' Matt said the thought aloud. The admission by the Commander that he knew his record answered why the helicopter crew knew his codename but left the question as to why they were bothering about him at all. Then he continued, 'On the face of it I am an administrator but could more properly be labelled a trouble-shooter.'

'And does trouble follow you around?'

'Not usually but it seems to have been doing so over the past few days.'

On the way to the Hangar where Matt was kitted out, the Commander asked, 'Have you ever flown in a service jet before?'

'No, but there has to be a first time for everything.'

'Well I hope you enjoy it, and good luck with whatever your people have got in store for you.'

Good luck, thought Matt. Was that for him or a wish for him to find the answers to their problem?

With a wave he was in the plane; it was lifted up onto the flight deck and he felt as though the breath was being knocked out of him as they were catapulted off.

The plane was a two-seat reconnaissance aircraft with the two seats side by side, and as they climbed and he looked back he thought of the ship as an island and another Status Quo song 'Living on an Island' came to mind. Also the line about 'getting high' and 'reach the sky' he felt were befitting as they rose above the clouds.

He had a good view above the clouds, occasionally seeing the ocean far below as the clouds cleared. Unbelievably, to Matt's lack of knowledge about such things, they only needed to refuel once at a US Pacific Air Base before they reached the US mainland and he realised he had not nodded off at all throughout the journey nor had he been consciously thinking things over.

But still no answers had come to mind.

Matt's plane touched down at San Diego and as soon as he had exited he was met by an officer from Homeland Security and transferred to the civilian side of the airport in a car with military driver.

Once there, he was taken to get his next plane by the quickest route, a route most passengers would never see as it went via all the airside back alleys. All the officer said throughout the walk was, 'They are holding the New York plane back for you. You sure as hell must be someone important.'

Here was another mystery. Why were the Americans pulling out all the stops to get him to meet his British Boss in New York? The more he turned it over in his mind, the less sense he could make of it all.

The plane had already pulled back from the air bridge and steps awaited his ascent. Before he was even seated the doors were closed and the aircraft was taxiing to the runway. His seat was the aisle one of two at the back, with plenty of room to straighten his prosthetic, and allowed him to sit more comfortably. He would have preferred the other side of the plane so the prosthetic on his right side could be more easily accommodated in the aisle.

His companion in the window seat was a lady, probably in her early forties and travelling on business. His 'sorry to have kept you waiting' was met with a grunt so he got comfortable and started to run the sequence of events from the past few days over again for the umpteenth time.

His thoughts were interrupted when the plane had reached cruising altitude by voices raised in alarm and two shots ringing out. Two men were standing at the front of this section of the cabin, and lower down the aisle a person was slumped sideways in his seat. Guns being discharged inside planes was not a good thing, was the first thing that came into his mind, but the plane was still going on its way. Must mean the bullets had been doctored like the ones used by Air Marshals. Still, not a good sign though; all it needed was one of them to be careless, and bam.

One of the men turned and went to the front section of the cabin whilst the other, who was stood down Matt's aisle, kept the revolver held in his right hand moving from side to side. In his other hand Matt could see he was tightly holding a grenade. How was it they were waiting at his every turn? But then his thoughts rationalised. No-one was going to kill him in such a public place and just be able to walk off on landing. They were not interested in him. Something else was going down.

Out of the frying pan and into the fire; his thoughts turned to the song he had heard by Meatloaf on a DVD. He had managed to get from one situation, which was none of his making and into another. He also remembered the aircraft carrier Commander asking if trouble followed him around. The way things were going of late, it was more like him finding trouble.

The PA system burst into life and a voice said, 'I am sorry this flight has had to be cut short but instead of the impersonal Big Apple we are now going to enjoy the bright lights of Las Vegas. Some of you will see them out of the windows as we flash by but this plane has now become a martyrs' flight. We are all going to die in the name of the almighty dollar. That will all change after our glorious achievement. One big bang and the US will become another third world country. Now everyone must stay in their seats or take the consequences.'

Matt's mind started racing. Two shots; presumably someone else was slumped in their seat. Whoever was calling the shots was on top of the situation and presumably knew any opposition which had been eliminated. Nothing had happened to him so he had to assume they were not aware of his capabilities. It was looking as though he could be the only hope for the passengers; if only he could incapacitate the hijackers. But were there any more besides the two? Had the voice over the PA been the other or was there a third or even fourth?

Following 9/11, security was tight but the two he had seen did not appear to be Al Quaida followers, if there was to be such a person to be identified. The language had been English, although with a slight accent and from what he could see of the man still in the cabin, he appeared to be Eastern European, but swarthy, as though from a southern country.

He had to do something. He was still wound up from the previous days and therefore on a high, but a cold calculating one. Quickly he appeared to massage his leg but the prosthetic one and pressed a release button. However, he was sitting on an aisle seat and to start ferreting would draw attention. He needed surprise to be on his side.

Out of the corner of his mouth he told the person on his right to reach into his trouser pocket. She did not move, so more aggressively he said, 'Reach into my trouser pocket,' and eventually he felt movement on his hip.

'Behind the flap and reach down the leg.' The trouser pocket had a loose flap of material which allowed access to his leg and the knife he carried in secret.

He liked the way she was now moving. Slowly and without seeming to be doing anything. He felt the fingers reach down his thigh and then nothing as the hand met the prosthetic. Working her arm further she touched the knife that had been released from its holder and slowly brought it out. 'Good girl' was all he said as he pressed a button on the hilt and the three-inch blade grew to five inches as the guard flipped out from sheathing the blade and more blade sprung out of the hilt. Taking it in his left hand, but out of sight, he then started to convulse, and when he had drawn the hijacker's attention he slumped slowly forward, hanging over the seat arm into the aisle. It appeared that his seatbelt was holding him in place but Matt had already released it and it was purely the pressure of his prosthetic pushing him into the seat that kept him in place. His other leg was bent, ready to move out.

Pudding time. Would the man come and see what was the matter, shoot him to make sure or just leave him? Nothing seemed to happen for a while, although it was probably only seconds, and then out of the corner of his eye he could see feet moving towards him. Legs became attached to the feet and eventually he was able to see knees as the man moved closer.

Matt dared not move a muscle, but the strain on the joint between prosthetic and thigh was beginning to tell. He was half expecting an executioner's bullet but eventually the man stood right in front of him. With the back of the hand holding the grenade, the man started to raise Matt's head. Surprise was his when he suddenly moved, grabbing the fist holding the grenade in his right hand and plunging the knife into the man's heart. He left the knife there and grabbed the gun from the other hand, moving out before the full weight of the body trapped him. At the same time as plunging the knife he had straightened his good leg and was moving out of his seat, holding the gun in one hand and gripping the man's grenade hand with his other. The push sent the hijacker against the side of the seatback on the opposite side of the aisle.

Standing up as best he could, he pirouetted with the body as it rebounded from the other seatback and slumped it down in the seat he had just vacated. Crosswise was the best he could do as the top half of the body rested face up on the lap of the lady, who was just staring nonplussed at the speed at which things had happened, the knife still sticking out and a red stain spreading.

Time was of the essence and he could not hold the grenade hand for too long. He pulled the lady's hand towards him and wrapped it round the grenade hand and told her to keep tight hold of it. He saw incomprehension on her face but her hand stayed there clasped. He was then moving down the aisle.

The other hijacker must have sensed the commotion and came into view in the opposite aisle. His reactions were fast but before he had time to assimilate what he saw, Matt had shot him right between the eyes. Luckily Matt was still moving as the other's reflexes were quick and he got a shot off before collapsing to the floor. He heard it slam into the locker above and then to his horror he saw the other's hand release the grenade he had been holding. Time seemed to stand still as he raced through the plane to the cross aisle as fast as the prosthetic would allow. Seeing where the grenade had lodged, by a toilet door, he grabbed the body and threw it on top of the grenade, adding his own weight as well just as the whole plane moved.

On the Flight Deck, the pilot and co-pilot had heard the initial shots and had notified local Air Control. As the second set of shots sounded, they felt it appropriate to lose height and after deliberation, put the plane into a steep dive.

The grenade went off; lifting both the body and himself and then he found himself rolling down the aisle as the plane went into an emergency dive. He ended up with a thwack against the forward bulkhead and with the breath knocked out of him and vision temporarily out of focus due to banging his head. All he could do was stay there semi-recumbent. Gradually his breath came back and he was also able to start focusing on things around him.

First thing he saw was the body of a stewardess as it was on the floor, at the same level as him. The red stain on her uniform was still spreading uniformly and he knew that must have been the original second shot. There had to be a third person involved, and then he saw him. A steward was stood at the opposite side of the plane, gun in hand and smiling as he raised it to shoot at Matt.

Matt, however, still had the dead man's gun in his hand and by slightly flicking his hand was able to shoot first from floor level without aiming. The bullet took the Steward in the chest, pushed him backwards against the side of the plane and then he seemed to bounce forward as though nothing had happened before keeling over forwards just as Matt was about to fire again.

Still feeling a little groggy, Matt stood up and looked around. The plane was now flying level again and he could see people in the cabin starting to straighten themselves after the dive. A stewardess came round the corner and started to scream. 'Don't worry,' Matt said, 'I am the good guy but you had better get the pilot here whilst I go and check on the other two I dealt with.'

He was curious about his second victim; the first was guaranteed to be dead but the second, although sure to be dead from the shot, had not been shredded by the grenade, and as he reached the body and rolled it over he knew why. It was a stun grenade and the pressure of the explosion had been absorbed by the body with just a little damage to the surroundings.

He was still holding the gun loosely at his side when the pilot came up behind him as he was examining the body. Still in battle mode he turned to face the person coming up behind him and the gun was level with the pilot's chest before he relaxed.

'Sorry about that but you should never creep up behind someone who is on a battle high,' apologised Matt.

'Who are you?' questioned the pilot. 'And what is with this hijacking?'

'Matthew Weston at your service. As to the reason for the hijack, I cannot help you there.'

'But you took them on.'

'I am required in New York in a hurry. They were going to stop me or delay me so I took them out.'

'You are the one we were delayed for.' A statement not a question.

'Yes, but you can continue on as normal now.'

'Unfortunately not,' responded the pilot. 'We have no control over this plane. Someone else has taken control and we cannot regain it. Wherever we are going or whatever we are to be used for is now in someone else's hands.'

'What! You mean to say I have gone through all that for nothing? I'll meet you on the flight deck in a couple of minutes but first I must relieve one of the passengers'

He could see the woman still keeping tight hold of the first killed's grenade hand. She was staring at it, oblivious to anything else and probably was not even aware of what had happened since Matt had left his seat.

'It's alright now,' he said when he arrived at her side and he retrieved the knife, cleaning the blade on the dead man's clothes. Pressing the point of the blade on a hard spot, he closed it and put it in his pocket.

'I'll take that now; you can relax,' he continued. As he eased her hand and took the pressure in his own she looked up at him and after a few moments of fear, she recognised him, sat up and started shaking.

After carefully removing the grenade from the dead terrorist's hand but making sure that the pressure was not released, he pulled the body into the aisle, laying it face down so that the blood was not showing, and sat down at her side. He put his free arm around her and as she leaned into him she started to cry.

'That's it, let it out. You really were brave back there.' He added a few more reassuring words, although he was not aware of what he had actually said as his mind was now on the new problem that was affecting them all.

Eventually she had settled enough for her to be left in the capable hands of a stewardess, who came at his behest and sat beside her as he got up. Before he went forward to the flight deck he tightly wrapped the grenade with some sticking plaster he found in the first aid box and put it in his pocket. By this time the gun was also out of sight, being tucked into the waistband of his trousers at the back. Then he moved the body out of sight at the back of the plane and repeated the operation for the other hijacker but could not find where that one's gun had fallen. On the way he picked up the steward's gun and tucked that into the front of his trouser waistband

'Where are we aimed for?' he asked on arriving.

'Not sure but it is Vegas way. It is as though we are being held by a tractor beam and pulled towards our destination,' the pilot responded.

'When did this happen?' questioned Matt.

'Someone or something took over as soon as we levelled out after the emergency dive.'

The co-pilot added, 'And we are still a loaded bomb with all this fuel on board.'

'Everyone's living nightmare,' commented the pilot further. 'Don't know what is going to happen and unable to do anything about it.'

That remains to be seen, thought Matt as, looking ahead, he could just make out the Stratosphere in Las Vegas and other tall buildings. His attention, however, stayed on the Stratosphere as it kept wavering from side to side. For a start he thought he was still suffering from concussion from being thrown around the plane earlier but then his brain started rationalising again.

'Why is the plane always correcting its direction? If we were being drawn towards something I would have expected a direct line.'

'Must mean that someone is controlling our flight, probably with a joystick or some such,' answered the co-pilot, without realising the implications of what he had said.

'To my mind that means someone close to us. Not miles away.' With that Matt raced out of the flight deck, grabbed the stewardess who was stood at the door and said, 'Have you noticed anyone playing with a games console?' Receiving a negative response he added, 'Well has anyone disappeared from their seat?'

'Can't be sure. I'll check,' and Matt followed her along the aisle. Regardless of the circumstances, she was showing true professionalism. 'That wasn't a vacant seat before we left,' pointing to another aisle seat.

Matt addressed the person in the next seat to the vacant one. 'Where has your fellow passenger gone?'

The man seemed startled and said, 'He is nothing to do with me.'

'Where did he go?' and the urgency in the voice made the other look up in fear. 'Where?'

'Don't know. He left about 10 minutes ago after the plane had finished diving.'

'What was he doing before he left?'

'Playing with one of those game things.'

Matt shot off and checked the nearest toilets but both were vacant and a check revealed no-one hiding there. The next two were the same but right at the back, one was occupied. Legitimately or not he shouldered open the door. A man was sat there playing with a games console which Matt grabbed off him, but it was only showing a game. Damn, he thought to himself, and as he was about to hand it back he saw the man's hand move. Instinctively he smashed the palm of his hand full force into the other's face, flattening the nose, and he just sat there stunned. A quick check through the pockets revealed a gun similar to the ones in Matt's waistband, which he dropped into his pocket.

The stewardess had followed him and to her he said, 'Secure him as he is dangerous.'

Matt knew then that the man had changed the screen just as he had broken in and started to press buttons to try find the right screen but without success. Unfortunately the man was in no fit state to answer questions so Matt, who knew little of such machines, went back into the cabin and found a teenager.

'How do you bring up different screens on this contraption?' he asked.

As if nothing had happened, the boy just took it and started playing around with various buttons and then asked, 'What do you want?'

'Something that looks as though it is flying a plane or similar,' and the boy flicked through again.

'Something like this?' he asked, handing over the console, and when Matt took it and touched the direction indicator the plane moved.

'Wonderful! Now come with me and we will see how we can land this thing,' and he led the boy to the flight deck.

'We have the controls,' he said to the pilot and then turning to the boy said, 'But can we stop this thing flying the plane?'

The boy took the console and started to play with various buttons but after a while handed it back saying, 'Nothing I do cancels it out.'

'What if we smash it?' Matt asked

'Probably means we would stay under whatever control it was at on destruction and that is what we would stay at until we run out of fuel,' the pilot answered and then continued, 'I have been onto Flight Control to make them aware and have now been transferred to the one at the Air Base at Nellis.'

'Do they have a longer runway there?' He received an affirmative response. A pause for thought and then he asked, 'Can either of you fly through the game console?'

'Hell we can give it a try,' said the co-pilot, who was the younger and took the box. Immediately he started to play with it, the plane altered course. 'Now on a heading for Nellis,' he said and then to the pilot, 'Better tell them what we are about. Everyone start praying.'

To the boy Matt said, 'Stay up here and look over his shoulder to check he seems to be doing everything OK. Get out as soon as we are on final approach and strap yourself into one of the stewards' seats. We could be in for a bumpy landing.'

With that he left and, for safety's sake, moved the other two bodies to the back where he found the one who had held the console with his hands tied and securely fastened in the toilet compartment.

Walking through the cabin he then spoke to the boy's parents, telling them what the situation was before continuing to his own seat. Sitting down and buckling himself in he could smell that his companion had had a stiff drink but could see she was still in some state of shock.

Short mousey hair; petite but pretty; and Matt had previously noted the green eyes. Probably the mother of two who had had to juggle family and work, although family should now have flown the nest. Well, she really would have something to crow about once she correlated her thoughts on what she had done and been through.

Taking her hand he held it tightly between both of his and said, 'You did wonderfully back there. Your family will be really pleased with you,' as he had seen her wedding ring. 'It's all over now,' he lied. 'Put it behind you and accept it as one of life's tribulations that you have successfully overcome.'

Any further conversation was cut short as the PA system announced the final approach to the airport and requested passengers to take up the brace position as the landing could be bumpy. As he took up his position, his mind was turning over on how it had felt to comfort someone. Was there more to life than his gadding about all over the world? Could it be his time to find someone and settle down? That thought seemed to warm him.

Up in the cockpit both the pilots were sure they could land the plane after a fashion but had not added after 'bumpy' that they were not sure if they could shut down the engines or if they would have to crash the thing at the end.

In the event it was a smooth landing and the plane slowed, followed a car to an allocated parking place away from everything else, came to a stop and the engines were shut down. Everyone sat up; sighed in unison with relief; and then started cheering. Was it for themselves in relief; or for the crew; or even for him?

As soon as the plane had started taxiing, Matt got up and headed for the front. The cabin crew requested that everyone remained in their seats until they were asked to move out. Eventually it stopped and one of the doors was opened. Two men in civilian clothes came aboard.

'I'm Atkins, CIA,' asserted one and indicating his companion said, 'And this is D'Angelo of the FBI. Please will everyone remain seated. At this moment in time we are seeking Matt Weston, will he please make himself known.'

'Right behind you.' The two men turned and found they were covered with the gun taken off the hijacker he had initially killed. 'How come the FBI and CIA are here when there cannot have been enough time to make the arrangements?' He still did not know who to trust.

'It's OK, we have been briefed. You have had a hell of a journey so far but you do not need the gun now. It just so happened that we were already at the Air Base on another joint matter when everyone went on the alert and the powers that be were happy for us to take the lead.'

Atkins held his hand out for the gun but Matt ignored it and tucked it back in his waistband at the front. He just stared coldly at the man who dropped his hand to his side. He was hoping if there was further trouble, and at this time he still did not know who was on his side, that someone might just concentrate on the gun in view and forget about checking for any other armaments he might have accumulated on the way.

D'Angelo, who was a little obese and appeared to waddle as he walked, led. Atkins, who being tall seemed to have a perpetual spring in his step, brought up the rear. The passengers were told they would be able to disembark shortly as transport was being provided. As he went down the steps Matt could see that the rear door had been opened and the bodies were being removed. On the tarmac and staring at him malevolently was the one he had smacked in the face in the toilet, who was stood there holding a bloody rag to his face. Matt smiled back at him as he stood there with two military personnel pointing rifles at him. Matt took out the gun from his front and pointed it at the man but his body hid the action from Atkins. Still smiling he aimed it from waist level but the man just stared back, daring him. Seeing this, Matt put the gun away muttering, 'Someone needs to be interrogated.'

A car was waiting, again with military driver, and whisked all three to the main building, and as they were travelling D'Angelo spoke for the first time. 'We have our orders to get you on your way as soon as possible and the Air Force is at present getting a jet ready, but we need a debriefing to find out what happened on board that plane.'

Once again the why as to the extreme help the Americans were giving came to mind.

Ten minutes later they were sat in an office and Matt had a Coke in front of him, sipping as he recounted the events as he could remember them. At the end he said, 'This operation took a lot of setting up, what with guns on board and the override of the controls. Why and what was the objective?'

'The objective was the Convention Centre. As to the why that we can only conjecture on,' said D'Angelo.

Atkins took up the response. 'At this point it is only conjecture,' he emphasised, 'but if we are correct, these were not ordinary terrorists.

Their mission had an economic purpose.'

Matt realised that these two were good at their job. Each was able to feed off the other, but he had no doubt that if need be one could be hard and the other soft, but which way round he had no idea. Probably able to take whatever stance was required at a particular time.

D'Angelo continued as though he had made the previous statement: 'For some time we have been aware that sources outside the USA have been trying to find ways to destabilise the economy but we did not know of anyone prepared to be suicide bombers to do it. If they had been successful, many top leaders of commerce, industry and politics, although the President was not there, would have been wiped out. The Convention Centre is holding a three day seminar for such people. Plenty of companies would have been headless, turmoil on the Stock Exchange and prey to God knows what.'

'It is a Godsend that you were in the right place at the right time,' commented Atkins. 'What I don't understand is why you were not sussed out.'

'As far as they were concerned I had probably replaced a nobody. I never travel announcing myself as a trouble-shooter. To anyone who does not know me I am an administrator who checks up on expeditions sponsored by the Government. Anyway who would suspect a peg leg of being a battler? Just their luck, or should that be bad luck, that I happened to be in the right place at the right time or perhaps, unfortunately for them, the wrong time.' At which all three had a good laugh.

'Right then, we had better get you on your way and then we can interview the others.'

'Fair enough, but can I suggest that the lady sat next to me and the lad who helped in the landing receive some recognition for their valiant efforts? Without them the outcome might have been different.'

'You can be sure we will look into that.'

Outside the same car and driver awaited, and as he was driven to another part of the airfield, one of his thoughts was on the Elvis song 'Viva Las Vegas'. Long live Las Vegas, which he had probably helped to do.

CHAPTER 3
A NEW YORK MINUTE

HALF AN HOUR LATER, Matt was kitted out and sat in the back seat of a tandem jet trainer. As the plane accelerated away he felt his stomach pushed against his spine, or so it felt, and the gun in his waistband pushed into his back most uncomfortably. Maybe he should have adjusted things earlier. Things settled down as they started cruising and the pilot conversationally asked, 'Have you been in one of these before?'

'No. It is a new experience for me.'

'Like to see what it can do?'

'Why not. It will help to pass the time.' But Matt knew the pilot was going to try make him feel ill; having a laugh at his expense.

Dive, climb, barrel roll and loop. Matt could feel his senses being disoriented but no physical problems.

'Great. Not bad for starters,' Matt stated as they were flying level again. 'Now let's see what she can really do.'

Someone had let slip before he had suited up that the rear seat was usually for the instructor, and that was where Matt was seated. Matt had the idea that the rear controls could well override the others, and when the plane started to dive again, Matt saw the controls move forward and applied pressure to keep them there. The pilot, realising what was happening when he could not lift the nose, screamed 'What are you doing?' thinking that Matt had panicked. 'Get off the controls. Do you want us both to be killed?'

'OK Cowboy,' responded Matt in a voice devoid of emotion and returned control to the pilot who then knew he had been hoodwinked.

'One of the tough breed, eh? Takes a lot to scare you.'

'Ex-combatant. Royal Marines. We are taught to assimilate before shitting ourselves.'

'Well you nearly had me doing it.'

'Shall we call it quits?' suggested Matt. 'And you can get me to New York in one piece.'

'OK Buddy. Hope I never have to face off with you at any time.' But there was a chuckle in the voice.

Two hours later they had landed. Within another half hour and minus the flying suit he was in a car being whisked to meet … who? He was wondering. The car entered a car park and went down three levels. As it was approaching a blank wall where Matt thought they were going to park, a wide door opened and the car went through, descending another three levels before stopping outside a door with a Marine sentry.

He must have been expected, as the sentry let him in and he found himself in an outer office with a few easy chairs but no-one in attendance. He knew he would be under surveillance, so straightened his clothes to show the gun still in his waistband.

'Welcome, Mr Weston,' a voice announced. 'Please leave the gun there,' and when he did the voice also added, 'And the one the one you have at your back.' Again he acquiesced and then the wall moved sideways from a corner to reveal his way forward.

As he walked along the corridor towards another Marine sentry, he was wondering if they knew about the other gun in one of his pockets or the stun grenade still in his pocket. See how far he could get, was his thought.

In front of the other sentry he spread the front of his jacket wide to show no apparent weaponry. Four doors led off from the ante-room and he was ushered to one. Inside, the first person he saw was his Boss who came up to him, shook his hand and said, 'Had a bit of a rough time of late. Glad you made it through.' Sexton Wilberforce looked dapper in the same pinstripe suit he always wore. All he needed was a bowler hat and furled umbrella to be the archetypal government officer. The hair was slightly receding from a clean-shaven round face, which always seemed to be smiling due to the crinkles around the eyes and mouth slightly turned up at either side. The eyes said different. They were hard and dark, the mirror image of Matt's, showing he had been a fighting man. About the same height as Matt, the body was toned from a rigorous gym routine. The erect bearing gave away his previous military service.

Inside the room were five other people, but before introducing them Wilberforce continued, 'We do talk to each other on certain matters and when you mentioned a submarine, alarm bells started ringing on both sides of the Pond. Because of certain worries the Americans have asked to take the lead and this is Alvar Mortenson, Director of Homeland Security.'

Alvar Mortenson did not look as though he had seen active service in his life. Podgy face with bleary eyes and button nose on top of a body with extensive paunch; no neck and short legs.

Mortenson gave an affable smile through his thick lips and invited him to sit down in the vacant chair; the one facing them all. All the chairs but his were in a semicircle but the room was devoid of any other furniture apart from a few chairs against one wall. He then introduced Calum with some unpronounceable name, who was one of his senior operatives but who remained silent throughout the discourse.

Also present were Appian of the CIA and Cortez of the FBI. Lastly he was introduced to O'Rourke who was British Secret Service and had come along with Wilberforce.

Jensen O'Rourke was someone Matt had not heard of before and he took an instant dislike to the man. He could not decide what to categorise him as but eventually decided he looked like a cunning rat. Thin face but not long and the eyes always seemed hooded. He always appeared to be uninterested in what was being said but Matt knew that was deceptive and probably hid an extraordinary brain. At about five foot six, he was slightly smaller than Matt but the body looked lithe and wiry. He always sat with his hands open on top of his thighs.

Mortensen took the lead and asked Matt to tell them what had happened in Antarctica, which he did in detail and saw some making notes, after which Cortez asked, 'Are you sure they were Russian?'

'A long time ago I spent time in their presence and whilst I could never get my head around the language I can understand some of what is being said. I am in no doubt that Russian was their native tongue.'

'What the hell are they playing at?' from O'Rourke.

'You tell me,' was Matt's response. Already he was getting bad vibes from him and he had hardly spoken as he continued, 'Your people are supposed to know what is going on. And why have I become their public enemy number one?'

'I'm more interested in this submarine,' continued Mortensen, changing the subject as he could tell Matt had an immediate loathing of the man and did not want to get into a position of having to give more information out than necessary. 'Describe it to me.'

'Looked to be about half as wide again as those submarines I have previously experienced, although I have to say it was dark and so I cannot be too sure. Maybe it was a little longer but I only saw it from an angle so things might have appeared deceptive. No conning tower, sorry sail they call it now, and at the back there appeared to be a countersunk space as though something should be sitting there.'

Mortensen rummaged through some papers and produced a photograph and passed it to him without saying a word.

'That's it. So that is what should have been on the back, a mini-sub.'

'Mmm. Well that's the second one accounted for,' mused Mortensen, 'but where are the rest?'

'How many do the Russians have?' queried Wilberforce.

'None as far as we are aware,' replied Mortensen. 'They had eight but one disappeared on its proving trials and they never did anything else in earnest with the rest of them. Then, of course, within a short time everything changed in Russia and they all disappeared one by one.'

'We kept watching over them in their home port and on one pass of the satellite all were there but then every so often one less was remaining but no-one thought anything of it until all were gone. It was like one month they were there, all mothballed; the next they had been made ready and were gone.'

The more Mortenson spoke, Matt became convinced that they were being sparing with their information. Why would Homeland Security be interested in ex-Russian submarines unless they were already being used clandestinely against America? The change of tack earlier had not escaped his notice either.

'The information coming out of Russia was that they did not know where they had gone and accused all sorts of people of stealing them.' This from the FBI man.

Javier Cortez. The name and slight dark complexion hinted at his Hispanic roots but he looked more like the all-American boy. Marine-cut blonde hair over a square face and his bearing showed a military background. Not that he had seen much active service as his sharp mind had brought him to the attention of other services and, after passing out with flying colours, he had been seconded to the military wing of the FBI where his ability to assimilate and correlate many things at the same time had fast tracked him to his current position – that of keeping an eye on activities which encompassed both military and civilian matters.

'Was there no-one on the ground keeping close watch on them? After all they were a new weapon.' This from O'Rourke.

'We were aware of them and were keeping an eye on them but when a decision was taken not to arm them, we pulled back and had to try and concentrate our resources on where all the other military hardware was going.'

'In the turmoil that followed the fall of Communism as we knew it,' Wilberforce confirmed, 'anyone who could dispose of any hardware cashed in. Did some minion take a bribe to turn a blind eye whilst some other organisation spirited them away? Anyone involved with them being recognised as having come into money which they did not have before?'

'If so they have managed to keep it quiet, although there have, of course, been a few people that have vanished without trace,' added Cortez. 'Some we are sure were eliminated for whatever reason and the bodies never found but there is no doubt that some could be living the lifestyle of the rich under a new identity somewhere.'

'What happened to the first sub to go missing?' Matt had been half-listening to what had been going on but had a nasty feeling in his gut that it held the key.

'From what we have been able to glean it was sent out for sea trials with a misfit crew and a commander who had recently been demoted.'

Before Cortez could go on Matt said, 'Vassilev.'

'How could you know that?' he asked.

'Because he is still alive. Don't ask me how I know. It is just a feeling caused by a dream but it is not unknown for two people to be thinking of each other at the same time and be aware of the other's existence.'

'Feelings, gut reactions, leave them out of it,' said the CIA man.

The curvature of the spine on Lazlo Appian was the most noticeable feature about him as he always appeared to be leaning forward. However, because of his deformity and the way he made light of it, he also looked the friendliest of those present. A neatly trimmed beard on the chin and a moustache highlighted a round face. Difficult to make out what was the true state of his misshapen body but strong legs showed signs of being muscular through his trousers. He was the only one to have removed his jacket and the rolled up shirt sleeves showed off the muscular arms.

'Obviously you have never been in a combat situation,' countered Matt. 'The heightened state of awareness can give some a clue as to what is happening around you. I know and I sincerely believe that this applies now.'

'Hang on,' said Cortez. 'We have always assumed that Vassilev died and so we eliminated him from our thoughts. However, records show that his younger brother was involved in the programmes for those subs and he has subsequently disappeared.'

'What is running through your mind now?' asked Wilberforce. 'I know that look. Something is developing.'

'True and it would give the lie as to why the CIA and the US in general are interested.'

'Well do enlighten us,' flippantly from the FBI man.

'Just suppose. The crew of the first sub to disappear would appear to be a load of rogues. Let us say that in their collective state of mind, after they have proved its worth, they decide to take it over and use it for their own ends. I am sure that for a few favours in any number of given areas they would be given safe haven in return. That submarine, with its mini attached, could be used for smuggling any amount of illicit cargo anywhere in the world, including terrorists into America. Am I right? That is why we are all gathered here.'

The question went to Mortensen who blanched a little before giving a studied answer. 'It is plausible but what happened to the rest?'

Matt had been watching as Mortensen had assimilated what had been said and the answer given. There was no doubt that Matt had hit on something. Mortensen kept most of his composure but, in addition to the blanching, there were some blinks and twitches; a giveaway that he had been on target.

'Now I am going into the realms of conjecture, but think how much more work could be carried out if you could get your hands on a fleet, especially if you had a man on the inside where they were.'

'I follow your line of reasoning but how do you hide so many? One is relatively easy and maybe two but a whole fleet …'

'Have them scattered about the world in secret locations ready for action in that particular area. Maybe that is what was going on in Antarctica; building a base near to the British Base for operations anywhere in the southern hemisphere. Knock out the communication systems whilst work is being undertaken so no trace can be found. I always did wonder why the system went down at the time it did without any real cause.'

'Got you there. We had a sub snoop all around the continent and could not find any trace of activity. We had the same thought but were ahead of you. The answer is a negative.'

'Then why was I targeted? It must have had something to do with stopping me snooping around down there.' And then as he saw possible enlightenment added, 'Or is it to do with my move to Greenland? What's going down there, Boss? Are the Americans just as worried by what is happening there?'

'I'll brief you on that later, but collectively here we are not worried about Greenland.'

Reading between the lines Matt could see that it was a very judicious answer. He had been going to say, 'Well I think they should' but felt it better not to. Together they were not going to act against the Greenland phenomenon as he was beginning to think of it, but in his own mind he had no doubts that certain aspects were going to start calling their own shots. He did not like it. When people started doing their own thing there was a chance of accidents and Matt could see that he was going to be in the middle.

'Well if there is nothing else you can add we will let you get on your way. You have had rather a hectic few days to get here but I know Wilberforce is wanting to get you over to Greenland as fast as possible, so off you go. The car is waiting outside to take you to your hotel.' This from Mortensen in a dismissive way.

Matt and Wilberforce left, going back out to the waiting car which took them to their hotel. He did not bother to gather up the guns he had left; after all what need could he have of them now? Famous last words, or at least thoughts.

On the way neither spoke about the recent events or the future, knowing that all they said would probably be either recorded or overheard. Instead they concentrated on chit-chat about various international happenings since they had last been together and points relative to his journey here; all of which had been spoken of back there.

Back at the hotel, Matt was able to change into some clean clothes as Wilberforce had brought some with him. Whilst he was changing, Wilberforce went into the other room of the suite and made a couple of phone calls and did not see Matt transfer the gun and stun grenade over to his new clothes; the latter he took the tape off and primed again ready for action.

Knowing that the room could be bugged in some way, both men headed for a nearby restaurant and it was only when he got there that Matt remembered when he had last had a good meal. He was ready to eat a scabby donkey and neither really spoke until the main course was over.

'Right,' said Matt, 'what is going on in Greenland that is causing such a fuss?'

'I don't really know what it is all about. What I do know is that in drilling an area for cores, they hit something really hard. That was only about ten feet down and so they cleared a trench to investigate. That was at the end of one day but when they came back the following day it had been filled in. Next they tunnelled in but the tunnel was collapsed, they think deliberately, before they had time to investigate.'

'Presumably this information is out. So why aren't the Americans sniffing around? Anything unusual so close to their shores usually has them getting under everyone's feet.'

'I agree. All I can think is that if the Americans seem not to be bothered about it, they must have a different agenda.'

'So you don't think they are involved in any way?'

'Not as far as we are aware. However, I am sure that they have an interest in what is going on. It is their apparent disinterest that tells me so. I can feel it in my water.'

'I agree. Back on the aircraft carrier I got the impression they were keeping something back and just now at that meeting there was a reluctance to divulge some information.'

'There is no doubt they are keeping something back but none of my contacts can fill in any of the missing spaces.'

'Why do I have this nasty feeling that I am the catalyst for something?' mused Matt and then continued, 'They are leaving me to open up a can of worms, if there is one, and then they will ride like the cavalry to the rescue; pick up the brownie points and look good on the international circuit.'

'You could be right,' and as Wilberforce looked at him, he continued, 'I have seen that look in your eyes before. Heaven help anyone who gets in your way or even tries to take the candy from you, whether they be friend or foe.'

Matt smiled but there was no mirth in it and the eyes remained as hard as ever. 'Have we any idea why I am being targeted?'

'Not a clue.'

'So you don't know if I touched someone's raw nerve in Antarctica?'

'I can assure you I am not playing any cards close to my chest. You are too good an employee for that.'

'Could it be that someone knew before me that I was to be assigned to Greenland and does not want me there?'

'If so, it would only be conjecture on somebody's part as I only took that decision about two hours before I spoke to you.'

Matt gave up on his conjecturing and concluded by asking, 'How am I getting to Greenland?'

'The Americans are prepared to help there, although it means a parachute jump on your part. Seems they have a group of Marines going on exercise further inland tomorrow and they are prepared to make space for you on the flight.'

'Sounds a bit too convenient to me.'

'Granted, but all we can do is roll with it at the moment and see what transpires.'

'Fair enough on that but what are you playing at with the Americans?'

'What do you mean?'

'Well it didn't take you long to arrange the flight out of the Antarctic. It was almost as though the fallback position was already in place.'

'That was as much a surprise to me. When I contacted them to advise them of the situation, they immediately offered the alternative; no asking, no pleading.'

'Definitely means they are up to something. Wanting information gleaned by someone else so they can act on it.'

'I cannot disagree with your surmise. However on a couple of occasions of late they have acted in haste on information they have been given and been caught out. I can see their difficulty. If things don't go according to any plan, we are the ones to be caught out this time.'

'Ah well, all I want now is a soak in a bath and a comfortable bed and see what tomorrow brings.'

Because he had been cooped up either travelling or in briefings for days on end, or so it seemed, even though it had been less than 48 hours, Matt suggested walking the three blocks back to the hotel and Wilberforce agreed.

They were still talking about the events of the past few days, trying to shed light on the happenings, and after a while Matt said, 'I still think there is something happening in Antarctica. The Americans must not have looked hard enough,' and then he paused as another thought came to him. 'Or they have found something and are keeping close-lipped about it.'

'You know our two countries are supposed to be buddy buddy these days,' commented Wilberforce. 'Well I do wonder how open they are at times. OK, there were times in the past when some of our networks leaked like a sieve, as you know to your cost, but of late all problems have emanated from this side of the Pond.'

'The less they say the less chance of another cock-up being placed at their door, eh?'

'Probably, but I do wish they would loosen up ...' Wilberforce, who was walking on the inside of Matt, was looking beyond him and into the street when he interrupted his speech and commanded, 'Down!' as he dropped to the floor.

Matt reacted automatically, complying with the order and following him down, hearing the sound of bullets flying over him and hitting the window nearby.

Whilst talking, he had been absent-mindedly playing with the stun grenade in his pocket, rolling it in his hand. As he looked to the side and saw a car almost at a stop with the muzzle of a gun pointed in their direction, he took out the grenade, pulled the pin and threw it straight through the open window of the car. There was no thought to the action; he just did it at the same time as reaching into his other pocket and drawing the gun.

As they got up the sound of the grenade going off could clearly be heard.

In the car were the brothers Demille. David was driving and Dennis was in the back doing the shooting. Having missed the opportunity and seeing the chance of bullets coming his way Dennis shouted, 'Get us out of here!' and the car sped off. The occupants of the car were oblivious to what was already in the car with them or not giving it much credence. After all, who walks around with a grenade in their pocket?

In the confines of the car the effect was disastrous. Dennis in the back took the full concussion blast and was killed instantly. The deafening concussion rendered David unconscious and forced his foot down on the accelerator. Straight on at a crossroads and through a red light, or would have if a large truck had not been crossing at the same time. The car crumpled into it and exploded.

Not wishing to get further involved, Matt and Wilberforce continued back to their hotel, where they were met by Appian looking worried, the stooping being more pronounced when he was standing. 'Thought I had better tell you, although some of the others wanted to keep it quiet. There is a contract out on you, Mr Weston. Seems as though your thwarting of the hijacking has upset someone and they want you dead.'

'There has been an attempt already,' responded Wilberforce.

'What? Where?'

'Just now on the way back; we were shot at,' he continued.

'Are you sure it wasn't the Russians or whoever they are?' the CIA man questioned.

'Two black guys in a car,' Matt spoke. 'The Russians do their own dirty work. Better put the local police in the picture; bullets in, I think it was a Deli window. The car that recently smashed into a truck and exploded, that was them, although I doubt there is much left worth investigating.' He did not mention anything about the grenade and was not asked any more about it.

'If it was more than a drive-by shooting, someone jumped the gun as proof is needed of your death, not just some report. How they hoped to get that is beyond me.'

'You know this gets better all the time,' Matt said, tongue in cheek. 'I'm looking over my left shoulder for the Russian mob and now I have to look over my right one for assassins.' Then he thought of a song he had heard The Eagles sing: 'In a New York Minute', which goes on to say everything can change.

As they parted, Wilberforce asked, 'Try and find out who is behind it.'

'Already on it,' was Appian's parting comment.

Matt was up early the following morning feeling refreshed and had to wait around until mid morning for the staff car to pick him up and take him to the airfield where he was to join the Marines' flight. They were all waiting when he arrived and a lieutenant took him on one side.

'Have you done any parachuting before?' he asked. 'I was told you had but I cannot let you board without knowing.'

'I am an ex-Marine and was fully trained although I have done very little since getting this,' and he tapped the prosthetic. 'I have used the wing type on a couple of occasions though, albeit only for pleasure.'

'That's OK. I'm sure it will all come back to you as we go along. Let's get you suited up, although the drop will only be from about 2500 feet.' And with that he led him to a table on which his equipment, basically coveralls, was laid out. He still had the last revolver from the hijacking but it was hidden away under his clothing and not attracting attention.

Within half an hour of his arriving they were in the air and he found himself sat near a sergeant who was rather talkative. 'They tell me you are nicknamed Pegleg.'

'That's so because of this,' and again Matt tapped the prosthetic, wondering how he knew. 'You people have call signs or such; what's yours?'

'My name is Antonio Pancetti so ever since I joined up they have called me Pancho, especially as I have inherited the swarthy Mexican looks of my mother.'

Born to an Italian father and Mexican mother, he looked like everybody's latino stereotype; one for the ladies to swoon over. Round face, with a large mouth that seemed to be perpetually smiling. A stocky body, with muscular arms and legs that were used to exercise. A solid, dependable companion, who looked as though he would be good in a tight corner. Confidence oozing from every pore, indicating a person who could be relied on.

Matt committed the call sign to memory as they kept on talking, never realising that he would need to use it before too long.

The plane did not even circle his drop zone. It was merely, 'here we are, get ready and go'. As he exited the plane something caught his eye inside that did not seem right but his main observation was for where he was going. He could see exactly where he had to aim for as there was the massive excavation in progress that he had been told about. Lazily he floated around; losing height and gradually making for the camp. Looking around he could see the lie of the land. The surf playing on a rocky beach, behind which was a slope for about 100 yards; snow-covered but a melt must have been underway as rocks could be seen exposed along the way. Then came a plateau for approximately 200 yards but the last few feet was where the excavation was taking place; the people there looking like ants.

Rising almost vertically behind the excavation was a snow cliff about 50 feet high, topped with a ridge. On the other side of the ridge there was a small valley before the land rose again in steps to the inland mountain range.

As he circled around losing height, he saw a shadow under the sea but ignored it as the next vista revealed movement on the ridge high above the workings. There was no doubt what the person was doing. Putting explosives into place which would take the whole snow mountain down if exploded and cover the excavations.

Obviously not expecting anything from above, the man kept on diligently with his work, setting one and then moving a few feet along before setting another. Matt altered his angle of fall and redirected the chute so that he was approaching the man from behind. At the last minute the man must have sensed his presence and turned, at the same time trying to draw a pistol. Too late – Matt was on him and with the solidity of the prosthetic kicked him. Over the edge he went and lodged in a crevice part-way down. As he continued his descent Matt saw no movement from the man before he was out of sight and ready to land. No-one below had seen anything and they were not aware of his presence until he landed amongst them.

'Who the hell are you?' questioned a man who appeared to be in charge of the party doing the excavation.

'The name is Weston, you should be expecting me.'

'Ah yes, but no-one said you would be dropping in. Only to expect you today.'

'Hitched a ride with some American guys but they kicked me out up there. Like to tell me what is going on whilst I get out of this gear?'

'By the way, my name is Steve McKracken but most people call me Mac. Supposedly I am in charge but sometimes I wonder.'

Mac was not what one would have expected a field scientist to look like. Over six foot, he towered over Matt. Beanpole thin; the sort who, to many people's disgust, could eat two potatoes more than a pig and still not put on weight. Neatly cut hair on top of a thin face with a long nose that did not look out of place. The long face was elongated further by the chin at the end of which was a goatee beard. His eyes sparkled as he talked about the work and around his neck was a pair of half-moon spectacles for reading.

Both returned to a nearby hut and as Matt took off his jump suit, the other said, 'We hit something hard as we were drilling. No bit would bite into it so we started excavating. Every time we do something there is always a setback. That is why we asked for you. Your success rate at solving problems of expeditions is legendary and we need some answers. We are now going big-time to uncover what we have struck and should have the area cleared by the end of the day. Then we can really investigate the phenomenon.'

Walking back out in his Antarctic gear, Matt felt a little overdressed as the days were getting longer and there was heat in the day. Soon he had to unfasten his coat. The winter storms were all gone, allowing more time for working outside. He was torn between finding out more about the excavations, but also the man who had been on the ridge intrigued him.

The latter won, as occasionally as he was inspecting the work he caught sight of a flash of light; sun reflecting on binoculars or something natural?

Making his excuses on the basis of getting his bearings, and leaving them to it, he worked his way up the ridge by the long way round. He had noticed a pathway and other features on his way down and instinct took over as he reached the top of the ridge.

There it was obvious that people had been around but, of course, no-one from the dig had thought to come up here; after all there were more important things going on down there for the scientists. Peering round a corner, he looked closely at the point where he had seen the reflection but nothing was visible. He kept staring at it and then there was a flash hidden behind the snow; camouflaged and well done.

He crawled over the ridge and saw a number of tracks all of which seemed to lead to a particular point and stop. Something else must be camouflaged there, he thought, and was about to investigate when there was a noise to his left and a man, dressed all in white like the one he had kicked off the ridge, appeared and seemed to check that the ridge where the other had been was OK before disappearing.

Taking a chance Matt walked along the ridge and found the canisters which had been placed there and threw all but one onto the snow pile that rose up where the paths seemed to disappear. The other he kept, and followed the pathway carefully to see an opening in the snow under an overhang, and slowly he moved inside.

It was only a short passageway which terminated at a point on the snow overlooking the excavations. A camera was moving from side to side, taking in all the activity below. No-one was there and he could not understand where the man had gone. Still he left his calling card of the canister hidden under some rags and quietly left.

He had only just reached the top of the ridge again when the man reappeared and then went down the passageway. There was a great burst of air and snow where he had thrown the canister which revealed a metal construction with a door in it. Under him he also heard another explosion at the same time and knew that the observatory had been put out of commission. He also knew then that there had been a previous attempt on his life in Antarctica. He had heard that sound once before when the avalanche had buried him.

Ducking down as low as he could in the little depression in the ground that he had found, he heard voices, again speaking in Russian. With his head on one side he peered over with one eye and saw that a door in the metal construction had opened to reveal a lift, and the voices were under him, no doubt looking for the man he had seen earlier.

Taking the opportunity of the noise they were making he left via the way he came and made his way back down without incident. Nonchalantly he walked back to the excavations and could now see what all the fuss was about. A slab about 20 feet by 10 feet had been revealed which, although seeming to be highly polished did not reflect the light. A couple of men were stood on it but try as they might they could not slide. They hit it with hammer and chisel but nothing happened. No pieces flew off and no scarring took place. Everyone gathered round at the edge of the excavation and many started to speak at once, which hid the noise of the activity going on behind them.

What Matt had been unable to see on his way down was that within 20 feet the shoreline under the water dropped more than 200 feet, whereupon it formed a large overhang before dropping away again. Under the overhang was a large cleft in the rocks that created an entrance. From that source had emerged a submarine and, with only the merest hint of deck above the waves, it had surfaced and disgorged a group of people and equipment before submerging again.

CHAPTER 4
THE CAVE

MATT HEARD THEM FIRST, a noise that he could not really fathom out. The others were talking in their group and with some voices raised there was no chance of them hearing the super-silenced snowmobiles which came over the lip of land behind them. Matt, stood apart at the edge of the excavation, turned round just as the four vehicles stopped and the men were spilling off them, two from each.

'Look out!' was all the time Matt had to warn them as he saw two with submachine guns aimed in his direction and he dived over the edge still looking back and realising, just as bullets started flying over his head, that he had made a wrong move.

The last thing he saw before disappearing from sight was two of the others lining up RPGs at the hillside beyond. As he hit the bottom he heard the whoosh as the rocket propelled grenades flew overhead and when they exploded on the hillside he was already running across the excavation.

Over the way he had seen a rocky overhang which might give him some respite when the avalanche of snow came tumbling down around him. Half-way across and a second set of grenades went overhead and exploded. He could hear the start of the avalanche and realised he was unlikely to make it, as having to throw the prosthetic as he ran he was slower than someone with two good legs.

Fear maybe gave him the extra spurt of speed and as the leading edge of the avalanche came tumbling into the excavated hole he dived head-first under the overhang.

He had expected to have a cushion of the snow that seemed to be packed into the crevice under the overhang and was surprised when his head went through a snow wall. Wriggling and squirming he made it through just as the light started fading into darkness as the avalanche thundered down. Knowing the fall would draw the air from whatever he had found himself in, he took a deep breath and held it as long as he could. Meanwhile the thunder of the avalanche seemed to get louder and louder as the noise reverberated around his hiding place.

As the noise subsided he started to let out the breath he was holding. Concentrate, cut your activity down to a minimum, just sit there and breathe slowly so as not to use up whatever air may be left inside. Shift brain into gear after the buffeting by the noise and try to think of a way out. After a few minutes of thought as he sat there, he realised that the air was still relatively fresh. Somewhere there must be a feed hole and if he could find it there may be some way of getting out or at least alerting someone of his plight. With the air, his nose told him that there was another smell mixed in with it and after a few careful sniffs he analysed it as being dank as if the air had been held for some time in a wet area.

His ears sensed the change in air pressure before he heard movement at the back of his dark nothingness; a slight hiss as an air seal was broken and then a light showed. The glow, as that was all it was for a start, showed that the cave he was in turned to the right after only about 10 feet and it was from the hidden part of the cave that the light was emanating and getting brighter. The increasing glow showed the hole he had come through and he managed to wriggle back through. The avalanche had not completely backed up into the entrance and he was just out of sight in a little square when the light shone right through the opening. Guessing that whoever was approaching was not going to be benevolent he hugged the snow wall at the side of the hole and waited. The light, and he could tell it was from a torch, seemed to probe into his bolthole but he was out of sight. The fist holding the torch came through and shone it away from Matt. At the same time a head followed through and was silhouetted against the back of the torch beam as it faced the same way as the beam.

Matt grabbed the head and pulled it backwards as fast and as hard as possible. No sound came from the person as Matt slid centre of the floor, using the head as a pivot, and pulled him through. The torch had dropped and rolled against the snow wall but still gave enough light for Matt to see what he was doing. The man popped through and dropped belly down on Matt's body with feet still trailing in the entrance, which meant he had no manoeuvrability. Matt still had hold of the head, gave it a vicious twist, first left and then right, which was followed by a snap and the body went limp.

Matt then had to rest himself for a while after extracting himself from under the body, before crawling back into the main cave. The exertion in such a cramped space with his own body twisted had caught him out. A quick search revealed that the man had no armaments and Matt put this down to him having been sent to see if there was any damage from the avalanche. Then with the torch held out in front of him he went exploring.

Round the bend and about 20 feet along there was a blank wall of rock but on closer inspection, when he got there, revealed an indented handle and when he lifted it, a rock door opened. He found himself in a vestibule-type room about four foot square with a door at the opposite side, but when he tried the handle of that door nothing happened.

Stood there, his mind went back and he remembered the sound he had heard. He was in an air lock; one door had to be closed before the other would open. Closing the one behind him and opening the other let him into a darkened area which proved to be a massive cave when his eyes became accustomed to the half-light that was showing ahead.

That was when he cursed himself for not having any assault weapons. Goodness knows what he would be facing when out in the open. Stealth would be his only option for a start so he removed the knife from his prosthetic and put it in his pocket, still folded, remembering he still had one handgun as well.

Looking around he did not see any cameras monitoring the area in which he stood but nevertheless he carefully moved forward until he could see the rest of the cave and what he saw amazed him so much that he almost stepped out into the open without thinking.

A small rock platform was immediately outside with a pathway leading away to one side. It was, however, what lay at the bottom of the cave that caught his breath. It was like a massive lake and moored at one side by a manmade dock were two submarines identical to the one he had sunk in Antarctic waters, and that was where the light was coming from.

Work was in progress either loading or unloading the submarines; Matt did not venture too close to the edge to see. Carefully scanning the area he could not see any signs of life or surveillance and realised the glow from down below was sufficient for someone to negotiate the path without being seen from below as they would be in semi-darkness.

He walked out onto the platform and waited, checking to see if there was any activity as a result of him being seen, but nothing happened. What clandestine operation had he uncovered and what could he do, one man, against whatever and whoever was there? Time to think. Who was controlling the operation? The Russians – and that was why he had been targeted; or could it even be the Americans, as they had not been really forthcoming about anything at any of the meetings he had with them. Then there was even the possibility of a maverick agency being involved.

There was no going back; he could only go forward, but before doing so he had a bite to eat from his secret rations. This time Kendal Mint Cake, which Wilberforce had brought through for him. He wished he had a drink to wash it down. Feeling against the side of the cave he found it damp but no water was running which would have afforded him a means of washing the food down.

What had happened to the scientists outside he was wondering, and what was happening now? Were they safe? Had the whole idea of the attack been to get him and cover the excavations? If so, were they now wondering about him – but anyone would think that he was buried under tons of snow with no chance of being alive. Escape or perish; it was entirely in his own hands. Rescue could not be expected. How could the cavalry come galloping to his rescue now?

Carefully he started his descent of the path, making sure of each step as he did not want to either slip or fall over the edge to drop over 100 feet or so into the water. The path kept curving round the cave wall but in such a way that it kept disappearing and every so often he had to peer round a corner to check the way was clear. After one such check he stopped as he could now survey the whole of the cave. There was no obvious way into it; no wonder they were using submarines, but who had created it and for what purpose? Had it been some secret lair for submarines during the war? He doubted it. The walls when he touched them appeared smooth and neither chiselled or blasted. Those thoughts he put to the back of his mind as he surveyed the operation below.

A floating dock had been created at one end, taking up about a fifth of the lake area with two fingers leading off, making a U-shaped bay within which the two subs were berthed, one to each arm. Built against the cave wall down which the path was descending was a three-storey structure which seemed to rest on the floating dock but was presumably secured to the cave wall itself. From above Matt could not see what the building was used for although some would no doubt be accommodation.

Walking further down the path he stood at roof level with the buildings, which were obviously prefabricated, and looking around could still not see any signs of security. Obviously, whoever was running the show felt safe from this approach. Or were they waiting for him one level below? So far so good, so on he went.

Stairs now led down to the working levels and he quietly worked down the first flight, aware he was becoming more and more exposed, and into an area where more people could be around with the obvious increased chance of detection. Behind the second level a corridor ran the full length with a number of doors leading off. The first door was partly ajar and he could see a man closely watching a number of screens beyond which was a large window overlooking the dock. Security, but obviously not in the area he had come from, as the man was still sat there.

The corridor was lit and he could not see any signs of a camera at this level so Matt walked casually along to the far end, but alert for any sound or sign he had been discovered. All that faced him at the end was a lift, presumably the one that reached up behind the ice ridge, and beyond was the continuation of the floating platform which formed the dock. Retracing his steps he tried the first door he came to but it was secured. The next one was not, however. Quietly opening the door and seeing no-one inside, he let himself in, closing the door behind him.

It was a working office and again had a picture window overlooking the dock. Looking down it was still difficult to know what was happening as boxes were being taken on and off the submarines. Suddenly a clicking noise made him turn suddenly with the gun in his hand, but it was only a printer. If that was going, would it be long before someone came to check and, with that thought, he let himself out, making sure the door was closed as he had found it.

If this was the offices level, what was the one below? He had to find out but that meant passing the open door of the security office again. The man was still intent on watching the monitors and Matt looked at the ones he could see clearly from the doorway. He still held the gun and wished he had a silencer on it as he went silently down the next flight of stairs.

Another corridor across the back and again he could make out the lift at the far end. Once again there seemed to be the absence of any security, so he went to the nearest door and tried it. No problem in opening it, although it squeaked. Not occupied though, as he was not accosted. Inside it was obviously dormitory accommodation. Four bunks, two on either side and a narrow wardrobe at each end of the bunks, one for each occupant. At the far end under a small window overlooking the dock was a narrow desk. No washing or toilet facilities.

Back out in the corridor after a quick check to see it was clear, he counted the doors. Seven, which meant there was likely to be at least 28 people around, although a closer check showed one door to be different. When he opened this he found the toilet, shower and washbasin where he cupped his hands under a tap and had his overdue drink. Twenty-four, then, but against one it was still tall odds and were there any more on the lower level still, a place he dare not check out as that was where all the activity was taking place.

Moving back up the levels he stopped at roof level and sat on the floor in the shadows. One gun with six bullets and his knife, not much to take on however many there might be. Twenty-four would be just about enough to man one of the subs so with two there must be serious overcrowding. Must mean some were still sleeping on one of the subs. He allowed his mind one short flight of fancy before returning to the problems in hand. This was because the words of the song 'I am a Mole and I live in a Hole' somehow entered his brain.

'Oh shit,' he thought to himself. Double the amount of trouble. Maybe best to wait until the activity ceased and then take some sort of action. No; whatever was going on had to be made public and the better time would be whilst activity was going on all round. That meant one thing: using the lift to get out and raise the alarm. The lift itself or the exterior would definitely have security cameras. That meant the first act had to be to incapacitate the man with the security monitors. Ah well. No time like the present. The longer he outstayed his welcome the more chance of being discovered. So once again with caution he went down to the upper level. Looking in on the security guard he noticed that one of the monitors, which had been blank the last time he had looked in, now had movement on it and the guard was looking at it intently with one hand on a microphone. Matt realised it was the view from a camera on top of the lift shaft and whoever was approaching was not welcome. He burst in and as the man turned to see his visitor, hit him hard on the side of the head with the gun. He went down and as he did so his hand on the mike made it click before he let go. A quick check through the window showed that no-one had bothered about the noise. Attending to the man, intending to tie him up, Matt found out he had hit in a vulnerable place and that he was dead.

Quickly he moved him to the side of the room out of view from anyone in the doorway and then closed the door. There were five monitors and three of them were trained on the dock area. The other two were situated outside, one on top of the lift shaft and the other overlooking the recently filled excavation. This camera was now only showing part of the area, but it was sufficient for Matt to see no bodies lying around, nor was there any sight of the people who had done the shooting.

Turning his attention to the monitor on which he had seen movement, the one over the lift shaft, he concentrated and saw people moving in a purposeful way. Perfect reconnaissance moves of some forward then prone as more moved forward. He knew then that his thoughts had been correct. These were the Marines he had flown in with. There had not been another exercise elsewhere. The cavalry had arrived, presumably motivated by the recent activity outside.

Looking down at the consoles he began to make some sense of them. The lift could be operated from here. Checking its position: ground floor. The system showed the door to be closed, so Matt sent it topsides. When the leading Marines were nearly on it he opened the door and, after angling the camera so it looked down on the entrance, could almost see the startled looks on their faces before they dodged away from view.

When nothing obvious happened, one came closer, no doubt covered by his colleagues. As he put his head in the door, Matt switched on the communication system to the lift and said, 'Step into my parlour, said the spider to the fly.'

The Marine quickly extricated himself but when nothing followed he looked back in again.

Matt opened the communication system again and said, 'I know you are a Marine force and I am a friend in dire need of your help. If Pancho is there bring him forward.'

It was obvious the Marines had their own closed communication system as he saw a man detach himself from the main body and defiantly march forward.

'Pancho, it's Pegleg,' he said when the man was in the lift.

'But you're supposed to be dead under that snow.'

'It is a long story and there is not enough time. I do not know how long it might be until they discover I am not their own man in this security booth.'

'Right. What's the plan?' Straight to the point. Maybe he had doubts but was prepared to go along with things for the moment.

'The lift will only take about four at a time. How many of you are there?'

'Nineteen.'

'Right, put four men in and I will bring them down to level three. This level is all offices as far as I am aware and I think they are unoccupied at present. Get them to check them out but not to be trigger happy until I can get more of you down. Oh, and one other thing. This security booth is the last office on that level, so tell them to treat me kindly.'

'Confirmed,' and he saw four men moving in with guns at the ready but Pancho was not one of them. He brought them down to his level and after they had left the lift and he could hear them checking out the offices he sent it back for the next lot, at the same time checking over the dock area but all seemed to be as before.

'Pancho,' and receiving an acknowledgement he continued: 'The next four will go to level two which is where the dormitories are. More care here although I think all are gainfully employed on the dock but there is still a need to check them.'

As four more got in Matt became aware of the door opening and someone behind him. He turned slowly after he had set the lift in its downward motion. A Marine was stood there with the gun aimed at him and Matt waved for him to see over the dock and the dead man. He also banged hard on his prosthetic and the Marine could hear the solid thud.

'OK,' said the Marine into his communication system. 'All systems are go down here.' With that Matt let the next lot out onto level two. Again a check over the dock area; nothing still appeared to be amiss.

'Can you stay there and guard my back?' and receiving an affirmative he spoke to Pancho again: 'Next lot to level two again but to go to the far end and be ready to go down the steps to the dock when others get there.'

Again the confirmatory wave and four more were brought down to level two and on their way. Still no consternation apparent from those working on the dock.

Things were going too easily. Matt could feel that something was about to go wrong, but the next four were in the lift and being taken to ground level with the instruction to spread out and conceal until the last had been taken down to that level. He saw on the monitors that, as they exited the lift, they spread out, taking up positions behind crates; still normal activity on the dock.

The last three were in the lift, including Pancho, when it happened. Three shots and the Marine who had been guarding him had not been doing his job right. Instead of watching out, his attention had been on what was happening on the monitors in the room, and the three bullets punched into his back and pitched him into the room on top of Matt who just managed to stay in his seat.

Someone out there was taking aim at Matt when other shots rang out and the man convulsed and fell over the edge into the water below. Another Marine appeared at the door and saw Matt shrugging off the dead Marine whilst still concentrating on the lift. As he was obviously OK, the Marine went up the pathway at a trot.

'Pancho,' Matt said, 'you are on your own when I open the doors. Tell your men they are on their own now.'

Down below he could hear a full-scale battle taking place, every shot reverberating around the cavern and making it seem as though whole armies were engaged in combat. Job done, and Matt picked up the fallen Marine's gun and spare magazines; also taking his headset and putting it on himself. Now he could communicate with all and might be of some use as he went outside.

There he met the Marine who had gone up coming back down the path. 'There is another level up there with a viewing area. He must have been up there. I think it was the smokers' area as there were a few dog ends around. No-one there now.'

'Damn, I must have missed that on the way down,' Matt spoke his thoughts aloud.

'Easy done,' was the reply, 'the opening is only obvious as you go up.'

They were then joined by another Marine coming along the corridor. He did not know where the fourth Marine on his level was but said to the two with him, 'Come on, let's give them our help,' and with that he ran up the stairs onto the roof and from the edge fired a few rounds at where he could see opposition on the dock.

Replacing the magazine, he then picked targets at leisure and heard shots from his side as the others selected targets for themselves. From below he could hear more shots with the same sound as his own gun and knew there were still Marines on the dock level who were firing as well.

A quick look round and he felt there was something different in the noise and checking to see he was not a target, it took him a while to fathom it out. Then it hit him. There was only one sub at the dock. Looking around he could see the other disappearing under the surface at the far end of the lake so he emptied the clip in its direction. It felt better but he realised as he put a new clip in place that it would probably have been like water off a duck's back.

From their vantage point on top the three of them were able to pick out their targets and eliminate them with only a little being returned, although some of it came dangerously close. Looking over again, something else was amiss and this time he realised the other sub was sinking at its moorings.

Then a movement on the water caught his eye and into the com system he shouted, 'Clear the dock, torpedo running. Just get out of there.' The departing sub must have fired two off as it went away and they were now heading towards the dock. Friend and foe were likely to be obliterated.

With no thought as to reason, he emptied a magazine into the water around one of the torpedoes. A massive explosion occurred as he got a lucky round in but the reverberations echoing around the cavern knocked everyone's senses for six, and when the second found a target and added to the cacophony inside the cavern it felt as though eardrums were about to burst. The shock wave from the first explosion must have altered its trajectory, and instead of hitting the centre of the dock area it blasted into the part that was furthest away from the buildings but still had a devastating effect.

When the noise diminished somewhat the three of them looked over the edge. Most of the dock at the side of the building had disappeared but most at the front of the buildings remained. By luck Matt had hit the torpedo meant for that area.

Inside one of the submarines, Khalikov, who was in charge, was not liking the job at present. There was no delineation of rank on board, everyone knew their job but he was the equivalent to the captain. He was quite happy to ferry people and goods around the world, no questions asked, but did not like enforcers being on board, hard men, and the leader, Roscov, just took over and commanded everything.

Worst of all he had recently had to surface in full view and broad daylight to offload the enforcers and their snowmobiles and then had to wait near the surface for their return. Less than half an hour later they came back, shipped their gear and they were away, but it seemed like a lifetime especially after the explosions occurred. When they surfaced to pick them back up, everyone was out on deck looking out for someone to discover them.

Back inside the cave he felt safe and everyone still on board breathed a sigh of relief until the shooting started and everyone was back on edge again. There was no need to sound action stations as, at the sound of the first shots, everyone went to their stations. The heavy machine gun was hydraulically raised into position and added to the cacophony.

Expecting the enforcers to get off and get stuck into the affray, he was taken aback when Roscov ordered him to get the submarine out of there and fast. A decision he was happy to comply with as he had no real wish to be part of a firefight and a couple of near heavy explosions gave everyone added impetus. As everyone was on board it did not take long for everything to be battened down and move away, stern-first from the dock.

When Roscov gave the next command, 'Fire forward torpedoes', he was gobsmacked. It would mean death to their own people, something he could not condone.

He hesitated and was about to refuse when Roscov grabbed him by the throat and menacingly demanded the same. Staring death in the face he had no option but to comply.

Summoning as much power to his voice as his squeezed windpipe would allow he ordered, 'Fire forward torpedo tubes,' knowing they were always kept loaded ready for anything.

'Torpedoes running,' came the response from one of those assembled in the control room.

'Then let's get out of here.'

As the submarine dipped beneath the surface, the first explosion occurred and the same voice from earlier added, 'Gone off short.'

They were in the underwater entrance when the second one came shortly after and all on board could envisage the death and destruction being heaped on their friends. Only Roscov seemed unperturbed by events.

Then the shaking began as disturbed water tried to push its way back out to sea, moving the submarine with its power, causing it to knock a few times on the side of the tunnel before it emerged into calmer waters. Once outside a quick rise to the surface revealed no significant damage, allowing it to submerge again.

At the first sound of gunfire, the four men outside the lift on the dock started shooting across it, mainly in the hope of pinning anyone else down until they could coordinate the rest of the team. At the same time the four on the stairs broke cover, shooting from the hip, and made their way onto the dock area to find cover there, followed by the four who had been searching the accommodation level.

Pancho, the Lieutenant and the last man burst out of the lift as soon as the doors opened and found their own cover. The opposition must have had arms at the ready as there was an immediate return of fire. The last Marine out of the lift was not so lucky and he jerked as bullets ploughed into him before going down.

A heavy machine gun then added its weight against the Marines, who launched a few grenades in its direction, although they could not identify its true position but it went quiet. From above Pancho heard the sound of breaking glass and the sound of a gun like his own. At least one above was still viable.

A little later he heard three more weapons firing from above, the sound meaning they were friendly also and the battle started to go their way, making it possible for them to advance. Two from each of the advancing sections went down but their comrades moved them under cover before moving forward themselves.

Suddenly everyone's earpiece crackled into life with a voice they did not know, but the urgency made them pull back as fast as they could. The first explosion came before they had got back to the cabins and then the second was a rolling one as first the torpedo exploded and then the munitions which were stored on that part of the dock. It all sounded like one big bang but those on the dock were able to detect each individual one.

If they had not been too preoccupied with trying to keep themselves sane from the noise and stopped from being rolled about by the heaving dock, they would have seen the side of the dock rise in the air in pieces and subside into the water, taking the other submarine, now partly submerged due to it having been scuttled, with it.

The blasts shattered the windows on all levels facing the dock and if anyone had been inside they would have been shredded by the glass. As it was the Marine shooting from the second floor dropped behind a desk at the noise of the first explosion and the shattered glass that followed the second explosion shot over his head. When he stood up there was not a piece of equipment suitable for any purpose left in the room; it had all been smashed by the pieces of flying glass which had also shredded the door and part of the wall.

The Marines at dock level regrouped and saw to their own injured before scouting around and finding two of the opposition injured. All were treated with first aid as best they could.

Through the com system Matt could hear the Marines regrouping and checked from his vantage point that no opposition were in confrontational mood. All was clear; there was no sight of anyone other than Marines moving about.

Another voice came on the com link checking off name after name, receiving answers including the two he was with, but there were about seven silences. Presumably that was whoever was in charge of the platoon, and then Pancho's voice came on: 'Are you OK, Pegleg?'

'Yep. We will come down and join you but check the areas as we go. How many did we lose?'

'Four in the initial action but three are still unaccounted for. They were a forward party by one of the subs and presumably got caught in the blast. Thanks to your warning we did not lose more.'

'Have we any prisoners? I really would like someone to tell me what it is I walked into.'

'Two with injuries being attended to at present. See you down on dock level shortly.'

The three of them went down one flight and found the other Marine who, as battle commenced, had smashed the window of the office he was in as well as smashing the light, and from his vantage point had poured fire onto those below.

A recheck of the offices revealed no-one in hiding, and nor was there anyone else in the dormitories or bathroom, and they joined the rest on the dock area or at least what was left. The explosion which had decimated the one half had also virtually wiped out anything on the dock. On arrival they could see casualties. Three were covered but the fourth was still in the Security Office. Six others were in various states of damage and being attended to.

'Lieutenant Cave,' said the man who came up to them. 'Glad to have you on board, but how did you get in?'

'There is another way in and I found it by accident as I was dodging the avalanche. What happened to the scientists?'

'Nothing. They hit the deck as the shooting started and when they looked up after it had gone quiet there was no sign of the, shall we call them, enemy. They called in and we came to the rescue. Whoever they were must have come from the sea and left the same way.'

'That would explain how that sub was able to get away so quick. Everyone was already aboard.'

'From down here we were unable to see what was happening over there as we could only shoot between the containers. If we put our heads above the parapet, as it were, we attracted fire and it was accurate.'

'Sorry. If I had realised I would have dropped more off higher up. We had a good vantage point from up top.'

'Glad you were up there. We would probably have all been taken out otherwise. How did you know it was us up there?'

'I knew you were somewhere in the vicinity waiting for something to happen, so perhaps you can tell me what is going on.'

'How could you know we were close by?'

'The last thing I saw as I left the plane was some of you getting ready for a jump. Not sitting there waiting but checking equipment although it did not really register at the time. Also Pancho knew my call sign. That should not have been known to anyone around here unless they had been checking me out.'

'As to the what, we are going to find out now that we are here. Our security people knew something was happening in the northern hemisphere but had no idea of what it really was. When things happened here they monitored activity and then when you were brought in we were sent as well. Backup ostensibly.'

'Well I wish someone would have had the decency to tell me.'

'Nothing to do with me. All that has happened today is a big surprise to us all. This is some big operation and how we would have got in if you had not been on the inside I hate to think. Looking around I think we would probably have been picked off one by one before we had reached the lift. By the way, what happened up there to set off the alarm?'

'We had an armed sneaker. He got the Marine guarding my back.' Matt said nothing about him not having done his job properly. 'He would have got me if it was not for one of your other men, as I was struggling to keep the lift working at the same time as disentangling myself from the dead one.'

'At least you had the forethought to pick up the com link. Without that we would have all been dead.'

'Nay. I just wanted to find out if you lot were saying derogatory things about me behind my back,' and they both laughed.

'I'll tell you what though. Someone is ruthless. That indiscriminate launch of torpedoes was meant to kill their own people as well.' With that the Lieutenant turned away, shaking his head in disbelief. 'Well I suppose we had better call the specialists in now to see what they can make of it all.'

Matt turned the other way, saying, 'I'm going to find a drink and then lay me down. This old body has had enough punishment for one day.' With that he left them to it, found a drinking fountain undamaged and then lay on a mattress in one of the dormitories after shaking the glass off it, and fell instantly asleep.

CHAPTER 5
A MAN UNDER PRESSURE

He was incandescent with rage. His vehemence was aimed at one man and one man alone. That man was Matthew Weston and his ears really should be burning; not just his ears but every other part of his body. All the man's woes were being heaped on Matt's shoulders.

He had stormed about in his office then into the underground harbour and workshop and now he was out in the compound. Cursing and swearing in his mother tongue and then in Russian, even interspersed with invectives in other languages which he had picked up on his travels round the world, some of which he did not know he really knew or what they meant.

His men had never seen Vassilev so wound up. When they heard him coming they just dived for cover or concentrated on the work they were doing. Anything not to catch his eye or displeasure. A few had been on the end of a verbal lashing from him when he had previously been in a foul mood and the tales had gone round so that no-one wanted to receive the same.

Normally his foul moods only lasted for short periods but this time he was still ranting and raving after over three hours. He had received news of the loss of the Base in Greenland and that had been the catalyst to send him ballistic.

Over the past few days, he felt as though he had aged years. Whenever he tried anything, he always seemed to be thwarted by that man Weston, who seemed to have a charmed life. At times he felt crushed under the weight of responsibility but a determination drove him on. Never mind what he had created so far; that only allowed him the time and money to pursue his ultimate goal – the Power.

His right hand man, his brother, was stuck in the Antarctic. At least he was alive, but Vassilev needed him here and he was not. Luckily he had not been on the submarine when Matt had sent it to the bottom.

Because the Base in the Antarctic was being prepared, most of the crew were not combat personnel, being there for their other capabilities. The second in command had taken the vessel out and would carry out orders to the letter but was slow to react to circumstances. That was the reason it had been lost.

His brother was the one who could defuse him; calm him when he got so wound up. The one who could usually see the way out of or around a problem. Close together they nearly thought as one and often would not need to speak to understand what the other was thinking. They really were chalk and cheese but the brotherly relationship was so sound that they never argued. In meetings one could be the hard man and the other the rational one but neither had the monopoly. It all depended on the circumstances and who decided to take the high ground. Many times one would finish off the thoughts that the other was speaking.

The loss of the Greenland Base was the last in a line of setbacks and even if Vassilev had been speaking directly to him about them, Matt would have been at a loss to know what he was on about in relation to some. If he had been present at the time, Matt would have likened it to the Queen song 'Under Pressure'.

It had really all started with the loss of the submarine in the Antarctic but then to compound that, the same man had now been responsible not only for the loss of another but the one that escaped from Greenland had suffered damage, although nothing significant, and was having to be recalled to the Caribbean Base for repairs before it could be used again. In addition to a few holes from Matt's burst of fire it had received a buffeting when the explosions had occurred and, again in the narrow entrance, it had received minor damage to the skin. It could still function but only in shallow depths where the pressure was not too great on the hull and the pumps could keep pace with the water that was being taken in.

To cap it all, another of the submarines, one that had been on a courier run in the Pacific, had disappeared without trace. Global positioning by satellite kept him aware of where his submarines were but this one had missed two checks when it should have sent up the probe for a few seconds to send its messages by short bursts of energy. There appeared to be no valid reason for them not to have made contact. Satellite viewing showed no adverse weather on the surface and from what he could gather there had been nothing untoward happening under the water where the submarine should have been.

Two others were being prepared for sea, one in the Caribbean Base and the other in the Pacific Base, but neither would be ready for at least a week. The submarines, once they had been purloined, had been mothballed until the time for their use. Such was the expansion of his clandestine business empire that the time had come to bring the last two into use.

Of the two submarines in the Aleutians, preparing a base for the North Pacific, one would now have to be transferred to ferry duties to ensure his contracts could be met. That would make it difficult for the workforce at that particular base, as two full teams could work better than one. In fact the two submarines only carried one complete team, and part of the workforce would now be decimated to crew the submarine that was to change its use.

In addition, two of his contracts had not been fulfilled. One because the landing of illegal immigrants in one country had been thwarted by the authorities. It was a one-way trip and the passengers had been left on an island off the coast. Vassilev knew he could rely on his own men, and anyway only a few knew of the cargo and destination before setting off. He felt that the organisation that had hired him had a mole in their midst but they would not admit to it. Now the same people were reneging on payment for another job.

All in all it had been a bad few days, each setback piling more anger and frustration onto him until finally it had become too much and he had exploded with rage. Eventually, after storming about both underground and on the surface where he had ended up, his thoughts seemed to gel and as he looked out over the ocean a calmness came over him. He now knew his course of action, and facing in a north-easterly direction anyone near would have heard him say, 'I'll have his heart on a plate.'

He had awoken from his dream this morning. His dream had been the same as Matt's, and it had been recurring over the last few days. Usually he had woken before the dream had concluded but this morning he had seen it through to the end and the outcome had been frightening. He had Matt in his sights and then the bomber had entered, whereupon Matt had disappeared; but something was still haunting him as he lay in the room where the bomb had gone off. That something was intangible but he had a gut feeling that history and the current situation were linked.

With that, and having realised what a foul mood he had been in, he now walked back as a different man. Through the compound and then the underground before reaching his office, calm and collected. Some of those who saw him returning made sure they did not catch his eye, but others recognised the change and greeted him, although getting no acknowledgement in return. His mind was set on a course of action and no-one was going to distract him from putting it into immediate effect.

Vassilev was now a man on a mission. No longer was he possessed by a consuming rage. Now he was possessed by a determination to remedy what had gone wrong and have the man who had given him so much grief here in front of him. Revenge would be sweet.

Back in his office he made contact with the base in Antarctica. He preferred communicating by the short message energy bursts but the base had not yet been set up for that and the loss of the submarine had stopped that means of contact. Longer calls over the airwaves could be monitored, but now he had no choice. If anyone did trace where the messages were being sent from or received, it would do no good. The antennae were hidden on a Pyramid in the jungle with radio relay to his office.

'Oleg,' he greeted his brother, 'we have a number of problems here and I cannot get to rescue you for a short time.' Then he proceeded to explain the situation. 'Can you cope there for another week or so?'

'If we have to, but Gregor here is nothing less than an engineering genius. At the moment I am his labourer.'

'What do mean?'

'We are carrying out adaptations to the mini-sub which should make it possible to leave here in it.'

'But I have just said I cannot get one of the submarines to you for over a week.'

'I know, but if we can reach a safe land mass you should be able to airlift us out.'

'If you can do that, then yes, but where were you thinking of?'

'Tierra del Fuego or thereabouts …'

'But that is some of the most dangerous seas, and the mini-sub will not have enough power to make the journey, and we can't have you putting in anywhere to refuel as it were.'

'There is nothing between us and there, but we have hatched a plan, or at least Gregor has. We have fixed one of the portable generators into the sub. Plenty of room as there will only be two of us leaving. Also we have put mountings on the back which will take a couple of outboards. We know it will be risky but we can surface from time to time to recharge the power in the sub from the generator and at the same time have propulsion from the outboards, which are being adapted so hopefully they will not be affected by bad weather or rough seas. We should be able to make it in a week or so.'

'Ingenious, foolhardy, dangerous, but knowing you two I feel that if it can be done, you will do it. How soon will you be ready to leave?'

'Hoping to undertake sea trials tomorrow. If that works we will load up, have a good night's sleep and set off the day after. We intend to make sure as much as possible that all is OK before we set off. We are under no illusion that it is, as you say, anything but dangerous. Nothing will be left to chance if we can help it.'

'Good, positive thinking, sounds promising. Keep me posted on progress so I know when to lay on transport. Now put Gregor on.' After an exchange of greetings, Vassilev said, 'If this works and we get you back here in one piece I have a position just waiting for a man of your talents.'

'I have heard the conversation between the two of you and realise you are now in need of an engineering fixer.'

'Just so.'

'That gives added impetus to our escape plans,' added Gregor. 'I have no doubt that we will be seeing each other in the not too distant future.'

'And we can all have a good laugh at the adversities that have recently beset us as we continue to build for the future,' added Oleg.

'What about the prisoners? Are you going to kill them?'

'Neither of us are killers but we need all the space on the sub for fuel, food and water for ourselves. We have thought long and hard about what to do and have decided to leave them to their own devices here.'

'They cannot be allowed to escape.'

'Worry not, brother. We have blocked the way out to the surface. A strategically placed explosion brought a few tons of snow down the chute and effectively blocked it off. Nothing that a few man-hours by people who know what they are doing cannot fix. Most of the machinery is being secured in one of the lock-ups and we will doubly ensure they will not be able to get in, but it will be readily available when we are able to come back and start work here again.'

'Positive thinking. I like that.'

'We also have a waterproof tank and we will put some of the last things we do not need in that and tip it into the water. It will take a crane to get it back out and divers suitably equipped. Again it will be awaiting our return.'

'That is good news indeed. I have only just shrugged off a bout of manic depression and what you have just told me has given me a spring in my step. I will let you get back to it. Don't work him too hard, Gregor,' and with laughs all round he cut the connection.

If anyone could do it, Gregor could. He was the engineering whizz of the Organisation. All the fitting out of each cave had been left to him. Where the cave was would decide the source of the equipment. Europe for Greenland, USA for the Caribbean, Japan for the Pacific, Australia for Antarctica, and the contract for the Aleutian equipment had been given to China.

This had been done as a deliberate ploy, as the shipping had been done by a tramp steamer, long overdue for scrapping. At sea the equipment had been trans-shipped to one of the submarines and carried piggyback in a container specifically designed by Gregor. The ship had then been ostensibly lost at sea and insurance claims made for ship and cargo. That way the equipment had cost him nothing and the owners of the ship had been paid twice as it had then been sold for scrap. All having taken part on different continents, there had been no suspicions about paying out each time.

A few moments later, after collecting his thoughts, he made contact with his Enforcement Team in America. After the usual coded words and an exchange of pleasantries with Korval, the head of the team, he gave his instructions.

'The immediate action required is to eliminate anyone from our side who survived Greenland. How or where is up to you. Just make sure no-one can talk.'

'But they may already have been talking.'

'More than likely, but they will no doubt be taken back to the US and a secure base for a detailed debriefing. That is what we need to avoid.'

'OK. Anything else?'

'Yes. That Weston man is causing us too many problems. We need to take care of him. I want to personally see him die in front of me.'

'You are aware there is a contract out on him. Can't we just leave him for someone else to deal with permanently? I do not particularly want to blow our cover here, but if he comes to harm at our hands the authorities might start delving too closely into us.'

'Your cover is safe, but I was not aware of the contract. Who has done it and what are the details?'

'Costain, and it is a million dollars for proof of his death. We could do the work and claim the reward. It would go towards covering some of the expenses that he has cost you.'

'No. I want him alive and here. I do not care how you do it. Just do it. Alive, do you hear, but no worries if he is harmed a little.'

'OK, you're the boss. We will get on with them straight away. Consider them done.' With that the line went dead.

The plan of action and the good news from Antarctica had put him on a high but the information about the contract out on Matt's life dropped him down a peg or two. The US team was one of the best he had and, whilst it had been right that they voiced their concerns, it also had an effect on his new-found morale.

He also knew that the next phone call would take all his effort not to lose his temper and be dragged down into the morass of despair again. Costain, a man whom he could do business with but could not get on with on a personal basis, and now he would have to talk to him in such a manner.

Using the private number he had, contact was soon made. 'Mr Vassilev, I thought that you might be calling before long.'

They both only ever addressed each other in a formal manner. 'Mr Costain, we have a mutual matter on which we need to speak.'

'You are not going to tell me that you are unable to fulfil the contracts?'

'Not at all. Everything is in hand.' It took him all his willpower to keep his voice and emotions under control, as he knew the man was goading him.

'I have heard that you have had a few setbacks of late.' This was Costain's interruption.

'True, we have encountered problems which were not foreseen, but,' and here he was able to get a dig back at him, 'I am also aware that one of your big schemes has been thwarted with disastrous results for your backers.'

'Alright, let's cut the crap. What do you want?'

'I suppose in a way it is a favour.'

'You! A favour. Now that is something I never expected to hear. What do you want? A delay in one of the contracts?'

'No. I want to cancel one – but not one between us before you get worried.'

'I don't understand.'

'The person who has caused your problem is the same as has been giving me grief.'

'Are we talking about the same Mr Weston?'

'Indeed. I want him dead as much as you but I want to be there when it happens. In fact I want to be a part of it but I will not bore you with details. All I am asking is for you to cancel the contract on his life and allow me to deal with him.' He did not add that he wanted to interrogate him first as he felt he held vital information about the past and its link to the present.

'Nothing doing. He has crossed me and I intend to make an example of him so that others will have second thoughts.'

'We can arrange for you to be present when I have him killed. All I want is for him to be alive when he comes in front of me. I too want to set an example.'

'I got things moving first and that is the way it stays. You don't live and work in this country. I do and want it to be publicly known that I will have anyone who causes me problems tracked down and eliminated. It's a matter of pride.'

'I know all about you and your pride.' He nearly said 'stupid pride' but just managed to leave out the single word that might have triggered Costain to terminate the phone call there and then. 'Just for once can't you set it on one side? If you leave it for my men to take him you could also save yourself from paying out the bounty.'

'The contract is live now. If I were to stop it there is a likelihood that those on his trail will not find out until it is too late anyway. As for the money, it will be worthwhile if the word gets round that I am not to be crossed. I will not help you. Goodbye.' With that Costain hung up.

Vassilev fumed at the intransigence of the man and then rang his US team back and ordered them to speed up Matt's interception. On being advised that a failed attempt had already been made on his life, Vassilev hoped Matt's dogged luck would hold out until his men could take him.

He needed to take out his frustrations on someone before they became all-consuming again. He dare not take it out on any of his men but he knew the exact person to call on.

Down below he went, and into a back room that had been turned into a cell. There was only one occupant: a man who, although having been beaten, deprived of sleep and tortured, still stared defiantly at Vassilev as he entered the room. That look wound Vassilev up a little more, making him grab the man and throw him against the far wall, following up before he had time to fall and had one hand to the throat, pinning him to the wall.

'Are you now going to tell me what it was about all those years ago?' Vassilev said with menace in his voice.

Although he felt as though he was going to be strangled, the man still stared back and shook his head.

Still holding the man by the throat, Vassilev spun round and threw him against the opposite wall. When the man dropped to the ground, he went over and kicked him hard but not enough to do any real damage. Nothing gained; he stormed out of the room, slamming the door behind him before locking it.

Slowly the man got up and gently exercised his body. The room was bare and he was having to sleep on the floor with no covers, but in his younger days he had encountered worse conditions and beatings but had survived. He had no doubt that he would again and be able to repay in kind.

There was no more he could do, so Vassilev went to the Temple and met with others, who greeted him as one of them. On the way he had changed into the traditional robes of a Priest, for that is how he was accepted by them. Someone who had been sent by the Gods to bring about the reincarnation of the ancient system.

'We will shortly have our first sacrifice,' stated Vassilev with confidence. 'Put the word out so that our followers can be ready to congregate at the appropriate time.'

'Is this person a suitable candidate?' asked one.

'Eminently suitable. A worthy warrior who has caused me much trouble over the past few days. The omens are right for the new ascendancy.'

With that he went back inside the Temple and in a secluded room lit only by a faint green glow, he sat on a stone throne and contemplated life as he went into a trance. In it he relived the events of years past but this time, after the bomber had struck, he had Matt's heart held on high.

CHAPTER 6
DEBRIEFING

THE NEXT MORNING MATT awoke from the same dream at the call of his name, but this time it must have been part of the dream. Something had been different though, but it was only later that he realised what. However, the smell that assailed his nostrils made him aware of the last time he had had a good meal. There is nothing like the smell of frying bacon to get one moving in the morning and he was soon amongst it, having washed and shaved.

Lieutenant Cave came up to him. 'Hope you had a good sleep. We heard you calling out at one time but when we looked in there seemed to be nothing amiss.'

'A recurring dream – or is it a nightmare? Neither really; it is a recollection of how I got this,' and he tapped the prosthetic.

'Boffins and all manner of people from various agencies are due with us today.'

'Can't wait, I'm sure,' came Matt's sarcastic remark.

'Can't say I blame you. Each will no doubt want their own debrief.'

'Well I wish I could sit in on some of their debriefings. Maybe I would find out what is going on.'

'Somehow the media have got wind of it and are already camped out up there. We have had to ship a contingent of National Guard in to secure topside.'

'More of your troops on standby ready for manoeuvres?' questioned

Matt without expecting an answer.

'Well, I had better get ready to receive the visitors. First ones should be arriving shortly.' And with that, Cave ignored the interruption and left him to finish the big American breakfast that had been put in front of him. His departure also meant he was not able to answer any of the other myriad of questions going around Matt's head.

Replete and ready for anything, he decided to have a nosy around for himself, but not knowing what he was looking for. He knew it was answers of some sort, but where was he likely to find them?

Part-way around he caught up with Pancho. 'Good to see you looking so good,' was his greeting. 'Last night you looked all in, and then when you shouted out in the middle of the night you gave us a bit of a start as we thought more of them had turned up, especially when you shouted out some Russian name.'

'I have been having a recurring dream of late. Well, as I told Lieutenant Cave, not so much a dream as recalling what led up to my losing the leg. Somehow, and don't ask me how, I feel the same man is now involved here. Only a feeling in my water, but when I have had that feeling before it has usually not been far off the mark.'

'The ones we took alive are not saying much but we have not interrogated them properly. Not our job. There are professionals who will be in today for that.'

'After all the problems they have caused me, I wouldn't mind having a session with either or both of them.'

'No way. You are not getting near them on your own.'

'So we do it together. Surely after being blown up by their own people they will be happy to talk?'

'That is not what I meant. You are likely to end up killing them if they do not give you answers.'

'That would have been last night, but after that good breakfast I am more mellow and would only use a little persuasion.' Both men laughed as they went their separate ways.

Matt continued his wanderings in and out of the various rooms and over the dock area, lost in his own little world. At the edge, where the dock had been damaged he saw a couple of bodies floating just under the surface, and called to the nearest Marines, one of whom went into the water and disentangled the bodies of two of their colleagues from the damaged area, whilst the other lifted them out.

'We always look after our own,' said one.

No answers but more questions were going round his head when the first of the visitors arrived. All of those who had been present at the briefing in New York. Wilberforce came straight over to him.

'Glad to see you are OK. I knew you would be the catalyst to all this but nothing on such a scale.'

'So you knew what I was getting into?'

'No. OK. We all knew something was going down but no-one could really put their finger on it. Hence just pointing you in the right direction.'

'You have usually been square with me on actions in the past but I have to say of late that I am having doubts about you.'

'I can assure you that whatever I know I will tell you. We have no secrets; never have had and hopefully never will. You are too good an operative for me to deliberately put in jeopardy.'

'OK,' said Matt and threw his arms in the air. 'Maybe it is just me getting paranoid after the past few days.'

'The Americans had no idea of what they were getting into or what they were sending you into but at least provided you with backup.'

'I wish they had told me.' Matt decided not to pursue the matter any further.

'Anyway, they are over the moon and O'Rourke is pretty chuffed as well.'

'Is he here?'

'Yes. Why?'

'Because that little bleeder knows more about this caper than what he is telling. Why is he interested in this operation? There is something greater going on here and if we are not too careful we will be dragged right into it to do his dirty work.'

'Impossible. The British Government would not be so covert with one of their own.'

'What do you know about him? It could be all a cover for something big he is pursuing for his own benefit. I don't trust him as far as I can throw him. Anyway, what have you found out so far?' Matt asked by way of changing the subject.

'Nothing much, but there is to be a meeting of all agencies this evening to which I have been invited and, whether they like it or not, you are coming along as my guest. If anyone can get an angle on this there is a good chance it could be you. Continue snooping, I mean mooching; I know that look on your face and something or someone better start coming up with answers. Am I right?'

Matt just smiled and continued looking around, coming across O'Rourke as he did so. In frustration at not being able to find answers, Matt grabbed him and slammed him against the wall. With his hand at O'Rourke's throat he said, 'I know you are up to something but the next time you want someone to do your dirty work don't look this way. In fact don't look my way at all or …' and he crossed his throat with his free hand.

He had watched for any sign from O'Rourke, and when the eyes had not given anything away he knew he was right and that this man was dangerous. The bluster came too late as O'Rourke said, 'How dare you handle a Government official in that way. I'll have you reported for this. You will never work for the British Government again. I'll see to that.'

'Good, that will allow me to hunt you down,' and with that he pushed him on his way. 'Just don't cross my path again,' and he left but could hear O'Rourke cursing him as he went.

Still searching for answers, Matt continued his mooching around, but nothing came to light. About half an hour later he came upon O'Rourke animatedly talking to Wilberforce, and as he came closer he could hear.

'… if he ever threatens me again.'

'You'll do what?' was Wilberforce's interruption, looking up and smiling in Matt's direction.

O'Rourke had his back to Matt and did not see him as he continued:

'When he gets back to England I'll be waiting for him and every agency I can muster will make life difficult for him. I'll teach the upstart that he cannot push a senior Government official around and get away with it.'

As he finished he found himself pushed off the edge of the dock and heard Matt's mocking words: 'You had better get swimming then,' before he stormed off.

His action had been spur-of-the-moment, but afterwards he had a couldn't-care attitude about it. Somewhere in his water he felt as though the two of them would never be destined to meet in England. In fact he had a premonition that he was unlikely to see England again.

Wilberforce, and others stood near, just looked on in amazement as Matt marched purposefully away. Seeing that the scientists had now arrived and were poking around, he felt the need to get away.

Knowing as well it would be better to keep a low profile for a while, he kept on wandering and, as he did so, he began to wonder. Who had created this vast cavern and why? The use to which it was being put now was obviously not the original intent or there would have been no need for the prefabricated buildings or floating dock.

It did not take an Einstein to be aware that the cave was not a natural phenomenon. Everything was so symmetrical, no cracks or fissures. He rubbed his hand against the wall and found it as smooth as he remembered the wall higher up, where the previous day he had tried to find water for a drink. Even the pathway down was not an addition, having been created at the same time, but why? And why did it seem to finish where it did?

Curiosity aroused, he went up the stairs and then could see that the path had continued all the way down but the building had been put up against it and the roof platform stretched out from the back wall, hence the need for the steps at the side of the building. On the passageways below, now he was not looking into the rooms, he could see the path continuing down at each level and then disappearing under the floating dock. How much further did it go and why had it been created in such a way?

He also had to admire the engineering that had gone into adapting it for its current use. Built so that it immediately faced the entrance, or so he assumed as that had been where he had seen the submarine departing. He had a feeling the entrance would not be the original one; these people would have had to adapt it to allow submarine entry. One had to respect the set-up and the way an existing feature had been adapted. But how had they found it in the first place?

He realised it was reasonably warm in the cave, even in the presence of so much cold water, but could see no obvious source of heat. Then he remembered that subterranean areas could be warm and in some places thermal heat was gained from the ground. The lights and equipment would now be creating additional heat; was this now permeating the rock above and being the cause of the melting of the Greenland ice cap? But he then dismissed it, as the operation had not been going so long. Then he had another thought. Where was the power being generated from? He could not hear a generator anywhere.

Later he found an inflatable and started paddling around the lake. Twice around, but each time something seemed to call him back to where he had seen the submarine disappear, and on the third visit he must have been at a different angle and the light caught something under the water.

Looking closer and getting the light to fall on them, he could see they were pictures. There appeared to be four in a square but he could only really make out two, which he committed to memory, and back on the dock found a pencil and paper in one of the offices and copied them down.

The evening meal was prepared early for all present. Matt, however, sat with the American Marines for his and every so often as he looked up he could see O'Rourke looking daggers his way whilst Wilberforce had the makings of a smile at it all.

One of the offices had been cleared, cleaned and commandeered for the debriefing. Matt sat at the back with Pancho and Cave, whilst the top table was taken over by Appian and Cortez for the Americans.

He had, however, walked in with Appian who said, 'Well, we have found a lot of information that was not destroyed that shows the scale of the smuggling operation to be carried on here. We know there are other bases from which they operate, but where they are exactly we do not know.'

'One of them is in the Antarctic,' voiced Matt but left it at that.

'Maybe,' said Cortez, who had joined them, 'but we ain't found it yet.'

'Anyway,' Matt continued, 'that is another of your submarines accounted for and another on the loose somewhere.'

After some discussion about the operations carried out from there, Appian then said, 'What we do not know is who created this cave and for what purpose. None of the scientists here can give a clue as to when or what, except to say that the walls appear to have been burnt and not blasted and nothing we know of could do such a thing. Even our most modern lasers would have trouble making a cavern like this.'

Stood at the back as others were entering and passing him, Matt posed the question, but to no-one in particular: 'Where does the power for this place come from?'

One of a group of scientists, who were entering at this time, turned and said, 'It is ingenious. Outside there is a heavy ebb and flow through a rock hole under the sea and a turbine has been placed there to generate the electricity for all of this. Any surplus is then stored in special batteries in one of the end rooms.' He then walked off without saying another word or allowing Matt to comment further.

That again left Matt wondering about the technical expertise which had been required to set the place up.

One of the scientists stood up and addressed the room as he would a group of college students. It was Mac from the above-ground site. 'There is no doubt whatsoever that this cave was hollowed out by some powerful force that virtually disintegrated the rock and left the smooth surface we can see around. OK, some additions have been done by blasting but they are only minor. If we could only find what did it, we could harness it for the good of modern man.'

Matt stood up and walked to the front, saying as he did so, 'What or when? I do not know but we may be able to uncover that tomorrow.

However, the why is really something. Someone ahead of their time was aware of the impact global warming would have in the future and created this cavern as a soakaway. If there is one here, we must assume there are others dotted around the world.'

O'Rourke was on his feet. 'Is this another of your flights of fancy? You'll be trying to make us believe next that the world is like a Swiss cheese waiting to soak up all that predicted water rise.'

O'Rourke was ignored as Mac said, 'On what do you base your hypothesis?'

'Pictographs at the far side of the cave,' and with that he handed the scientist the drawings he had made earlier. Mac digested what he saw and then said, 'You could be right.' Then he placed them on the table and everybody started crowding round.

The first showed a mountain that was obviously covered in snow and at the side something that resembled a hollow U with a top on surrounded by water. The second showed the mountain again but without the snow and the U was filled with water and its top had gone.

'And there are more under the water where those were but I could not make them out,' added Matt, at which he went and sat back down again.

Looking around he saw that only O'Rourke was not concentrating on the pictures, although he appeared to be looking at them. That only served to convince Matt that he definitely knew more than he was letting on. It was as though he was one step ahead of them. Probably knew more, and that made him dangerous.

Mac, who had now assumed the role of spokesman for them, came over and said, 'Will you show us where they are?'

'Now?'

'Please.'

'I thought it would be better in the morning.'

'The light does not matter in here so time of day is of no importance.'

'I suppose you're right.'

'So can we go then?' He was getting excited.

'No problem. Have we an underwater camera, as that could make life easier?'

'As a matter of fact we do, although it is still topside,' and with that he rattled off instructions. Someone to get the camera, someone else to get other equipment, as the camera was digital and could therefore be played onto a screen.

Within half an hour Matt was taking the inflatable dinghy back across the water, with a Marine doing the rowing and himself and two of the other scientists on board.

Matt had to search for the pictures again when they were near but when he pointed them out the two scientists nearly capsized the boat in their eagerness to see.

When stability returned, one scientist leaned into the water with the camera and photographed what was there. After a check on the camera screen he did it again, only more deliberately. It took three takes before the man was satisfied with the images captured and they could return to the dock.

They had left the meeting with everyone talking, and the hubbub was still going on as they walked back into the room, at which time everyone went silent. The first thought in Matt's mind as he entered was the title of a song he had heard, 'Send in the Clowns', as everyone seemed to be talking their own stuff and not listening to others.

Not a word was spoken as Mac set up the system, and the first image appeared on the white wall of the room. It had been decided not to use a small screen so everyone could see easier.

This showed the four pictographs, but at the side was a figure holding a staff on which there was a bulbous end. Something Matt had not seen earlier. The second was a better image of one of those drawn by Matt earlier and the third was his other drawing.

The fourth showed what appeared to be the excavation of the cave and the fifth the creation of a cap and the opening of the cave below the external sea level. The photos had been taken left to right on the top row and similarly on the bottom row, but the cycle was obviously anti-clockwise.

The last one was a more close-up detail of the figure with the staff, showing no features but wearing a long robe from head to foot. There was no further detail of the staff.

'Well, what do we make of that?' asked Mac as everyone then closed round for a better look after they had managed to get all the images on the wall. All, that is, except O'Rourke who, although still appearing to be interested at the back of the throng, was, to Matt's eyes, anything but.

'Can we get the paint or whatever carbon dated?' someone asked.

'Has anyone come across that person's image before?' asked another.

'What's down below us now?' Another voice.

'Let's open up this place and let the water find its own level. It will stop this being used again and could save some of the low-lying land already at risk,' came from someone else.

'We need to check out the engineering first to see if it can be used elsewhere,' piped up a different voice.

Matt had stayed back as he did not think he could add to the conversation, but when all that came were questions and no answers, he volunteered, 'The Bible tells us that Moses struck a rock with his staff and water flowed. Was this something similar?'

A few of them looked at him disdainfully but he continued, 'I'll leave you with one last thought. Eric von Däniken asked if God was an Astronaut. Is this the proof?'

With that he left the room, fed up with all the voiced questions. Staying pensively on the dock, his opinion of the 'Clown' song was reinforced. He had plenty of questions of his own but not about the creation of the cave. There was to his mind something bigger in the offing: a greater goal aspired to by some, and these thoughts sent a shudder down his spine.

In his reverie, he was aware of O'Rourke leaving the meeting long before everyone else and going off alone. The others eventually left, all in their own little groups, whether it was scientists or security. Wilberforce came and found him. 'Your comments caused a stir in there, and by the end some were beginning to believe you. But only because they could not put any other reason for it.'

Matt shrugged his shoulders, Gallic style, and said, 'Who or when I do not know, but it is obvious to me that someone in the dim and distant past expected the planet to be taken over by global warming and created a means of alleviating it, if only in part.'

'Everyone in there agrees with that. It is thought that when the pressure in the cave builds up because the increase in water level outside compresses the air inside here, the top will blow off and allow the water to rise inside the cave.'

'It's a wonder the double explosion did not raise the roof,' stated Matt, 'it felt powerful enough.'

'Must be fixed with superglue,' was Wilberforce's humorous retort.

'This on its own will not compensate for the rise in sea level. There must be others dotted around the world. Gut feeling says there is one in Antarctica close to the British Base.'

'The Americans found nothing.'

'That is because they did not know what they were looking for.' Then he emphasised, 'There must also be others, but where are they?'

'That is what a few people in there want to find out. Not the scientists, of course. Everyone has a lot to think about at present and so there is to be another meeting of those that matter tomorrow morning. You included. I think some people will be wanting you to lay your life on the line again.'

Matt just raised his eyes, said goodbye and went to lie down.

The next thing he was aware of was the same dream, but being woken before the normal conclusion by Wilberforce. 'Sorry to wake you but this morning's meeting is not taking place here. We are all going back to the US and the transport is here, so wakey, wakey.'

Matt got up and did not bother to wash or shave. He had not removed his prosthetic the night before so he followed Wilberforce up in the lift and out. A Chinook was there waiting and they were the last to board.

As soon as they were seated it took off, and Matt could look around at those present, seeing that O'Rourke was not amongst them. The others were Appian, Cortez, Cave and Pancho.

'Where's O'Rourke?' asked Matt, putting his mouth close to Wilberforce's ear.

'Doing his own thing. Does not see the purpose of this meeting having any effect on HM Government.'

'Why do I have a feeling that he is going to crop up again?' thought Matt as they continued on their way.

The helicopter landed on an aircraft carrier, and it was everybody out. 'We are to hold the meeting on here,' said Cortez. 'You cannot get more private than this, and no-one should have any surveillance around. Do you want a change of clothes, Matt?'

'I'll stick with what I've got. They have grown comfortable on me.' He did not want any of them to see the arsenal he had about his person. The more surprises he had the better was his way of thinking, as he had no way of knowing whom he could trust.

He still had the gun from the hijacking, but in his wanderings around the cave he had also found a diver's knife, which was now attached to his good leg, and an automatic with a spare clip, now ensconced at his back.

The same men who had been on board the helicopter sat in the room, each waiting for another to open the dialogue. Eventually it was Appian who said, 'Mr Weston. We have a problem. Hopefully you will be able to help us out. Mr Wilberforce here has agreed to release you from other duties. But I cannot force you to do anything. The road ahead is bound to be dangerous and you have been through more than enough and done more than anyone could have expected.'

The dialogue was stilted, as though they did not know how to approach the issue without putting him on the spot.

'No problem,' responded Matt. 'I do so wish to be re-acquainted with Vassilev. Am I not right about who is behind all this?'

There was a collective sigh of relief from the Americans, including the two Marines. 'Yes, but we have two issues here. How many and where are these caves, and how many are being used for nefarious purposes?'

'What did your people gather from the Russian prisoners?' asked Wilberforce.

'Nothing much. They named Vassilev as their leader but did not know where his HQ was. His brother was around as well. They were a new team brought in to run the Greenland operation, and had only been taken to HQ by submarine and then out to here. Any R&R was taken in Russia itself as they were waiting to get their families out. Then they would be brought to the central place to live when not on duty. They had the impression that a new base of operation was starting up somewhere and the former Greenland people were going there.'

'What you mean is that you want to find his HQ – or more to the point, want me to find it for you. Correct?'

'Yes,' although it was said hesitantly. 'You seem to have a knack of being able to hit him where it hurts and we would like you to continue being a thorn in his side.'

'Do you have any idea at where this loose cannon should be aimed at now?' Wilberforce asked.

'Not really, and that is the problem.'

'The two prisoners; did they say how long it took to get from HQ to Greenland?' This from Matt.

'Don't think anyone thought to ask them that. I'll get onto it straight away.' With that Cortez left the room.

Then addressing Appian, Matt asked, 'Do you have any idea where the Russian ex-pats are gathering? There must be places somewhere in this world where there are more than would normally be expected, especially as they seem to have their families with them.'

'I have got our people onto that at present. We had not thought of things being that way before or been too worried about them collecting together somewhere.'

'Hopefully the clues will be there for the finding,' put in Wilberforce.

Cortez came rushing back in. 'We have lost them!'

'Who? What? How?' from Appian.

'The van they were travelling in was blown up. Everyone killed.

Guards, interrogators and prisoners.'

'You should have let me at them yesterday,' was Matt's aside to Pancho.

'That means we are going to have to be very careful with you, Mr Weston. The two Marines will be with you at all times.'

'On the contrary. I want to be left alone.' Matt suddenly realised the significance of the changed ending to his dream. 'The dream I have been having has altered. Vassilev, I now feel, wants me. Not dead, although that might come later.'

'But what about the assassination attempts? They are going to continue.'

'A risk I am going to have to take. Are you any nearer finding out who put the contract out on me?'

'Our other people, who came in at the end of the hijacking, are following up leads, but nothing concrete has come to light so far. A few strands seem to be leading in one particular person's direction, but still early days and the communication lines have been well hidden.'

'OK then. Turn me loose and let anyone who wants to come and find me.'

'If that is the case we insist on a tracker being fixed to you.'

'I want more than that, so let's get started.'

CHAPTER 7
A WAITING GAME

SAT ON THE VERANDAH of the motel where he was staying, Matt felt content with the world, even though he knew his life was on the line. The sun was out and, although it was still early in the year, it felt spring-like to Matt after his time in the frozen areas of the planet. In his reverie, the words of the song 'Take Me Home Country Roads' came to him and he did wonder if he would ever be able to settle down with someone.

He was in short sleeves but knew that once he left the shelter of the building, which would not be long now, he would have to cover up because the wind was still on the chilly side. The fresh air had never smelt so good.

The Sheriff, who had just left him, wore a pullover as well as a coat. Matt found himself musing on how fate had played its hand in making him come this way and the way things had worked out for the best. Also his thoughts were on how easy it had been for him to turn back into a killing machine; no thought or compunction, just changed as though he had never been away from it. The thought frightened him, however, as it was totally at odds with his thoughts of settling down.

He had been two days in New York, getting himself prepared. His prosthetic had been adapted, but by someone he knew, and the Security Services were not aware of all the modifications. They did allow him to keep the arms he had accumulated but had insisted on him wearing a trace that could be satellite-tracked, and this had been incorporated into his belt buckle.

The agencies had found a couple of clusters of Russians in Northern Panama: one on the Caribbean coastline and the other on the Pacific. At the present time two companies of Marines should already be in position awaiting his identification of the Base. The Americans had taken the Pacific side whilst the British, after Wilberforce had insisted on their participation, were on a ship in the Caribbean in readiness for a dash to land at the appropriate time.

A few more details about the hijack had come to light. It seemed that the Airline kept a spare plane at San Diego in readiness for any problem on the west side of the country. This had been infiltrated to allow the arms to be secreted and the fitting of the control override. All that remained was to get it into service at the appropriate time. The damage had apparently been done accidentally to the scheduled plane but the man who had caused it had subsequently disappeared. That meant the other plane had to be used. The damage had only been done as the plane was ready to push away from the Terminal and so there had been about an hour and a half delay whilst the other was prepared, luggage etc. transferred over and passengers re-assigned, which had meant it still being at the terminal when Matt had arrived there.

More details of the hijackers had come to light between his leaving for Greenland and now. Three were unknown but from the emerging Eastern Europe. All had fake papers in which a cursory glance showed them to be American citizens. They might have even been able to use their own names, as the national makeup of names there was international. The steward had all the correct papers and must have been a sleeper, but there was a question mark over whether he knew it was a suicide mission. Why they had been determined to be suicide hijackers was still a mystery.

Additional information about the contract on his life was now known and the leads were all pointing in one corporate direction. It all seemed wrong; more clarification was required and Matt was assured sufficient staff were on with it.

The Agency had given him his pick of a car from their pool and he had chosen a sports car with a bonnet that seemed to slope almost to the floor, and he had put it through its paces as he had travelled upstate. Although a hard-top, it would detach if necessary and, if the weather had been better, he would probably have had it as an open tourer.

Luckily for him he had not, as suddenly out of a side road a big off-roader, with giant wheels and high off the ground, had appeared and started chasing after him. For a start Matt ignored it, thinking that if he wanted to pass, let him. However, when it rammed him from behind, he knew another game was in play.

It matched him speed for speed on the country road, giving him another couple of taps as they went. When the road climbed into the hills it started to be twisting. This gave Matt the upper hand as his car stuck to the road better and he was able to get away from them, albeit not too far. The truck must have been customised for it also stuck to the road like glue and its straight-line speed was phenomenal.

Heading round a bend, there was a wide patch of road immediately in front and Matt turned the car round as if on a sixpence by a judicious use of the handbrake, and started driving towards his pursuers as they came round the corner. The 150-foot lead had given him the advantage of being able to do it out of sight of the others. He went straight for them but then jigged from side to side at the last minute. The others did the same and Matt saw his opportunity. At the last minute he braked hard and the nose of his car dipped down. He had hoped the other would ride up his nearside and leave the road over the edge but the other's jiggling left no option but for the off-roader to ride up the offside and Matt only had enough time to lean into the passenger seat before one big tyre smashed the windscreen in front of him and continued riding over the roof, which popped and detached itself with the pressure.

The motion of the other vehicle, building up speed after it had come round the corner, eventually left it driving on two wheels only. Inside, the driver, who had not been trained in stunt driving, could not hold it, and veered to his right, hitting the rock wall where the road had been cut through the cliff, and throwing him totally off balance. Not wearing a seatbelt, he tried to brace his body against the seat back, which meant he still had his foot hard on the accelerator. The side of the cab hitting the rock wall caved in, knocking out the passenger and throwing him against the driver. Another problem for him to contend with and no time to react as it bounced off the rock face, dropped back onto four wheels, travelled drunkenly but at speed behind Matt and then flew over the edge as there was no barrier to stop it.

Matt saw the other disappear through his rear view mirror, just as he was about to accelerate away. That made him stop and get out of his car to look over the edge, at which time he realised that the drop was more than he had anticipated there. Two hundred feet or so down and near vertical. He had expected a gentle slope, allowing the other vehicle to run off whilst he got away. Instead it had dived and hit nose-first and just crumpled; no chance of anyone surviving such a drop, and he could not see anybody having been thrown out on the way down or any living person who might have got out in flight.

The bashed-up car he was now driving, albeit with difficulty because of the damage, drew more than a few stares as he made his way to the next town. One of the front wheels was now out of alignment, making it a wobbly steer, and damaged bodywork hung off. The roof he had picked up and it now graced the passenger seat.

Once there he sought out the Sheriff's office, which luckily was at the edge of town, meaning he did not have to drive the car in that state through it. Going in, he reported the accident. Having seen the vehicle mount over him, the registration number was imprinted in his brain, and when he mentioned it, the Sheriff almost did cartwheels. The Sheriff took him back to the scene of the accident, and using the pulley on the front of his Jeep, went down for a closer look.

He only had 150 feet of rope on the pulley, but it was sufficient to get him down the vertical cliff. Matt had the controls and lowered him gently. At that level he was able to then release himself from the harness and descend a steep scree with care to where the wreck lay.

It confirmed all he had hoped for, and when Matt had hauled him back up he said, 'All the law enforcers in this and the adjoining two counties are in your debt. You have rid us of a problem. The Jackson boys were always causing problems, but we were never really able to make anything stick. Any idea why they decided to pick on you?'

'I thought it was because it was a strange car in their area and they thought they might be able to make some money out of me in some way.'

'Not their usual style.'

'In that case it could be because I have a price on my head. Proof of death would have made them really rich, although how they could know the car or my whereabouts beats me.'

The Sheriff looked stunned and then asked, 'Who are you, and why?'

'If you must have that information you will have to ask the FBI. I can tell you, though, that my name is Matt Weston; at present I seem to have been seconded loosely to your Security Service.'

The Sheriff tapped Matt's prosthetic and then said, 'You were in Greenland with Tony Pancetti,' although emphasised as a statement and not a question.

'Pancho. Yes we had a bit of an adventure there.'

'He is my brother-in-law.' A pause as he collected his thoughts. 'Not strictly true.' Another pause. 'His wife and mine are sisters and we get together whenever we can. We spoke on the phone only the other day and he mentioned certain happenings but did not go into too much detail.'

'That is because the detail is still being worked out. I think I can be a little more open with you than maybe I could otherwise.' And with that he told him about the contract, without being too specific as to reasons, and the hoped-for abduction.

The Sheriff had insisted he stay in town, and got him into the motel, showing him where the good place to eat was. This was his second day there; yesterday had been all about getting his bearings. The room was simple, with minimum requirements, but comfortable. His was the middle of a row of five but the only one to be occupied in this the out-season. The front overlooked a gravelled square around which the rooms were set, but the back had a verandah that looked across a wide valley.

Last night he had been for an enjoyable meal at the Sheriff's house.

The Sheriff had insisted he should come to tell more of his adventures. This he had done, but had been a little less than totally truthful about some of them, especially the recent ones.

The sheriff's name was Onslow, and out of uniform he looked less formidable, but still towered over Matt, who thought he must be six foot four. Being tall made him look like a beanpole, although closer inspection revealed a fit body. The full head of hair was well turning grey, which he put down to the three women in his life – wife, daughter and stepdaughter. Having seen him and Tanya together, Matt somehow doubted it. Dressed in jeans and a thick shirt, he would not have looked out of place on the Range.

Tanya, the Sheriff's wife, was obviously younger than him, and it transpired that her husband had been killed in the Army, and when Onslow's wife had died in a car accident, Tanya had looked after his son whilst he had been working. She had a young daughter at the time and, although romance had been slow to ignite, they had eventually married and now had a daughter of their own.

Tanya was a damn fine cook and Matt had really enjoyed the homemade food and the excellent company. It was in one of those mellow moments in the conversation, when Onslow had cuddled Tanya in passing, that he realised something was missing from his life and wondered, after this was all over, if he should find someone and settle down.

This morning's breakfast had been in the only café, which doubled as general store and gas station. The locals, who frequented it for breakfast, eyed him a little suspiciously, but word must have got around about his friendship with the Sheriff and some even wished him 'Good morning'. Otherwise he was left alone.

Today he wished he had some binoculars, but did not want to ask the Sheriff as that might have made him do something if he had known the reason why. Yesterday morning he had seen a flash of light way over on the far hillside, and again it had appeared this morning. Matt was sure he was being observed and the flash had been the morning sun reflecting off a spyglass; but which party?

He was in open view and could have been an open target for anyone with a powerful rifle. Getting proof of death from a body in the middle of a town might be a problem, but not insurmountable, if someone was determined. He was hoping that it was the Russians keeping an eye on him and awaiting the opportunity to take him.

He was also left wondering how would-be assassins knew where to find him. It was almost as though someone was pointing them in his direction. Was there someone in the US Security circles with a hidden agenda; not wanting him to be taken by the Russians in case he was able to destroy that organisation?

There had been two other attempts to kill him: one even in New York as he was leaving Security HQ. Bungling fools had shown themselves with arms drawn too early. Matt had not seen them nor expected anything so near a secure place. The Marine sentry, on the ball, saw what was happening and opened fire first, making every shot count.

The other had been last night, after the Sheriff had dropped him off and he was walking the last few yards to his motel room. A high-powered silenced rifle had been used, but for some reason the bullet had passed in front of him and thudded into the building. A second followed but lower, and would have caught him if he had dived forward. Instead Matt had fallen back to allow him to get his gun out, but when he was ready he could not see anything and thought he heard scuffling in the distance as someone ran away. He had not reported it to the Sheriff, thinking it would be one less thing for him to worry about.

Yesterday he had driven the car he had hired in town, the other being in no fit state to drive and awaiting collection, up to a place he had found that seemed to be an ideal place for an ambush or abduction. All he had done there was take a walk around. Now was the time to go back there for today's visit and another walk, although this time in another direction as there were plenty of pathways leading off from there, and it had to appear that he was just another hiker. Better not to give anyone the idea that they were being set up.

Getting his coat, he set off. There had been enough time for everything to be in place. The timing had to be spot on because the Sheriff, who had now been brought in as part of the scheme, needed to be in place, but he had to get there by a circuitous route.

Arriving at the spot, Matt parked on his side of the road and got out of the car. Gazing around to get his bearings, he became aware of a movement on the other side of the road, and saw two men rise from hiding and point guns at him. Before they could do anything they were felled by a hail of bullets from rocks over to his left, even before Matt could throw himself to the floor or get one of his guns out.

The Delaneys, Peter and Paul, father and son, were bounty hunters. Each had arms covered in tattoos and sported a ponytail; with unkempt beards it was hard to tell which was the elder. Quite happy to take on either dead or alive cases but preferring the dead ones, which meant taking less into account of the requirements of the law. They were not aware of either Matt's background or the other current aspect of his life. To them it looked like an easy number; an Englishman out of his depth here.

The previous day they had seen him park here and take a walk. After last night's failed attempt, and nearly having been caught by the Sheriff, they had decided that out of town was best and to lie in wait in the hope he would return to the same place. They thought everything had fallen nicely into place for them when Matt arrived.

Rising from their hiding place, guns at the ready and concentrating on their target, neither saw the others. The first they realised they were not alone and that something was wrong was the powerful bullets thumping into them, hurling them backwards. That was the last thing they knew, as they were dead before their bodies hit the ground.

Two men appeared from where the shots had emanated and started moving the short distance towards him. Matt caught a part of their instructions to each other: Russian, so he feigned a mistake to his stance as he cleared his gun and fell against the car, seeming to bang his head. The next thing he knew was a jab in his arm and, as he entered a nothingness, he knew he had been correct about the abduction.

Higher on the hillside, but on the opposite side of the road to where Matt had parked, the Sheriff had been in place for some time, as he had been aware of the two strangers in the area. He was sure they were the same ones who had taken pot shots at Matt the previous night, when he had almost caught them in the act. As Matt had not said anything, he thought he must not be aware of the attempted assassination and, not wanting to worry him more, kept quiet.

He had had them in the sights of his rifle ever since they arrived, but when Matt arrived he was taken as much by surprise as Matt was by the shots from the others, whom he had not seen. They must have been in hiding well before he arrived. Turning his attention to the newcomers and lining up the rifle on them, the sound of their voices reached him, if only faintly.

His mind went back a good 10 years to a time when, as a Deputy, he had to keep a couple of Russians on a visit from the Embassy under surveillance. Neither had spoke English in his presence, always their native tongue, and that is what he heard now. He kept them covered and saw Matt fall, but they reached him and did nothing apparently untoward, and so he just kept observation, but still covering them with the rifle.

One of the men stayed with Matt, who had now been moved to the other side of the car away from the road, whilst the other disappeared. The one who remained moved the bodies so they were hidden from view, and then cleared up the spent cartridges from their shooting. A couple of times he had to dodge out of sight as someone drove by, but no-one seemed to notice anything wrong, and each continued on their way. Three quarters of an hour later the other Russian re-appeared in another off-roader pick-up, which had been well hidden, as the Sheriff had not even seen it. They heaved Matt unceremoniously onto the back alongside a package and, covering both up, drove off, going further away from the town. A short while later the Sheriff heard but did not see a helicopter take off. At which time he rang Appian.

'Looks as though the abduction has taken place. He was driven off by two of them unconscious, and as far as I can tell has just been whisked away in a helicopter,' and then he explained what had happened in detail.

'Good luck to him. All we can do now is wait, hope and pray.'

'Amen to that. What action should I take in relation to the dead bounty hunters?'

'Keep it as simple as you can. For me you can lose them. By the way, thanks for your help.'

As the line went dead, a smile came to the Sheriff's mouth. He did not want to formally deal with the dead ones, as it could lead to complications for a few people, including himself, and publicity was the last thing required now as it could put Matt's life in more danger. The Sheriff in the next county was of the new school, having been educated in law enforcement before taking up the job. Really he was more suited to a city post but liked to crow about how good he was. There were a few unsolved cases on his books and he was about to get another. Definitely needed taking down a peg or two, and now was the time.

The local Sheriff had progressed through the ranks, as it were, sometimes working by the seat of his pants, but there were no outstanding unsolved cases. The other Sheriff could now have an abandoned vehicle to sort out, if everyone had left in the helicopter, as the abduction had taken place close to the county boundary. It would be only fair for him to have a couple of bodies as well to worry about.

Having decided his course of action, the Sheriff found the would-be killers' hidden car and heaved the bodies into the back. Then he drove over the county line and sent the car hurtling over the edge of a ravine. They were now someone else's responsibility. He saw no-one throughout, and then returned cross-country to where he had parked his own vehicle.

He drove back home, picked up his wife, and travelled back to pick up Matt's car, putting her in the picture as much as he dared. He had secured the car before disposing of the bodies, and now he drove Matt's car back to the rental agency whilst his wife took his to the office, and when they joined up later it was off to pick up Matt's belongings from the motel.

When the Sheriff entered the room there was nothing to show anyone had ever been living there. Everything of Matt's had been removed. He had come in the front door but the back door onto the verandah was ajar.

Going through to the outside he could see that someone had used a grapnel to climb up from the track below. Now he knew why the Russian had been so long in returning, and what the package in the back of the truck had been.

Back home after the evening meal, when the kids were doing their own thing and they were sat alone, his wife said, 'That man needs a woman in his life. No-one can keep living on the edge like that. Anyone would think he was gay.'

'He is not as far as I am aware. But what makes you think that he needs female company?'

'Simple. He keeps everything to himself. That cannot be good for him. No-one to talk things over with like we do. No chance to relax.'

'Normally in his line of work you could be right, but just at the moment it is probably as well he has no-one else to worry about. He will have enough on his plate keeping himself out of harm's way, even though he seems to have put himself in that position deliberately. I like him, and only hope he is able to keep one step ahead.'

'I rather like him as well. He would make any woman a good husband.'

'Never mind matchmaking. His work would keep him away for periods of time, which probably would not be good. Anyway, who did you have in mind?'

'Was it that obvious? I was thinking of Widow Hardy. She's about his age and an adventurous person. If he comes back, and it would be good to see him again, I think we should introduce them. In fact I would have invited her last night if she had not been on her way back from the West Coast after seeing her specialist.'

'She has seen off three husbands. I'm not sure I would wish her on my worst enemy. Wasn't she going to try to see her sons on the way back?'

'Never mind changing the subject. They would be ideal for each other. Maybe not for marrying, but they would be good together. Take my word for it. As to your question, I would think she will try to see her stepsons even though they never make contact with her.'

'I know she feels a responsibility for them since their fathers died, but with no reciprocation on their part, and they were the ones who left of their own volition, I would give them up as a bad job.'

'Yes, she will no doubt, as usual, watch from a distance.'

'Well, he may never come back this way again. Even if he is successful in what he is now involved with, there is still the problem of the contract out on him. How do you get rid of that without being killed? You know, though, I would like to see him again. I feel a little responsible for him. Don't ask me why.'

'I know. And I also know you have not told me everything about what happened out there today.'

'What you don't know will ensure you are not caught up in any conspiracy later if the shit hits the fan. But you are right. It is great to come home to someone. Come here and give me a kiss.'

Appian had known, even before the Sheriff had rung, that something had happened. They had been keeping tabs on the tracking device and suddenly it started moving at speed. They followed it as it went westwards, stopping twice as transport changed or was refuelled and then rested near Seattle. A day later it continued westwards out across the Pacific and later onto the land.

Had they been wrong about the destination, or had they been sold a bum steer? Either way, they could now only sit and wait for Matt to give them a sign.

CHAPTER 8
OLD ENEMIES

Hearing was the first of his senses to fully return, although Matt had been semi-aware of the noises and sensations going on around him. He lay still, just listening, allowing the drug to wear off, and knew instinctively he was on a submarine. In his active service days he had been conveyed in such craft a number of times and the sounds were exactly the same, even though he knew he was on a newer one.

As the rest of him came alive again, he realised he was strapped down on something soft, but not restrained, as he was able to firstly move his arms and then his legs. The fastenings were purely a safety device. He also became aware that he was naked and that he lay in his own bodily fluids. Loosening the straps he eventually sat up at the sixth or so attempt and remained so until someone looked into the cabin.

'Ah, we have life,' was spoken in English with a heavy Russian accent. 'Welcome back to the living as you English say.'

Matt looked himself up and down and said, 'I think I could do with a clean-up and some clothes.'

'No problem,' came the rejoinder. 'Follow me.'

'But we do have a problem,' added Matt. 'One leg only does not allow me to walk.'

'Ah, the false leg. Here we are.' With that the Russian reached under the cot and handed it to him.

As he put it on, Matt noticed that the knife had been removed, but he was glad to see all the toes were intact. Standing up made him go a little dizzy again but it soon passed and he was able to follow the other.

It was strange walking through the submarine naked. Were they trying to humiliate him by not having offered him even a robe? It did not bother him, even when everyone stared at him. He just kept on, with an enigmatic grin on his face. So far things were playing into his hands, as he had hoped. Even so, he was still aware that there is many a slip twixt cup and lip and that things could quite easily go pear-shaped.

The man led him to a shower room, and when he had washed himself the man appeared again with some of his clothes. Matt realised they must have removed the whole of his wardrobe from the motel, as they were different to the ones he had been wearing when taken.

Back outside the shower room, there were a number of people crammed into the corridor, and they started shouting in unison at him. Although it was in Russian, he was left in no doubt that it was a chorus of abuse and that he was not welcome. One man, who appeared to be their leader, pushed his way through and then shoulder-charged him.

With no room to manoeuvre, Matt had no chance to take evasive action, and was knocked off balance. He did manage to stay on his feet, but then the rest crowded round and punched, jostled and kicked him. Because the area was so tight with people, he still kept standing but leant against the bulkhead.

Eventually the crowd moved back and their leader was the only one stood in front of him. He was nearly as broad as he was tall, which was only about five foot three, probably made up of solid muscle, as he hit Matt in the chest with the flat of his hand. Matt, who had just managed to stand upright again, was knocked back against the bulkhead with the wind taken out of him, expecting a follow-up, but none came and the crowd all just melted away.

The remnants of the drug in his system and the punches he had received made him feel nauseous and dizzy, but he managed to stay on his feet. As he came back to his senses, he was aware of another man stood in front of him and, although still panting, asked, 'Have you come to use me as a punch bag now?'

'My dear fellow,' the voice had only a trace of an accent, 'I am in charge here and was not aware of the welcome you have just received. In fact, I have only just been informed you were moving about. Better come to my cabin and have a seat.'

Without waiting for a reply, he turned and led the way along a corridor to his cabin, stopping along the way to pick up a tray of food, which he placed before Matt when he was sat in his cabin. 'Please enjoy the food,' and he then poured out two glasses of liquid. 'Sorry it is nothing stronger than a cola.'

Although it was only a cold buffet snack, Matt attacked it with relish and then asked, 'Is that the usual way of welcoming guests in Russia?'

'No, but can you blame them? They know who you are and that you were guilty of getting some of their colleagues killed. They consider that to be murder, and if it was not for the demands of Vassilev that you arrive in one piece they might well have put you out of a torpedo tube – alive!'

'People should not try to kill me. I, as with most people, tend to fight back when attacked. Granted the sinking of the sub in Antarctica was not intended; that took me as much by surprise as it probably did the crew.'

'Not only that but your interference in Greenland caused corporate grief ...'

Before he could go on, Matt interrupted with, 'But more deaths were caused to your people by the departing submarine firing torpedoes. That wasn't you, was it?'

'No.' It was emphatic. 'For your information you are now in the Pacific. We had to be taken away from preparing a Base in the North Pacific to pick you up and become the Pacific Courier boat. It was an Atlantic crew responsible for the destruction there.'

'And yet I am getting the blame.'

'In the heat of battle many things happen, including collateral damage and the wrong apportionment of blame. Also the launching of those torpedoes was nothing to do with the crew. Enforcers, sent to eliminate you, forced the issue.'

'Presumably the same people also killed the survivors before they could talk to the authorities.'

'I was not aware of that but cannot say I am surprised. I for one would not like to tangle with them. A bad lot; a very bad lot. Ex-Secret Service.'

Matt rubbed his chin thoughtfully and realised he had not had a shave. 'About two days by the feel of this since you took me. How come you got me here so fast?'

'Helicopters, planes and a loading facility on this side of the US. You would be surprised how fast we can move stuff around. Your shaving tackle is in your cabin. Do you think you can find your way back?'

'Sure.'

'Well, stay there – and no moving about the submarine on your own. If you want the heads, ring for service.'

With that, Matt considered himself dismissed and went back to the cabin, aware of the shadow that followed him. Obviously he was not to be trusted alone.

Back in the cabin, where the cot had been remade, and after a shave, he lay down and tried to make some sense of what he had been told.

About an hour later there came a knock at the door and the same person who had greeted him before poked his head round the door and asked, 'Would you like a tour of this thing?'

'I would like that very much.'

'Good. Then come along, and no tricks as we will not be alone.'

'But are you taking me for another beating?'

'Goodness, no. But if you ever find yourself alone, no-one can guarantee anything.'

Walking along, Matt was aware of the armed man following, and pointing to him said, 'He is not necessary. I have no intention of sabotaging this vessel. I really do want to renew my acquaintance with Vassilev.'

Despite that, the guard remained as they toured from one end to the other. At one time he saw the leader of the pack who had assaulted him, but nothing happened and two hours later he was sat in the canteen with those off duty, having a proper meal. He had to sit alone and he could feel the crew staring at him from time to time. Ignoring it he considered it prudent not to antagonise anyone. It was obvious Vassilev had given the no-damage order, but would anyone abide by it if they felt slighted in any way?

For the rest of that day and all the next he remained in his cabin, with food being brought to him, and only going out escorted to the heads as required. Someone had found a couple of American magazines for him to read, but they were not ones to hold his attention. His mind was thinking about what was to come when he and Vassilev met, and what would then befall him.

At the end of the second day of his known confinement on the sub there was a great deal of orderly activity, and he felt they had reached Base, but where, and was it one of the places that was being targeted by his allies?

Eventually all was quiet and the same man came to collect him, this time entering without knocking, and ordered, 'Time to leave. Let's go. Your things will follow,' and when he was slow to react, 'Come on, chop, chop,' was added.

Up onto the deck he followed the man, with the same armed guard following. A gangway had been placed between the dock and the sub, and looking around, Matt could see they were in a similar cavern to that in Greenland but on a bigger scale. More buildings and docking bays, the furthest away being occupied by a similar submarine.

As he stood looking, the man with the gun prodded him to move, and seeing other crew members leading off, he moved into line, deliberately selecting his place. Two in front of him was the one who had thumped him; retribution was due, regardless of the consequences. At the appropriate time he stopped, steadied himself on the prosthetic, and extended his good leg between the legs of the person in front.

His quarry had a foot hooked and could do no other than tumble off the gangplank. Matt's action had been so quick that no-one realised what had happened, apart from the man immediately behind him, who had steadied him when he seemed about to fall, and when Matt looked back at him he was sure there was a smile. His quarry, he was now sure, had been a bully, and a number of people would be likely to have a laugh at his expense, albeit maybe in private.

If there had been water between the dock and the sub, the man would have had splashdown. Unfortunately the sub was snug up against the dock, but because the deck was not as wide as the body of the sub there was a gap into which he fell, and his size trapped him there. He did manage after a struggle to extricate himself, by which time Matt was on the dock. Looking back, he could see the enmity of the man, and so to make matters worse blew him a kiss. This time he did hear a few titters from around him.

There was no mistaking the man who came to meet him. The same erect bearing, although time had not really been good to him. The dark hair was now a dirty grey and cut short, revealing the part ear. The thinnish face had puffed out somewhat and there was about him the air of a troubled person. That had lifted the moment he saw Matt on the deck of the submarine, and the smile of greeting said, 'Gotcha.' Although he looked somewhat fit, there was the hint of a paunch from good living, sitting behind a desk, running a business and generally lack of action.

'So, Mr Weston, we meet again. You have given me a bit of grief of late but now is not the time to remonstrate with you. Follow me and we can talk over old times in better surroundings.'

'You can call me Matt, Piotr. Let us seem as though we are all friends together for a start.'

Receiving no answer as Vassilev turned on his heels, Matt followed, but this time there was no armed shadow.

Once they were in a room off the dock, Vassilev turned to him angrily and said, 'The name is Vassilev; nothing more, nothing less, and you will address me so at all times and not refer to my Christian name again, especially in public.' With that his demeanour mellowed and he continued, 'Let me show you around outside, I am sure you have had enough of enclosed spaces for the present.'

'Fresh air would be rather enjoyable, but where the hell are we? Is it cold or hot out there? Am I suitably dressed for the occasion?' He had been in so many seasons over the past few days, from autumn in Antarctica to spring in Greenland, and wondered what season he was going to encounter now.

'Come and see for yourself,' and he led the way, with Matt intently watching every direction and every move.

Outside it was a pleasantly warm evening with a cooling breeze blowing off the sea. They were stood on a cliff top overlooking the sea, but behind them was a small town, some of which was built into the cliffs that reached higher, and other buildings under a jungle camouflage net.

'I see you note your surroundings. This is just a little added security. Down there is the Pacific and we have eyes above and below the water. The mountains behind us are almost impassable, but we have a warning system in case anyone decides to come calling. We also have early warning of any aerial approach, and appropriate defences should they be required. In and out is either by our own helicopters or over or under the sea.'

'Most impressive. For a clandestine operation you certainly have covered all the options. How come then that I was invited, if that is the right word, to visit?' he added, hoping to keep up the pretence. At the present time he had no way of knowing if they had fallen for the ruse or if he was now being taken for a ride.

'Because I have need of some information from you, but more of that later.'

'What's it all about' was the song title that crossed Matt's mind, but instead of 'Alfie' he substituted 'Piotr'.

'You think this is impressive. Just wait until you see our headquarters – but for that we need to go back down below.'

Again Matt just followed; rather nonplussed, but still focusing on the route he was being taken. What he had seen here was good enough to be a main centre of operations, but it seemed there was some other place. Where he was now would, he thought, be in striking distance for those waiting to come to his assistance, but where else was he being taken?

Back down to the dock area, but to a quiet side where they both got into an outboard inflatable and set off across the underground seawater lake. They seemed to have been steering in silence towards the blackness for what seemed about half an hour, but was probably less, when there came a discernible faint glow ahead. When he looked back, the dock area was now itself only an illuminated intangible blur.

The faint glow was subdued lighting which increased as Vassilev, on reaching the side, hit a switch. Climbing up the side of the cave was a set of rungs fixed to the wall, and Vassilev started climbing as soon as he had tied up and cut the motor. Matt could do no other than follow, but lost sight of him at one point as the ladder went over a rock protrusion, which left anyone climbing it hanging over a long drop. At the top he found that he was not breathing as heavily as Vassilev.

'We have a lift but exercise is good and I like to check that I am still capable. At one time I timed myself, but now just making it without being too much out of breath makes me feel good.'

'You need to have a head for heights, especially where it comes out over the belly,' was Matt's response.

'Just a feature of the cliff face that we have made into an additional security feature. If anyone was being chased up or down, they could have a slight advantage if they chose to take it. Anyway, time waits for no man. Follow me, as we need to go through the airlock. Cannot do with losing pressure as the water level would rise by a good three foot, which would not take that long and the dock would be under water.'

Again Matt followed. Through the airlock and into a long wide corridor that had obviously been recently hewn out of the rock. Two rails sat side by side, and on one was a cabin capable of taking about 16 people, and into this both men got.

'Electromagnetic propulsion,' was all Vassilev said as he sat at the controls with Matt immediately behind him. Contact, and he felt the carriage rise slightly and then power away on the monorail.

Just as they seemed to have reached maximum speed the carriage slowed and came to a stop. Here the rails parted and on the opposite side was a similar carriage which had also just appeared, but no-one was in it.

'As one goes the other automatically comes the other way,' spoke Vassilev by way of explanation. 'That way we are sure to have one at either end if required. It is not usual to stop half-way but I wanted to show you something else.' With that he got out; Matt did likewise.

Between the rails was a large slab of stone, four foot square and 12 inches thick, towards which Matt was looking and wondering what it was for.

Noting his questioning looks, Vassilev explained: 'If you look up you will see where it fell from as we were excavating this passage. It killed two of my men and injured three others.'

Matt looked up and saw a black square in the ceiling about 12 foot above them, and then saw Vassilev reach down the side of the stone and a rope ladder streamed down. Obviously there was some radio control at the side of the slab.

'This was an existing passage between two underwater lakes which we enlarged to facilitate movement between the two centres. What we had come across we did not know until we started clearing our way upwards. Come along and I will show you.'

'Follow my leader' came to Matt's mind, as that was all he seemed to do. He waited until Vassilev had climbed and disappeared through the hole before venturing up himself, whereupon he found himself in a chamber about 15 foot square, dimly lit by electric lights. From one side a staircase disappeared, and he was just in time to see Vassilev going up it and set off after him.

Up and up through four levels of chambers of various sizes all similarly lit, and then they came out. It was the top of a Pyramid and below them the green canopy of the rainforest was spread out. All sides of the Pyramid and the top were overgrown and would be invisible from the air.

'I am surprised you did not make this into your headquarters …'

Before he could continue, Vassilev turned to him and said, 'If we had not already got ourselves sorted we might just have done that. However, there is now a better use for it. Come and see what you cannot from up here.'

Once again Matt could do no other than trail after him down the steps on the outside, noticing that they had been cleaned and made safe but then camouflaged again. Below the canopy level of the trees was a large clearing and people were going about their daily business. All obviously had a bloodline from pre-Spanish invasion times.

As they descended, Matt was informed that, whether it be Mayan, Olmec or Toltec, the history by word of mouth passed down through the generations indicated that power came from one source and the disciples from that place went out to found their own groups; Aztec, Inca or other. Everything pointed to this Pyramid being that source, hence all the others erecting Pyramid-type buildings as their Temples.

Vassilev stopped within view, but not venturing any further, and spoke quietly: 'Although these people are living in the Twenty-First Century with all its creature comforts they are happy to recreate the great times past when they were a superior race. With my help they will be again. The Shaman and Leader is of true Mayan decent, as is his wife. All the people here have only a small amount of Spanish blood in them. I made sure of that before inviting them to become a part of the great rebirth of their nation. My son is now one of them.'

'But that will surely spoil the true bloodline.'

'True. But my bloodline comes from the great Cathars, and once I have the source of all power, they will be happy to receive my family into theirs as they will then have the ability to rule over, who knows, maybe the world.'

With that they retraced their steps and Matt then realised the steps were large and he really had to lift his good leg to climb them. They must have been eighteen inches from tread to tread. Ideal for defending from people climbing, or maybe they were meant for people over seven feet tall. The last comment was forgotten as he was more interested in how he was going to get the upper hand and wondering where he was going to be taken next.

As they regained the summit, Matt asked, 'So why the hole in the bottom of this thing?'

'Good question. It was only just resting on two pieces of rock jutting out and, of course, when we took them away, it fell. The fit was so neat you could not tell it from the surrounding rock roof and we did not have the amount of light we now have.'

'Had to open upwards then. Sure would take some effort.'

'There are lugs on the underside as it is now. It turned over as it fell. We think there was a pulley system inside.'

'You still have not told me what it was for.'

'Because we do not know. It was not a means of escape, as this passage only led to the Lakes.' At the mention of the plural, Matt pricked up his ears as Vassilev continued: 'We have created the ways up to the surface from them. The only way out at the time this was being used was under the water.'

Matt made an inspired guess. 'Did seawater feature in their rituals?'

'There is not a lot of history about this place, so could be. Why?'

'The lake is seawater. If the priest appeared to the people with seawater or fish that only lived in saltwater, he really could be looked on as a wizard. After all, even from up here you cannot see the sea.'

'It is as good a theory as any. But come, we must go now.'

Once back at the monorail they continued in the same direction as before. At the end it was out of the carriage and through another airlock. They could have been in a mirror image of the underground lake they had recently left. At the foot of the ladder was a manned inflatable waiting but this time they took the lift. Across the way, Matt could see the working dock again just as an illuminated picture.

As they went, Matt asked, 'Presumably the water levels were rising in the cave once the Pyramid was built, especially when the trap was opened.'

'There would be nothing to stop it, but at that time there was not the same effect of global warming, and the fluctuation of water level would not have been so much. When we came here the sea level outside was half a metre above the inside level, and when the slab fell nothing much happened. It was only as we cleared the inner stairway that we realised what was happening. Air started rushing out so we stopped up the gap and put in the airlocks before continuing further.'

'Gave your people a scare, eh?'

'And me. I was there. We had to act fast as we already had most of the lakeside structures in place.'

When they arrived, Matt marvelled at the virtually duplicate area of where he had left the submarine. Two submarines were tied up there, and as Vassilev saw him look, said, 'One of those is the one you damaged in Greenland.'

Through the dock area and up, where Matt found himself inside a stockade made of stone. 'This used to be a Spanish fort which we have refurbished and made stronger. Out there is the Caribbean.'

There were two walls to the fort, one at each end. The back was a vertical cliff and in front a 200-foot drop to the sea. Matt had no doubt it was as secure as the place he had just left. How would help be able to get in?

Outside the gate was a small village, with all the buildings looking contemporary with the fort. 'That's where most of our people live when they are working here. Some have integrated with the locals and live in the nearby villages. Others, who have families from Russia here, normally live in the town about 10 kilometres down the coast.'

'How do you keep your clandestine operations under wraps with outsiders being so close?'

'No problem. Most of the money hereabouts comes from our operations, whether as earnings or grand gestures. Crime is virtually non-existent thanks to the company's enforcers, so the police do not need to concern themselves too much with this area, for which they are grateful. A few backhanders keep anyone else sweet. Hey presto, we can do what we like as long as it does not interfere with the Government.'

'Very nice too. Got it all worked out to your advantage. On an international scale too, and then along comes me and things start to fall apart. How much have I cost you in lost equipment and aborted contracts?'

'Millions, and that is only an estimate. Once you are no longer of use to me you will be made to pay for that. I was originally going to hand you over to the Temple worshippers so that they could make a ritual sacrifice of you, but your treatment of Kharlov on the submarine has rather altered the complexion of things. He is one of my hard men; there is one on each submarine. You, however, have made him a laughing stock and I may just have to turn you over to him so that others will see a lesson.'

'Oh good, something to look forward to.' Matt made light of it but added, 'Although something tells me it will not be allowed to be a fair fight. Mind you, if you play your cards right you could eliminate me and claim on the contract on my life. It would reimburse you somewhat.'

'Ah, the Cavalcade Corporation of Seattle and Mr Costain. We already do business together and my taking care of matters might just help ease the current pain we are both experiencing thanks to you.'

'All part of the service,' was Matt's sarcastic rejoinder, but mentally he noted whom he would need to visit if ever he got out in one piece. It also gave the reason he had been brought in via the Pacific. The contract on his life needed to be terminated, one way or the other.

Vassilev ignored that comment but said, 'Come with me to my office. We need to talk. You have information that I need. Hopefully a vital piece from the last time we met.'

Matt was perplexed by this but said nothing as the follow-my-leader started again and soon they were in his office, an inner sanctum with no outside windows. The desk was large and solid and end-on to the doorway, facing a wall on which were a number of large TV screens. On the desk was a computer, a notepad and photographs, presumably of family but Matt could not see clearly, nor did Vassilev enlighten him. The wall behind the desk was full of cabinets but all doors and drawers were closed. On either side of the door were bookcases full of various types of volumes. The remaining wall was solid rock.

Once they were sat at opposite sides of the desk, although in comfortable chairs, Matt opened by saying, 'I should have killed you all those years ago and all the current problems that you have been causing various Governments would never have started.'

'You were sent to kill me! My orders were to kill you as you had become a thorn in the side of my masters.'

'Why had I?'

'No idea. I was just following orders, just like you. I do not suppose you know why your side targeted me?'

'No. Anyway, what was the lure that you were told about for getting me in your clutches?'

'An informant to be grabbed and taken away.'

'Likewise. The bomber man was not part of any plan I knew of.'

'He did not feature in mine either.'

'So someone set us both up to take us both out. Who?'

'That is what I had hoped you could tell me.'

'I do not know. It is something I have pondered on deeply in my quiet moments, but there seems to be no logical answer. However, I do feel that in addition to the set-up for us, someone else was pulling strings and had a separate agenda.'

'I have to agree with you there. I have recently had the opportunity to interrogate the person who sent me on that fateful mission, and even under extreme pressure he did not know anything more.'

'For what it is worth, and it is only a feeling, I think that same person is now pulling the strings again. Who and for what purpose eludes me. I feel as if the ball is in play and we are all heading for the final goal right on full time.'

'But what team is going to win?'

'That is the $64,000 question.'

'I have heard of your gut feelings. Oh yes, I have my moles in various places. However, I tend to agree with you. No action will be taken against you over the next few days, as I want you to think long and hard without any other worries about the events of that time. Although it now seems an aeon ago, I still feel it as though it was only last week, and you have more reason than me to remember. Every day you see its legacy.'

'If I came up with an answer, I don't suppose you would keep me around to participate in any retribution?'

'That might depend on how fast such could be undertaken. Now, if you will excuse me I have work to do. Someone outside will show you to your quarters. You may wander around the complex but on no account must you leave. Just to make sure,' and Vassilev reached into a drawer, 'you will put this on,' and threw a bracelet over to him. 'It is a tracker device but also sounds an alarm if you leave the compound. We will meet again to have a further conversation this evening over dinner. Until then I bid you farewell.'

'If it ensures that I am not confined to four walls then I have no problem,' and with that Matt put it on, noting that it could only be removed by a special key, and wondering how easy it might be to cut off. He had an idea it would be difficult, but at least he would be able to reconnoitre the place.

Outside, he was met and taken to his room, where his clothes and other belongings had already been placed. 'I must commend room service around here,' but the comment was lost on the other person, who had not spoken at all.

It could be any motel room. Backed against the outer wall of the compound with windows to the front only. A bathroom, double bed, wardrobe, couple of chairs, which were comfortable enough, and Sky TV. A desk-cum-dresser completed the furniture; the other creature comforts being a hairdryer and tea/coffee making facilities. No refrigerator or trouser press, and not even a lock on the door.

On the bedside table was his watch. No doubt it had been checked to see if there was anything untoward with it. From his recollection of being outside, it looked as though it was set at the right time, and with a few hours to kill before dinner he had a shower and lay naked on the bed, thinking. Try as he might he could not get his mind to totally dwell on the events of years ago. More recent happenings crept into his thoughts, and then his mind would head off at a tangent, trying to find the means of calling reinforcements and ending it all.

By the time he was collected to go to dinner, he had been dressed and ready for an hour. It was a dining room into which he was shown, as there was only a dining table in it. At the head of the table but on one side, Vassilev was already seated. Although the table could seat at least 20, there was only one other place set. That was opposite Vassilev and Matt took it.

'Sorry to have kept you but something came up at the last minute requiring my attention. At times I seem to be working 24 hours. I hope you are hungry as there is plenty to eat. I had intended to introduce you to another guest but he refused to come. Said he did not look his best.'

Matt wondered who else was incarcerated here. Did he know him? Could either assist the other? Was it the man referred to earlier as being interrogated?

The homemade tomato soup for starters was excellent. Someone knew of his liking in food, as a well-done steak with plenty of potatoes and vegetables followed. Vassilev had a fish course. Dessert was an individual cream-filled pavlova with fresh fruit.

No wine was served with the meal but afterwards a liqueur appeared and they both retreated to another room, one with a magnificent view over the sea. That was Matt's original impression, but then he realised it was a giant plasma screen depicting what was going on seawards from the compound. Comfortable chairs were the only furniture, each facing the screen, and both sat in quiet contemplation for a short while.

Conversation over the meal had been light and general but now Matt interrupted the silence with a question. 'How did you make the first submarine disappear with all those men on board?'

'Curiosity at a sea tragedy near where we were carrying out sea trials. Someone drilling for oil broke through into one of these type of caverns and when we got close we also got sucked in. Luckily there was no damage apart from losing the mini-sub, and when everything had stilled we waited for the nearby storm to pass. To find the way out we had to send out divers and one of them found the markings relating to the reason for the cavern, which you are also now aware of.'

'But that was not this one?'

'Correct. But if you look closely near to where the designation markings are, each cave gives the direction of the next one. That one had two waymarkers, and when we did eventually leave we made our way first to the other but could not find a suitable entrance. And so we came here and the underwater entry was large enough to allow the sub to enter with ease.'

'What made you start working for yourselves?'

'Most of the crew, like myself, were disgruntled. We were all misfits put aboard a totally new concept. If it had sunk, the authorities would not have been bothered, but if all turned out successful, they could see it as a way of us coming back into the fold, as it were.'

'But setting up for yourselves?'

'When it occurred to me that we had the makings of a business outside the fold most of the men embraced it willingly. A minority had their reservations but eventually came round when it was promised that their families would be brought out. In the end only half a dozen had to be removed.'

'But did you keep your promise to bring out the families?'

'Oh yes; promises need to be delivered to keep everyone happy. It did take a little longer than anticipated though. We did it eventually right under the noses of the police. We just spirited them away and have done the same with all new recruits ever since.'

'Nice one having your brother on the inside for taking the other subs.'

'It took a while to set up the organisation, but then my brother had become Commandant of the facility that was charged with deciding what to do with these apparently obsolete subs. No-one knew what had gone wrong and no-one would give the order to sea-trial another. Changes in leadership, both political and military, also led to inactivity about them. Easy then to find people prepared to be skeleton crews when the Communist break-up started, and easier still in the confusion at that time to spirit them away before anyone knew what was happening.'

'So are you making full use of them all, then?'

'Goodness no. There are still two in reserve, although we will now have to speed up the fitting-out of them for our purposes and utilise some that are already preparing new bases as courier ships, as you have managed to waste a couple.'

'Something was going on under the Antarctic, then?'

'Yes. Another base was being prepared. My brother was there …'

'Did you lose him when …'

'No. He was not on board. However, he and another are now preparing their own rescue craft as for the moment I cannot spare one, having to try to limit the contractual damage you have done.'

'Sorry, I don't think.'

'They were hoping to get away a couple of days ago,' Vassilev continued, ignoring Matt's sarcastic comment. Technical problems and bad weather have delayed their departure, probably by about a week.' A pause, but as Matt said nothing he continued: 'Well, before I bid you goodnight, have you had any thoughts on what we were speaking about this afternoon?'

'Unfortunately not. I did try but all my thoughts keep getting jumbled. Past and present. If I could only get the thread, there may be the answer.'

'Well, get a good night's sleep and maybe by tomorrow your thoughts will have gelled into something coherent. And now I will bid you goodnight as I want to see my wife and also get a good night's sleep.'

With a 'goodnight', Matt left and was allowed to find his own way back to his room.

CHAPTER 9
AGAINST THE ODDS

THE NEXT MORNING VASSILEV got up, having had the same dream, but this time the ending had been fine as it had showed him getting the upper hand.

Matt on the other hand had had a restless night, although the nightmare had not returned. All through the night he had been turning things over in his mind and only sleeping fitfully. At least his thoughts were in some sort of order, even if he had not been able to see the way forward. That was something he decided not to worry about. Up to press on this caper, something had turned up and he would just await the omens that said 'the time is right'.

The two of them met up in the dining room where they had dinner the previous evening, Matt having been summoned. Vassilev made do with a continental style breakfast of fruit, followed by muesli and finished off with a croissant dunked in his coffee. A fully cooked breakfast awaited Matt and he did it justice, working on the basis that if things happened suddenly it might be some time before he could eat again.

After the small talk over breakfast, Vassilev asked, 'Are you any nearer knowing what our previous meeting was all about?'

'I think I am a little nearer although the why eludes me.'

'Go on then, enlighten me. Let us see if it follows my own line of thought.'

'The why is the cause of the set-up. If I could work that out maybe we could find out the who.'

'Sounds plausible, but what brought us together?'

'The who fed information to both our superiors or, more probably, their superiors, as I would not be surprised if the ones giving us our orders were not well up in the hierarchy. The why I am sure was something separate, which we were both about to stumble across and had to be eliminated, but the blood had to be on someone else's hands.'

'The bomber?'

'Oh no. It had to go back to whoever was likely to have sent him. Some Mullah or Warlord, it does not matter as they were only a pawn like us.'

'I don't like being looked on as merely a pawn.'

'OK but we were dispensible nevertheless. The ruse was to sneak the informant out but with the elimination of anyone else present. That was both our briefs, wasn't it?'

'True.'

'Then the same notified our joint opposition of the fact that we two – who knows what we were described as but it must have been something grand to warrant the suicide bomber – would be in a certain place at a given time. Somehow it went a little wrong as we both survived; perhaps we were too professional. Does that help? It is only the bottom part of the conundrum but have you any ideas about either the who or the why?'

'I think you have put it succinctly and although I had not totally thought it out that way, feel I must agree with you. However, as to the other part, I really do not have any idea, but it will give me something to think on whilst I am deciding what to do with you. In the meantime, keep thinking. You now have some building blocks in your mind to work with.'

During the interim silence Matt wondered just how long he had before a decision on his future would be taken.

Vassilev then continued, 'I now have some work to do, but I will send for you this afternoon and give you the full guided tour myself. Now if you will excuse me. But remember the bracelet.'

Matt considered himself summarily dismissed and after returning to his room and resting for half an hour, he went out exploring the compound. The two walls were about three quarters of a mile apart, with the guest accommodation being on the wall at the far end. Matt poked his nose into a couple of rooms either side of his before setting off, and they were clones of the one he had been placed in. The other wall was entirely Vassilev's domain and he had no doubt there would be a private way out into the nearby village.

Surreptitiously he had searched the room to see if it was bugged for either sound or vision, but had been unable to ascertain anything. However, he had a feeling he was under observation both inside and out and knew he had to be on his guard when preparing for action. In his wanderings he noticed cameras discreetly set on some of the buildings, and at each end of the walls were watchtowers, which seemed to have been built around the same time as the walls themselves and not put up as a recent afterthought. He could see a man in each but, apart from the assault rifles they carried, he did not know if there were other arms of a heavier nature, as the wall came up to waist height. Four uprights carried a thatched roof to give shade from the sun and they looked new, but was that just because they had had to be replaced?

The plateau on which the fort stood was about half a mile from sea cliff to back cliff at its widest, but curved a little to the walls which were not as long. The streets were set out as a grid. Matt walked the streets, peering into doorways that were open, but none gave him any idea for escape. Tools and equipment only. He also looked into doors that were not open but not locked, revealing a canteen, a recreation room, dormitories and other ancillary domestic services. Some doors were locked, and he made a mental note of their locations in case chance in the future allowed him to investigate further. With the security cameras he had his doubts, but it was always as well to be prepared.

Satisfied, after a couple of turns around the place, that he had the layout committed to memory, he went to the edge and looked out to sea. The next thing would be to gain access to the walls themselves. He only had a brief look when he arrived from the top of one, but at around 10 feet high it was impossible to guess what was really on the other side when stood at ground level.

To all intents and purposes he appeared to be wistfully looking out to sea as if for help, but his gaze fell on nothing in particular as he used the time to collect his thoughts on what he had observed. Maybe Vassilev would take him behind some of the closed doors this afternoon.

'A penny for them,' spoken at the side of him made him come back with a start.

He had not heard anyone approach. Either his senses had left him or he had been too engrossed in his thoughts. He turned to face the stranger and said, 'Sorry, I was miles away,' which he thought added to the previous distant look.

The man was a little shorter than Matt and probably 10 years older, although it was impossible for him to be sure because of his appearance. It was not so much the dishevelled clothing as the puffiness and bruising to the face, and Matt was sure by the way he held himself that other parts of his body had been abused.

'I have to thank you for getting me out of that pokey hole downstairs.'

'Me? How so?'

'Your musings to Vassilev this morning have taken the pressure off me. I have said all along that I knew nothing about that matter years ago but until now he has not believed me.'

'So you were his superior all those years ago. Any idea why he has suddenly got wound up about it now?'

'I understand he feels someone is trying to horn in on his set-up, and for some reason has a bee in his bonnet that the same person is behind it.'

'I agree with him. The who and the why of the past are now inextricably linked to the now and possibly the future.'

'How can you be so sure? You are just a fighting man, a troubleshooter. What do you know of what is going on in the higher echelons of politics or commerce?'

'It is by being on the outside. It enables me to look in. However, I feel it in my water; something is going to happen shortly, but what, I know not.'

'I'm sorry to have interrupted your thoughts, but escape that way is out of the question. I have tried it but did not get far and ended up being beaten for my troubles. We are both here until Vassilev decides what to do with us. By the way, my name is Malkovich, Sergei Malkovich.'

'Pleased to meet a fellow incarceree, if there is such a word. I'm Matt Weston.'

'I know who you are, where you come from and what you have done. Let me shake your hand. I have no time for my fellow countrymen who back themselves instead of Mother Russia.'

'Then we will have to see if we can topple the man. Don't suppose you have an army hidden away close by.' Matt did not know whether to trust him or whether he was on Vassilev's payroll.

'No. I know you are being facetious. I can, however, tell when someone is up to something; it's in the eyes. You have that look, and if you want my help at any time I am now only a couple of rooms away from you. Now I'll leave you to your ponderings.' With that he turned and walked stiffly back to his room.

Matt ruminated on the matter. If he was an ally and really wanted to help, how much use would he be in his current state if action became the order of the day?

In the afternoon Vassilev did take him into one of the buildings that he had been unable to gain entry to, but it was only the top of the lift shaft to take them down below. Secured so that, the airlock incorporated into the lift doors could not be tampered with. Coming out of it a couple of days before and seeing all that was round him had blurred his knowledge of that building.

The dock area was more or less the same as in Greenland, although on a larger scale. The two submarines he had previously seen were the only ones in the bays. The platform area being twice the size allowed buildings at either side this time, five storeys high.

Vassilev took him this way and that, into most rooms, and those he did not enter he was advised were the same as those he had already been in. He saw no reason to doubt it as they were on the same level and the standard layout seemed to imply that all rooms on each level were for the same purpose.

Vassilev chatted happily away throughout the tour, explaining what was going on. All seemed to be the usual requirements for a commercial organisation, albeit nefarious. On top of each building Matt noticed an armed guard, but were they usually there or ready should he try to do something? At this moment in time he had no plan or purpose, merely gathering information as to layout in case it was needed in the future.

The one thing he did note was that there appeared to be no security room, and that must be topside. He would have liked to see into it and maybe ascertain what the hidden surveillance might be. One thing that did stick in his mind was the two ways into Vassilev's own quarters. One was a private lift that came out in the foyer of his office, but when Matt followed him down again because he was wanted, they came up a stairway and into his office by a hidden route.

On the way down the second time, Vassilev said, 'I know you were staring out to sea this morning. Were you perhaps hoping to see a rescue flotilla on its way? Highly unlikely. The GPS bug you had on you was removed and is now somewhere in the middle of Russia.'

'I knew you would find that, but the Americans were adamant I should have one. I told them it would be a waste of time and that your Organisation was not run by fools, but they insisted. Serves them right if they are now mobilising a clandestine operation in the wrong place.'

'Does that mean that you have another one, I wonder?'

Matt realised in saying 'that', he had used the wrong word and hoped he had got away with it. Trying to keep his voice even, he continued, 'No, or I am sure you would have picked up on it by now. It's just that you get fed up of doing other people's dirty work and then them coming to the rescue at the last minute, to claim the rewards. Let them do their own legwork for once.'

'Well said, but no doubt you are able to call up reserves if needed and you get into such a position.'

'I would like to think so, but how long would it take for anyone to get here? By the time they arrived I would be done for.'

'But yet your mind is calculating all the time; waiting for the opportunity. Don't deny it.'

'Any man would wish to go down fighting and not be executed. Of course, given the opportunity I will take whatever action I can against you. That is a promise so you better make sure your guards are alert.'

'Thanks for the warning, but what chance do you think you would have of getting away with that bracelet on?'

Matt let that go without an answer. He was not going to escape. He was going to go active within the complex.

As he did not get a reply, Vassilev then went on: 'I see you have met my other guest. He should thank you for getting him out of jail, as it were.'

'He already has done.'

'Ah, but can you trust him to help you in anything you plan?'

'He is older than me, in no fit state to become active. What help am I going to get there?'

Vassilev smiled and then continued, 'Is there anything else you would like to see?'

'Yes. Over the walls. Always curious to see what is on the other side, and the other night I did not get much chance.'

'There is nothing to see really. The village on one side and a rocky scree to the sea on the other. But if you so wish, it will at least show you that there is no escape in those directions.'

They walked out into the sunlight and onto the wall that separated compound from town. From here he noticed that the watchtowers were also armed with RPGs, and also, in a cradle that could be swung up into play any way quickly, a heavy machine gun. On the outside of the wall was a building that nearly stretched the whole length, stopping only when it reached the gate. This was a substantial building and Matt knew instinctively that it was Vassilev's own personal comfort zone. He was sure he had seen the way through from the office foyer during one of the times he had been there. There was then a 100-yard gap to the start of the village itself. A quick glance took in the geography in case it was ever needed, but what really caught his eye was a well-camouflaged building at the far end.

'What is that?' he said and pointed with his hand.

Immediately, audible warnings were to be heard and the guards at either end came running.

'Oh shit. I had forgotten about the bracelet.'

'Well, you know it works now,' said Vassilev as he motioned the guards to relax. 'That building is the helicopter bay. Sections of the roof open to allow direct entry or exit.'

'Well at least you found out the guards here were not having a siesta,' commented Matt. 'I better be careful in future.'

They went over to the other wall, and here Matt had an idea. Immediately below on the outside was a steep slope of loose scree which went down towards the sea, but only at one point did it reach there. For the rest there was a 50-foot drop onto a rock-strewn area in the sea itself.

'Satisfied now that neither side allows a means of escape?'

'Perfectly, thank you. And thank you for the tour, most enlightening, or it would be if I knew how to do something about it.'

'You are a resourceful man and I am sure, given time, that you would find a way to become a spoiler. We will have to hasten your demise. I have sent for Kharlov to come over tomorrow. That should provide some fun and a lesson to everyone.'

That set Matt's mind wondering and he immediately thought of the Beatles song 'Help'. That was going to be something he would really need shortly.

He and Malkovich dined alone in the dining room that night. Not much conversation was ensuing between them as Matt was more concerned with his wellbeing on the following day. His timescale for action had just been ratcheted up a couple of notches.

In the morning he breakfasted alone but made sure that he had as much as possible as he had no idea when his next meal would be. Before going for breakfast, and hoping that it was away from any prying eyes, he removed two of the middle toes from the prosthetic and prepared them.

He had gone back to his room after breakfast, and to lull observers into a false sense of security he did the same as he had the previous day and stayed for about half an hour, allowing his breakfast to settle somewhat. Then he went walkabout; here and there but eventually ending up on the wall nearest the town. Arriving there at a different time of day he was able to see a steady stream of people coming and going from what appeared to be part of Vassilev's quarters. Those going in were different to those coming out, and it gave him a clue as to a mystery from the previous afternoon. When they had come up the secret route to Vassilev's office, they had first climbed what appeared to be unrestricted stairs. It was only after they had gone through the airlock that Vassilev had revealed a hidden door, but the stairway continued further. This was no doubt the top of that stairway; another piece of information to store away.

As he went across to the other wall he hoped that his mind was not being overloaded with useless information which might clog up the system when it came time for action.

On the other wall was where he hoped to start the mayhem, but the timing had to be right and the initial move really had to look like an accident. Luck was on his side again. The opportunity came shortly after he had arrived. A speck on the horizon grew larger and revealed a helicopter. Matt called to the nearest guard, 'What's that?' and pointed out with the arm wearing the bracelet.

Immediately the alarm sounded again and Matt pulled his hand back and looked sheepish at the guard. One of the false toes had been a GPS transmitter, and Matt had activated it just as he put his hand out and let it go at the other side of the wall. He did not see where it went but hoped that if they realised one was now in operation the signal would have been picked up before they could destroy it.

As the tiny transmitter dropped, it hit a ledge, bounced and then rolled part-way down the slope, becoming lodged in a little crevice and sending its signal out for all it was worth. Being so microscopic the battery would not last that long anyway. In the Security Centre the escaper alarm took everyone's attention. By the time they realised it was a false alarm and picked up on the signal being transmitted, all hell was breaking loose and they had to concentrate on keeping tabs on Matt and advising their enforcers, who had been alerted and were sent on his trail.

On the wall the other guard came up running, and when he saw that it was not a security breach and reported the same to Security Control he stopped to talk to his colleague. One had his back to Matt and was blocking the view of the other as Matt prepared the next surprise. Things could not have fallen better into his hands if he had tried to contrive it.

The other false toe was a simple garrotte made from a weight on the end of a piece of strong fishing line. With one action he swung it. Round the neck of the guard with his back to him it went and tightened. Surprised, he dropped his weapon and grabbed for his throat. The other guard did not know what was happening and his first thoughts were for his colleague. Matt would have liked to have utilised more of the length of the cord attached to the weight but the proximity of the other guard required a short one. However it circled the neck twice.

Nearly in the same fluid movement of flicking the garrotte, Matt then hurled himself at the same man, pushing him into the other guard, who immediately lost his balance. Following through, Matt picked up the dropped gun and before the other guard had regained his balance, shot him in the head. The other was still struggling with the garrotte, but his efforts were getting weaker and weaker so Matt ignored him.

He then looked across to the other walls and saw one guard there getting ready to shoot. Instead of dodging Matt pressed the trigger and loosed of a quick burst, seeing the other tumble back, and heard the bullets that had been fired his way go harmlessly overhead. Then he dived into the nearest guardpost and ducked low as more bullets came his way. A change of weapon and he popped up with an RPG and fired at the remaining guard in his post. The rocket-propelled grenade found its mark, and once the dust had settled it was as though there had never been a guard post there. Total obliteration. He now had control of the high ground, as it were, but for how long? He needed to get out of there but first there were other things to take care of.

On his visit to the wall yesterday – and his observations had been confirmed today – he had seen that one of the buildings was not what it seemed. At ground level it appeared similar to all those around it, but from up there it could be seen that behind the parapet the roof was totally different and made of modern materials. This, thought Matt, had to be the control and security centre, and taking that out would help him.

The next grenade he fired at the roof, but it just bounced off, flew over the far wall and exploded out of his sight. He assessed the roof again and saw a lip at one corner. This time he carefully aimed and fired. Bingo, bang on target and after the explosion he could see that part of the roof had peeled back. The next grenade he launched into the gap.

Now was his time to get out of there. He darted out and grabbed the other rifle before being forced back into cover by a burst of gunfire. He had seen the rooftop where it came from and quickly he squeezed a burst off from the rifle he was now holding. Without waiting he then darted for the stairs and was part-way down when there came the explosion he had anticipated, followed immediately by an almighty explosion.

The sound was greater than the actual explosion because it took place in a confined space. He realised then that the building had not been security control but the place from where missiles could be launched either to sea or in the air against unwanted guests. His last grenade must have triggered something, and the whole of the roof burst out in pieces, showering the surrounding streets with shards of metal.

Before the pieces came raining down, Matt jumped off the stairs, hoping his prosthetic would hold up to the 10-foot drop, and hobbled to the shelter of the nearest building. He remained there for a little while, catching his breath, and then, with a look round the corner revealing no-one, he set off at his imitation of a run; a way he had found of moving over distances fairly quickly with the prosthetic, providing the surface was relatively straight, which these were.

He had now selected single-shot on the assault rifle in an effort to conserve ammunition. Hearing a noise behind he stopped, turned and fired a couple of shots randomly, seeing someone duck into one of the street entries he had passed. Gun at the ready, he darted into the next side street, and then at the next junction turned off into another. Another such move at the next intersection and he found himself at the side of the building that had exploded.

It must have been made of strong stuff as there was not the destruction he expected to see. The walls must have been made strong, because they had cracked but not disintegrated. Maybe the power of the explosion had followed the line of least resistance and gone through the damaged roof. Then he realised the building would have been reinforced to take the blast from any launched missile. He had no way of knowing how much internal damage had been done, but hoped it was sufficient to put it out of action for when rescue came.

In the street a number of people lay injured, but Matt could not tell whether they were security or otherwise. Only one man tried to shoot at him, but by then Matt was so close that he just slammed the butt of the gun into the man's face and continued on his way.

He needed to keep moving, as he had no way of knowing how soon the cavalry, in the shape of the Royal Marines, would arrive. Try as he might he could not get away from the compound. Every twist and turn put someone against him. Good shot or bad shot, he had no way of knowing, but if anyone showed their face he fired.

Eventually he realised they were herding him, tracking his every move and anticipating what he was going to do. It was as though they had a homing beacon on him, as he could not see any eye-in-the-sky. If they had been tracking him on camera they would have been reactive, but they seemed to have the upper hand.

Then he remembered what Vassilev had said when handing over the bracelet. It was both an alarm and a tracking device. He had to get rid of it, but nothing was to hand and so he had to use what was at his disposal, namely the rifle. Luckily it was a loose fit and so he found a stone, and with fist down the edge, rested the bracelet on top. One-handed he put the muzzle of the gun against the bracelet and fired. The shock wave as the bracelet with bullet against it tried to break his wrist almost made him faint, and then the burning from the bullet's discharge hit him, making him cry out in pain.

The bracelet parted and he was able to shake his arm to help ease the pain. He was aware that he could not stay there, so grabbing the bracelet in the same hand as the gun he went on his way, still shaking his hurting arm. Throwing the bracelet behind a pile of rubble as he went, he then ducked into a building he had noted on his first tour of inspection; one with two entrances, or exits if you prefer.

The building was empty, but to be on the safe side he hid for a while near the other door, just in case anyone decided that was the way through. Nothing happened, and then he heard shouting outside the door he had come through and departed by the other way after first checking the way was clear. Now he could make his way to the gate and get out where there was more room to manoeuvre.

He did however continue with his zig-zag route, and just before he reached the gate he heard a helicopter overhead, obviously searching for him. The helicopter was on a seek-and-destroy mission, as when he was sighted bullets from a man leaning out came in his direction. It was a long time since he had done target-shooting on the move, but he used it with success as the man dropped his gun and the helicopter moved out of the line of fire and he heard it fly into the distance.

That, unfortunately, had highlighted his position and must have given them the idea as to where he was making for. Looking round a corner he could see a number of armed personnel at the gate, waiting for him. A quick change of style on the rifle was called for, and a burst made them dive for cover, although one was not so lucky. Matt then darted the other way. There was only one other way to get outside and that was over the wall.

He could hear sounds in the streets behind him, and that urged him on, still zig-zagging through the streets. At one time an armed man came out in front of him, but surprised at seeing the quarry, delayed raising his gun, and Matt, who was back on single shots and at the ready, dropped him. Not being sure how much more ammunition he had, he threw his gun aside and grabbed the man's rifle; a quick check revealed another magazine in his pocket. Less than 15 seconds, but he now felt better, making sure that the gun was on single fire as he still needed to conserve ammunition.

He made it to the wall. Good, no-one on top, and he raced up the steps to where the guard post, the one nearest the back cliff, was now non-existent. Someone had seen him, as a few shots came close, but he was either firing in a hurry or a lousy shot. Matt saw the man on a roof a few streets away and made a clean kill before jumping over the wall. The explosion had also knocked out part of the parapet, and he did not have as far to drop onto the roof of Vassilev's quarters as he might otherwise have had. Always hoping it would take the strain; it did and then he dropped where the stairway was and ducked inside.

Before taking the stairs down he paused a few moments to catch his breath, but did make sure there was no-one lurking there ready to take him. It also allowed him time to take stock. Provided they did not throw in a grenade, he was relatively safe, as he could cover the entrance and the way up, but time would not be long before they realised a two-pronged attack would have him.

From the entrance to the stairs was a 10-foot corridor, and he hugged the wall as he moved back to the entrance. Peering out, nothing seemed to be moving and no sound came from behind him. More valuable seconds to catch his breath and collect his thoughts. Then he heard sounds on the roof above; someone was waiting there, but what for? From behind, the sound of the airlock going made him aware of their intention. They were going to chase him out and let him be taken from above. Time for bluff.

He scuffed his feet as if coming to the entrance and then put the gun out as though ready for a shoot-out, drawing back just as fast, but as he hoped, the man above had already started to drop. As he landed, Matt grabbed him with one hand, nearly screaming out with pain and only just managing to keep hold. The action had reactivated the pain from him shooting off the bracelet, which the recent activities had pushed to the back of his mind. Before the man had regained his balance, Matt pulled him in, at the same time shooting him. Dragging him behind him he went to the head of the stairs and loosed off a volley downwards.

There were some screams and the sound of bodies tumbling, so he looked over the edge and with deliberate shots took everyone out, not caring if they were already dead. He replaced the magazine and then stripped the one who had tried to jump him of all weapons. He now had a veritable arsenal. Another rifle with a couple of spare clips, an automatic handgun, although he could not find a spare magazine for it, and a commando knife. Now he really could take the action to them.

How long had it been since he threw the transmitter? It seemed a lifetime but was probably less than 30 minutes. Definitely not enough time for the Marines to arrive. He knew the location of their jumping-off point and that it would be at least an hour before they could arrive, provided his location was the anticipated place. Even if they had been on full alert it would have taken a little time to get airborne and then it was to be a low-level run to target. There was also the question in his mind as to whether he had, albeit by accident, knocked out the reception missile system.

There was no way he could go back out into the open. They had had too much time to cover all their options there. That meant he had to go down and through the airlock and see what sort of a reception committee awaited him there. Down he went and opened the airlock from his side. No-One was waiting for him there. A little stage production came next as he lugged three bodies in with him and set them in position by the exit. Then he closed the one behind him and released the one in front.

Being a part of the stairway, there was only a small platform area outside, and two armed men were waiting. What they saw, when the door opened, was one of their own men obviously dead and two more semi-upright as though injured and needing help. As they started forward Matt rose up from his hiding place behind the corpses and shot them both at point blank. Both were sent backwards and ended up rolling down the stairway.

It had obviously been thought that these men were sufficient to contain the situation, as no-one else was ready as Matt went down the stairs as fast as the prosthetic would allow, firing at anyone who showed themselves. Of the men on the roof the previous day, there was no sign; presumably they had been there to watch him. Before doing so Matt had pushed two of the bodies in the airlock forward so that they prevented the door from closing. No-one could come at him from behind, but what he was going to do he had no idea.

It hit him as he gained the dock level and moved to the quieter side. Get across the water and into the corridor between the lakes. Escape might be possible through the Pyramid and into the jungle. Sending people scurrying for cover meant that no-one was immediately following him, and he had time to disable two of the boats moored there by shooting into the outboard engines before taking off in the third.

He took the long way round so that the darkness of the wall hid him but made the sound of the engine echo all round, a ruse he hoped would disorientate any would-be pursuers. There was no other boat at the ladder so he cut the engine and tied fast before climbing up. On this side there was no overhang, and he had not seen anyone up there before starting to climb. However, he was doubly cautious at the top, but it was clear.

It would not take them long to realise his intent and maybe send reinforcements from the other side. He could not stay on that ledge too long even though it had a commanding view. He had to go through and get the car moving so that one was not at the other end to give them a chance to come at him.

Into the airlock he went. This was different in that there was a window in each door. Closing one behind him he could see no-one through the other, and the car was still in place. He let himself out and immediately had the rifle grabbed from him, and he was pushed away.

CHAPTER 10
SURPRISES GALORE

WHEN HE HAD REGAINED his balance he found himself facing Kharlov. 'Hello lover,' he said. 'Good of you to wait for me.'

The smile on Kharlov's face turned to a fixed stare of hate as he threw the rifle to one side. This was going to get personal and painful for Matt. Kharlov was going to take retribution, even if not in public. He had been humiliated, and that required payback, with interest.

Matt did a quick pirouette and was reassured to see no-one else present. Before he could arm himself, Kharlov charged and Matt managed to avoid the full force although an extended arm caught him and rocked him. The automatic was tucked in his waistband at the back, as was the knife for safety's sake as it did not have a sheath. Neither were the grenades he had purloined earlier of any use.

Kharlov, regardless of his stature, was quick on his feet and was charging at Matt again before he had a chance to do anything. All he could do was keep dodging, but each time he received a blow, whether to the head, shoulder or arm, and always on the same side. Ducking, diving, unable to get a stance, eventually it happened. Kharlov gave a glancing blow to the wrist from which the bracelet had been shot off.

Momentarily a shock wave of pain shot up his arm and stopped him in his tracks, but thankfully Kharlov's action had caused him to over-reach himself and he was unable to take immediate advantage of the situation. Matt's brain kept working, though, giving him the incentive to climb over the rail in an effort to make time, but Kharlov rolled over as well. Back through the carriage, but Kharlov was only seconds behind. As was to be expected, the strain started to tell. He was not fully recovered from the previous bout of exertion. Obviously he was getting too old for sustained active service; in fact it had been some considerable time since he had needed to be so active. At close quarters dodging, the false leg was also a hindrance. On one occasion Matt was not perfectly balanced on the prosthetic. One off-second was all it took and Kharlov had him.

Sinew and muscle gripped him from behind, pinning his arms to his sides, and started to squeeze tighter and tighter. Matt struggled and tried to get leverage for his foot but to no avail. Just as he thought he was about to pass out, whilst shaking his head from side to side to try to alleviate some of the pain, he noticed the car had risen on the rail and started to move. Kharlov had his back to the rail, and with a last-gasp superhuman effort Matt pushed backwards; took Kharlov still holding him off balance; and he fell against the rail.

It was Kharlov who, now disadvantaged, loosened his grip somewhat, and Matt managed to bring his forearms up to squeeze against Kharlov's, and also lifted his feet off the floor. The car, now having some momentum, hit Kharlov and bounced both of them away, making Kharlov release his grip. Matt, being aware of what was going to happen, managed to gain his balance as soon as he was let go. He was the first to recover and, before Kharlov could do the same, had the automatic out. The last thing Kharlov saw was the business end of the gun as Matt got off two shots, both of which hit Kharlov in the face.

'You're not pretty any more, lover boy,' he thought, but then added, 'Probably I don't look anything to write home about now either.' He could feel bruises and bumps starting where he had taken a buffeting in the fight, and the wrist was still killing him.

Realising the car had gone meant opposition were now probably on their way. There was no time for him to catch his breath. Adrenaline only kept him going. Back through the airlock he went, dragging Kharlov behind him as best he could with one good arm, to leave him in the outer doorway, thus ensuring the inner one could not be opened. Looking through the window had shown no-one outside, and nothing assailed him as he came out.

No reception committee waiting below, so he went down the ladder and set off back in the boat. Part of the way across the lake he stopped. Time to take stock of the situation and, more particularly, his body, exercising his limbs as best he could in the boat without upsetting it, and massaging the parts that hurt the most. He did get back to a feeling of normality, or what resembled that in his current situation.

Short of the dock he cut the engine and paddled the rest of the way, but not to where he had set off from. That was where he expected a welcoming committee if there was going to be one. Instead he came up against one side of a submarine, and with a little difficulty as there was nothing to assist him, climbed on board. Racing off down the gangplank and across the dock, waving the automatic made people seeing him dive for cover. That allowed him to reach the stairs without confrontation.

At the landing a man was trying to move the bodies from the airlock door, and he clubbed him, completed the job and closed the door behind him. Without him doing anything the opposite door began to open, but whoever was there was expecting a colleague, and Matt shot him and dumped the body in the open doorway before continuing up the stairs as fast as he could go.

At the top, rifle fire was sounding, and as he reached the corridor there were two of the opposition firing outwards. That must mean that his rescuers had arrived. Catching his breath without them being aware of his presence, Matt clinically despatched them and came to the entrance just in time to see the cavalry arrive. Not what he was expecting, as they were US Rangers. When he stepped out to greet them, having tucked the automatic back in his belt, as they came through the village, they just passed him by as if he did not exist, and went into the stairway.

Matt was nonplussed. This was not what he had been expecting. The old adage of expect the unexpected came to mind, but the hairs at the back of his neck started rising. Things were not what they seemed, and Matt sought cover in a ruined building close by, realising as he did so that the grenade he had fired and which had bounced off the roof must have landed there. Before he loped across from the stairway entrance, he picked up one of the dead men's rifles.

It was as though they had been there before and knew exactly where to go. Matt could sense danger all around and was not really surprised when a bullet tore into his prosthetic. He just had time to see a man on the ramparts above duck down before he could return fire. He aimed the gun in the general direction but the man did not reappear and then he sensed someone at the entrance of the stairs.

When he looked, he saw it was one of the Rangers, and indicated that there was a sniper on the roof. The man gave no sign of understanding and Matt saw him raise his gun and look towards him. In that moment Matt saw the hardness in his eyes that said more than 'Ranger'. This man was a trained killer like himself. Without thinking, Matt dropped the muzzle of his rifle, which had been pointing in the approximate direction, and fired twice, just as the other lined his assault rifle up on Matt.

The first shot hit the man in the body armour and knocked him off balance sufficiently for the second to find a fleshy home. The man did not seem to realise he had been hit, and continued to try to shoot at Matt, but Matt took careful aim and shot him again in the face. What the hell was going on when even the 'goodies' seemed to have it in for him?

A movement on the ramparts caught his attention. The sniper had raised himself, but in a different position. Matt fired twice, but only one bullet left the gun; out of ammunition. It was sufficient, as he saw the sniper fall backwards, but whether hit or just dodging he knew not. Even the ruins were a dangerous place, so he darted back for the stairs and relieved the dead Ranger of his rifle. With it at the ready he went to the head of the stairs, but there was no-one on them.

He had no idea of what was happening or what to do next. All the Rangers had gone down, but Vassilev's men were still in control on top. Why had they not taken command of the surface before going down below? He just wished he could be a fly on the wall and listen to what was going on, and then he spied the dead Ranger's communication system.

He put that on and also appropriated the dead man's body armour and spare ammunition. Nothing was coming through on the communicator and Matt realised it had been deliberately switched to a channel that was not open to all. He kept switching channels; eventually hearing a voice saying, '… where are you? Captain, come in. What are we doing down here?' When there was no answer the voice continued, somewhat pleading: 'Sergeant, where are you when you are supposed to be down here with us? Sergeant, what the hell is happening?'

Matt realised the Sergeant was the one he had just killed, and responded, 'Your Sergeant is dead, but where your Captain is I have no idea.'

'Who the hell are you?' came the challenge. 'And what are you doing on this communication system?'

'I'm the one you all charged by at the top of the stairs, and it is obvious you have not been sent to rescue me. As far as you need to know, just call me Pegleg, but I do not know if we are on the same side, as your Sergeant tried to kill me, but I was faster on the draw.'

'If you are not one of them, why should he want to kill you?'

'I have no idea. Just as I have no idea if you really are Rangers.'

'I can assure you we are,' came the vehement reply. Matt could visualise him thinking how dare this unknown person impugn the integrity of the force.

'Anyway, what were you supposed to do here?'

'Secure this area under here.'

'Then I suggest you do just that. How many men do you have? I didn't count you in.'

'Fifteen when we came down, but the loss of Captain and Sergeant takes us to 13, but that must have been unlucky as we lost one more when we came in here. Another killed and two injured, but partially active subsequently.'

'Try to gain the high ground on top of both buildings, but watch your backs as there are other ways in.'

'Can't you get us out? The airlock on the stairs is not working …' the voice was cut off by the sound of gunfire

'You OK down there?'

'Yeah. We just found one of the other ways in, or at least the opposition did. One of our injured guys got them as they tried to sneak out of a lift.'

'Just make sure that the doors on your side remain open. No-one can get in at the other side.'

'Their bodies are doing that.'

'It's the same reason why you cannot get out of the stairway.'

'Can't you remove the blockage for us?'

'Sorry, but I have troubles of my own at present,' and with that he loosed off a shot in the direction of a movement outside.

'What's going on up there?'

'No-one thought to secure the outside before you lot raced downstairs.'

'There was supposed to be more on the way but if they have not arrived by now there must be a problem.'

'One big problem for all of us. Just get on with what you are supposed to be doing, and by the way, watch out for the subs, they have heavy machine guns, although if they have not started up already you may be lucky.'

'Sounds as though you had better watch out for yourself.'

'True. Oh, and another thing, four doors away from the the lift that just opened and to the left is another. Better secure that in the same way as the other.'

Over the system, Matt heard orders being given and then the voice came back. 'Found it. Any more problems we might encounter?'

'Two. But by the way, what are you called? Or at least give me your callsign.'

'Corporal Paragem at your service; callsign Toff, as I had a rather privileged upbringing.'

'Right Toff. One: keep a lookout across the lake. There is another way in over there, but no boats, and the way should be blocked.'

'And two?'

'If the water suddenly starts rising you will know that one of the ways in has been breached. The water level with you is lower than the sea outside. If the air in there is allowed to escape, the water level will rise and you really will have to find your own salvation. Now good luck, I'm going to see if I can make my own.'

Matt signed off and went to the edge of the tunnel. Looking outside he could see no-one and cautiously moved out, quickly drawing back, but nothing happened. He knew he had to find the Command Centre and went back into the compound through the gate, but it was all quiet. Too quiet for his liking.

He worked his way up and down the streets, trying to find something that would be the giveaway as to the whereabouts of the Security Centre, but after traipsing throughout the compound he was no wiser. He did however come across a body, the head of which was at a crazy angle. Someone had obviously caused the neck to break. The same someone had taken any arms but had left the grenades, which he purloined for his own use. Strange for someone to be so armed in the compound. He also bethought himself to check the lift, but the door would not open and he knew they should be safe from that quarter down below.

Failing to find anything at ground level, he made his way onto the ramparts where he had started the escapade. Everything was quiet; no-one moving. Were they all trying to get into the cave, he wondered? A quick scan of roof levels failed to show anything up, and he was about to descend the steps again when a movement below caught his attention. Purely a shadow, but he was on alert and ready when an armed man came round the corner into view.

The man was concentrating on the street ahead and did not see him above. Where had he appeared from? Matt had not seen anyone on his way through the compound. Matt moved to give himself a better line of fire, and that must have caught the other's attention, as he looked up and steadied the rifle he was holding. Now he knew who had been responsible for the dead man from whom he had taken the grenades.

Neither shot, as each recognised the other. It was Malkovich, and Matt joined him at ground level.

'I see you are still alive then,' was Malkovich's opening remark. 'Where's Vassilev, and what exactly is going on?'

'Search me on both counts. I've been shot at by all and sundry, and even the American Rangers that have appeared on-scene.'

'So that's why everyone disappeared suddenly.'

'Don't think so. The Rangers seemed to arrive with not much opposition.'

'So maybe they are now meeting opposition.'

'Possibly, but why aren't we hearing anything?' With that, Matt called over the com link, 'Toff, you there?'

'Sure, what's up buddy?'

'Nothing, I hope, but have you encountered any surge of opposition recently?'

'No. We are now working through this place bit by bit, with only the occasional shootout. Why?'

'Well, all personnel from up here seem to have disappeared and I cannot find out where. Carry on then.'

'Will do, and watch your back. Whoever you are, you seem to be on the right side. OK to contact you if we come across anything untoward?'

'Sure, and anything unusual as well. Out.' Then to Malkovich he asked, 'Any idea where their Control Centre is up here?'

'Down that walkway,' and he pointed. 'Only one door and it is unlocked at present.'

'Cheers,' said Matt and went the way indicated, not bothering to wonder how he knew. The last he saw of Malkovich in the flesh was him continuing on his way.

It was little more than a passage and two people could not have walked side by side down it. Matt had seen it earlier and assumed it was only a rear access. He looked down and could see nothing; visually it appeared to be a dead end. He went down cautiously and at the end found it turned sharp left. What was more frightening to him was the fact that a machine gun, probably under remote control, had been facing him all the time he had been walking down.

At the end of this short section was the only door of the whole passageway. At the door the way turned sharp right and as he continued another right was followed by a left, and within a short stretch he was in the next street. Looking back the way he had come, it again resembled a dead end, but now knowing what he was looking for; he could see the lie of the land. What better place for a Control Centre, as any attack in such narrow confines would easily be dealt with.

Walking back along the passageway, he put his ear to the door and could hear the faint sound of machinery humming. Testing it, he found it unlocked and pushed it open without entering. Nothing happened so he went in, gun at the ready, but there was no-one alive there. Two bodies still oozing blood were sat in the chairs they had been occupying. Now he knew why he had not come across Malkovich earlier in his wandering around the compound.

The humming was from all sorts of technical equipment, but it was the bank of televisions that caught his attention. Eight screens in all, although one was blank, and each altering the image as they automatically switched from one camera to the next, but on none could he see any signs of life. On the desk in front of the screens were any number of controls, so Matt started playing around with them and eventually found a way of moving cameras at his command, but as soon as he did, the screen jumped to another camera.

Each screen covered a specific area and there were differing numbers of cameras feeding to each one. One screen covered the north/south streets of one half of the compound, whilst another covered the rest. Two screens were similarly set up for the east/west streets. Two further screens covered the village, and the last one, which was working, viewed over the helicopter complex. That left the blank screen, but try as he might he could not activate it. If it was not pointing out over land or sea, which he doubted, it must be inside the dock area, but what had happened to take it off-screen?

With the keyboard on the desk in front of the screens, he started pressing various combinations of buttons and found that certain combinations could keep a particular camera on the appropriate screen. He froze each one of the seven working screens, after letting them go through their full cycle, on what he thought was the best camera. No-one was anywhere to be seen. It was like a ghost town. Try as he might though he could not get the eighth screen to function.

Then he spotted a baguette on the other desk. Partly eaten, but it reminded him that it was some time since he had partaken of food. He cut off where it had been eaten into and ate the rest. He could not make out what the content was, and it was not really appetising, but it was food nevertheless. He washed it down with a part can of Coke he found and it made him feel better.

'Pegleg,' called the Toff, 'if you can hear me we have taken the Control Room down here and just as we were watching all the viewing screens have frozen on one particular view.'

'That could be me,' answered Matt. 'I'm in the Control Room up here and have had a little fiddle around. How many screens have you got there?'

'Eight,' came the response, 'although the one covering the dock area is still working normally.'

'You must have control of that, as my eighth screen is blank.' At that the blank screen in front of Matt came to life, and as it went through its cycle he could see that all down there was under control.

'You seem to have things all sewn up down there.'

'Mostly thanks to your various hints and warnings. Stiff opposition for a start but we now have about 20 prisoners, but we do not think they were operational guys.'

'How many did you lose?'

'Too many, but it could have been worse, so thanks again to you. If all is quiet up there, are you coming to join …' The voice trailed off and then continued in another vein: 'What the hell is going on out there? That's Captain Delaney who shoved us down here, but who is that with him?'

Matt checked the screens to see what had attracted Toff's attention, and saw people by the helicopter bay. 'The other is Vassilev, the mastermind for this organisation.'

'But who is that third guy coming into view?'

'That rather looks like another enforced guest here. Name of Malkovich. Could be he has a bone to pick with Vassilev, and I cannot say I blame him. Pity there is no sound from those cameras as well. It would be interesting to hear what is going on.'

The camera could only give an overview, but down on the ground Captain Delaney had Vassilev covered with his assault rifle and stood in such a way that his back was to the newcomer. He was actually partway through saying, '… and the new proprietor of this organisation will be here shortly. You can work with him or die now. You have the key to the Power.'

Something in Vassilev's eyes or demeanour alerted the Captain to the presence of someone else, and as he turned he saw Malkovich with a rifle aimed at Vassilev and then could hear him rambling on in Russian, the gist of which was about the treatment he had received and that it was time for retribution.

He never got the chance to go further as the Captain shot him. Whether Malkovich flinched or started to move to avoid the bullet no-one will ever know. Suffice to say that it caught him in the shoulder and spun him. At the same time his finger tightened on the trigger and with the gun set on automatic, bullets flew in a semi-circle as he was falling.

Neither Captain Delaney nor Vassilev were hit, as they were out of the line of fire, but the spread of bullets raked the nearby helicopter, killing the pilot, and continued into the hanger. As the magazine emptied and Malkovich landed on the ground, there came an almighty explosion from within the hangar and a fireball spread out through the open door. It engulfed the helicopter, which itself exploded, and the fuel from it added to the intensity of the fireball, making it expand and expand.

Before anyone could do anything they were all consumed by the fire, and when it was all over there was nothing to be seen except a few incinerated remains and nearby buildings on fire. Those watching on camera could only stare in horror at the scene which had unfolded before them in the previous two minutes.

'What the hell happened there?' came the Toff's voice.

'Something got triggered and blew.'

'With a vengeance,' commented Toff. 'We felt the tremor down here.'

'I got showered with dust as well.'

After a short while, during which all assimilated what they had seen, the Toff came back with, 'Hey, look out there – the cavalry is arriving. About time too.'

As soon as Matt saw on screen what was happening he almost screamed. 'Shit; that is more trouble. Look at the way they are indiscriminately throwing grenades into the buildings. Those are mercenaries and, if I am not mistaken, the worst kind. Prepare to batten down the hatches. I'll be down shortly to let you secure the stairway from your side, but I have another important job to do for a start, so over and out for now.'

Wondering whatever next was going to be thrown his way, the words 'knock on wood' from the song chased about his brain and he did just that on the table, not knowing if it was proper wood or not but hoping beyond hope that luck would be with him. He now realised why the body he had seen earlier had been so armed; he had been off to defend the perimeter.

With that, Matt found the radio and selected a certain wavelength and said, 'Pegleg to Marauder, Pegleg to Marauder, come in.'

'This is Marauder, Pegleg. We will be with you within 10 minutes. Sorry not to have got there sooner but someone stopped an early take-off when your beacon came on line.'

'Never mind that. Abort the mission. I repeat. Abort the mission. Return to Base. Everything has gone arse-up here. I'll try get out as best I can but you lot go back. Do you understand?'

'That's an affirmative, Pegleg. We are now turning to retrace our flight path. Abort is understood. Luck be with you. Over and out,' and the radio went dead.

Matt left the room, but not before chucking a couple of the grenades inside, and set off for Vassilev's office. They went off as he was in the walkway, decimating the electronic systems there and rendering them useless to anyone who might want to use them later.

He had seen that the mercenaries were making good progress, and knew he would have to hurry. Time was against him, for, as he was hurrying the last few yards to the office complex entrance, a stranger dressed in the same camouflage that he had seen on the mercenaries appeared in the doorway.

Both fired together and Matt felt a punch in the top of his left arm which sent him spinning back into the side street he had just left. He saw that the other man was on the floor, but just where Matt had been the earth was being churned up as bullets gouged the ground, and he heard the chain gun from above, although could not see or hear the helicopter. Although injured, he realised the other had done him a favour and actually kept him alive. Maybe the wood he had knocked on had been good.

As the chain gun went silent he dashed across the intervening space and into the office entrance just as it started off again and bullets followed him. Over the dead man and straight to the inner sanctum, even as the bullets from above started ripping into the roof above. It stopped as soon as it started, presumably because they had either lost him or presumed him dead, and he soon came to the private office where he had been previously with Vassilev.

Sat on the chair, he ministered to his arm. The bullet had gone clean through and for some reason there was not a lot of blood. Using one of the field dressings in the body armour he had taken, he wound it round and secured it as best he could with one hand.

Then it was on the move again. Dropping down the secret way, he called Toff and said, 'Get someone to the stairway. I am going to give you the chance of securing yourself from the inside. Just be there if I need to come through in a hurry later.'

'On with it,' came the response.

Matt carefully opened the door onto the stairway, but there were no persons around, and he heaved the body that was keeping the outer door of the airlock open inside and closed the door.

'All yours,' he said and heard the other side open as it echoed through the rock wall.

Back to the office, and he was glad that no-one had yet made their way there. He was expecting someone to come in, but that someone would probably be expecting to find Vassilev. It was now too late for him to have the answers, but Matt hoped that he would be able to find out what historical and current events were linked, and how.

He had just sat down at the desk when the telephone rang and, out of curiosity; he picked it up to hear a voice he had last heard in Antarctica. Vassilev's brother. A short conversation took place, but when he started talking in Russian, Matt put the phone down. He was more interested in who his visitor might be and did not want any distractions.

No sooner had he cut the connection than Toff came on. 'Pegleg, are you picking up anything on this communication system?'

'No. Why?'

'I am getting someone calling for you. The callsign seems to be Pancho.'

'He should not be anywhere near here. There was no reason for him to be coming to my rescue. Just as a way of checking, ask him who Onslow is married to.'

'He says his sister-in-law,' reported Toff after a short delay.

'Sounds as though Pancho is around. Find out what he wants.'

Another short delay and then the response came back through Toff. 'Says he and his men are trapped in another system like ours and wants a way out. He is secure for the moment but cannot go back up to the surface as Government troops are stationed there, shooting at anything that moves.'

There was only one thing to do, and that was to bring him through the tunnel. 'Tell him to look across the lake and you do the same. A green light.'

After a short pause there came the response: 'Got it, and Pancho has also given the affirmative.'

'He needs to get across to that light up the ladder and through the airlock. There is a lift if he needs it. Get him moving, but he will have to leave any dead ones behind. And tell him to watch for bogies when he gets there.'

A short pause and then, 'He says he has encountered some undesirables coming across the water already but is on the move.'

'Right. You need to get someone across the other side as well. Same applies, but there is a body blocking the airlock at this side. That obstruction needs to be removed or else they cannot get through. Just make sure you have enough boats or flotation devices to get them back to you.'

'Affirmative. Setting it up now.'

'Good. By the way, do you have someone there who is injured and unable to be of great help?'

'Yes. Dannyboy has caught it in both legs. He will be OK but can only be a guard. Why?'

'Shortly I will be having a visitor here. It is imperative that there is someone else who hears the story and can pass it on to the appropriate people if I do not make it.'

'Why don't you just get out of there and leave that problem for another time?'

'Because another time will not arrive. There will be only one shot at finding out what all this is about and that information needs to be got out.'

'OK. You seem to know what you are doing and no doubt you have your reasons. Good luck.'

'Thanks, but before you go you need to be preparing to leave here yourselves.'

'How do you mean?'

'Strikes me that there will be no way up, and like Pancho you are trapped down there. You have prisoners. See if there are enough to take one of the subs out with everyone on board. Check if Pancho has any as well. Now out, and put Dannyboy on listening.'

A new voice with an Irish accent came on: 'Dannyboy here. Toff tells me you want me to listen in.'

'Correct. If I don't make it there needs to be someone able to tell the story. Does not need to be verbatim. The gist of the matter will suffice, and no doubt the people who want to know will be able to make sense of it. Are you OK to do that as well as stand your guard?'

'No problem. Just tell me when.'

'As soon as I greet someone here. Then start to take a mental note of what happens.'

Matt just had time to rearrange the bandage he had previously put on the bullet wound in a hurry, making it more comfortable, but in so doing spread the blood a little wider to make it appear the damage was worse than it was. Additionally he angled the microphone on his headset so that it would pick up what any others in the room might say.

The door opened and the visitor walked in, closing it behind him. 'Weston. What are you doing here, and where is Vassilev?'

'Mr O'Rourke. Welcome. I knew we would be bound to meet up again in the not too distant future, although I do not know what the name of the game is.'

CHAPTER 11
TRIBULATIONS AND PROBLEMS

CORPORAL DAVE PARAGEM WAS the last man down the stairs, as taking Sergeant McDermot's orders had allowed the rest of the platoon to pass him. Now, because of his position on the stairway after passing Matt, and in the limited space, he could not lead from the front.

The leading man out of the airlock took the full force of the firepower from the man sent to guard the way in. However, before the dead man could drop, the one behind had pushed him forcefully forward, which took him into the guard, and as the second man kept pushing, both dead man and guard tumbled off the platform and down the stairs.

There had been only one person on guard, and the second Ranger followed down and shot the guard before he was able to recover. He then continued on his way, firing indiscriminately as he went. The third Ranger exited the airlock and immediately vaulted the barrier to drop 20 feet below onto the dock itself; again shooting at anything that moved and not caring whether he hit anything or not. The fourth stepped onto the platform but stayed there, seeking any movement and firing in that direction.

Paragem was in the next lot out, having been able to move into that position once the other men had left and hearing the commentary over the com link from the first ones out. He stayed on the platform as the three Rangers of his tranche went down the steps. That left two on the platform, and both took up positions on either side, randomly firing to keep heads down and allow the next group of his men through. In between shots he was able to check his surroundings and marvel at the buildings, the dock and the submarines, the like of which he had not seen before.

Success was originally theirs, as when the third and fourth groups, each of four men, came through; they were able to disperse without any real trouble. The Corporal was a little perturbed when neither the Sergeant nor Captain followed, and became really worried when he found it impossible to open the airlock to go back and see what was happening. That was when his tribulations started and he came out in a cold sweat despite his training.

Realising it was now down to him to ensure the success of the mission, he started talking to his men, and between them they were in a relatively strong position when the counter-attack came. Although they were spread widely they had a good field of fire and most of his men were able to cover at least one of their comrades.

However, the counter-attack was not a feeble one and some ferocious fighting took place, some of it hand to hand, before the Rangers eventually regained the upper hand. He saw one of his men overwhelmed by four opposition attacking simultaneously from different points, and although three of them were killed, one got through and shot the Ranger before going on without seeming to take a hit.

Another Ranger was killed by a thrown grenade and two others wounded, one by the man who had shot the other Ranger, but this time was killed before he could inflict any more casualties. And then the fighting stopped, just as suddenly as it had started. He knew that they had not accounted for all the opposition, and now expected hit-and-run skirmishes and warned his men accordingly.

That was when he tried to raise the Captain and Sergeant on the com link and ended up talking to a complete stranger, one with an English accent at that. His mind started doing somersaults when he found out the Sergeant was dead and he began to wonder what the hell was going on. This was not part of the game plan he had been ordered to undertake. Everything was getting crazier by the minute.

Neither Captain Delaney nor Sergeant McDermot had been part of the group which had been sent down to check out where certain pulses of energy were being received on Earth. All they had found was an ancient Pyramid and a group of people seemingly living in the past.

They had appeared the day before, after the original ones had received orders to deploy elsewhere. It had felt odd when that had happened, as the two new ones seemed in a different league. More specialist services than shock troops, but the change of orders to attack this place had come through and once again it seemed as though the wrong people were being used, and now the Sergeant had gone off on his own and been killed, whilst the Captain was also missing. Could things get any worse?

They probably would have if it had not been for the advice and instructions of the one he could only refer to as Pegleg. Who was this man who was already on the inside? Could he be trusted? But there was nothing to do but act on the information he was giving; after all he had a call sign even if he was not giving anything else away.

Having told his call sign he then continued: 'My father was in the US Forces, married an English girl and spent most of his time in Europe. I went to various boarding establishments and naturally picked up a few upper crust foibles and speech. Everyone called me "The Toff" when I joined up Stateside and that is what has stuck.' Just as they were speaking the lift door opened and more opposition tried to come out. Fortunately for the Rangers but unfortunately for them, Dannyboy had been seated facing the lift and, although in pain and being ministered to by one of his own, saw the danger and opened fire. Two others alerted also joined in and no-one came out of the lift alive. In fact, dead bodies stopped the door closing and so nobody else was able to use it.

On being advised of the other way in, Paragem noted that one of his men was by the door. 'Vanman, the door to your left. Check it out but with caution.'

It opened easily and Vanman, so called because his previous job had been a delivery truck driver of sorts, had his rifle at the ready, but no-one was there. Paragem heard him say, 'Pass me that box Collegeboy,' and he jammed the door open with it.

Following the advice from Matt, he redistributed his men, and then, just to make sure any opposition were kept on their toes, each man took a target and fired. Some at the subs, others through the windows that overlooked the dock area and others through doors at dock level. The cacophony from the firepower was deafening to the Rangers. To anyone hiding from the continuous hail of bullets the sound must have been like a rolling wall of noise and death to anyone who happened to be incautious. Windows shattered, sending shards of glass flying. Bullets ricocheted round rooms and clanged against the subs, mainly penetrating the nearest one. Others smashed into packing cases on the dock, sending slivers of wood flying as they exited.

All firing stopped at Paragem's command and he then shouted, 'Time for surrender. Come out now with hands up and you will be safe. If we have to come and find you it will be shoot first and ask for surrender afterwards.' Nothing happened for a while and then in ones and twos from the buildings and the subs people started to appear with their hands held above their heads. The Rangers were amazed at the number as the trickle seemed never-ending. Actually, there were about 20 when a headcount was finally taken.

'What the hell do we do with this lot now?' questioned Paragem in general.

Vanman came up with the answer as he found a room with an outside lock on the door. It was a storeroom with a few crates in, but in the hurry to get things settled, no-one bothered to check the contents.

The prisoners were moved in there in single file, each being roughly searched before being allowed in. Only one of them was found to be carrying a weapon, and as his place in the line was closing in on the Ranger doing the searching he pulled out a revolver and started to aim at the searcher. No chance. All the Rangers were on high alert for trouble and he took three bullets before he could even get off one shot.

'If anyone else has any fancy ideas, forget them. See what happens when you try and be brave,' shouted Paragem and allowed his rifle to traverse along the rest of the line.

Vanman saw what the Corporal was doing and did the same through the open door at those who were already inside.

Once all the prisoners were secure and locked inside the room, with Dannyboy on guard outside facing the door, propped up against a packing case, a minute search of the whole area began. His callsign was from the nickname he had all his life. He had been brought up by his grandmother, who herself had been an Irish immigrant, and he had picked up the brogue during his formative years, never having lost it completely. In fact he could also speak Gaelic.

Two opposition lay in waiting, and one managed to kill another Ranger before dying in a hail of bullets. The other was discovered but had no chance to do anything. After the previous actions the Rangers took no chances, and whether he was frightened or in waiting did not matter. He was found hiding and shot. Well, they had been warned, although it was only later that Toff found out that some of them did not speak or understand English.

Eventually they discovered the Control Room, and that was the same time as Matt had found the one outside. Those present could only stare in horror as the scene by the helicopters unfolded. It seemed as though their Captain had found the man responsible and taken him into custody when the other appeared on the scene; and the conflagration occurred. It was then that they saw the new arrivals, but it was only after Matt had pointed things out that they realised the newcomers were taking no prisoners. Those in the Command Centre watched in horror as they systematically went through each building, throwing in grenades. Paragem managed to get one of the cameras to close in on the jungle at the side of the village, from where the latest arrivals had appeared on the scene, and the carnage could be seen. Dead bodies littered the place. Now they knew where the people from upstairs had gone. Warned of approaching hostiles, they had gone to defend their perimeter, not knowing what they were up against. Some of the mercenaries were already lying in ambush when they got there. It had been total annihilation. Here and there he could see the bodies of some in camouflage, but not many. The newcomers had won decisively and were now ensuring, in the only way they knew how, that there was no further opposition.

Taking his cue from Matt, he directed one of his men to the stairway door, and soon it was secured from the inside. Whatever happened now, it was imperative to keep anyone else out and his own men alive. The mercenaries above were super-professional and his men would be no real match for them, although he knew they would give a good account of themselves.

That was when, to add to his problems, he started receiving requests for help from other American troops somewhere else in the system, and answered by saying, 'Pancho, this is Toff. Pegleg cannot hear you as he is above ground. You will have to go through me. Just to make sure who you are, he has a question for you.'

The response came back followed by, 'Who are you and what are you doing in this mad world we are caught up in?'

'US Rangers,' Toff replied, when Matt had confirmed it was Pancho. 'What the hell we are caught up in is anyone's guess. What's your problem?'

'Government troops followed us into the compound outside and acted hostile, especially as we are here without their permission. We are inside a massive cavern but there is no way out except under the water.'

'Likewise here, only we have mercenaries topside and it looks as though they want us dead. Our way out is similar to yours.'

Here he was, passing on information like a messenger boy but over the airwaves as the chit-chat carried on. Then to cap it all the one they called Pegleg asked him to check out if one of the subs could be made operational as a means of escape, and if the prisoners could do it for them.

'Pancho. Pegleg asks if you have any prisoners, especially ones who might be able to operate the subs.'

'I have some prisoners who appear to be non-combatant. I'll check them out and bring them along. Seems strange, but Pegleg usually knows what he is doing.'

Toff then had to arrange to meet them at the other side of the great underground lake, and ordered, 'Vanman, take Collegeboy and get some boats over the other side where those green lights are.' He had seen them earlier when Pegleg had mentioned them, and pointed them out. He then added, 'You had better take another two just to add weight if there is trouble.'

'OK,' came back as they went on their way to see what they could scrounge that floated, 'but what are we going for?'

'Marines. US Marines. Don't ask; just go.'

How the hell was this one man able to think about the rescue of others, escape for his men, and at the same time trying to get to the heart of the matter? He must be superhuman. Dannyboy and Pegleg were now on a separate wavelength. He could not listen in and control his men. He would have to ask Dannyboy later what he had heard.

At the same time as the Rangers were given the go-ahead to attack one base, Lieutenant Cave and his party of Marines were told to go for the other. As they were expecting such a call, no-one thought to check the order out, after all it came through with all the correct codes and appeared to be from a true source.

The two helicopters swooped in from either side and dropped their troops before flying off. Neither on the way in or out did they encounter any enemy fire, which gave concern to the Lieutenant as he led his men in from one side. On the other, Sergeant Antonio Panchetti, better known as Pancho, led his men. Neither of the groups met any opposition, but they were not to know that the guardians of that Base had been instructed to reinforce the other because of Matt's activities.

People were around, but if they posed no threat, their orders were to leave well alone. Not a shot was fired in anger, although just to make sure anyone kept their heads down, a few were fired into the air or ground. As both parties met up, everyone was looking querulous; they had expected serious opposition but none had come.

They found the Command Centre, but the two who were in the room surrendered; there was nothing they could do without colleagues to send on the offensive. Whilst there, they saw shadowy figures moving in from the jungle, and these eventually materialised into Government troops.

LEGACY OF THE ANCIENTS

Lieutenant Cave said, 'I had better go and meet them and make sure there is no real problem.' With that he set off accompanied by three of his men.

Quite openly and with his gun over his shoulder, he moved out to meet the incoming troops. As soon as they saw him they just opened fire and shot him in cold blood. At least three guns poured automatic fire into him.

Seeing this, the three who had accompanied him and had stayed back opened fire themselves and the three assassins went down. The shooting had brought other Marines who were nearby, and they also created a firewall, keeping the Government troops down, whilst one of the Marines recovered the body of the Lieutenant. Any of the Government troops who showed their heads had them blown away.

That left Pancho in charge, and seeing more Government troops coming their way, he ordered his men to fall back. What he had witnessed had sent him mentally reeling. They were well and truly trapped. The helicopters could not come back for them and it was obvious there could be no surrender. That was when he knew his problems had started.

Some of the men, hearing of the trouble over their com links, started to look for places to hide and create a defensive position. One of the Marines stumbled on a stairway going down, at the bottom of which was a door. Realising that it could possibly hold their only way of salvation, at least in the short term whilst they were able to sort themselves out, he called in his position.

'Pancho, I have found a way down to the underground. It is at the end of the passageway between the village and compound.'

Pancho felt that he was grasping at straws but nevertheless gave the order, 'Meet on the stairway where Veteran is now, but give each other cover as need be. Now go.' To the two with him he said, 'You as well.' He followed them out but threw a couple of grenades into the Control Room as he left. The explosion which followed wrecked the equipment and rendered it useless for anyone who might want to track them.

As he went, Pancho could hear bursts of gunfire; some he recognised as from his own people but mixed in were other sounds which meant the Government troops were also fighting back. He was the last to arrive, and two of his men gave covering fire as he raced down the open passage. Three more of the Marines had been killed but no-one had been able to count the number of Government troops lost. All four bodies had been brought into the stairwell; Marines don't leave their friends either dead or alive on the battlefield if at all possible. The stairwell was crowded, and all had to keep low as bullets were coming in, although the two at the entrance had sufficient cover to shoot out at anyone attempting to rush their temporary place of refuge.

At the bottom, Veteran, so called because he was the oldest and had seen more action than any of the others, was trying to get some sort of order and allow Pancho to make his way down the crowded stairway. One of the new recruits, who had not been in action in Greenland, had opened the outer airlock and gone inside. When he could not get the second door to open, and as he was the explosives expert, he placed a charge against the other door, came out and partially closed the other door.

Veteran, on seeing the position and instinctively knowing what had happened, shouted, 'Nooo …' but it was too late and his voice was drowned by the sound of the explosion, which in that confined space and the narrow stairwell was deafening to all.

No sooner had the sound vanished up the stairs than there was a different sound. The second door had been blasted out; the explosives expert did know his stuff. A whooshing sound became a roar as the first door was blown open, crushing the explosives expert to death. Then it sounded as though all the inmates of Hades were trying to get out.

Still reeling from the noise of the explosion, all were caught off guard as the air inside the Base was expelled at a great rate as water entered via the underwater entrance. Some were sent tumbling, others held onto colleagues and tried to withstand the pressure, but eventually all were face-down on the stairs. Dust, dirt, debris and anything not fastened down came flying out and up the stairway, and for about five minutes no-one dared move. At the entrance the two guards were nearly blown out, but they were able to hold on because the doorway was smaller than the internal passage and they could brace themselves into a corner each. The force was so great that it travelled part-way across the village before dissipating a little, which kept the Government troops' heads down.

As the unseen force abated somewhat, Pancho was able to get his men moving through the airlock, telling them to expect trouble on the inside, but none came and again he was puzzled. The dead Marines were also taken through. Two men from the entrance were the last through, and one had left a calling card at the top of the stairs – a grenade on a tripwire. Pancho and the last two, with a great deal of effort, even though one was a heavyweight, managed to shut the one remaining door on the airlock, and when Pancho tried it he found it could not be opened, so presumably those on the outside could not get in. Just as they got it closed they heard the exploding grenade at the top of the stairs and realised they had done it in the nick of time.

Pancho, when he got outside the airlock, realised why there had been no opposition. The place was a shambles. The rising water had lifted the pontoons onto which everything was built, and the buildings had crumpled like a pack of cards as they had been braced from the roof as well. Broken glass, half panels and even some girders spread over the dock area, and the two submarines in there, because they were free-floating, had risen faster than the dock, and one was on the dock and the other crosswise on the loading pontoons with its nose buried deep in the other.

People were stumbling about in shock, not even looking at the intruders as they tried to make sense of their new surroundings, looking for friends, trying to find a comfortable place to rest after the turbulent times they had just encountered.

Pancho knew that the destruction would have rendered any other way in as inoperable, and instructed, 'Get down there and help them, but keep a lookout for any would-be troublemakers.' With that he followed them down and moved about, trying to coordinate the needs of the people there.

Some men went looking amongst the structures which still resembled buildings whilst others tended to the wounded, and gradually the walking wounded joined in looking after their friends. Twenty minutes later, and after he and two others had checked out the submarines, there were about 20 people in various states of fitness. How many had perished there was no way of knowing. His men had encountered some bodies as they searched and it was obvious that others were missing as those left were looking around.

Seeing the state of the people, it was obvious that they were not fit to create any opposition, and the Marines started to relax as they took stock of their situation. Those remaining alive knew they were safe for the moment, but if the Government troops found a way in they would be trapped rabbits.

Veteran, as ever, was looking around and nosing into various places to see what he could find, when a movement out on the water caught his attention. Somehow the lights had remained on, which meant he was looking into the darkness, whilst illuminated himself. As he moved to get a better view of what was out there he saw a twinkle and before the sound of gunfire came to him he was on the deck with the bullets whirring overhead.

'Pancho, we have company over on the backlot coming across the water.' Pancho did not need telling, the sound of gunfire had already alerted him and with a few men he was already heading in that direction. Standing in a darkened recess he was able to see three boats coming in, each heading for a different area.

'Get out of the light,' he shouted to his men. 'Veteran, you and two more take the boat on the right.'

He then heard Veteran call two men and all three started pouring fire on the indicated boat.

Knowing where one of his other seniors was he than commanded, 'Donkey, get a couple of men by the subs and take out that left boat.'

Again he heard calls as Donkey, so called because his laugh was like that of such an animal, collected two men, and he heard gunfire from that quarter.

'You three with me,' he said to the three men standing near. 'The centre boat is ours,' and with that he opened fire, followed shortly afterwards by the others.

Each group fired two magazines each and then stopped to survey the damage. Meanwhile Desperate, who had been one of the last down, had found a battery-operated torch, but it was like a searchlight. Dan was his Christian name but he was built like a shithouse wall and so he had been nicknamed after the comic book hero.

From a hiding place, knowing that his light could be a target, he shone it out. All that could be seen was the wreckage of three boats and a number of bodies in the water. Two men were swimming towards the dock, and they were allowed to come in unharmed, but as soon as they were out of the water they were roughly manhandled and checked for weapons, revealing none.

The searchlight was played out further over the water, but nothing else was moving as Pancho sat down and tried to collect his thoughts. The instruction to go in had been received, and therefore Pegleg must have gone on the offensive. Perhaps he was somewhere around and could hold the key for getting them out.

Using the open channel of his com link he called out, 'Pancho to Pegleg. Are you there?'

Receiving no response he went through three other channels before getting an American voice answering him after a short pause: 'Pegleg cannot pick up your frequency where he is at present so you will have to go through me. However, he does have a question for you. Who is Onslow married to? Does that mean anything to you?'

'Of course it does.' Pegleg must be around as it was not a question he would have expected from anyone else, but where was he? 'Tell him he is married to my sister-in-law.'

'Right Pancho, this is Toff, and Pegleg confirms your reply. What can we do for you?'

'Get me and my men out of this hole. And by the way, who the hell are you?'

'Corporal Paragem, US Rangers. As for getting you out, that might be a problem as we are in a hole as well. What is your position?'

When Pancho, having no option but to trust the voice, told him what had happened, he then received the information that the Rangers were trapped underground by mercenaries.

After a three-way conversation Pancho was eventually asked, 'Have you any prisoners?' After responding he was then asked if they were from the subs.

The question seemed somewhat strange but he went to check and found most of them were involved in some way as submarine crew, and received instructions and directions to get out.

On being told where to look he had seen the green glow referred to and now felt that he had to trust whoever and go for it. No good sitting around waiting for something to happen. Someone must have a plan for escape for all of them. There was no doubt in his mind that it had all been a set-up, but who, and more to the point, why?

'Veteran, take Donkey and see what you can find that floats and will carry people. We are going over there,' and he pointed across the water.

'All of us, including the prisoners. Pegleg needs us somewhere over there.'

Veteran looked a little askance at being given the order, but the mention of Pegleg, whom he had seen in action in Greenland, sent him on his way without demur. A quarter of an hour later they returned to the edge of the ruined dock in a dinghy with outboard motor, towing a number of liferafts.

'Could be a tight squeeze and there is not much power in the engine but it is the best we can do.'

Whilst they had been away he had spoken to the Russians again, through one whom he had found earlier who spoke reasonable English, and explained what had happened topside before they had come down. None of them had any wish to be left behind to face whatever it might be, and all were willing to take a chance with him.

Before they left, Pancho collected his men at the dockside and said a prayer over the bodies of their colleagues, who were wrapped in whatever could be made into a shroud and weighted before being tipped into the water to sink out of sight. The Russians decided to leave their dead where they were.

Everyone managed to squeeze into the boats, and they all set off in line astern to find out what actually lay on the other side. None of the Russians let on about having been there before and no-one knew what to expect. Pancho and a group of Marines were in the dinghy, whilst the Russians were in the lifeboats with a Marine at bow and stern. The last lifeboat held the remainder of the Marines and a few of the Russians.

Pancho had one last job to do before leaving. Entering the subs one at a time, he left a timed charge in their control rooms and left. Before he had got into the dinghy, he heard the muffled explosions and hoped they had been rendered useless, at least in the short term.

All crossed safely without a hitch and the motor on the dinghy was able to pull them all without problem as the water inside the cave was calm. Once at the ladder Pancho ordered Donkey to go up and reconnoitre, and received the all-clear. Unfortunately the rising water level had knocked out the lift and so it was up to everyone to climb.

Pancho and two more Marines then went up, and he found himself on a small platform. That meant people would have to come up a few at a time. Donkey had not ventured from the platform and so he found the airlock and opened one side. Through the window he could see no sign of life, and taking one of the other Marines with him he closed the door and opened the other. Nothing happened and they both marvelled at the sight of the car and the rails.

He had a few more Marines come up and posted them through the airlock. Then, half a dozen at a time, he had the prisoners come up. The first lot were put in the airlock whilst the next set came onto the platform and others were on the ladder but held below the overhang. Then it was a chain: one group through the airlock and as the next entered, the ones on the ladder emerged onto the platform and more started up the ladder.

There were a couple of mishaps with the prisoners as they made their way over the overhang. Two men fell to splashdown some distance below. They were winded but otherwise unharmed and the Marines in the last lifeboat were able to drag them on board. At last they were all up and the boats sunk. Now there was no going back, but also it was imperative that anyone following was not immediately aware of where they had gone. Before they were all through the airlock, Pancho sent the first group of Marines and prisoners, with Donkey in charge, in the car to face whatever might be at the other side. When the car on the other rail appeared, everyone was through the airlock and as with others it was left so that the door on the platform was inoperable.

Pancho went with the next mixed group and marvelled at the ease with which they went, wondering why at the point where the cars passed, the rails went either side of a large, obviously man-made stone. At the other end he found himself facing a Ranger. 'Hi, I'm Vanman. Welcome to what could be another hell hole. Your first lot are through and waiting. How many more?'

'About the same again.'

'Right, can't take you all at one go. Do you want to take the first lot, including some of your party and then send the boats back for the rest of us?'

'OK. Sounds a plan.' With that he then spoke over his com link: 'Veteran, I am going to find out what is in store for us here. You and your party will have to wait for the next shuttle boat over here.'

With that he went through the airlock, down the ladder and took charge of the motley array of boats that were waiting there. He could see the lights in the distance and headed out that way. The Marines with him were on the alert both for activity from the prisoners and anything else. They had been welcomed at the portal into this new cave but did not know what further trouble lay in store for them.

All the time that Pancho was getting his men organised in one cavern, Toff was busy sorting out his side as requested by Pegleg. He realised what the proposed means of escape was going to be and so his first job, like Pancho's, was to commit his dead colleagues to the deep. He left the opposition's dead where they were.

Following that he went to where the Russians were being held and asked, 'Any of you understand English?'

Two responded that they did and under armed escort he took them to the Control Room, which one of his men was monitoring. He showed

LEGACY OF THE ANCIENTS

them what was happening topside and explained who they were and what they had done. They just stared.

'Now you can stay here and await their arrival, but I do not think they will be well disposed towards you. Or you can help us escape and get away yourselves.'

'What is it you want?'

'Have you enough people there to be able to take one of those subs out with all of us, all of you and more on their way?'

'We are submariners and I know others who are but cannot vouch for all,' said one.

'Some of the others have been helping dockside,' added the other. 'Usually that means they have a working knowledge of submarines as they may be required to man them.'

'Then let's go and find out,' and off back they went to question the others.

As they went, Toff was mulling over in his mind what the second Russian had said, or rather what he had not said. There seemed to be a question mark over some of the prisoners which no-one was speaking about.

Toff had hardly had time to get there when the man in the Control Room came on the com link, saying, 'Toff, get back here fast. There are more problems topside.'

The urgency in the voice made Toff sprint back, just in time to see Government troops coming in fast, furious and heavy. He switched to Pegleg's channel and almost screamed, 'Get out of there fast. More trouble topside heading your way – in fact they have just shot a gunship out of the sky.'

Could it get any worse, he thought, all the time willing Pegleg to get down to them.

CHAPTER 12
ESCAPE

'I ASKED YOU, WHERE is he?' After a pause when Matt did not answer, he demanded again, 'Vassilev; what have you done with him?' O'Rourke's voice started to rise and continued to do so with each additional phrase.

'He got frazzled,' was Matt's response as he tried to wind him up even more.

'Don't answer so stupid. What have you done with Vassilev?' This time the tone was even and hard. 'And where is Donovan?'

'Was he your pseudo-Ranger?'

'Never mind that. Where are they?'

'They got all fired up.'

'You are making me angry.' With that O'Rourke started to raise the machine pistol he was holding, but stopped as Matt raised his rifle.

'You must have passed the remains of the helicopter. Well, they were two small piles of smouldering ash at the side. Not of my doing.'

'Well who did then?'

'He had another guest who wanted retribution. He is the third pile of remains.'

'Blast you, yours and every other interfering busybody. Now I will have to search through here to find the answers.'

'The answers to what? What is the link between the happenings of yesteryear to the both of us and the now? Vassilev wanted to know, and whetted my appetite for information as I seem to have become involved. Neither of us could work out who was currently pulling strings.'

'You and your sort were interfering once before. Pity you were not permanently taken care of then.'

'Why? You are obviously too young to have been involved at that time. So what is it that you are trying to find out now?'

'You don't begin to understand the part of it. The Power is what I am seeking and Vassilev was part of the way to discovering it. All I want is what is mine. My family should have had it years ago.'

'Ah yes. The Power,' said Matt as though he knew about it. 'Vassilev mentioned it in passing but I thought nothing of it then.' Matt's thoughts flashed back to the Greenland cave and O'Rourke's lack of interest when the photographs were being discussed. 'Now I realise that the wand in those pictographs is what you are seeking. Pity I cannot help you; not that I would, if I could.'

'I wouldn't ask you. Vassilev was getting close to finding it and it was only going to be a matter of time before he handed it over. I have known about the man and his operation for some time, and just to make sure I held the upper hand, I had one of his subs sunk and a couple of his contracts thwarted.'

'OK. So you can find your own answers now, but why was I targeted deliberately all those years ago?'

'If you must know, not that it will do you any good, my grandfather was an amateur archaeologist working in the Middle East. He had found various references to the powerful wand and was following through on information which could have led him to finding it. You and your colleagues, with your clandestine operations in that area, and Vassilev's interference in local politics, were causing difficulties. Remove both of you and he could continue. Unfortunately things did not go to plan and my grandfather was held responsible for subsequent counter-actions against the Tribes. The locals killed him, but not before he had sent his findings back home.'

'So what has that got to do with me now?'

'Hear me out,' and he held up his hand, 'although your interfering has now jeopardised the entire operation again. I must admit that you have a charmed life. Knowing where you were and the price on your head, I pointed people in the right direction, but they failed to take you out.'

'You should not use amateurs,' was Matt's response.

'Anyway,' continued O'Rourke, ignoring Matt's sarcastic comment, 'my father had been seriously injured in a car accident and was unable to follow through. That is why there was a delay before I could get going, as first I needed to gain respect in Government circles. All the time I was in touch with those who had supported my grandfather and little by little we were getting closer to our goal.'

'So you are not alone in this. Who else beside you would become all-powerful?'

'There are many organisations who would like to rule the world, some of which I have used. I just wanted to ensure I got the Power first and then I could select who would join me in creating a brave new world; led by the Irish of course. About time we took possession of our own destiny.'

'And now it has all turned into a big fat zero.'

'Not necessarily so. A setback, yes but the search will go on. The Irish will rule over many countries, as thanks to the mass exodus my countrymen are now scattered throughout the world.'

'But why are you carrying the flame?'

'Six of my great-grandparents were related to the old Chieftains. My lineage is as good as it gets. I will be the one to lead the people again.'

'You are already corrupted by the thought of the Power.'

'You have some room to talk. You are already corrupted as a killer, so don't talk to me about corruption.' Matt missed any more of O'Rourke's tirade as the building rocked with an explosion that sent dust dropping through the air, and at the same time his earpiece crackled with Toff's instructions to get out. 'Government troops are harrying the mercenaries and gaining the upper hand. If you want to use the portal, better get a move on,' were the added words.

O'Rourke had also become aware of the commotion and shouted,

'He is in here, come and get him.' Before the final word had left his lips, Matt had started firing the rifle, which was on automatic fire, from where it lay on his knee, and traversing it up O'Rourke's body. Not waiting for anything else, Matt then dived below the desk, where one pedestal was turned to one side to reveal the way down. With one fluid movement, despite the false leg, he was down the hole and securing the pedestal closed from underneath when he heard shots from above.

Matt's first few shots had not found a target inside the room and had gone straight through the wall. Outside were two of the mercenaries acting as guards, and the bullets coming through found one of them. As the line of fire was angled upwards slightly, the mercenary, who had been looking towards the door at the sound of O'Rourke's command, took two full in the face. The other mercenary immediately returned fire in the area where the other bullets had come through. Then he barged the door open just in time to see O'Rourke's body slipping off the edge of the desk where his bullets had propelled it.

Of anyone else there was no sight, and after a quick look round he left the same way and went out to join the fire fight outside.

Along a short rock corridor and Matt was at the secret door onto the stairway. A little spy hole like in hotel room doors allowed him to see what was happening on the stairs. Three mercenaries were trying to force their way into the airlock. Matt slightly opened the door and threw one of the grenades he had picked up earlier on his travels through the compound, and then said into the com-link, 'Stand by to receive, I am coming through after the explosion.' Immediately after the explosion, he came out through the door, and as he said, 'Close the inner door,' he sent a few bullets up the stairs towards the corridor in case anyone was lurking there.

He had to move two of the mercenaries' bodies before he could open the door at his side, and as he was closing it there was an explosion from the top of the stairs.

Some of the shots fired by Matt had been at such an angle that they had ricocheted and gone outside. Three of the Government troops had been approaching when one had gone down. Without thinking, another had thrown a grenade into the passageway and brought down masonry from above, effectively sealing it off and burying the body of the Ranger Sergeant.

Out into the cavern Matt emerged and propped the inner airlock door open with the crate that had been left there. Down to dock level, he followed a Ranger who had obviously released the door for him. A Corporal was coming towards him but in the distance Matt had spotted Pancho, who had just arrived with some from the other cavern. He ran past the Corporal, who just stood there in amazement, and went to greet Pancho. As he did he saw people in the party whom he recognised. Without thinking he raised his rifle; two shots rang out. One body fell back into the water, whilst another dropped where he was.

Matt then noticed the man who had showed him round the sub, and shouldering the rifle made straight for him, grabbed him and propelled him away from the group and behind an adjacent wall. As he did so he shouted at Pancho, 'Keep out of this,' but winked as he did so.

When they were both out of sight, Matt released his hold and said, 'Sorry about that, but I don't know whether I can trust you or any of those that have come through. Do you know what is happening up there?' and motioned upwards with his hand.

'Yes. I have spoken with the Sergeant and we are all agreed there is a need to get out of here and rather fast.'

'Good. What I want to do is use one of the subs. Have you enough men to do it, even if it needs help from the rest of us?'

'I do not see why not. It really does not take all that many to move a submarine around.'

'Good.' That seemed to be has favourite word at the moment. 'How many of those with you are submariners? Really I need to know which are not.'

'The only two that I was not sure of were the ones you shot. Why did you pick on them?'

'I remembered one as a guard who looked at me in an evil way when I first left the submarine. Could not feel safe turning my back on him. As for the other, I had seen his dead twin in the Control Centre here. I could not imagine Vassilev being so naive as having one man in a secure place with another roaming where the two could get up to mischief.'

The other man smiled and, when asked, said his name was Leonid. The hair was turning grey and receding although he was still probably in his early thirties, hinting at his European ancestry. Short of stature but well built. Dark eyes in a round face that retained its impassive look at all times. He did add his surname but to Matt it was so unpronounceable that he immediately forgot it.

With his arm around the other, Matt escorted the man back to his group and then went to Pancho and gave him a big hug. 'Good to see you, my friend. I wish it could be under better circumstances but I am sure we will get out if we all work together.'

Then he turned to the approaching Corporal. 'You must be Toff,' and held out his hand.

Toff ignored it and took him in a bear hug. 'Pegleg, it is good to meet you in the flesh. After all you have done for us a handshake is too little.'

The dark hair on a square face had a military cut. A tidy moustache but the shadow on his jaw showed it had been some time since he had a shave. It was the mouth that was the feature of note. When he smiled all his upper teeth showed but the mouth had a downward twist at one side which allowed part of the lower teeth to be revealed at the same time. Of average height, but the hug he gave Matt hinted at toned muscle.

'I don't know about that. All I seem to have done is get us all into a sticky situation.'

'Not of your doing,' answered Toff.

'We were catapulted into something,' added Pancho as he approached Toff and said, 'Thanks for the invitation to join your party. Together we may have a better chance of getting out of here and he,' pointing at Matt, 'seems to have the luck of the devil.'

'Let's hope it has not run out,' added Matt before adding to Pancho, 'You can stand your men down from guarding your group. Just keep a careful eye on them, but I think they are in the same boat as us and want a safe way out.'

Turning back to Toff he said, 'You have some prisoners also. Where are they?'

'In that storeroom where Dannyboy is facing the door.'

'Is there any way they can be seen without them knowing they are being observed?' asked Matt.

'Actually there is. We only found it later but there is a one-way mirror in the next room. Why anyone would want to spy on a storeroom I do not know.'

'Good.' There was that word again. 'Leonid,' he called to the Russian and indicated he should come over.

'Leonid here,' he said to Toff with Pancho listening, 'is going to help us get out, but I want him to see those you have under guard in case he can identify any possible problems. Are you up for it?' to Leonid but without waiting for an answer continued: 'Let's go look them over but without them knowing.' And with that he followed Toff, who had understood what was happening.

As they went, Matt said to Leonid, 'I saw you talking to your people. Do they know what is happening and what is proposed?'

'Yes. They are wanting to get on with it as they do not feel safe here. Some of them do not trust your people here and one or two are actually afraid of you, but overall there is a desire to get out and fast.'

'Do you trust me?'

'At the moment I can see no other way and so I have to go along with you. Trust is a word that maybe is questionable but I do not intend to cause you harm, and if we do get out then I know you are a man of your word. Your people here seem to hold you in respect, and that for the moment is good enough for me.'

'Fair enough. On that basis I will respect your judgment.' By this time they were in the next room and could see the other Russians grouped next door. 'Any of those you recognise as possible problems in our escape bid or afterwards?'

'A number of them I do not recognise. Sorry, but it was rare for the teams to meet so we only ever saw each other in passing. The two at the front I do recognise. They are both senior submariners like myself.'

'Those are the two that I have been talking to and have explained the position to,' interrupted Toff.

'The small one I only know by sight,' continued Leonid, 'but the other is my senior in length of service. We both have our different ways of doing things and I am afraid I cannot work with him.'

'Fair enough,' commented Matt. 'Is there any way you can talk to them and try to find out if they are all submariners or if any are security in disguise? I want to get out in one piece and stay like that afterwards.'

'I can try, but what are your proposals for us when we have got out of here?' asked Leonid.

'There I have a dilemma. How best for us to part company. I am sure you do not want to meet American security, and neither am I bothered about that. There is a need to ensure this operation is shut down. However, what is the best way for us to go our own ways in safety and comfort?'

'There is always the mini-subs for one of us,' commented Leonid.

As they had been talking Matt had also been idly watching what was happening in the other room. Suddenly he ordered, 'Get them out of there,' swung the gun off his shoulder and smashed the butt against the glass. It shattered but the initial resistance aggravated the wound on his arm, which he had forgotten about. Before the glass had landed on the floor he was shooting into the roof and shouting, 'Everybody out.'

Toff did not wait to see what was the matter. He rushed out and pulled some of his men together and unlocked the door to get the prisoners out and under guard.

'Stay here and listen,' was Matt's instruction to Leonid. 'Pancho,' who had stayed close, 'with me,' and as they went outside he added, 'I am going to stick the muzzle of this rifle up the tall one's throat. You do the same with the other. Rough interrogation required.'

Everyone was taken by surprise as the two of them ran up to their individual targets and pressed gun muzzles to throats, threatening to shoot upwards. 'How many of these are not submariners?' he demanded in a rough voice.

When no answer was forthcoming he pressed the muzzle harder and demanded, 'Which of them are not submariners?'

It was Pancho's prisoner who answered. Matt's just stared back at him, so he relaxed the muzzle from his throat and as the man had the makings of a smile appear, thinking he had faced him off, hit him with the butt in the stomach, wincing with pain as it caught his arm, and then swung the gun one-handed in an arc over his body and crashed it down on the other's back to drop him on the floor, and then ignored him.

As the other started to speak, Pancho had also withdrawn his gun. 'All of us have something to do with submarines. None are security. They all fought to the last. We are not fighters in that sense and are aware of what awaits if we do not get out of here.'

'Good. Leonid, did that sound right?' but thought to himself that it was similar people in Greenland who had put up one hell of a fight. Knowing they were all in the same predicament, he let the thought lie.

Leonid came into view and said, 'Seems OK, and as they left most seemed to have that marine gait. All you can do is trust them and hope for the best.'

Before commenting further, Matt addressed Toff, saying, 'Get some men to check what is in those cases in there.'

Then, turning to Leonid he said, 'You are in charge. Take what men you need and give me a true assessment of the status of the submarines. I'll hold you responsible if there is any trouble. You know what I can do if I am angry.' Pancho made as if to send some men with him but decided against it when Matt shook his head. Then he forgot all about questioning the decision as the exclamation 'Bloody hell' came from inside the room where the prisoners had been, and Toff's voice added, 'Come and see what we have found.' The Marines and Rangers had now mixed together and some stayed out, watchful, as some followed Matt and Pancho into the room. The sight that greeted them was an amazing one. Boxes had been opened and all revealed bars of gold; small bars, the type that could be fitted into a jacket pocket.

'No wonder this room had a lock on it,' commented Toff.

'And that is why there was the spy mirror,' added Pancho. 'What put you onto it?'

'Just the way they were acting. They had obviously found it and were looking to keep some. It was just the way they were acting, but my first thought was that they had found weapons.'

'There must be a fortune here,' one of the men who had followed them in commented. 'They won't miss any of it now.'

'Toff, keep it under lock and key for now until we can decide what to do with it.' Matt gave the order in a commanding voice and then added, 'Everybody out, now!'

Back outside he was met by Leonid and his team returning, and asked, 'What is the status?'

'The far submarine is relatively unscathed. No problem with taking it out, although I would not like to try it at any great depth as there are a few bullet holes. The other sub is more damaged, although some of the damage looks old. It would be a risk to use it.'

'That could well be the one from Greenland. At least that gives us something to play with,' commented Matt. 'All we can do is go with the flow. Get it ready. Take what men you need and let's get this show on the road, or at least into the sea.'

Pancho's prisoner, who turned out to be called Sergei and had followed Leonid, then added, 'Both the mini-subs are in good condition and could be used as well.' This one was obviously of Slavonic origin and about the same stature as Leonid, probably a height suitable for submarines. His eyes were bright and once he was given something to do they sparkled and his whole face lit up.

'Right. Get them both ready as well, but before you go, call all your people here.'

Pancho and Toff looked at Matt, wondering what he was going to do next. They were expecting something, but when he made the request, 'Bring out two of those bullion boxes' it really was a surprise.

When all were gathered and staring at the contents of the boxes, Matt started speaking. 'I intend that we should all leave here. Only those necessary to take the sub out will be allowed on board. Everyone else will have to go in the mini-subs. One of those will go piggyback and the other will follow. You people cannot be allowed to keep the sub and start carrying out bad things again, so once we are out and at a safe distance you will be allowed to go on your way in the mini-subs. These two boxes will be placed on the mini-sub being carried out, as you will need some funds to get you on your way wherever you make landfall.'

He could see that his speech, which had been translated for those with limited or no knowledge of English, had been well received, so he ordered Toff to place the two boxes on the mini-sub and add another for good measure. Then he added, 'Leonid, there remains just one more thing. You will have to teach a few of the Rangers and Marines how to control the sub for when we part company. OK?'

'No problem, provided you do not want to go into action.'

'I think we have all had enough action for the time being. A place of safety is all any of us, your lot included, want at present.' He was about to say 'go to it' when there came a warning cry from the assembled Russians. Everyone had been watching them and not the man whom Matt had knocked out previously. He was now charging head-down at Matt, who turned and saw that there was limited time to react. He fell back, intending to hit the floor and trip the man up. Pancho was right behind him and, thinking he was off balance, caught him. Matt, leaning there, raised the prosthetic. The man hit the foot head-on with a crunch, knocking both Matt and Pancho to the ground with the force of the charge. They were able to get up, but the other was dead, a severe indentation in the top of his head from hitting the solid false leg.

Once he had stood up again, Matt bowed to the Russians as the only way he could think of that all would understand his gesture of thanks. Then he said, 'Let us get ready to leave this place. Leonid, you are responsible for getting the sub ready. Sergei, you have the responsibility for making sure the mini-subs are ready.' Then to Pancho and Toff he said, 'Select some of your men who might have a technical bent to learn what they can about running the sub after we part company.'

The two buffetings he had given his wounded arm and the fall against Pancho had caused the wound to bleed again, and Vanman being the first to see it said, 'Come on and let me see to that arm before you lose any more blood.' Matt allowed himself to be led away for treatment. Ten minutes later, with a new dressing professionally applied and some painkillers, he felt a new man, ready to take on whatever was to come his way. Whilst he was being ministered to, he allowed his mind to relax, and the first line of an Animals song came to him; the words of which were, 'We've gotta get out of this place if its the last thing we ever do.'

Within the hour everything was ready and the spare mini-sub had been winched off the mother submarine and set in the water. The Russians had been divided up so that they were equal in each mini-sub, albeit with a tight squeeze. Only those Russians necessary for running the sub were being allowed onboard.

Before they left, however, Matt made the time for everyone to have a good meal, which one of the Russians fixed up. Something of a cross between Russian and American cuisine but it set everyone up for whatever lay ahead. In the presence of Sergei he also allowed each Ranger and Marine to take one of the gold ingots, and it was also agreed that one should be taken for the families of each of their fallen comrades.

He emphasised that care would have to be taken in disposing of them, adding, 'We do not want to be accused of theft, nor do we want others trying to get in here to help themselves to the rest. But I think we have earned it.'

It was then left to Toff to secure the storeroom and the gold that remained. He went into the adjoining room and secured that door from the inside before climbing through the broken window and coming out of the storeroom door before locking it. He was going to pocket the key but Matt took it off him and hid it on a ledge he found under the edge of the dock.

'No-one can now accuse us of trying to keep things for ourselves,' he said by way of reason.

One of Toff's men had been keeping an eye on what was happening topside, and Matt had a last look just as they were about to leave. Close-quarter fighting still seemed to be going on, and that meant it should be propitious for them to leave without trouble. That was always hoping that a welcoming committee was not awaiting them outside.

Matt was just about to climb down into the sub when he realised there was one outstanding matter. He shouted down for a grenade, and Veteran popped up with one. He then went onto the other sub and down to the control room, where he threw the grenade and heard the explosion, hopefully rendering it immediately useless, as he was leaving.

The submarine led the way out with either a Ranger or Marine watching every move the Russians made so that they would be able to take over at the appropriate time. The mini-sub followed at a pre-arranged interval. That was to make sure that if trouble was lurking outside, both would not be caught at the same time.

Nothing happened and, once in clear water, the mini-sub was taken in tow, using an articulated arm on it to hold onto the tail of the other mini-sub still being carried piggyback. Southwards they went, as had been agreed, for a few hours until they were near the South American coast.

The time of separation came and the Russians who had been crewing the sub made their farewells, with Leonid climbing through the hatch into the mini-sub last. Matt secured the hatch inside the sub, but then locked all mechanisms so that it could not be released.

'What are you playing at?' demanded Leonid.

'Just a little insurance,' replied Matt, 'to check that no-one has sought to do any damage when you leave. We will wait a few hours and see if anyone starts to sweat. That goes for you as well, Sergei,' who was in charge of the other mini-sub and had been listening in. He then cut the communication system and walked away.

An hour later, after rifling through the contents of the captain's cabin he returned. 'Anyone getting worried?' he asked Leonid as he undid the hatch and poked his head inside the mini-sub.

Everyone was calm and Leonid answered, 'We are all happy to stay here for as long as you want.'

He looked through the observation dome at the other mini-sub, which was still holding on. All he saw there were people sitting around getting a little restless as they were more cramped and had to rely on their own air supply, whereas the one he was in was being supplied from the parent sub.

'Everyone there OK?' he asked Sergei.

'No real problems but we might have a problem with the recycling machine as the air is getting a little thin.'

'OK then. Prepare to cast off,' and with that he went back into the sub and closed the hatches. 'Best of luck to you all. Take care.' Then he released the mini-sub, and as that started moving away the other one let go its tow. Both rose to the surface and Matt breathed a sigh of relief, as there had always been the possibility of sabotage which could have happened as they parted company.

Back in the control room he said, 'Let us go and find friendly company. Northwards to America.'

CHAPTER 13
A CATCHING OF BREATH

THE USS GALVESTON WAS on station off the Atlantic coast of Florida. The crew's concerns were in relation to surface traffic in the particular area as the countdown to a shuttle launch was under way. They were also there to pick up the booster rockets after they had been jettisoned, and also, should the unthinkable occur, pick up the crew of the shuttle if the flight had to be aborted immediately after take-off.

No-one was paying any particular attention to what was happening under the sea, and the submarine surfaced right alongside without detection. The first the ship knew anything about their presence was when a crewman heard an English voice call up, 'Ahoy the Galveston. Permission to come aboard.'

The crewman looked over the side and gawped at the apparition which had appeared. A few seconds' delay and then he dived inboard and hit the emergency klaxon. Everyone wondered what the commotion was all about and it took a couple of minutes for the Captain to get the facts, after which he appeared on the Flying Bridge and stared down as Matt, who had originally called out, was joined on the deck of the submarine by a Marine Sergeant and a Ranger Corporal.

Matt saluted the Captain and again said, 'Permission to come aboard. We also have casualties who need proper medical attention.'

'Who the hell are you?' asked the Captain as more Marines and Rangers appeared. Then something triggered in his mind. 'You lot wouldn't happen to be the personnel who disappeared in Panama a few days ago, would you?'

'Could be. That is where we have just come from,' responded Pancho.

'The airwaves have been fairly buzzing about you. A number of people will be wanting your reports, so you had better come aboard.'

'Good, but can you take this in tow? It's a remarkable bit of kit for its age,' Matt added.

Whilst waiting for the arrangements to be made to take them on board and Matt knew they would be communicating with the powers that be, he reflected on how they had kept just under the surface after they had parted company with the mini-subs, feeling their way carefully around the Atlantic side of the Caribbean until they reached American waters. It was then they had decided, as the men operating the sub were getting their hands in, to see how near they could get to the first US ship they found before being challenged. It had surprised all on board when they had actually surfaced alongside without a problem.

A hatch in the side of the ship opened to reveal men with arms, one of whom, presumably the Master at Arms said, 'Come aboard singly with your hands where we can see them.'

'What do you need those for?' asked Toff. 'We are on the same side.'

'Orders from on high,' came the reply.

'If we had intended harm,' added Matt, 'we could have sunk you long ago. This baby has some fearsome defence systems that could be used aggressively, so put your playthings away before the men on here get riled at the welcome. They have been through a lot, none of which was their own making, and are ready to tear someone apart to find out why. Don't be the ones to start them off.'

Below deck on the submarine Matt could hear some of the other men getting their arms together. The last thing he wanted at this time was a fire fight between the two groups, but the Captain arrived himself and told his men to relax before coming on board the sub.

'Get the injured up,' he said. 'There is a Coast Guard chopper on its way to pick them up and another for the rest of you. I am to take command of the submarine, so perhaps you would be good enough to show me round.'

'It would be a pleasure,' commented Matt. 'Step this way. By the way, my name is Matt Weston and these are Sergeant Antonio Panchetti and Corporal Dave Paragem. I see you are Captain Waylon. Welcome aboard your new command.'

'I do not know what to make of you all. Rangers, Marines, an Englishman and a submarine the likes of which I have never seen before.'

'I know we look a right motley crew but we have all been through hell together and will be looking after each other. Toff, see to the injured, will you. Pancho, will you get the rest ready to leave, but keep the men who have crewed it at station until the Captain's men relieve them.'

Receiving affirmatives, he then went inside, followed by the Captain, who was marvelling at the manning of the submarine by Rangers and Marines; men who had never handled a submarine before.

Twenty minutes later the injured were on their way to shore and medical treatment. A short while later and two more Coast Guard helicopters appeared, by which time the transfer of the submarine was complete and took the rest of them to shore; a military camp offside of Cape Canaveral.

When the tour of the sub was over and Matt and the Captain had gone on board the ship, Matt persuaded the Captain to call the Director of Naval Operations. When he came on, Matt asked, 'Could you let me have the use of the submarine you have in Antarctic waters?'

He got no further as there was a spluttering from the other and an emphatic 'No. What do you mean by asking such a stupid question?' with the line going immediately dead.

'Don't think I asked for that favour in the right way,' commented Matt, staring at the dead microphone in his hand.

'What makes you think he would have complied?' asked the Captain, looking at him in surprise.

'Obviously he has not heard of my prowess with submarines, either sinking them or using them. He will come around to my way of thinking.' And he left it at that.

Once they were in the Camp, Matt, Pancho and Toff went into separate debriefings over the radio with their respective superiors. Matt found himself on a three-way system with Appian and Wilberforce. A quick resumé as to what had happened and then Matt made the same request for the Antarctic submarine again, this time saying why.

Ever since boarding the submarine, Matt had been holding a log which he had found in the Captain's cabin. A log which gave the directions for gaining entry to all the caves that the organisation had been using.

A short while later, when Matt had had his injured arm properly attended to, the Director of Naval Operations came back on line, very apologetic. 'You seem to have some friends in very high places in the Pentagon.'

'And beyond,' added Matt, thinking it would do no harm for him to think he was better connected than he really was. At the moment it was only friends of friends that were pulling strings but Matt did not want the Director to realise that.

'Regardless. I have been told that if you want a Fleet I should put it at your disposal.'

'Just the sub, thanks. I would like to control the operation but you may listen in. I have nothing to hide and you could have everything to gain.'

'I am all ears and am now handing you over to Lieutenant Da Vinci.'

With that the line went dead and then another voice came on. 'Da Vinci here with the Bradenton at your service.'

'Not Leonardo, I hope.'

'No. Harlan actually.'

'Right Harlan. You can call me Matt or, if you wish, Pegleg which ...'

'Pegleg! You the one who sank the sub down here?'

'Yep. That's me.'

'In that case, me and the crew are right with you. What is it you want?'

'To go searching for a cave. And before you think I am mad, hear me out. I am going to give you some coordinates. To all intents and purposes they appear to be on the Antarctic continent itself. You need to approach at 750 metres or deeper.'

'We have been looking for something for days now without success. Why should we trust your information? I do not mean that disrespectfully but I do not want to put this submarine in harm's way at all.'

'Understood. I am reading from documents seized from another sub. I know you found nothing, but you were not actually looking in the right place. Trust me.' With that, Matt read out the coordinates and a short while later Harlan came back. 'OK, we are on our way. ETA should be just over two hours.'

'Right. When you get into position you should line yourself up on a north-northwest alignment. All the directions I have are in metres, so I will leave you to do the necessary calculations. You will then rise to 500 metres. Do you copy?'

'With you so far. We are playing along for now but if the first reading does not pan out then we will pull out. You realise your reputation is on the line here.'

'I am well aware of what is at stake for both our countries. But I am glad you stopped me in full flow. You will need to take care when coming up to the 500-metre mark. The calculations here are for subs without a fin but which are longer and broader than you.'

'Right. We will take things very carefully but you could not have picked a better sub for the work. We have sensors all over and should be able to tell if there is a problem before we hit it.'

'Glad to hear that. At 500 metres you need to turn through 90 degrees.'

Before he could go on the response came back. 'Good job we have thrusters then.' Matt ignored the comment as he was concentrating on the sheet in front of him which was in pictographs rather than in Russian. 'Forward then for 200 metres, at which time you will be able to surface. It does not tell me how far below the surface you will be but based on others I have been in I would anticipate less than 50 feet.'

'If we are able to follow through your instructions we will definitely proceed with caution.'

'Do so at all times. I do not know what you will find there, so be prepared for trouble. Now read the instructions back so I know you have them correct.'

Harlan's voice clearly read out the instructions and then said, 'OK?'

'Spot on. I'll let you get on with the work. Out for now.'

Matt sat back in the chair, stretched himself and then started to work his body to rid himself of some of the aches and pains. He was still thinking and not really aware of whoever else was in the room when he felt hands on his neck. He stiffened, ready for action, but then they started massaging the neck muscles.

'Oo, yeah. That feels good, whoever you are.'

A man's voice answered, 'Thought you looked all stiff and sore when I looked in just as you finished talking. Hope you did not mind my interruption, but in a small community like this camp, it does not take long for things to get around, and we all have a good idea of what you men have been through recently. All on camp want to help in any way we can.'

'Just carry on. That really is helpful. I can feel the stress of the past few days leaving me. Carry on like that and I'll be a new man.'

'I am not a masseur but have found that I seem to be a natural when I have helped others.'

'You definitely do feel to have healing hands. We are now in a waiting game, so do your best.' At that, Matt turned round to find himself facing a young civilian worker, who then continued the massage onto his good arm and then other parts of his aching body.

The man left after half an hour or so, by which time Pancho and Toff had joined him, along with the Base Commander. Matt put them in the picture as to what had happened and what they were waiting for.

A buffet meal was brought in for them and then a radio conference was set up, with the three of them able to talk to their superiors and the FBI and CIA.

Appian took the lead, as he had on so many other occasions, by saying, 'Each of you has spoken direct to your leaders, but now we need to try get a few things straightened out amongst ourselves. Matt, will you start as you were the first in.' Matt outlined what had befallen him since being taken, followed by Toff and then Pancho. All were heard without interruption, but at the end the two soldiers' commanding officers nearly spoke as one together.

'I did not order you to go in, so who did?'

'Matt saw Pancho and Toff looking blank and could visualise those he could not see bearing the same expression. 'Only a thought,' he said 'but perhaps we should be looking for an Irish connection.'

'But how could anyone from Ireland infiltrate our communication system?' This from one of the commanding officers.

'And for what reason?' rejoined the other. 'They are a friendly Power.'

'I said Irish connection. Not a direction from Ireland. How many Americans are of Irish ancestry? Maybe there are those in high places who would have pledged their allegiance to the Chieftains, not realising it was only O'Rourke.' And he wondered how many Irish eyes, as in the words of the song, would not be smiling now.

Before anyone could go on, the communication was interrupted by Harlan saying, 'We have approached the coordinates and there is a void above. We are now proceeding further with caution.'

'Good luck,' said Matt in unison with the other three who were with him in the room.

That effectively killed any further conversation as everyone was waiting on tenterhooks for an outcome.

The seconds stretched into minutes and the minutes seemed to be hours, but a look at the clock revealed only 40 minutes had elapsed before Harlan came back on and in an elated voice said, 'That was some place you sent us into.'

'And?' said Matt as there came a pause.

'Firstly, we have a couple of dents in the upper part of the superstructure but nothing serious. Even with careful manoeuvring we seemed to have a tight fit in places. Secondly, no opposition was met. Seems two who were left when you sank the sub, went on their way yesterday in a converted mini-sub. Actually we think we picked them up as a contact, but it was too far away and so indistinct that we did not follow through. Pity, they could have been very helpful. Thirdly, what a base it was that was being prepared there. Not far from operational.'

Matt had a feeling that Harlan was holding something back. Was it something he wanted only his people to know? So he asked, 'Is that all?'

'No. There were still two people left, and death would have been their only way out if we had not arrived. The bastards had just left them with no food or communication system.'

'They were not called McPherson and Colton were they?'

'Why, yes. How did you know?'

Matt was laughing at that, and took a couple of minutes to compose himself, with the others looking on incredulously.

'Sorry about that but I seem to have gone full circle. My original brief for being sent to Antarctica was to find out what happened to those two. It seems I have done just that, even though it might, to some extent, be by proxy.'

There was laughter and cheering over the airwaves, and someone slapped Matt on the shoulder.

When the merriment had settled, Harlan then said, 'These two are adamant that they are OK and are demanding to be put ashore by the British Base. Our Medic on board can find nothing wrong and we have given them a good meal, so I propose to do just that. Over and out.'

'Gentlemen, I think overall we have gained a good result from what we have achieved,' concluded Matt, although he knew his services would be required further but hoped for a rest before anything else.

The following day Pancho and Toff, with their respective commanding officers, together with Matt and Wilberforce, met with Appian and Cortez in the camp. In the 24 hours since the general debriefing it had transpired that three senior officers had disappeared from duty and two more were being held by the Military Police. All, it seemed, had some Irish ancestry. It was known from where the commands to enter the compounds had emanated, and the Irish network was now being investigated.

When they were all together, Matt asked 'What about Dannyboy?'

His commanding officer said, 'We are not aware of any connection between him and the Irish network, but he is only junior rank. He has, in fact, confirmed all you have said.'

'Sorry, that is not what I meant. Although, given the way things went down the tubes, I would not have tried to vary the report if I was involved. I was more interested in how he is.'

'Oh. He will recover and return to active service. From the Corporal's report on his actions we would be more than happy to make sure he can return to our fold. Guys like that we do not want to lose.'

After again going over the activities of the past few days, Matt then asked, 'Where do we go from here?' Knowing full well that he would be required to give his services further.

'Glad you asked that,' said Appian. 'On the way here we all agreed that you three should remain together as a team. Somehow you seem to have gelled together, despite not having known each other long. Mr Wilberforce has given us carte blanche for your services for as long as we need them.' Matt was just about to butt in but Appian held his hand up and continued: 'Yes, we know we have no power to force you to work for us. But yes, we would hope you will continue to do so until the whole of this matter has been resolved.'

Before Matt could speak again, Cortez came in with, 'What we had thought would be the end of the matter seems to be only half of it. There is still the need to try to find out what the power is and where we can find it.'

'Why can't we just leave it hidden?' came from Wilberforce. 'If no-one has found it by now, is anyone ever going to?'

'Unfortunately,' began Cortez, 'we do not know how many people are still seeking it. The Irish network will probably never be totally disbanded, and if Vassilev was onto it as well, are any of his cohorts still looking? It would be a disaster if it fell into the hands of some tin-pot dictator or the Axis of Evil as our President calls some countries. Safer overall if we can get it.'

Matt was not convinced of the argument but did not want to become a part of it. 'I was going to say that if my services are required I would hope that a little R&R would be allowed. After all I do have an injured arm and a few days not having to worry about anything, except for avoiding assassins, could be beneficial.'

'I think we can agree to that,' commented Appian, 'but these two,' and he pointed to Toff and Pancho, 'will accompany you wherever you go.'

'In that case,' Matt interrupted, 'you two had better start calling me Matt.'

'I'm Tony.'

'And I'm Dave.'

Matt went over to them and made a show of shaking their hands, saying, 'Pleased to meet you.'

When he had finished, Appian continued: 'Where is that to be?' It was a statement and not an option, but Matt did not really want to be encumbered with protectors. However, appearing to go along with it he said, 'Where I was before seems as good a place as any, and we know we can rely on the good intentions of the Sheriff and his staff there.'

'Good. I could not agree more with your choice.' Before anyone else could say anything, Tony interrupted: 'I do not know if the others have given it any thought, but I have been wondering how the Panamanian troops knew to come in when they did. It was almost like clockwork and as though we had been expected.'

'From what we have been able to gather,' responded Appian, 'Vassilev had some agreement with a General that if there were real problems, he would send in troops to help out.'

'But it was as though they were on hand in readiness,' continued Tony. 'There was no time to have them mobilised.'

'I was going to say, before you interrupted, that they were aware, don't ask me how, of all foreign troops in their country and had anticipated something was about to go down.'

'Can't see the Irish mob with their mercenaries wanting backup,' Matt spoke thoughtfully. 'So does that mean we have a spy in the camp somewhere?'

'On that, your guess is as good as the next man's. Now I have to get back, so I will leave you to make what arrangements you want.'

Before he could get away, Matt took Appian on one side and asked, 'Have we found out any more about who put the contract out on me?' not letting on that he already had some knowledge.

Appian paused and then said, 'Come again?' Matt could tell it was only a ploy to gain time to come up with an answer as he repeated the question.

'It seems to be a well-hidden trail that we are trying to unravel.'

'Liar,' thought Matt but said no more. It was obvious he was not going to get any help from that quarter. But why? Then he asked, 'What about the hijackers?'

'All but the steward were illegals and were all terminally ill. Their families had been promised big money if they did this.'

'Would that have been honoured?' mused Matt aloud.

'That is something we will never know.'

'So the steward was not terminally ill.' Seeing a shake of the head, he continued: 'Did I take out the wrong person then? I saw someone with a gun and a dead body and assumed two plus two equalled four. Perhaps this time it did not.'

'What are you getting at?'

'Did anyone check out the dead stewardess? Was she the baddy and he had got the upper hand?'

'I follow your logic, and that is something we need to follow up.' After a slight pause, Appian went on: 'Would it be on your conscience if you had killed the wrong person?'

Matt shook his head. 'No. As far as I am concerned, someone was going to shoot me. In a me-or-them situation, I always prefer it to be them that fall.'

When he and Cortez had left, Dave, Tony and the commanding officers also took their leave. Matt and Wilberforce were left to talk to each other.

Wilberforce opened by handing Matt duplicates of his credit and debit cards, saying, 'I have arranged for funds to be available here in the US, so it should make things easier for you moving around. Additionally you have been given temporary honorary US citizenship, and here is the card you need. At the end you will have to hand it back but it should ensure all the help you need if you require it.'

'Thanks. I was wondering how I was going to live, having left my own cards somewhere in Panama. The other will help me get lost easier if need be.'

'How do you mean?'

'Well, as much as I trust Tony and Dave, they are there to ensure I bring home the bacon. I am not sure that this porker wants killing. All it needs is a future President or even a top-ranking official to be a little paranoid for the Power to be used indiscriminately. After all, if it is what we think, it is a weapon of mass destruction.'

'So what are your plans now?'

'To go where I said, but first I would like to suss out the opposition, or at least the ones who have put the contract out on me. I know who and where, as I am sure Appian does too, but is not saying for some reason. All I have to do is work out the how of having it terminated.'

'I won't stop you, I know it would be no good, but I would urge caution. Firstly because you are not in your home country, secondly because our friends here are relying on you to find the answers, but thirdly and mainly, I want you back working for me in one piece. Those two are supposed to be there to protect your back, don't get caught out.'

The next day the three of them were taken by staff car to Orlando Airport where they boarded the shuttle for Atlanta. Matt saw how the citizen card worked wonders, and so at Atlanta he managed to get himself separated from his minders and, as it was the hub for Delta Airlines, got himself on a plane to Seattle instead of New York.

He was sure that by the time he arrived in Seattle they would be aware of his movements, but when he got there a few planes had arrived at the same time and by staying in the middle of the mêlée to get out he was not spotted, or if he was, no-one could get to him. Instead of using a car rental agency, he caught the shuttle downtown and booked into the first hotel at which the shuttle stopped.

He did not leave the hotel until well into the following morning. All the time since checking in he had expected to have a visitor but no-one made themselves known and nor was he aware of anyone shadowing him as he left. He spent the next few hours at various public establishments, finding out all he could about Costain and Cavalcade Corporation, eating lunch at a Subway.

Towards the end of the afternoon, but whilst there was still some natural light, he decided to observe the headquarters of the Cavalcade Corporation and checked the map for where he wanted to be. The quickest way led him down a side street, and although there were a few people around he became aware for the first time that he was being followed. There were three of them and their demeanour said they were not security.

As he hurried his step he realised that two more had emerged ahead of him. There was no mistaking their intention. He was in a trap and had no weapons except for the knife in his prosthetic, which he proceeded to get out in readiness. What method did they intend to take him – after all, with other people around they could not just kill him there?

That same morning Her Majesty's Submarine Avenger had entered the Aleutian lair of Vassilev's Organisation. Wilberforce had insisted that the UK play its part, and the fact that Avenger was in the area had swayed them. One of Vassilev's submarines was still in the Base that was being prepared as they were waiting to see what was happening, having heard of the destruction of the Organisation. They felt that to delay going anywhere for a few days would allow the clamour to die down and they would be able to disappear.

The coordinates for entry to the Base were also on the papers that Matt had taken from the submarine that had carried them to safety. Accordingly Avenger was able to negotiate its way in without any trouble. Unfortunately, as it surfaced, the other submarine was checking it armaments and on seeing a strange submarine arrive, opened fire on it. A fierce fire fight ensued and Avenger's Captain decided the only way to terminate it was to fire two torpedoes.

One found its target, decimating the area being prepared around the other submarine. The other was a little off line and seemed to explode harmlessly against the wall of the cavern. Unfortunately, being part of the Pacific Rim of Fire, the explosion weakened the cave wall and allowed molten lava to come to the surface, whereupon a volcanic eruption occurred. When it was all over there was no sign of the cavern or anything that had been in it. All had been obliterated and the island was taking on a new shape as molten lava cascaded out.

Back in Seattle, Matt was trying to work out his best plan, intending that attack should be the best means of defence. Looking beyond the two who had appeared in front of him he saw things start to move. He shook his head but it was not a hallucination; there was a shaking and it was approaching nearer. He did not know that the volcanic eruption in the Aleutians earlier in the day had set off movement in the Pacific Plate, causing a minor earth tremor which was now coming his way.

Judging his time as best he could, he started moving towards the two men as fast as he could go. The earth tremor reached them first and threw them off balance. Matt, being aware of what was happening, was able to keep his footing and as he passed one of them he used the side of his fist to hit him on the back of his head. Then he was out and made his way into the nearest building, a relatively new hotel which had been built to withstand earth tremors.

Sitting there in the lobby, he felt naked. He could see anyone entering, but the lack of armaments left him feeling vulnerable. No-one followed him in, and as he sat there looking out and at his map, he realised he was in the street for the Cavalcade Corporation Headquarters. Looking out, he could see it diagonally across the street. If they had a room overlooking the street he would have a chance to observe things.

His luck was in again. The hotel had a room on the 12th floor, and when he checked it out it was perfect. A diagonal look along the street gave him full view of the Cavalcade Building. Half an hour later he had checked out of his original hotel and was settled in his new room. He would have preferred a balcony but the window jutted out in the shape of a horizontal V, giving a clear view either way along the street.

The chair was hard and after a few hours of viewing he had only seen the people from the offices leave at the end of the day. He knew from his earlier gleanings that each floor was a separate office for one of the Cavalcade Corporation's operations. No 13th floor, which was not unusual in some American buildings, and the top floor, the 14th, was Costain's private quarters.

Once it was dark and the offices had gone into darkness themselves, he gave up and went to find something to eat. On his return he found the room already had two other occupiers; two whom he had been expecting.

'Hello you two,' he greeted Dave and Tony. 'What took you so long to find me?'

'We just missed you at the other hotel,' answered Tony. 'What made you move out so fast? Surely it was not to keep us off your tail.'

Matt motioned for both to come over to the window, saying as he did so, 'I knew you would catch up sooner or later but quite by accident I found the Cavalcade Corporation HQ. Right down this street,' and he pointed. 'That is where the contract comes from and Costain is the man at the top.' Then he told them how it had come about.

'What do you intend to do if you see this Costain? One man against – how many?' This from Dave.

'I had nothing in mind. Just checking out the opposition. Seeing if there was any opportunity which presented itself.'

'Well, we are here to make sure you go where you originally said. A lot of arrangements seem to be in train up there for your safety.' Tony would know because of his brother-in-law.

'So are you going to drag me there kicking and screaming? Or will you stay close to me here for a few days whilst I check this thing out?'

'Nobody gave us a specific timescale, did they Tony?' questioned Dave.

Tony looked towards the ceiling before answering. 'Nooo. But we will have to report in that we have found you and what is happening.'

'OK. I know you have to cover yourself and I have no problem with that. Nothing appears to be happening over there at the moment, and I do not intend that we watch it 24 hours, but I do need to see what happens in the morning and then I want to take a floatplane ride. I suggest you two check in here as well, go and get something to eat and we will meet in the Bar in a couple of hours.' As both looked at him quizzically he added, 'I promise, I do not intend to run away again. I just have one of my feelings that the way ahead will be revealed.'

When they met up again later, they were like three old friends as they talked through the evening before going to their separate rooms. By six in the morning, Matt was up and keeping observation, but only a few people had gone into the building by the time Dave and Tony joined him at seven. Matt had arranged Room Service breakfast for all three in his room, and each took short spells at looking out whilst talking amongst themselves.

Dave was at the window when he said, 'Hey. Come and look at this.' Both the others joined him, and whilst it was difficult for all three to clearly look out at the same time, they were able to observe a man come out onto the balcony of the 14th floor of the Cavalcade Building accompanied by two others, who were obviously Heavies. The balcony was covered and the man sat down to breakfast, which one of the Heavies brought out.

Dave produced binoculars and each man was able to study the one on the balcony. That had to be Costain. At the same time they could see the other office workers arrive but there appeared to be nothing untoward in that. Thinking he had seen all he was going to, Matt was turning away when something caught his eye. From the underside of the balcony an awning was moving out for the floor below but it went way out over the street. He also then became aware that the floor below also had a balcony, albeit not as big. A closer look at the awning showed it to be covered with netting and the inside edge was very loose. The man on the balcony looked over and then went to sit back down at the table and the awning retracted itself.

'Weird,' was Tony's comment when Matt pointed it out.

'Mm,' came from Matt, who was thinking over what he had just seen and the reason for it. There was obviously a good reason or else why bother to check?

By 10:30 they were on a floatplane. One part of Matt's brain was still thinking over what he had seen earlier whilst the other was watching the coast of the Olympic Peninsula as it went by below them. He knew where he wanted to be, but had not been specific with either the others or the pilot. Cruising one way he saw the property he was interested in, and then from another angle as they came back. Exactly as he had seen it on the plan. Returning, he asked the pilot to circle in over the town so he could get an overview of the area of the Cavalcade Building and noted cranes at a building site on the next block.

Back at the hotel Matt explained what he had been looking for. 'Vassilev told me that he had dealings with the Cavalcade Corporation but there was no way he could bring a submarine into Elliott Bay unseen. There had to be another drop-off point. Costain has a retreat where we have just flown over with a large building at the water's edge. Two storeys high and it appeared to go down into the water. What better place to dock a sub for unloading?'

'I saw the property you were looking at closely,' commented Dave. 'I was watching you closely until you showed an actual interest in it. I can follow your line of thought, but it did not seem long enough to hide a submarine, especially one of the size we are familiar with. After all, you are not the only one to fly that area and these local pilots would surely note anything out of the ordinary.'

'Agreed, but arrive at nightfall, unload overnight and be away by dawn and no-one would be any the wiser. Now, any of you trained in scuba gear? I would like to get a closer look at that building.'

'I have been trained,' said Tony, 'but I am not sure it is sufficient for what you are wanting.'

'You will have to rule me out,' commented Dave before continuing, 'But what about you?'

'I have done some in the past, but this,' and he patted the prosthetic, 'is not a lot of good when covering distance, and the arm has still not got a lot of power in it. I would hope for a tow.'

'Would you be happy to bring someone else in on this caper?' Dave asked. 'One of our wider circle of friends. I know a man who could do it for us. Vanman.'

'If he is able and willing, go for it.'

Within half an hour Dave had tracked down Vanman, and within two hours he was with them, as he had only been in Montana for his R&R and had quickly flown across. After they had explained what was wanted, Vanman left them, to return a couple of hours later to say everything was organised for the following day. His legs were long in relation to his body, which made him lope along rather than walking or running. Looking at him face to face there was no doubt that he was his own man and completely in control of what he was doing. The face had a hint of East European ancestry, and with a gold tooth shining when he smiled, he appeared more a wide-boy, which is what he had been at one time before enlisting and finding his true vocation.

'Because I have the appropriate licences,' explained Vanman, 'there were no questions asked. The appropriate equipment will be delivered to a boat that I have also hired for our own use.'

Matt put his fists out, thumbs up. 'Now I feel as though I am taking control a little.'

That evening, Matt noticed the same escape of people as the previous day, and in the morning the man on the balcony did exactly the same thing as the workers were arriving. As this was happening, Matt, for no apparent reason, counted the floors. Fourteen, and then he checked again. Same result but with the 13th floor missing there should only be 13. Then it hit him: what the situation was over in that building and what the awning was for.

The rest of the day was carried out in underwater exploration. Dave stayed with the boat as Vanman and Tony, with Matt holding onto a sea-sled, examined the structure under water. From there it became obvious that the cliff face to which the structure was attached was an overhang and the underside of the building was definitely made to accommodate a submarine which could stay there for days undetected.

The following day they all left, with Vanman continuing his vacation in Montana and the others flying off to New York State.

CHAPTER 14
PARTY TIME

ON THEIR ARRIVAL AT Newark Airport, a car was awaiting them. Tony took the wheel, as there had been a request that this car not be written off like the other. Matt thought the other would not have been if various agencies actually spoke to each other. He was still miffed that the CIA seemed to be dragging their feet over identifying the source of the contract on his life.

Tony had driven that way many times and on a couple of occasions took shortcuts over rough roads, but as the vehicle was an SUV it took them in its stride. Tony dropped Matt off at the same motel he had stayed at previously. Dave was also left there as he was taking an adjoining room. Tony then went on to join his wife at home.

Matt had barely had time to unpack his clothes when the telephone rang. 'Hello,' he answered, and before he could go on:

'Matt, welcome back. It's Onslow. Tanya and I hoped you would come visiting this way again. Tonight you will come and have a meal with us.'

'Sheriff, I have been travelling most of the day and really do feel like a rest.'

'Rubbish. Good company and a good meal is what you need. Tony is coming over and your other colleague is also invited. Oh, there is one other thing, we would like you to meet someone.'

'Some of Tanya's cooking is a worthwhile invite but …'

He did not get any further as Onslow said, 'If you don't come I will personally come down there and bring you here in handcuffs.'

'OK. OK. You win. Who is it you want me to meet?' But the line went dead after the question had been asked.

As they had no idea of timing for the evening, Tony had to chivvy them up when he arrived early in the evening to pick them up.

Once on their way Matt asked, 'Is your wife not coming?'

'She has been there since early afternoon helping to prepare the meal for tonight.'

'We were expected then?' suggested Matt, and Dave looked on, bemused.

'Of course. Up here we are one big happy family and you will find most of the locals will be looking on you as some sort of hero. In fact both of you. The whole town will be looking out for your safety.'

'What about you? Are you not classed as a hero, or is that because you live here?'

'Don't worry. The whole town would lay on the full red carpet treatment for the three of us, but have been told to keep everything low-key.'

'Onslow wants me to meet someone there. Any idea who it is?'

'Not really. I have gleaned that it is a female, as Tanya thinks you need a woman in your life. Just go along with it. Tanya likes to think she is a good matchmaker and many times she has been proved right, but tonight it is all a matter of having as many men as women there.'

'What about me?' interjected Dave.

'You will have to make do with the lovely Katia, Tanya's daughter,' came the response. 'As I said, just for this evening go with the flow.'

They were the first to arrive and there were introductions all round. Dave and Katia hit it off straight away and went off together. Tony's wife, who was called Isabella, was a slightly younger version of Tanya, but there was no mistaking the family likeness.

They both had round, nearly heart-shaped, faces with brown eyes. Tanya wore her brown hair short but Isabella favoured a longer style which curtained her face. When they smiled, they were exactly the same and their bodies showed they both followed a fitness regime.

With Dave gone, Matt and Tony were left talking over their drinks when the doorbell rang. Tony, who was nearest, went to answer the door as Tanya came into the room from the kitchen. Before either could undertake any introductions, Matt rushed over to the newcomer, took both her hands in his and kissed them.

'If it isn't my helper from the plane,' he said. 'I never got the opportunity to thank you for your help in the hijacking. Even though I do not think you knew exactly what you were doing, your help was really appreciated.'

The mousey hair was shorter than he remembered, but it was the sparkling green eyes that he had to force himself to look away from. Stood there, he realised his original impression of petite on the plane had been wrong, as she was only a couple of inches shorter than himself. Still, she was definitely pretty in a simple casual outfit.

Tanya, Tony and Onslow, who had been with Katia and Dave but had also come back into the room at the sound of the doorbell, stood there amazed.

Onslow was the first to recover. 'You two know each other then?'

'We have never been formally introduced,' conceded Matt, 'but we were thrown together in unfortunate circumstances, you could say.'

'Right then,' said Onslow. 'Hilary, this is Matt Weston. Matt this is Hilary Hardy. Now tell us the story.'

By this time the rest had joined them in the room upon hearing the slight commotion and exclamations. 'What's it all about, Hilary?' asked Isabella, who probably knew the least of all those present, being only aware of the circumstances in which Matt had met her husband.

'Well, I have been told not to talk about it,' she said.

'Don't worry,' commented Matt, 'you are among friends here and most are aware of my involvement in the hijack. It's a long story and perhaps it would be as well told over the meal, as that smell coming out of the kitchen is one to make the mouth water.'

The two sisters hurried out to get the meal served, eager to hear the tale and how one from their own community had helped foil a hijack. Matt told the most, with pieces from Hilary as they went through the meal, but did not add that there was a contract out on his life as a result of it. The four in the room who were in the know did not mention it either.

Matt found himself at Hilary's side all evening, although the conversation was much generalised after the meal and involved everyone. Matt found himself attracted to her but could not tell whether it was because of their previous joint involvement or if Tanya's intuition was on target. He also wondered what they would have to talk about if they had been left on their own.

Hilary was the first to leave, as she had to be up early in the morning as it was her turn to be the carer of one of the old people in town. Tony and Isabella were ready to leave shortly afterwards, and that was the signal for the party to break up, as they were taking Matt and Dave back to the motel.

Before leaving, Tanya said, 'It is Hilary's birthday next week and the town is giving her a celebration to remember. Will you be here for it?'

Matt had a feeling that something was being unsaid, but looked at his two minders and said, 'Are we in any hurry?'

Both shrugged their shoulders and Dave answered, 'Depends on whether anyone winds us up for action. Personally I have had enough for a while and am quite happy to relax here. What about you, Tony?'

'I am at home with my family. Nuff said.'

Matt smiled. These two were very good at interpreting their instructions as liberally as they could. As they were driving back, Matt felt that he could not wish for a better team around him.

After they had been dropped off, but before they had gone to their separate rooms, Matt said, 'You seemed to be getting on with Katia like a house on fire.'

'I have to admit I am smitten,' answered Dave. 'She is beautiful, brainy and a joy to be with.'

Back in his room he could not get her out of his mind. She had obviously taken after her father for being tall, towering over her mother, although Onslow could still look down on her. Her brown hair had not got the body of her mother's, so she wore it in a ponytail. Her body was really something to look at, showing her bent for sporting activities, as she wanted to be a PE teacher. No wonder he had been smitten.

At breakfast in the deli the following morning, all the locals expressed bonhomie and seemed to know about his introduction to Hilary. Each of them had their own tale to tell and Matt was able to pick up a picture of his anti-hijack assistant.

It seemed that she had been, until recently, one of the leading lights in the town; involved with many of the organisations, some of which she had helped set up – like the Cub Scout pack of which she had been leader. A few months ago she had become ill and had had to cut back on the number of activities she undertook to allow for the treatment.

She had been married three times. Her first husband was a helicopter pilot who had been killed in action. Unfortunately there had never been any children of her own which, following the departure of her stepsons, had caused her to use her energies for the benefit of the town.

She had then married a man who had been divorced and took responsibility for bringing up his son. That man had committed suicide when his business went tail up and he could neither cope with the financial problems nor his failure as the breadwinner. That had sent the son on a spiral into drugs and the wrong people, and eventually he had disappeared to the big city. Another remarriage brought another stepson, but when the father died through a smoking-related illness, the son had put his efforts into studies and now worked for the Government.

The one common thread through all this was that they never came to visit, nor did they seem to keep in touch, even though she had done so much, or at least tried to, for them. Everyone was determined to make this the best birthday party for her but no-one had anything good to say about the stepsons except to comment that they would probably not remember it was her birthday.

Matt stopped off at the Sheriff's office after his lengthy breakfast with all the people talking to him and asked, 'What is it with the two stepsons that they never visit their stepmother?'

'At least two or three times a year she goes to see them, but only from a distance. She never makes contact and has said they are the ones who left and it is up to them to make the first move. I know she would like to see them but it is probably six of one and half a dozen of the other that makes neither side give way first.'

'Could they be persuaded to come to the birthday bash?'

'Possibly, if they knew the full story. Hilary is terminally ill and has only months to live. When you met her on the plane, she had been out to the West Coast to see the top specialist in that field but there is no more he or anyone else can do. Most people are aware to some extent of her position, and that is why everyone is pulling together to make this a party to remember for her.'

'So that is what was unsaid last night as we were leaving. I had a feeling there was something being kept back. Puts paid to Tanya's matchmaking though, does it not?'

'Yes. But do you think you could make her last months happy?'

'Well, we did seem to hit it off, but you know the problems I have and the further action I have to carry out. I am not sure that I want to get involved with anyone. If the circumstances were different, I could be tempted. Now what about the stepsons?'

'One is a Diplomatic Courier for the Pentagon, so whether he will even be around is anyone's guess. The other is more of a problem. He left here a tearaway and became a small-time crook in Washington and has worked his way up the ladder to become a serious contender for criminal of the year but manages not to get caught.'

'Is it worth a try?'

'I am sure she would be glad to see them, given the opportunity.'

'Right, then. I think me and the lads will have to go to Washington. Give us all the information you can on them.'

His thoughts on the plane had been right about the children having flown the nest, although he had not expected them to be stepsons. He had, however, been wrong about juggling home and work. Just as she must have been on a low ebb on the plane, he had given her something to take her mind off the illness for a while.

Matt had already offloaded the gold bar and another he had managed to conceal. With the money he was able to hire a private plane to take them to the Capital and await the completion of their business there. Later on he was also able to use more of the money to pay for additional mouths to feed at the party.

It was nearing the end of the working day when they were on the road out of the Airport in the hire car. First stop was the Government worker and they arrived just before him. They were in the parking lot under his apartment block and aware of his particular parking place. Before he had time to get out, Matt had opened the passenger door and was sat in the front passenger seat.

Karl Berenger was surprised, but his reflexes were quick and his hand went for the gun under his jacket as he said, 'Who the hell are you?'

Sizewise, as they were both sat there, he seemed to be as tall as Matt, but the blonde hair was slightly longer than a military cut and the round face with the blue eyes kept looking directly at Matt. Matt had been in such situations before, and just stared back at him. The most noticeable part of his features was the missing section of eyebrow over the right eye; it started, stopped and continued again. No beard or moustache, but there was more than a hint of five o' clock shadow that indicated he had been up and on the move very early that morning.

'If you feel safer with the gun pointing at me, then feel free. I am but a messenger.' Matt could see it in the eyes. This man was no mere courier. His eyes were those of a killer, although perhaps it took one to know one.

Karl kept his hand on the gun but did not draw it from the shoulder holster. 'What do you want?' he demanded.

'To give you a personal invite to a party next week. Your stepmother's.'

'So she could not come to me in person. Always looking on me from a distance. I have seen her. Why she cannot make the first move I do not know. And now she sends an intermediary. How wonderful!' It was said sarcastically.

Matt could feel his anger rising but managed to keep his cool as he retorted, 'You are both alike. More like mother and son than step-relatives. She feels you should make the move as you left her and were not kicked out.'

'Maybe, but life goes on and we have nothing in common anymore. Not that we did have to start with.'

'OK.' Matt held up his hand to stop him interrupting. 'Hear me out. Your stepmother is terminally ill. This is the last birthday she will have, and the townsfolk are making it a big one. If she comes to see you, if only from a distance, it must mean something. I am sure that your attendance at the bash would be welcomed by her.'

'We'll see.' There was bravado there but Karl looked a little taken aback.

'The invite is there. Take it or leave it.' With that, Matt got out of the car and into the other, and as they drove off he could still see Karl sat in the car.

Next stop was a Club owned by Larry Fontaine, the other stepson. This was a bona fide business, but it was also a front for other activities. This would be more difficult, so they parked the car a block away and went to reconnoitre. There could be a few people in the way of getting to Larry.

Walking down the back alley, they found the rear entrance to the Club, with one man stood outside an adjoining door, which suggested an entrance to an apartment. Larry must live over the business.

Matt, with the other two, walked up to the man and said, 'I have come to see Larry Fontaine.'

The man looked him over as he stubbed out the cigarette he had been smoking. 'No-one sees the Boss without an appointment and no-one is due tonight, so bugger off.'

He made as though to reach for a gun, but Matt acted first and pushed a fist into his solar plexus. As the man doubled up he caught him by the arm and swung him round to where the others were. Tony caught him and held him in a vice-like bear hug whilst Dave relieved him of the gun. Then all four walked inside. Well, three walked, the other was almost carried.

Stairs led up from a hallway but no-one else was in sight. Tony stayed with the man whilst Matt and Dave went upstairs. Another door, but locked. Dave went back downstairs and took the keys from the one who was now coming round. First one fitted and they entered a kitchen. Music was coming from the next room and Matt indicated Dave should stay but be ready if needed.

Matt opened the door and entered as bold as brass. His hand was behind his back, holding onto the gun in his waistband, but he need not have bothered. Larry was in a clinch with a female and had his back to Matt. The woman saw Matt for a start, and as her eyes widened, Larry became aware of someone else's presence. He carefully turned round, and seeing only one man, shouted, 'Rollo.'

'If that is the man who went for a smoke, he is otherwise detained at present.'

'What is it you want? You must know that you cannot get away with anything. I control this area. You will be dead before you leave.' He had obviously had to fight his way to where he was now, as the nose was squashed to one side. Heavy-set but muscular, which seemed to indicate good living, as did the jowled face, topped with crew-cut dark hair. No moustache, but immediately under the bottom lip was a tuft of hair but no more.

'What a lot of bluster. I got in without trouble and will leave the same way. However, I am not here for anything other than to give you an invitation.'

'To what? What makes you think I would want to go anywhere where you are? I could be walking into some sort of trap.'

'True. But I am only a messenger. The invite is to a party next week. It is your stepmother's birthday and the townsfolk are giving her a big do. However, I am sure that a highlight for her would be if you were to come along.'

'Why, when she has never made contact? Oh yes, I know she keeps looking on from a distance but why should I make the first move?'

'Because you are a fool.' Matt saw him stiffen and thought he might have gone too far, but continued: 'Just like your stepmother. I don't know about step-relatives. You could be from the same mould. Anyway, she is terminally ill and will not see another birthday, so maybe this is a chance for you both to make peace with each other.'

'What good would it do at this late stage? She despises me for the road I have taken.' Matt could see a change in the expression as the reason struck home.

'I am merely a messenger. I cannot force you to attend, but the invitation is nevertheless delivered.' With that Matt backed out of the room, collected Dave and then Tony, who released the man, and they were gone; hurrying back to the car and away before there was any chance of pursuit.

Back at the apartment, Rollo came into the room and started to say, 'Sorry Boss …'

'No matter. We are going to a party next week and we will become very rich in the process.' Then in a lower voice he said, 'I know who you are, Mr Weston.'

Straight back to the plane and on to New York, where it was overnight in an Airport hotel. Early the following morning they were at Appian's office, but he had beaten them in. The secretary started to say, 'He is in but not available,' but Matt resolutely ignored her. The other two with him, out of uniform, looked frightening as they put on hard faces. Not knowing what to do, she just sat there doing nothing. She had no idea who they were, but they looked determined and more than a little dangerous. To her feminine side, the two left with her looked interesting.

Matt barged straight in on him and he said without looking up, 'Miss Brzinski, I said not to be …' at which time he realised it was not the secretary. 'What the hell do you mean by barging in here?'

'I have come to see what you lot are playing at. You are expecting me to put my neck on the line, but doing nothing to help in relation to the contract out on my life.'

'You have to realise these things take time and we have to be sure that we are targeting the right person.' Matt realised it was bluster, although said with conviction.

'Bullshit. You know as well as I do that it is Costain and the Cavalcade Corporation. However, seeing as you do not wish to help me, I am withdrawing my services from you.' It was a lie but he had to force the issue somehow. Also he wanted to see through what he had started. Then continuing he said, 'I will have to concentrate my time on eliminating said people myself.'

Before he could go on, Appian interjected: 'You cannot go taking the law into your own hands. How do you know it is who you say?'

'Vassilev told me at the same time he confirmed he did business with them. And don't tell me you did not know. You have been lying to me right from the beginning.'

'No I have not. I have been as straight as I could with you. My hands are tied but I needed you to go along with us on the other matter.'

'Tough. You had the chance and blew it. Now I need to eliminate one problem before we go on.'

'OK. You win. I will be open with you. We have been told at the highest level not to interfere in the Cavalcade Corporation. Revenue have given us the warning not to encroach on their patch as they are after them. Money laundering amongst other things. My bosses have said pull back and that is what I have had to do. There is no option open to me, and I am sorry if I have not been open with you, but it was none of my doing.'

'So who in Revenue has closed the door on me? Maybe I should pay them a visit.'

'The top man is La Roche but you will not get near him.'

'Then tell your bosses to get me an appointment or I walk.' With that he walked out; forgetting to enquire further of the dead stewardess; collected his minders; went back to the Airport; and all flew back to town.

The following day Appian rang before Matt had gone for breakfast. 'I have been on to my superiors and they say you are bluffing. They know you would like to see this caper through. So nothing doing there. I know you would like to follow through on what you have started; don't deny it, but I am also concerned for your wellbeing and would not like to have that hanging over my head whilst trying to sort out other problems.'

'Sure I would like to see things through, but the termination of the contract has got to be my priority. So where do we go from here?'

'I am now going to put my head on the block for you, but if anyone asks, we never had this conversation. In fact I am calling from a payphone just to be safe. La Roche is a man of habit and every day after work he has the chauffeur collect him from work and he goes to a bar for a drink alone before going home.' Then he gave him the various addresses before adding, 'I am sure your two minders will be quite happy to assist in anything you might do.'

'Right. Now we have things in the open, let us at least seem to be getting this other show on the road. To my mind we need to revisit Vassilev's headquarters to try to find more info. Set things in motion for an undersea approach. I do not want any strangers involved, so get Vanman for the underwater work. He seemed quite capable when we visited Costain's submarine mooring.'

'You have done what? You were a busy little bee in Seattle.'

'I do not let the grass grow under my feet if I can help it. Anyway, thanks for the information. We'll take it from here. Cheerio for now.' Matt replaced the receiver in its cradle and wondered if Tony and Dave would go along with him, or even if he should involve them.

When eventually he did consult them later in the day, after much deliberation on his part, they were both in without hesitation. By the day of the party they had formed some sort of concept for getting to La Roche, although they would still be somewhat playing it by ear.

On the day of the party, it was left to Matt to keep Hilary company and away from the preparations. The school hall had been taken over and a marquee erected in the grounds. Instead of giving a present, all in the town had either given time or money to allow the event to be one to remember, both for Hilary and the rest of the townsfolk.

The longer they were together, the more Matt realised they were actually kindred spirits. Both were to some extent loners but able to get on with most people in company. Matt did learn that her one real wish was to go away from the town and experience something new before she died, even if it meant being away on her dying day. Death held no fear for her; she had accepted what fate had dealt her, although she wished that there would be no pain in her final days. To go out in a blaze of glory and cheat the predictions of the medical profession would have been her preference; something in the nature of the hijacked plane crashing would have suited her.

As they talked, Matt had an idea start to form in his mind. There was something he could possibly do to make her wish come true, but that all depended on him being around at the appropriate time and there were too many imponderables at the present time to really make plans.

At the appointed time, Matt escorted Hilary to the Party, and when they entered the marquee, all the townsfolk who could make it were there and all started clapping. She was somewhat taken aback and felt self-conscious, but Matt squeezed her arm and gave her the courage to go on and greet as many as she could in passing. Matt felt good to be taking a part in it.

Part-way through the throng she said, 'There are a few people here that I do not recognise.'

'Don't worry. If they are wearing a earpieces like Tony here they are there for my protection. If you do see anyone you do not really recognise, point them out to one of us so we can keep a close eye on them.'

Both of the stepsons did turn up, but at different times. As they approached he saw her eyes light up and left them alone for a short while, merely acknowledging them as he came back to her side and she introduced them.

Four of the residents were musicians and had formed a combo for the evening. They played, and then food, a buffet and drink were served in the Hall and the band played some more. As other people came up to greet and talk to her, Matt would leave and receive updates on the security situation for himself, only coming back to her side as she seemed to be looking for him. Overall a fantastic night was had by all, including the extra minders who were from Matt's wider circle of friends in the Marines and Rangers and had been specially brought in. It was for these that Matt had paid. There was plenty of home-made food for them and the alcohol could have flowed free, but they knew they were there for a purpose and kept it within reason. Matt appeared to be drinking the night away, but in reality, he would get a full glass, have a sip and then surreptitiously empty most of the contents, only leaving a little in the bottom which he kept sipping before getting a refill.

Tony stayed close to his wife as much as he could, although he was called away on a couple of occasions. Dave kept close company with Katia, the new love of his life, whenever he was not called away. Both were coordinators, as Matt knew full well that the evening would be a fantastic opportunity for anyone to get him.

Out of uniform, some of the Rangers and Marines, who felt they owed him something, looked totally different. Each had jumped at the chance to come along and all hoped to see some action. In fact it was all very subdued. Only Larry had brought people; it was as though he had given out the word to keep off this patch tonight. He had rolled up in a minivan with Rollo as chauffeur, who stayed with the vehicle for most of the night. All the while they were under observation and when, as the party really got going, three people emerged from the darkened interior of the vehicle, they were immediately followed. Each went to a different position and started to lurk there, but not for long. As soon as it became obvious to either the Marine or Ranger shadowing them that they were preparing for action, they were taken care of by a tap on the head that put them to sleep. Each was then tied up and gagged before being unceremoniously carried back to the vehicle. Two men approached the vehicle after being told the three had been taken care of. One built like a shithouse wall approached the driver whilst the other gave a bray like a donkey as he opened the back of the van to check that no-one else was there. It was empty and the tied up incumbent forms of Larry's men were dumped inside.

Rollo had started to say something to Desperate, but as he wound the window down a fist came through and Rollo just slumped across the front seats. Tied up and gagged like the others and secured in the front seat, they were then left whilst Matt's security team checked elsewhere.

The Sheriff and his men had been told that unless there was anything really untoward occurring, they should ignore any unusual activity.

Karl was the first to leave, saying to his stepmother, 'I have to go as they are sending me to the Caribbean tomorrow and I need to be off early. I really am sorry that we did not make time for each other before, but I promise I will be in touch again as soon as work permits.' With that he left. Matt, however, had a feeling that their paths were to cross again.

Throughout the evening Larry looked at Matt very strangely every time he came across him, and Matt, knowing why, just smiled back. Each time Matt left Hilary's side he made sure he spoke to one of the minders to keep abreast of what was happening. Eventually it was time to go, and after he had said his goodbyes to his stepmother, he came to find Matt, little realising that Hilary was following to link up with Matt again. 'What the hell have you done with my men?' he demanded.

'Are we talking about the ones you brought in to take me and claim the contract reward?' questioned Matt, who had seen Hilary come up behind.

'How did you know?'

'Saw it in your eyes when I gave you the invitation. I would probably have tried the same thing if I had been you.'

'How dare you use my party for your own criminal activities?' stated Hilary in an angry voice. As Larry turned round she slapped him hard across the face and then stormed away, almost crying.

'You knew she was there, you bastard, and encouraged me to say more. I'll get my own back, don't you worry,' he snarled and then added, 'What have you done with my men?'

'They are all asleep in your van. Some may be awake now but they are a little tied up,' and with that he turned to Donkey, who was the nearest of the minders that had moved close on seeing the confrontation, and said, 'Escort Mr Fontaine off the premises and make sure he drives away.' With that he walked off in the same direction as Hilary, and found her sobbing in a quiet corner away from all the guests. 'Come on,' he said, 'time to get on with the party. Put on the brave face and let's go.'

'Why did he have to do it?' and she sobbed on his shoulder.

'Dollar signs in front of the eyes. I have big bucks riding on me. Who could resist what should have been a golden opportunity? So many people around, and I probably would not have been missed for some time. Glad I took precautions.'

'But why at my party?' she repeated.

'Look, you have known for a long time what he was doing, Why should this surprise you? I know you feel some responsibility for him but it is time to let go. There will be no turning him; you have seen that tonight. Time to get on with enjoying the rest of your life.' Then he added in a severe voice, 'Pull yourself together.'

The shock of the way the last comment worked made her take note. She was about to lambast him when she saw the kindness in his eyes. For a moment she did not know what to do, but then her brain told her it all made sense and she straightened up and took a few deep breaths before saying, 'You are right. My people await me tonight. Cannot have them seeing me like this. I'll just go into the ladies and powder my nose as you English say.' With that she turned and less than five minutes later returned bright-eyed and linked up with him as they returned to the party.

Ten minutes later Donkey found him, and whilst Hilary was speaking to some others he said, 'I watched him drive off. None of the others had come to, and one of the other minders has followed just to make sure. He stopped following after a while as Mr Fontaine continued on his way, but is holding station for a while just to make sure he does not double back.'

'Thanks,' was all he said but inwardly he was thinking of the words of the Beatles song, 'With a little help from my friends'.

After the stepsons had gone there was a surprise visit from the State Governor. Matt had suggested some recognition for Hilary after the hijack, but it would take too long in view of her illness. He had therefore come with a Certificate of Courage as a means of thanking her for the assistance rendered.

At the end of the night, when all the guests had gone and those who had set it up were clearing away, Matt escorted Hilary back to her house. Inside she told him to sit down in front of the log fire, which she stirred up and made a roaring one. Then she sat down at his side and leant against his shoulder, so he put his arm around her. He had thought she intended to talk to him about the evening, but when there was silence, he looked at her and realised she was fast asleep. That was when he realised the exertion of the evening had probably been too much for her considering the illness and medication.

Not wanting to disturb her, he stayed like that into the early hours of the morning, and would have continued to do so until she awoke. He was only dozing, thinking how good it was to be close to someone, and so heard the catch on the door go as someone tried to force their way in. If they had been in any other room or he had consumed the alcohol he had appeared to be doing through the night, he would have not heard a thing.

Immediately he went into action. He moved off, allowing Hilary to lie on the sofa, but as he did so she looked at him. 'Just stay there,' he instructed as he took the knife from its place of concealment and headed for the door.

He was just in time to stand behind it as it opened and a hand holding a revolver moved slowly through. The fire, although now having burnt down somewhat, still gave enough glow for him to see what was happening. When the shoulder appeared, Matt grabbed the wrist with one hand and forced the gun to point to the floor. At the same time the knife in his other hand touched the skin under the intruder's chin and the man stood there frozen.

His partner outside was just about to move in behind him, when he became aware of someone else being there, and turned to find himself staring down both barrels of a sawn-off shotgun.

'You alright in there Matt?' asked Desperate. 'This one is looking at twoeyes.'

Matt knew that was the affectionate name for Desperate's favourite close-encounters weapon; a multi-load sawn-off shotgun, which looked like a toy in his hands. 'Yeh. This one has got the point. How did we miss them?'

Before an answer came, there was a thud outside and Matt just had time to move his knife before his intruder crumpled. A bang on the head from the side of Desperate's fist was enough to render them unconscious.

'They were crafty. They had settled themselves inside our cordon and waited. It was only as they moved that I saw them and came across.'

As everyone was still linked up to the communication system, reinforcements soon arrived. The Sheriff, who had been at home, was the last to arrive, and said, 'What shall we do with these two? It could be their car we found just outside the town, abandoned behind an empty house.'

'Search them and if there are keys that fit then we will know you are right,' a voice from outside said.

A search revealed other weapons, which were removed, and a car key. Someone went to check and it confirmed they were the owners of the car.

'Now what?' questioned Matt. 'I don't suppose you want them in the lock-up. Too many questions. Can we not just dump them somewhere?'

The Sheriff's eyes lit up. He was getting good at losing things he did not know what to do with now. 'I know just the place. An old quarry, but the cliff face road in is narrow. I would not like to try and reverse out of it. That should keep them out of our hair for a while.'

Desperate picked up the recumbent forms, one under each arm, and said, 'Lead on.' Taking the initiative so the Sheriff had to follow.

The rest of the night passed without any further trouble. Hilary went to bed but Matt stayed on the sofa, only dozing and half expecting more trouble, but none came.

Hilary awoke a new person in the morning and cooked Matt a full American breakfast, and when his minders came round, each one was treated the same until the house was full of Marines and Rangers, but out of uniform they looked like a bunch of roughnecks spoiling for a fight. Joking and jesting whilst telling tales of the previous night, they passed the morning away, but come lunchtime it was time for all to go their separate ways, with Matt, Dave and Tony heading off for New York.

Before he left, Matt said to Hilary, 'If the Gods permit, I will return and we will go on that journey of exploration you have been talking about.' With that he gave her a kiss, full on the mouth, saying, 'That is to remember me.' Then he was gone before she could reply.

CHAPTER 15
RETURN TO THE LAIR

THINGS WERE UNDER WAY for their return to the Caribbean to try to get back into Vassilev's HQ without drawing too much attention to themselves. The submarine with Vanman and the necessary equipment was already on its way from the Base in Norfolk and Matt, Tony and Dave were due to join it later before it left US waters.

In the meantime they had a little project of their own to undertake: that of contacting La Roche. Back in New York, Matt once again used his ill-gotten gains to hire a rental car, this time a minivan, in his name, and by late afternoon they were sat in it parked near to the bar frequented by La Roche. All it needed now was for him to turn up as usual, with Matt hoping nothing had caused a delay.

Bang on time a limousine drew up and a man got out, tallying the description which Matt had been given of La Roche. When he had gone inside, they knew they had less than a quarter-hour to effect a means for Matt to meet him.

Tony and Dave crossed to the car and before the driver knew what was happening he had a revolver thrust in his side and orders to move out, with Tony saying, 'Just do not do anything stupid and no-one will get hurt. We are just substituting you temporarily to allow a secret meeting to take place.'

The three of them returned to the minivan and the car driver was put in the back with Dave. Tony was about the same size as the driver and quickly took his place in the limo. Matt also crossed the street and stood outside the bar as if waiting for someone.

They had all just managed to get into position when La Roche returned to the car, and as he opened the door to get in, Matt raced up behind him and shoved him in, following almost immediately, and as both landed on the floor, the limo set off.

Matt was the first to recover, and then helped La Roche to sit up. He was tall and distinguished, with hair going grey at the temples. No fluster as he took in the situation, showing he was used to taking control, whether in the boardroom or elsewhere. The suit was expensive and well cut, showing no sign of armament, but he had no need of such as he just seemed to take control of matters. Dark eyes from under bushy eyebrows stared at Matt unflinching as he spoke in a forceful but not loud voice. As he did so, Matt caught a whiff of alcohol-fuelled breath as he faced him. He had either downed more than one inside the bar or had been drinking previously.

'What is the meaning of this?' Then, without seeming to wait for an answer, shouted, 'Frankie, stop the car!'

'That will do you no good,' commented Matt. 'It is my driver who is at the controls. But let me introduce myself, Mr La Roche, and perhaps things will become clear. I am Matt Weston and I have it on good authority that you have scuppered any chance of people terminating the contract on my life. I have to say that I do not like being treated in that way when I am expected to put my life as an Englishman on the line for another country which is not prepared to help me.'

'At least I know what you are hoping to do, but what makes you think that I am prepared to now help you? As soon as you leave, I will call the relevant authorities and you will be arrested for kidnap.'

'No-one is being kidnapped. After our conversation, whatever the outcome, you will be free to go on your way and your driver will be able to join you. What I do need to know is why there can be no action taken against Costain and the Cavalcade Corporation.'

'Simple. We want to take it down in total. Any action against the top man there will only result in someone else taking over. We know that the Corporation is working on various illegal matters but we are having difficulty in finding out where that is taking place. All the Cavalcade Group offices in their Seattle building are legitimate. Each of the 11 floors above ground level is taken up with a separate legal entity. The first floor, what you would call the ground floor, is meeting rooms and stores. What would be the 13th floor is known as Number 14 and is Costain's private quarters. Nowhere is there any room for the illegal practices to take place.'

'Who told you that?' questioned Matt.

'We have an operative out there keeping a watching brief, but he has been unable to come up with anything that would lead us to where the action, as it were, is taking place.'

'It all happens on the 13th floor of the building,' stated Matt. 'If anyone had bothered to check the outside of the building as I did, there are actually 14 floors. Make it so the 13th seems to have disappeared and, hey presto, you have a secret?'

'How do you know all this?'

'Because I have been and seen it, as well as Costain's retreat on the coast and the large covered dock he has there where submarines would come and dock undercover.'

'You what? That confirms a rumour going round the office that our operative there is not up to scratch.'

'Or maybe he is on the take?' suggested Matt.

'Mmm,' and Matt could see the cogs whirling round in La Roche's brain. 'Right. In that case we need to take it down quickly. You will excuse me if I verify what you have said.'

'I would have been disappointed if you had not. But can you trust your man there to confirm matters?'

'No. I want independent corroboration and I know just the man. One of our operatives has been based abroad for some considerable time but his father is terminally ill and it will not be long before he dies. Accordingly our man has come home on sympathy leave. He will be able to see things through there for me. Thank you for pointing me in the right direction. I am sure you are right in your assumption as I am aware of your track record. Now all I need to do is work out how to move against them, as we are also sure the local police have a mole in Cavalcade's pay.'

'Maybe I can help you there,' added Matt and explained all he had seen. 'And if you want more manpower to act as shock troops I think you might find that a number of Marines and Rangers would be quite willing to add some muscle power.'

'Whoa there. We cannot go assaulting the building.'

'Did not mean to suggest that, but there are a number of floors to take out. Can you muster enough personnel with a knowledge of active service of this nature?'

'I can soon rustle up enough manpower, but I see where you are coming from. I will give that some thought.'

'OK. Tony, drive us back now will you,' and receiving an affirmative continued: 'I have now to go away for a few days to deal with the other matter, but when I come back I will put myself at your disposal.'

As the limo stopped, both Matt and Tony got out, crossed to the minivan and let the chauffeur go before driving off. Within a couple of hours they were in the air, flying down to Florida and across to the Space Center. Because it was night when they got there, they slept on the Base and in the morning a helicopter was waiting to ferry them out to the submarine to rejoin Vanman. The submarine was on the surface and they had to abseil down from the helicopter onto the deck. Luckily the weather was good, the sea calm and the three boarded the submarine without any difficulty.

As soon as they were inside, the submarine slid beneath the waves. This was a clandestine operation and they did want any nosy people watching their progress. Vanman had taken the time to check through the equipment with a qualified underwater expert and was satisfied everything was A-OK. Now came the wait until it was time for them to leave the submarine.

That was at nightfall on the following day. After checking that there were no boats in the vicinity, the submarine surfaced and the sea-sled was brought on deck, bolted together and launched. It was basically two power units fixed together with a bar at the front and another at the back. It looked like a strange catamaran. Each man wore a harness in addition to the breathing apparatus, which Dave had been given a quick guide to using. Vanman and Dave attached their harnesses to the front bar which also had controls for Vanman to guide the contraption. Matt and Tony attached themselves to the rear bar.

Under the water they went and the sled towed them along with it. They had a rough idea of where the entrance to the cave was but it still took them a little while to find it and Vanman was getting a little worried, although not sharing it with the others that they might not have enough power to get back to the submarine which was waiting submerged for their call.

Through the entry tunnel and they surfaced, but only so that their heads could see above the water to check if anything awaited them. Nothing moved and the dock area, which they approached with caution, was bathed in an eerie glow from the emergency lighting. Where the power for that came from they did not know but were grateful for it, as they did not have to rely on night vision goggles, which they had brought with them.

The sea-sled was moored out of sight and before going on a tour of inspection, they each armed themselves with an assault rifle and revolver which had been towed behind them in a waterproof bag. This showed that no-one had been down to look, as the bodies which had been left in airlocks were still there. They all knew what they were there to do, but Matt had an additional mission to carry out. Whilst he had been relaxing, he had read up about the new Mayan Organisation that was going on outside. It was more widespread than just the Pyramid and Matt had wondered if Vassilev knew exactly what they were doing. Had they just been going along with him because of the protection he had afforded them?

It was a culture shared by many of the people across Central America and it used funds it collected to provide schools, social welfare and help for the slum dwellers. The eventual hope was to create a new government in those countries and it numbered some politicians in its ranks.

It was also there to try to better the lives of those living there. Matt had access to plenty of funds, as he had been wondering what to do with Vassilev's gold. Here was a worthy cause.

The others were not too sure of the idea when he broached it to them but he managed to persuade them that if better living conditions were to apply to those countries, there would be less economic migration to the US, and what better way to kickstart it than by using the ill-gotten gains of one who no longer needed it?

The key was where they had left it, and they opened the strongroom door. The gold was still there. Four boxes waiting to be taken away. Matt knew he would be having more expense before too long, and clandestinely secreted a few bars in his clothing. He did not know if the others helped themselves, and did not care. As long as the bulk of the gold was going for a good purpose, that was all that mattered.

They found a couple of inflatables and put two boxes in each, with one man accompanying each box. It was possible that all would have gone in one, but Matt did not want an overload and it would be easier for them to paddle them as there were no motors to be found; not that they wanted to use anything that might make a noise and alert someone to their presence. Were the monitors still working that covered the dock area? That was a risk they had to take.

Across the water they paddled until they reached the climb to the connecting tunnel. Here, because they were not sure if the lift would be working, they had to haul each box up with a rope that Tony had conveniently found. Once they were all up on the ledge, the decomposing body of Kharlov was moved and they went through the airlock. Vanman went first with caution, but when all was clear the rest of them soon followed with the gold.

They tried to use the railcar but there was insufficient power, although it did try to lift off the rail. Dave realised it had not made full contact with the power source, and with all four pushing, full contact was made. The lighting in the tunnel dimmed, but after a while the dials on the car started to glow. After an hour they tried again, and it rose and moved. Impatiently though, they gave it another two hours before setting off, hoping the charge would be sufficient to get them there and back.

When they arrived at the base of the Pyramid, Matt found the switch for the ladder and that still worked, which he was glad of as he had not thought about how to access the Pyramid if it had not. Once again they had to use the rope to haul up the boxes into the base of the Pyramid, and then up they went, each carrying a box of gold, until they emerged onto the platform at the top.

The first hint of dawn was showing as they emerged from the Pyramid, but there was no sign of life down below. Looking round, Dave saw a ceremonial drum, and with a nod from Matt started a tattoo on it. That soon made people come out of their houses and look towards the Pyramid. Matt stepped forward, but the others remained back out of sight. He had no way of knowing what the reception would be and if he suddenly hit the deck, the others would come forward with weapons at the ready.

In the event two people, who were obviously the Leaders, came forward and shouted up in Spanish. Tony translated the opening comment as being, 'What is the meaning of this intrusion and how dare you play the ceremonial drum? What do you want?'

'Tell them we come in peace and bear gifts,' were Matt's instruction, and Tony, having come forward, shouted down in Spanish.

Matt then moved to one side and the others came into view. It was obvious to those below that they were armed but the weapons were at rest. Matt laid his box on the side of the Pyramid and let it slide down the sloping side. It gained momentum, and when it hit the floor it burst open. The people down below just stared in disbelief and a voice came back when translated asked, 'What do you want from us?'

'Tell them "nothing",' said Matt and as Tony translated Dave slid his box down to them, which once again broke open on landing. 'Tell them we hope they can make use of the gold as Vassilev has no use for it now.' Again Tony translated and the two remaining boxes slid down, but these did not burst open and those below had to open them to see their contents.

With that, Matt started climbing down the steps with Tony behind, remembering how deep they were from last time. The others kept station above, just in case of trouble. The person who had spoken earlier started climbing to meet them, followed by a woman, and spoke in English, albeit with an accent, when they met.

'You are the man Vassilev was proposing to use as a sacrifice, aren't you?'

'So he told me. But your Organisation pays obeisance to the Crystal Skull and does not go in for such things now, does it?'

'No. We have better things to do, and one of them is not attract too much attention by acting like barbarians. We heard of Vassilev's death and the demise of his Organisation and had wondered whether to enter his lair to see if there was anything of use that would help us, but decided against it, knowing Government troops were in occupation of the compounds.'

'I am sure you will be able to make good use of the gold.'

'Indubitably. Do you mind me asking, the way you came down those steps makes me think you are injured in some way.'

'Have been. This is a false leg,' and he tapped it.

'Then you are the one we have been waiting for.'

'How do you mean?' Matt was perplexed by this statement. How could they have known that he was going to come to them?

'Prophecies from our leaders centuries ago said that a warrior who was not whole would come and lead us to a renaissance. You must be the chosen one.'

'Hold on. I have my own battles to fight at the moment. I am not taking anything else on. There must be someone else in the offing for that.'

The woman then spoke, but as it was in Spanish, Tony had to translate. 'Some of the people over time have said that the person referred to as the saviour of our culture would bring the means of achieving that goal, and perhaps this is a truer interpretation in view of the gift.'

'That I can go along with,' Matt spoke and allowed Tony to translate before adding: 'All I hope for is that this gold will be used to better the living standards of your people. And now we must go to fulfil our part of a quest. Farewell, and may the Gods be with you.'

With that he turned and climbed back up to Vanman and Dave, with Tony following. The words 'Spread a little happiness' from some song he had heard a long time ago were going round in his head. As they entered the pyramid, Matt had a feeling that something was not quite right about it. The sun had now risen above the surrounding hills and, although the base of the pyramid was still in shadow, the top was bathed in a beautiful glow. As they walked along the passage to the stairs, in front of them with the sun shining on it was a kaleidoscope of colour to which Matt's attention was drawn. The three others kept on going but Matt lingered, taking it in, and when eventually he did follow them, he had various images imprinted on his brain, but he could not make head or tail of them. Also he had noted on the way up, and confirmed it as he went down, that the interior walls of the pyramid were smooth like the caves and not hewn stone as would have been expected.

Retracing their steps they exited the bottom of the pyramid but left the ladder in place. Another walk along the passage through the airlock, which they left insecure, and they just took one of the inflatables on the basis that with all four paddling they would make quicker progress.

Back on the dock, they had the rest of the day to kill before it was time to find out if the secret way to Vassilev's office had been found. They checked around to see if there was any clue as to what they were after, but nothing was revealed. All was as they had left it those few days before.

When it was a suitable time to go, they moved the decomposing bodies from the airlock at the bottom of the stairway and went through, where they found the bodies of the ones decimated when Matt had thrown the grenade as he escaped. The smell was horrible as, in the sealed area, with the top of the stairs still being blocked by rubble from the other grenade, all it could do was increase as putrefaction took place.

That made them move quickly into the secret corridor under the office, and Matt stood on a ledge, which allowed him to raise his head into the hollow of the desk pedestal. No-one was to be seen through the one-way spyholes that had been incorporated into the sides of the pedestal, although someone had obviously been there since Matt's previous visit, as books and sundry other things were strewn all over the floor.

Matt unlocked the pedestal and swung it to one side. He was the first into the room, followed by Tony, Dave and Vanman, who bringing up the rear, swung the pedestal closed again. All the books had been taken from the bookshelves and whatever had been on the tables had similarly been scattered on the floor. Matt had a feeling that someone had only recently left, as the light was on and when he picked up a book there was dust under it but not on top.

'Where do we start, and what exactly are we looking for?' asked Dave.

'To be quite honest I do not really know,' answered Matt. 'Somewhere there must be something to show what information Vassilev had gleaned for finding the Power, but what format I do not know.'

'Well it's obvious someone else has already been looking by the methodical way these books have been taken off the shelves,' commented Tony.

Vanman just looked around in amazement and went to the door, where he put his ear against it. 'Someone moving in the next room,' he said. 'Turn off the light and let us see who.'

Matt said as he turned out the light, 'That is the outer office. There is one way in from the compound, another from the outside, and an elevator down to the dock.'

Vanman quietly turned the handle and opened the door ever so slightly. Light was on in the outer room but he could see no-one and had to open the door wider, but did it slowly. Eventually he saw a person dressed all in black moving about, but that person must have sensed the opening of the door and turned. An automatic was already in his hand and a silenced shot rang out. Vanman pulled back and the bullet gouged into the door.

Vanman had his own revolver out as soon as he had pulled back, but when he put his head round the door again, this time on his knees so that he was at a different level, there was no-one there except a shadow leaving down a corridor. Vanman leapt out in pursuit and the other three, who had also armed themselves, followed.

'Stay here and keep watch,' Matt ordered Dave and Tony as he followed Vanman out, noting as he did the three bodies there still oozing blood. Outside the compound walls they went and, as the fugitive did not seem to draw any attention, they followed regardless.

All three hugged the wall, but there was a goodly distance between fugitive and chasers. Past the entry into the compound the man went and then turned round to face them, pointing the gun in their direction. A shaft of moonlight came through the compound entrance and fell on the man. Matt was a little further out from the wall and was aiming his gun in the man's direction when he saw who it was. Quickly altering his aim he fired at the wall above the man, who then turned, without firing, and ran straight to the edge of the cliff, where he seemed to just disappear. When they got there they found a rope attached to a grapnel, and looking over they could see the person deathsliding down it. With a superhuman effort, Matt lifted the grapnel and the weight of the man pulled it out of his hands. The man on the rope dropped the last 20 or so feet into the sea, and then they saw a boat come out of the shadows, pick him up and power away.

Matt's gun had not been silenced and the sound of it going off had seemed to reverberate loudly all round. But as they retraced their steps to Vassilev's office, no-one came to see what the commotion was all about. Back in the outer office they found Tony holding another person dressed in the uniform of the local Militia. Dave was looking around to make sure nobody else was there.

'I have told him we had nothing to do with the deaths of his colleagues.' That was the greeting from Tony as they came in. 'As far as I can make out, these are the nightwatchmen. Others will be here to replace them come the morning.'

'That means we need to be quick in searching for whatever,' commented Matt. 'Tie him to that chair over there and let's start looking.'

'Maybe it would be best to tie him up in there,' said Vanman, 'where we can make sure he does not do anything stupid.'

'You are right. Go for it, and then we need to look for anything that might be a secret hidey hole.' Matt left them to it and went into Vassilev's office, where he sat on the desk and looked around. Where would be a suitable place to secrete a safe or something similar?

When the others came in he was banging the backs of the bookcases but unfortunately all had a backboard and gave the same sound back. Then he tried to see if any of them would move but they all seemed to be firmly fixed to the wall.

Seeing what he was doing, the others started closely looking at the other walls, but there was no hint of a hollow wall. Vanman even stamped around the floor but no hollow sound was revealed. They did the same in the outer office and then in Vassilev's dining room, but still nothing. Time was running out for them, as they did not know how long it would be before the relief arrived. They had to give it up as a bad job and get out, as they could hear a helicopter approaching.

They rushed the tied-up man into the outer office and then behind closed doors they made their way to the desk to get out. Vanman was in the lead but went to the wrong pedestal. Matt was about to tell him, when it moved to the side like the other and revealed a floor safe. It needed a key but a quick search revealed none and it had to be assumed that Vassilev had kept it on his person. If so, it was now no good. Was there a spare, and if so, where?

Voices outside made them close the pedestal, open the other and just in time disappeared with it closed as more Militia came into the room. Matt watched as they tried to find the secret way out, but they never thought about the desk pedestals and left, complaining.

Time for them to get back down to the dock where they should be safe whilst they thought out their next move. Along the secret passage, into the stairwell and through the airlock where, instead of bodies, they wedged a crate. Then they ensured that the other ways into the dock were secure before they could think about relaxing. The one thing about them having been seen upstairs was that none of them were wearing any uniform or insignia. The guard they had left alive would only have their voices to go on.

As an extra precaution, Vanman went to the control room there and smashed all the machinery, hoping that it would have rendered any upstairs useless if Matt's earlier grenades had not taken everything out. When they eventually settled, it was to allow two to sleep and two to watch, and they kept well in the open so that they could hear any movement.

Later in the day, when they had all had two sessions of sleep, a round table was called. Matt opened up by asking, 'Dare we go back up there tonight and try to liberate the safe or at least its contents?'

'I would like to,' commented Dave, 'but feel we would not be safe. They know where we disappeared from, and in their shoes I would be waiting there for any return.'

'It would be obvious to that chap we left tied up that we had not found what we were after.' This from Tony. 'I agree it is a big risk to try another go.'

Whilst they were talking, Vanman appeared to be miles away, but then he said, 'Has anyone properly searched that secret passage? Does it go under the safe pedestal, and if so, could we tackle it from underneath?'

'Hell, it's worth a try.' Matt came to life. 'There is no reason why we cannot check it out now. Let's go.' With that he led the way back to the stairway.

As they went, Dave said, 'Nothing has been happening for them to worry about topside. Maybe they will have become lax and any noise we make might not be noticed.'

'Good point,' said Tony. As they went they agreed how to tackle it. Dave stayed by the airlock, but on the inside, to make sure they were not met with anyone on their return. Tony stood guard at the entrance to the secret passage and Matt went forward with Vanman, who, ever ready, had brought along a torch.

After they had oriented themselves on the underside of the desk, it was obvious that the safe did in fact sit into the secret passage, but it had been so well camouflaged to look like rock that to a casual glance it would not be noticeable. There was no way into it from this side, but could it be removed from below?

Vanman prodded around the perimeter with his knife and gave a little chuckle. 'I think it was inserted from here so that it could not be removed from the office. How it was fixed I do not know, but shall I try to remove this plaster from around it?'

'Definitely,' and with that both started scraping away at the plaster with their knives. A lot of it came away easily, but then it revealed that from inside the safe itself, bolts had been inserted horizontally into the surrounding solid rock.

'Damn,' said Matt, but Vanman seemed unperturbed by the setback.

He said, 'Back in a minute,' and departed, shortly to return carrying a laser cutter. 'Short of nothing these people were. I noted this last time here and wished I could have taken it then. State of the art machinery this.' Switched on, there was a steady hum and then the laser shot out, almost looking like a light sabre from Star Wars. Vanman let it warm up and then sliced through one of the bolts with ease. A second and third followed, but the power of the laser had gone by the time he came to the fourth one.

'Damn and blast,' were Vanman's words at this setback when all had seemed to be going so well. 'Ah well, we will have to finish it off the old fashioned way.'

'Brute force,' said Matt as he tried to force the safe downwards.

'No. Explosives. I have brought some along just in case they were needed. I know it will alert them to our presence, but if it works we will just have to make a quick getaway.'

'Right. Start making your preparations. Dave and Tony can stay on guard and I will get the sea-sled ready.' With that they returned to tell the others what it was about and all four got back into their underwater gear which they had discarded once they were on the dock.

Whilst Matt brought the sea-sled round to the front of the dock in readiness, the others went about their business. Dave controlled the airlock and Tony took charge of the entry into the passage. Time was running out, as they could hear the sound of rubble being moved up top.

Vanman hurriedly put the explosives in place but came back behind the door with Tony before setting them off. Going back in, he had to fight through swirling dust, but the explosion had worked and the safe was on the floor. Unfortunately it had also shattered the pedestal above and he could see into the office.

Quickly he made his way out as he heard footsteps above. He and Tony were just closing the airlock when distant voices could be heard behind them. Dave blocked open the inner airlock door as the other two hurried to where Matt had the sea-sled. The safe was secured to the sled as best they could and the three of them were harnessed to it when Dave joined them. All four just discarded their weapons; after all they would not be required now.

Just in time they felt a surge of water which could only mean one of the ways in had been breached. Instead of going to the entrance on the surface, Vanman immediately slipped the sled below the water and proceeded slowly, as he could not use any light which might reveal their whereabouts. Looking back, Matt and Dave could see lights waving about on the dock they had just left as someone tried to find them.

Out through the entry they went, gingerly feeling their way, and once outside they continued away from the place still submerged. Three of them had flippers and were helping the sled along, but Vanman knew they would not have enough power to be able to make the rendezvous. Even after the power had gone, they still kept paddling but eventually had to give up as they were fighting unsuccessfully against a current. They had plenty of air in their tanks, and Vanman took the sled down onto a shelf and parked it behind some rocks, which gave some protection from the current which had become stronger.

Vanman had come prepared. As soon as they started to drop to the seabed, he tripped a switch which sent out a homing beacon to the mother submarine; in effect a distress call to let them know there was a problem. Two hours later and the air in their tanks was starting to get low, but Vanman kept them all calm, telling them that help would be on the way.

Just as they were about to go onto their reserves of air, Vanman saw movement coming towards them. A signal from him was answered, and within minutes they were being supplied with new tanks. Four divers had come for them, each with a power torpedo, and soon they were being towed back, one behind each of them, to the submarine. The sea-sled was left where it was, along with the empty tanks, but Vanman took it upon himself to have responsibility for the safe and kept it with him even though it meant he was left behind the others. No-one thought anything about it, after all he was the underwater man.

It was an undersea transfer into the submarine, something that none of them had ever done before, but each went in with their new buddy and all worked satisfactorily. When Vanman arrived two of them were already inside and the third was already entering the chamber. Dave's first words when he was inside, and to no-one in particular, were, 'Well I'm glad that's all over,' as he sat and caught his breath. Bearing in mind that it had been his first experience of underwater activity he felt he had acquitted himself well, even though he had been frightened at times, especially towards the end when air was getting low.

Once everyone was on board the safe was placed in a secure compartment and the submarine headed back for home waters. This time the landfall was to be at Norfolk, the submarine's home port, and everyone hoped for a couple of days to relax.

CHAPTER 16
WINNER TAKES ALL

A TIME FOR RELAXING there was not to be. Matt was aware that other people within the USA were after the information he had now hopefully gained, but he was not expecting things to happen so fast. The four of them had changed into the more casual clothes they had left on board. Matt deliberately dressed so that his trousers went on first, followed by the shirt. He made it appear that he could not be bothered to tuck it into his trousers, but he meant it to be that way as he had an automatic secreted at his back in readiness for action should it be needed later. They had barely sat down to eat their first good meal for a few days when the Captain came in with two armed men. 'I will have to insist that you give up your weapons,' he commanded. 'We are now taking responsibility for the safe and its contents. Thank you all for your assistance in getting the goods, but the Navy now intends to become the powerful element of the armed forces. Hopefully this will tell us where to go to retrieve one of the power weapons.'

Covered as they were by the two sailors with machine guns, Dave, Tony and Vanman had no option but to divest themselves of their guns. Matt had thought about making a move to see if they would open fire in such enclosed quarters and maybe hole the submarine from the inside, but decided against it. The two holding the guns looked eminently capable of shooting first and asking questions later.

'And the knife in your false leg please,' requested the Captain, after

Matt had divested himself of the automatic. Covered by that amount of firepower, Matt could only obey, and removed the knife and handed it over.

'I'm sorry, but you will have to make yourselves comfortable in here for the next couple of days until we get back to Base. No harm will befall you if you do not try anything on.' With that the Captain withdrew, followed by the two seamen, and they heard the door lock.

Matt was furious with himself for not anticipating an early move for the goods. Knowing who he had been chasing back at the compound, he had not expected action until they had got back to dry land. However, he had suspected that someone might try something on and had prepared himself somewhat. None of the others knew what he had hidden about his person, as he was not sure if any of them would have tried to take responsibility for any information they had gleaned to ensure it got to their superiors' hands.

The clothes he was wearing had offered some concealment of weaponry but they had known about it anyway. Very few people, though, knew about the hollow top part of the false leg. Unfortunately, to extract the weapon concealed there would mean revealing it to others present, and he was still not sure if they were going to be with him all the way.

He remembered a previous conversation with Wilberforce. Someone had taken the candy and he was not going to take that sitting down. 'I don't know about you, but I have not gone through all the troubles of the past few weeks just to have some jumped-up cretin take the kudos. I don't know how we get out of here, but given the chance I am prepared to go on the offensive.' This was Matt's comment as he looked around the room for a means of escape.

'Count me in,' came from Dave and Tony almost simultaneously.

Vanman did nothing more than reach into his pocket and bring out a wad of explosives and from another pocket there appeared a detonator. 'Does this count for anything?' he asked.

Matt put his hand out, palm up, and each of the others put their hands there, creating a pile of four. Woe betide anyone now who got in the way. All that remained was for the means to offer itself, but what could they do to take over the submarine and its crew if they did get on the loose? They could only play it by ear as all hands were raised in the air.

Then it was Matt's turn to surprise them. It became a little bit like James Bond's gadgets as first he removed his watch, which was rather thick and bulky, and removed the straps with a quick hard tug. Next he removed his belt buckle which detached easily from the main part of the belt. That again was solid and bulky. He then pulled his trouser leg up and from the false leg removed a sheet of thin metal that encircled it. If it had been around any ordinary limb it would have cut off circulation, but on the false leg it was of no consequence. Once removed, it tightened itself into a tube about three layers of metal thick. The others could only stare as he then took off the shoe and sock and removed two of the inner toes from the prosthetic by unscrewing them. One was forced into one end of the tube and the other followed in the other end. At the back of both the watch and the buckle was the female screw and when the toe screws were fitted in he had a fighting barbell. Gripping the tube in his hand he shook it up and down as well as bashing it into the palm of his other hand to make sure everything was secure.

Vanman just shook his head and grinned before saying, 'What can you two offer?'

Dave just reached into his trouser pocket and produced a pepper spray. 'This any good?' he said.

That left Tony, who did nothing for a start, as though he had nothing to offer, but then dropped his trousers and lifted his shirt to reveal a strip of metal strapped to his back.

'So that's why you were always to attention,' said Matt, laughing, as he helped him undo it.

'Picked it up back there and I don't know why but thought it might come in useful.' With that he took his handkerchief out and wrapped it round one end. That end he held in his hand and it looked as though he had a sword. With the flat of the so-called blade it would do damage to anyone on the receiving end, but if the side of the metal, even though it was not sharp, caught someone it could be fatal. Even though it was not particularly long, it was still a weapon and in Tony's hands it would be lethal.

Matt rubbed his hands and said, 'We will wait a while to see how things stack up and lull them into a false sense of security. We only need to be in a commanding position when we get near to land.'

With that he leaned back in the chair, put his feet on the table and appeared to go to sleep. However, he was mulling things over as to how it might be possible to get the upper hand. The other three similarly relaxed and when the next food was brought they looked as though they had accepted their lot and merely acknowledged the seaman who brought the food and the armed guard outside.

Matt was the first to need to go to the heads and called the guard. Another armed seaman came to escort him and one by one the others went as well. Matt took the opportunity to assess the outside of the room, and saw that there was only the one guard on duty. That gave him an idea, but it all depended on the same configuration happening when they were next fed.

Matt outlined his plan and then moved to the head of the table, which they had moved against the wall opposite the door, but with his back to the door. Tony had angled himself so that he had a good view through the door when it opened, and the others got themselves into positions where they could act fast.

At the first sign of the door being unlocked, Matt put his feet on the table and rocked back on two legs of the chair. As the seaman entered, Tony nodded. That meant that the guard was stood behind the seaman. Matt appeared to lose his balance and the chair tipped him backwards. The seaman just stood waiting for him to get up, but instead he did a backwards roll and kicked both feet into the seaman's stomach. That man dropped the tray he was carrying and was pushed back into the guard, who became off balance, and before he knew what was happening Dave was through the door, leaping over the seaman, who had dropped to the floor, and used the pepper spray on the guard. There was no other movement in the corridor as Dave commandeered the guard's gun, and Vanman, who had followed, dragged both into the room.

Tony had come forward at the same time, and closed the door behind them all as the guard started spluttering. Vanman just hit him into unconsciousness as Dave searched him and found a revolver. Two guns were better than nothing, but they still had to get the upper hand and now was the time for action before the two crewmen were missed.

Vanman said, 'I have been through this submarine earlier. If I go and create a diversion with the explosives, it might give you a chance to somehow get to the controls. I will not use it against anything which might cause us a problem, but there are many internal bulkheads which could be damaged without sinking us.'

'Let's do it. The longer we think about it the less chance we have of creating a surprise.' This from Tony, who checked the revolver. Seeing this, Dave checked the assault rifle which had been removed from the guard.

A quick check outside revealed no-one, and Vanman was on the move, followed by Matt, who went the other way and dodged into the heads. It was occupied, but a quick blow from Matt's barbell and the seaman slumped to the ground. Matt looked out and indicated the coast was clear, and was joined by Dave. Tony was staying in the room as backup for when the big bang came. Matt left Dave there and proceeded cautiously towards the control room, although that was not his destination, or at least not immediately.

The Captain's cabin was his goal and once outside he knocked and, receiving the bid to come in, did so but with speed. He saw where the Captain was and because he was not expecting trouble, he was slow to react. Once again a blow from the barbell and the Captain sagged to the floor unconscious. Locking the door, Matt then tied up the Captain before seeking out the safe keys. Out came Vassilev's safe. Matt, when he had been an operational Marine, had had to use lock-picking and this safe was no real problem. It just needed an old fashioned key and, although it was not to hand, Matt was able to be inventive and soon had it opened. Looking at the papers, they were all in Russian and so he put them on one side before closing the safe and locking it again.

Now it was time to reveal the other surprise with his false leg. He dropped his trousers and took the prosthetic off. With a twist he removed the base of the cup on top and revealed a secret compartment.

The composite of the leg made it so that even an x-ray machine would not show it was hollow. He removed the automatic from its resting place and tucked it into his waistband at the back, but under his shirt, which was still outside his trousers, hiding the bulge. Into the cavity went the papers and the base of the cup was replaced and the leg refitted to him. Now he had an additional surprise if anyone else was to try something on.

The explosion, when it came, made him jump because he had been so engrossed in what he had been doing, and it had taken longer than he had originally thought so that he had forgotten about it. There was a lot of noise in the corridor and someone banged on the door. Matt, with barbell in hand, opened it and a surprised seaman fell asleep immediately and was pulled inside before he had time to fall on the floor.

Matt went out into the corridor and headed in the direction of the control room, arriving just behind Dave who opened fire with the rifle at the equipment that lined the bulkhead. Everyone was at sixes and sevens and did not know what to do. Explosions, bullets flying, what was to come next? That was the arrival of the armed guard who had escorted them to the heads and whom they had forgotten about. On hearing the shots, he had come running. He was about to try to regain control of everything when his leg gave way at the sound of a single shot. Tony appeared with smoking revolver and picked up the rifle that the seaman had dropped when he saw blood flowing from his leg.

'You better see to him,' said Matt to the nearest crew member. 'Can't do with him bleeding to death. We are just taking control of our destiny again. Do not try anything funny. We are all killers if we need to be. So far there have only been injuries, but that could change if someone makes us angry. Your Captain is incapacitated at present, so you will be taking orders from me.'

From the other side of the control room, Vanman appeared. How he had managed to get from one end of the sub to the other was of no consequence to Matt at that particular time. For the moment they had the upper hand, but there were far too many crew members to keep tabs on all the time. Time to go with the flow again and hope for the best.

'Right. It is obvious that we will not be welcomed with open arms at your Base, so we will have to find some alternative way of getting ashore. Just keep this sub on a course for the US and we will leave as soon as we are able. Meanwhile, one of us will be here to watch over you; so no funny stuff. Vanman, will you take first stint?'

Receiving the affirmative, Matt made his way back to the Captain's cabin, where that man was just coming to. He could have been a clone of the commander of the aircraft carrier. Were the Americans cloning their Naval officers these days? Was Matt's thought on seeing him for the first time. Blue eyes, sandy hair and about Matt's height. Long face, clean shaven with ears sticking out. Matt could see the brain behind the eyes assessing the situation.

The other seaman was still comatose on the floor. Matt untied the Captain and said, 'Your submarine has been taken over. Neither myself nor my colleagues take kindly to someone else taking over after we have done all the hard work.'

'There was never any intention to harm you.' A statement from the Captain. 'We would merely keep you out of circulation for a short while to let our superiors assess what you had found. Now you really have caused a commotion. Some people will be wanting your hides.'

'It won't be the first time and I am sure it will not be the last. There is already one contract out on my life, so what does it matter if there are any more? Now let us get down to business.'

'What do you mean?'

'Well, there is a need for the four of us to depart this sub before we get to your Base. I just wondered if you had any ideas.'

'If you think I am going to help you get away after what you have done to my sub and my men, well, think again.'

'I thought that might be your answer. In that case maybe we should go on a further wrecking spree and then maybe someone will come up with a useful idea. Might as well get hung for a sheep as a lamb. Temporarily, you and the injured will have to occupy the room we have just vacated, as it is one which can be secured from the outside. So move it!' That last statement was emphasised with a raised voice.

No sooner had all the injured and the Captain been secured in the room than Vanman shouted for him. He arrived at the same time as Tony and Dave, who had been searching the sub to try to find some means of getting away.

'Toff did not put all the instruments out of action,' stated Vanman when they were all there. 'We have something strange happening on the surface,' and he indicated a screen.

Electronic interpretation of the information it was receiving showed a light floatplane alongside an ocean-going cruiser. 'Drugs or something similar,' was Tony's comment.

'Either of those would get us away nicely, and if we thwart some clandestine operation in the process it can only be to our good in view of what we have done here.' Matt was thinking out loud. 'Take us up right alongside,' he commanded the crew. 'I don't want either to get away.'

On the surface, to the consternation of those involved, the water started boiling and suddenly at the side of the plane the submarine appeared. This was something the crew were used to. They did not need a captain to tell them what to do. Immediately the sub was on the surface, men were on deck and guns manned. Tony was amongst the first out, and the pilot of the light aircraft found himself blocked in between the cruiser and submarine with a rifle aimed at him. As the man was obviously South American, Tony shouted at him in Spanish: 'Where are the drugs?'

On being told they were on board the cruiser, which was now trying to make its getaway, a heavy machine gun from the top of the sail fired over the plane and bullets could be seen smashing into the stern of the cruiser. Suddenly smoke started coming from the rear deck and the bow wave dropped to nothing as it became dead in the water.

'Good shooting,' shouted Matt, who was one of the last to arrive, being the least agile, but to no-one in particular. He had also taken his time to allow himself to retrieve Vassilev's safe, which he now carried with him to keep up the pretence of it still holding the goods. 'The boat is all yours. We are taking the plane.'

On his way to the deck, Dave had seen a coil of rope hanging near the hatch. Seeing the position with the plane and the disappearing cruiser, he had gone back, collected it and now it firmly moored the plane to the sub.

The plane was only meant to take three passengers and the pilot, but Tony, without consulting the others, said, still in Spanish, 'It is going to be a little tight, my friend, but you are going to take four of us for a flight.'

'Impossible,' came the response. 'It will be too heavy to take off.'

'In that case you will have to ride the waves to shore,' and before the pilot could respond again, Dave had the passenger door open.

Matt, Vanman and Dave contorted themselves into the rear seats and then Dave used his rifle to cover the pilot, by pushing it into the back of his neck, to allow Tony to occupy the front passenger seat, with the safe at his feet. As the only Spanish speaker, it seemed prudent to have him sat up front, and it had all been done without anyone saying a word.

One of the crew loosened Dave's mooring line and the pilot started the engine as the two craft started to drift apart. He drew forward of the sub and then at a suitable distance, turned and, gunning the engine, came back towards it. By the time it was at the side of the submarine again it had gained lift-off speed and the pilot used the still water on the lee side of the sub as the best place to lift into the air; a place where he was not fighting waves.

It seemed like a struggle for the little plane, but little by little it gained height and, under Tony's directions, headed for the US coast. They put down in a creek by a quiet town and when all four were out with the safe, Tony told the pilot to scarper and fast. He needed no further bidding and by the time they had reached the end of the jetty on which they had been dropped, he was airborne and away.

Matt asked a man mending a fishing net, who looked agog at what had just happened, the way to the Sheriff's office. He was told they would find a Deputy having a coffee in a deli round the corner. The Deputy nearly choked on his coffee when four somewhat unkempt men, two of them armed, although the guns were at the relaxed position, walked in. 'Come on,' said Matt, 'we are going to your office.' The

Deputy meekly obeyed and all five got into the Deputy's car outside. No-one spoke during the journey.

Once in the office Matt demanded the phone and rang Appian who asked, 'Where are you? You have really caused a stir with your action on the sub and I am getting it in the ear.'

'I'll cause more than that if anyone else tries to take over. We are in ...' and he told Appian the location once he had got the information from the Deputy. Then he proceeded to tell him most of what had happened. The Deputy could only listen and his jaw went slack the more he heard.

'I'll get someone from our office down there to pick you up.'

'Can they be trusted? I am starting to get paranoid about who our friends really are.'

'Stay there. Let me get back to you when I know who and give you some identifying information. By the way,' continued Appian, 'your surmise about the stewardess was right. She was terminally ill. Looks like you shot the wrong one.'

Matt looked skywards and said aloud, 'Sorry mate.' Then he thought of O'Rourke's comment about him being corrupted by killing as he felt no remorse. Maybe he had been right.

Ten minutes later Appian called back and described the man who would be picking them up in about an hour and a half.

Tony and Dave, almost simultaneously and without bidding from any other, checked their guns were safe and threw them one at a time to the Deputy, saying, 'You better keep hold of these.'

Bang on time a minivan rolled up and there was no mistaking the driver from the description they had been given, who got out and opened the rear door to show that there was no-one else with him. Bidding the Deputy goodbye, they climbed in the van and it took less than two minutes from arrival for them to be on their way.

Straight to the Airport where an executive jet from the company was waiting. Without any formalities they were soon airborne, landing a couple of hours later at a private airfield where they were met with another minivan. Appian was waiting for them this time, which gave reassurance, especially when Wilberforce popped his head out of the back. Then it was off to another regional office of the company.

When they were all sat in the conference room there, Appian said, 'In view of the problems you have recently encountered, I thought it might be appropriate to meet somewhere out of the way and without any others having knowledge of our whereabouts.'

'That suits me fine and I am sure the others will agree,' stated Matt. 'I am getting paranoid about anyone I don't know. We have not gone through hell and high water just to have the goods whisked away at the last minute for someone else to gloat over.'

A full debriefing then took place, except for a mention of what they had done with the gold, including the action on the submarine. They were just about to discuss the next stage when the door burst open and an Army Colonel with two Sergeants burst in, each holding an assault rifle at the ready.

Appian was just about to demand an explanation but the Colonel signalled him to be quiet with a wave of the gun. 'For reasons which I am unable to go into, I am forced to take responsibility for the contents of that safe.' He pointed to Vassilev's safe, which was on the table. 'We are grateful to you, Mr Weston, and your colleagues for liberating it, but now your part is over and the Army will take it from here.'

With that he reached over and took the safe as Matt said, 'How is your man from the Caribbean? I hope Mr Berenger was not too shocked by his soaking. The Colonel ignored him as he produced a set of skeleton keys and proceeded to try the lock. Matt continued talking, but wondered if the Colonel had heard him or was deliberately ignoring the question, or even if he knew the answer. 'I knew we would be having a visit from someone in the Army. Does the Pentagon know you are here, or is this working for yourself? Anyway, how did you know where to find us?'

The Colonel stopped what he was doing and said, 'My reason for being here is top secret. However, now we have the goods I see no reason to keep quiet about the mole in your team.' Turning to Vanman he said, 'Well done, Krasowski. You have earned your Sergeant's stripes.'

Vanman saluted and moved to join the two Sergeants, who stood there like matching bookends. Hard men, devoid of any emotions, but as they covered the party, their eyes kept darting about, watching for any untoward action.

The Colonel went back to the task of opening the safe, having put down his rifle, and when he did and found it empty he exploded with rage, came face to face with Matt and demanded, 'What have you done with it?' When Matt did not answer he gave a back-handed swipe which knocked Matt to the floor. The other armed men made sure no-one decided to make a move.

Matt landed on his back, but intentionally bounced to one side and lay, apparently recovering, with one arm tucked behind his body. As he started to rise, seemingly groggy, the arm that was under him reached the gun in his waistband. All this action had been semi-obscured by people, chairs and the table, and as he stood up the gun was out and pointing forward. Three shots rang out, nearly sounding as one. The Colonel crumpled to the floor with a bullet in his leg. The two guards dropped their assault rifles as each took a bullet in the shoulder of the arm holding the trigger.

Vanman made a move as if to get one of the rifles, but found himself looking at Wilberforce's revolver. His reflexes had not diminished with age. Dave and Tony dived for the fallen rifles, and as they got up Matt asked, as he kicked the Colonel's rifle to one side, 'Either of you two under orders to take the goods, because if you are, first you have to find them.' Neither answered, as they turned to face the door when it burst open and another group of soldiers stood there. It was a Mexican stand-off. Neither side could face being the first to fire.

Appian was the first to exert his authority, and showing his badge said, 'Everybody relax. Believe it or not, we are all working towards the same end.' Then turning to Matt he continued: 'I don't know how you made the contents of the safe disappear but it certainly caused a stir.'

Matt said nothing but went to the Colonel and swiped him, albeit lightly, across the face with the gun, saying, 'That's for hitting me.' Then, turning to Appian, he demanded his mobile phone. He was reluctant to hand it over but eventually had to as Matt came menacingly closer, swinging the hand holding the gun.

Taking it, Matt scrolled through the contacts and said, 'I knew you had to be better connected than you would have us believe. You have been stringing us along all the time. Always telling the truth, eventually, but not the whole truth.' With that Matt selected a number and pressed the transmit button.

A voice answered that Matt recognised from having seen newscasts from the White House. 'Good afternoon, Mr President. I know you would have expected Mr Appian to be calling, but this is Matt Weston.' All others present, apart from Appian, looked on in amazement.

'Ah, Mr Weston. I have heard much about you and am now getting reports of your recent exploits. By the way, how is Mr Appian?'

'Safe and unharmed, you will be glad to know. However, we have just had an altercation with representatives of the Army intent on taking information I and my colleagues have risked our lives for.'

'Army you say. That is news. I am aware of the Navy trying to muscle in. I have this phone on open voice here and the Secretary of State for Defense has just looked as shocked as me.'

'Mr President, we are going to have to trust someone and it looks as though it is going to have to be you. I am prepared to hand over the papers to you and you alone. It will then be up to you to decide who should have them.'

'Fair enough. As Commander in Chief I will accept responsibility for ensuring they are put into the correct hands. Now, how do we go about meeting?'

'I was hoping you would come here. At the moment I seem to have the upper hand, but moving onto other territory I will not be sure who to trust.'

'Unfortunately I cannot get away at the moment. Just hold the line, will you.' At that Matt could hear indistinct voices over the phone before the President came back on. 'The Presidential Helicopter is coming down for you and your party. The Secretary of State for Defense will be on it. Does that give you the reassurance you need?'

'Just as long as there are no others on board apart from the Secretary of State and cockpit crew.'

'Agreed. It will take about three quarters of an hour. Just keep watching outside.' With that the line went dead before Matt could respond.

Whilst he had been speaking, Vanman had been tending to the wounded Sergeants and Wilberforce had bound the Colonel's leg. He was sat on one of the chairs, and Matt turned to him, saying, 'You have heard the conversation. Are you prepared to let your men stand down and guard us until we get on that helicopter, or are we going to have to fight our way to it?'

He had the same military bearing as Wilberforce when Matt had first become acquainted with him. The 10 or so years difference between the two was now noticeable, but the Colonel was twice the size of Wilberforce. The military haircut showed he had lost an ear and there were other scars on the head, but the steel eyes glinting in the light made him look wicked.

'You are a resourceful and dangerous man, Mr Weston, and I have to give you respect, although why you had to hit me as well as shooting me I fail to see.'

'Sorry, but that was just to make sure Mr Appian would hand over his phone. Do we have a deal?'

'Yes.' Then to his men he said, 'Relax, but guard the perimeter in case anyone else has ideas. I think Mr Weston has dealt fairly with us and I think that when the President is apprised of the position, the Army will have the information handed to it. By the way, Mr Weston, where are the contents of the safe?'

Matt was not going to give away his secrets and merely said, 'Microdots,' which he knew they were not, 'can be hidden in any number of places on a person.' He still had the information despite the setbacks, and the line 'Winner takes it all' from the Abba song came to mind and he started humming it to himself.

The helicopter arrived, and the Secretary of State stood in the open doorway. Appian and Wilberforce went first and when Matt received the all-clear in a pre-arranged signal from Wilberforce, he, Tony and Dave went on board. It landed on the usual place at the White House, and people looking on saw a motley group of characters exit the helicopter and be received into the portals of that building.

Inside they had to wait a half hour before the President could see them, but then they were all ushered into the Oval Office. 'Welcome, gentlemen,' opened the President. 'Let me first thank you for what you have achieved so far despite the adversity which seems, in part, to have been of this country's own doing. I am indeed grateful that no-one has been killed during the recent, shall we say, disagreements. Have you got the goods, Mr Weston?'

'I have indeed, Mr President, and as I said previously, will hand them over to you, but would ask that we do this in private as I would not want too many people to know my secrets. I would hope that you will not divulge anything you see.'

'I agree. I know of your exploits and trust you. Come this way.' With that he led Matt to an ante-room where Matt took off the leg and produced the papers. 'I see what you mean about secrets and can assure you it is safe with me.'

They returned to the others, with the President holding the papers, but realising when he looked at them that they were in Russian, he said, 'I will have these translated and then decide in view of the content where they should go. Is that satisfactory to you, Mr Weston?'

'I have handed them over to you. It is now your decision as to future action. Now my priority is to get the contract on my life terminated, one way or the other.'

'You will have no problem there. I have given instructions that the closure of the Cavalcade Corporation, even though they gave to my Presidential fund, should be made a priority. Now I must bid you farewell as I have another meeting shortly.'

They were dismissed. A limo was waiting outside which took them to the secure HQ where Matt, Dave and Tony found their clothes, which had been left behind when they had set off on the latest escapade. Changed and refreshed, they joined Wilberforce and Appian for a meal.

'I have just heard from the President,' was Appian's greeting to them.

'The Army is being given the information, although there does not seem to be as much in the papers as one might have wished for.'

'So does that mean we went through all we did for nothing?' This from Tony.

'No. I understand the papers give details of where it would be expected to find the, what would you call them, power staffs.'

'I suppose if one thing has come out of this it is the fact that more of your country's agencies seem to be working together,' Wilberforce commented.

'True. And the Financial Security Regime is preparing to smash Cavalcade. You three will be flown out there eventually, but first, and I do not know why, the Army is taking you to look at something in Nevada, whatever that is. For some reason it is being kept on a need-to-know basis at the command of the President. You are to be flown out there tomorrow and then on to Washington State.'

Matt, Dave and Tony looked at each other in bewilderment.

Come the morning and they were taken to the local Air Base, where a plane awaited them. As they got on, the first person they saw was the Colonel from the previous day, and Matt gave him a mock salute and received an acknowledgement in return. The other two, although out of uniform, stood to attention as they entered the plane and executed a proper salute.

'Sit down, gentlemen, and make yourselves comfortable. No hard feelings from yesterday?'

'Yesterday is dead and gone,' answered Matt. 'Today is another day. I do not bear a grudge as long as you are not going to try to get your own back for that,' and Matt pointed to the Colonel's injured leg.

'People get hurt in any action. You only did what you thought necessary. I will admit I underestimated you and paid for it. Knowing more about you now, I am glad you only decided to injure me.'

'Am I to assume you are the one that finally got the papers?' Matt asked the question that had been on all their lips.

'Yes. For reasons you will understand when a secret is revealed to you. The men with you were sworn to secrecy when they joined the

Service, but I cannot make you. However, the President has given me an assurance that you are to be trusted and I will have to take that as gospel.'

Matt thrust his hand forward. 'Here is my hand as a gentleman. I will not divulge anything that you may show me unless it actually affects my wellbeing.'

The Colonel shook it and said, 'Accepted.'

Matt asked the question he had posed the previous day. 'Was Karl Berenger working for you, or at least the Army?'

'That name meant nothing to me yesterday, but the additional information from Sergeant Krasowski led us to investigate. No-one is sure who sent him but he has not returned to the Pentagon.'

'So was he working for the Irish connection?'

'I am aware of their involvement, but there does not appear to be any Irish blood in his veins.'

'Another loose cannon then,' murmured Matt.

By this time they were airborne and nothing more was said about it until they arrived at their destination. Instead the talk was of what they had done over the past few weeks.

At Nellis Air Force Base they were met by a blacked-out van, in which they had to sit in the back whilst the Colonel sat in front. They had no idea of where they were going but had to trust that they were safe. In a cavern they were allowed to get out, but were ushered immediately through a door so that they had not enough time to see about them.

In this room Matt and Tony had the shock of their lives. There in the room was a body not too dissimilar to the pictograph from Greenland. Also there was the staff exactly as shown, but in addition there was something that resembled an egg.

'You recognise those, don't you?' asked the Colonel.

'How could we not,' answered Matt. 'Where did they come from?'

'Discovered by Park Rangers after Mount St Helens blew. We provided security at the time and took them under our wing, not having a clue what they were. Just part of the aliens scenario to be kept out of the public eye.'

'Had you done anything with them until we turned up more information?' A question from Tony.

'We thought the egg thing was the key, but no matter how we try it will not break open. Jackhammer, laser, you name it and we have tried it to no avail. It was not until you raised the spectre of the staff being something powerful that we started to concentrate on that. Not that we have had much success there either. We know it needs sun to be activated and we have had it powering up somewhat but it has not become fully charged, or if it has we have not been able to discover the trigger to make it work.'

'Maybe the sun is not strong enough now. Ozone and other pollutants are now masking it. Although we are aware of global warming, back whenever these people,' and he motioned to the body, 'were around, the sun could have been more direct. Perhaps you should consider it as a space weapon.'

'Mr Weston, you are a wonder. I have people around me with degrees in higher this and higher that but no-one has come up with that conclusion. We will definitely be trying that, Thank you; thank you. It was worth allowing you to see it just to get that one suggestion. Now, any ideas what the egg thing might be?'

'Sorry there. If you have not been able to open it up, I am not sure that I can hazard a guess.' Matt did not think it was any concern of his.

'Could it be the space ship that transported them here?' Dave suggested and then went on before anyone could pour scorn on the idea. 'I know it is small but did they arrive small and grow once they arrived?'

'It looks more like an egg to me,' ventured Tony. 'Could it be that this is what created life on this Earth's barren landscape? Maybe we are all related to what came out of that or a similar one.'

All the Colonel could say was, 'Your guess is as good as ours, and we have thought of both them, but without being able to see what is inside, and x-rays do not penetrate it, we are stymied.' As nobody there was able to add anything else, they all left the way they had come and went back to the airfield, where a plane awaited to take the three of them away.

CHAPTER 17
TERMINATION OF CONTRACT

THE BASE FOR THE operation against the Cavalcade Corporation was the HQ of the State National Guard, which was on operational duties elsewhere. Situated south of Tacoma near the Air Force Base, it was sufficiently distant to avoid questions about any activity going on there.

The first person they met on arriving was Vanman, who came towards them a little sheepishly, saying, 'I really do want to help. I know it might not have appeared so the other day, but then I was under orders. I suppose really I am asking for a second chance to become friends again.'

'Orders are orders and not to obey is to pay the consequences.' This was Matt's comment after a general greeting. 'If I had been in your boots, I would have probably had to do the same. As far as I am concerned what has happened is now in the past. Providing you are here to help, then welcome.'

With that he extended his hand, which Vanman shook, and in turn was accepted by the two others who also shook his hand, after which Matt asked, 'Have you still got your Sergeant's stripes?'

'Yes. I helped deliver the goods safely and that was the deal.'

'Good for you,' commented Tony.

'There is someone else who wants to help also,' said Vanman, and as they walked round a corner, there was Dannyboy in a wheelchair.

'I had to make it to see if there was a chance of being able to repay you for what you did back there. Is there anything I can do? I know I am not mobile but I would welcome anything to do my bit.'

'As it is, there could well be. When the action starts I will want someone to be watching my back. You, with a rifle in such a position that you do not have to move, will fit the bill and release an able-bodied man for other duties. So welcome aboard.'

Matt had previously outlined a sort of plan to La Roche, who was there in person to supervise, and work was already underway on adaptations to certain of the contractor's equipment from the building site near the Cavalcade Building.

It had been agreed that wherever Matt went, Tony and Dave would accompany him as personal bodyguards, and so the three of them met La Roche in what had been taken over as the Briefing Room. As they had gone there, they had seen the camp was a place of activity and been acknowledged by a number of people they knew from action at Vassilev's place.

Another man was with him and introduced as Peter Wender, who it turned out was the man sent by La Roche to assess the situation. He stated as soon as they were sat down, 'The information you gave has been proved correct and I even managed to get inside the building and have a quick look around. Just as I was passing, the Fire Department turned up as there had been a false alarm on a faulty appliance in the building. I just followed in amongst all the confusion and did manage to reach the 12th floor before being apprehended by their security. I just babbled away in a foreign language and so they kicked me out.' Matt saw that he was small and wiry, relying on brains rather than brawn in any given situation. The eyes were steel grey and piercing but Matt was able to give him a cold stare back. Behind the mask of blandness one could almost see the brain working overtime.

'So you did not find out anything about the 13th floor?' questioned Matt.

'No, but I did find out that there is no stairway beyond the 12th floor, or at least nothing that was apparent. We are all agreed that there is a 13th floor and I did blag my way into a building opposite and looked across but the windows were all covered up.'

'We have taken up your suggestion, Mr Weston, about approaching Costain's level, and things are in hand with the appropriate equipment alterations.' La Roche now came in on the conversation.

'I saw that as we came in. Glad it worked out OK, as it was only really the germination of a thought when we spoke.'

'We are looking at a dawn start the day after tomorrow. The local team is being sent to take over the house and dock, ostensibly on the grounds of investigating information supplied by you. They will be aided by the local police. That will happen shortly before we go into the HQ building, and maybe Costain and Co might just be distracted long enough for us to gain the upper hand.'

'A long shot,' commented Matt, 'but anything like that would be welcome. Suck it and see is all we can do at this stage of the game.'

'The contractors on the other site have indicated there is no problem with the way you want to approach Costain, but I have to emphasise that we cannot be seen to be a part of it. You are on your own for that part.' La Roche was making it clear that he could not expect any help from that quarter.

'Understood. Since arriving I have already sorted out my backup, so yes, you can concentrate on securing the building.'

'You will have a quarter of an hour before the arrival of the helicopter squad, and that is the timescale we have to get our people into the building. Tight, but not impossible. Your time will start when most of the office workers have gone in,' La Roche finished.

Wender then took over. 'There is just one Security man on duty inside the lobby and we need to find a way to take him out. As the door opens there is a clear view of the control panel behind the desk and we intend to blast it with microwaves every time we can. That should cause some confusion as well. Trouble is we can only get in when all the workers are in because we do not know who works where, and someone might just be in a position to raise an alarm.'

Dave looked pensive for a moment, thinking back to when he had looked on from the hotel when they had caught up with Matt. 'After we had seen Costain at breakfast, I glanced at the entrance. There appeared to be two latecomers arriving for work in the building. They did not appear to be hurrying because they were late. Is that their regular arrival time? Are these the last to arrive and is that the time to go in?'

'Come to think of it, I am sure that there were a couple of late arrivals, but I really did not pay them much attention. I will check that out tomorrow.' This from Wender who then continued: 'Obviously you have a reason for mentioning that.'

Dave looked at Tony and said, 'Are we up for a bit of mayhem?'

'Count me in,' was the response. 'What did you have in mind?'

'If we were to accidentally on purpose follow those two in, perhaps we could then keep the Security man occupied whilst those two workers disappear; and then take him out to allow the rest of our people in. Job done.'

'I'm game. How does it sound to you?' With that Tony looked at Wender, sensing he was the man to put it all together.

'We had wondered how to take out Security without a massive invasion. Your suggestion might just work, especially if he is somewhat confused, but we need to get the controls on the blink for that,' La Roche answered, and he was getting excited. 'Let's build it into the scenario.' This last statement was to Wender.

Further discussions then took place as to the rest of the proposed action, and a particular job was built in for Vanman with his specialist skill.

Next day the fine tuning of the proposed offensive took place, with everyone being briefed as to what they would be expected to do. That night the specialist equipment was taken to the building site and put into place. Before dawn and once the team taking on the dock and house were known to have left, Matt, Dannyboy and two others had an early breakfast and were in the building site and ready. It all depended on other people now. If all the pieces of the jigsaw did not fit, the whole plan could descend into farce.

Felix Costain was up early that morning. There was a night vision camera set up in the grounds of his house which monitored the dock.

The mole in the Financial and Securities Authority team had tipped him off, but had also requested more kickback. Today he would be paid in full and final settlement. Nothing would be found at either the house, which was only his retreat, or the dock, which had not been used since Vassilev could no longer get the goods in. Time to draw a veil over that part of the operation and make sure no-one else outside knew of the clandestine parts of the Organisation in this building.

The situation of the house was such that it caught the rising sun. Just as it was starting to get light the alarm from the house sounded to indicate intruders and the camera picked up movement at the dock. He knew that the lock could easily be picked because he had made it so, and soon three people entered. He could see others outside but they soon followed. When he could no longer see any movement outside, Costain reached for a console and pressed a button.

Inside the dock all the people heard was the door closing automatically and the lock being engaged. Try as they might they could not reopen the door, and all other exits were similarly secure. To all intents and purposes they were in a prison, and then they heard explosions outside.

After locking them in, Costain had pressed another button and explosive charges went off at the bolts securing the dock to the land. At the same time, hidden motors in the pontoons on which it was resting started up and the whole dock moved out into the Sound. At a prescribed time, where the water became deep, the motors stopped and undersea vents opened. The air vents on top of the building were already open and within a minute the dock had sunk, taking everyone in it to a watery grave. The mole and its associated problem had been solved.

Once there it had been decided that the Police would take the house, with the Financial and Securities Team going to the dock. On hearing the explosions, the Police Chief leading the raid looked down and, seeing the dock moving, ordered his men out of the house. Was it similarly booby trapped? All he could do was stare as the building just disappeared. Nothing happened at the house, but they remained outside until the all-clear had been given later in the day.

Costain had a slight stoop and a deformed ear, which he had had since childhood. Being different meant he got picked on for a start, but fighting his corner was what had made him what he was now. Early in life he had found he had an ability to get back at people without seeming to be involved, and that still applied today. Throughout his educational life his brain had been able to assimilate facts, and at University he had been able to help others in various ways, some of which were not legit. Those favours he had called in but had not recoursed to blackmail where he could. That meant those people were still friends and at times they had all been able to reciprocate, helping one another.

He was a happy man as he went out onto the balcony to enjoy his breakfast, but became a little concerned when the builder's tub at the end of a crane came into view. This was followed by another above it and both lowered down at the side of his building and drew into the side with the top one at his level. An extension had been added to the boom of the building site crane to give it a longer reach, which allowed it to be lowered into the gap between the Cavalcade Building and the one across the street. Luckily, although there was a wind blowing down the street at pavement level, up there it was not as noticeable and there was very little sway.

A man stood up in it and hailed. 'Good morning, Mr Costain. My name is Matt Weston and I have come to have you terminate the contract on my life.'

At the sound of the name, the two men guarding Costain on the balcony took out their revolvers. Matt seemingly had both hands on the edge of the tub but in fact one hand only had the thumb hooked over. Hanging loosely on the fingers was an automatic with a silencer. As the two men started to bring their guns to bear, Matt revealed his surprise and shot both in the head. All this happened whilst the tub was moving closer, and when it reached the edge of the balcony, Matt, keeping Costain covered, climbed over.

'As I said, time to terminate the contract. I hate having to look over my shoulder for trouble. You are the one that set it up and you are the one going to end it.' A statement rather than a suggestion.

'What makes you think that I will do that? You have come in here expecting to leave alive. How stupid is that? There is no way that the contract will be terminated except on your death, and you coming here means that I will not have to pay out a million, just a bonus to one of my men.'

'Maybe, so perhaps I should kill you here and now, and then there will be no-one to pay out.'

'The Organisation will continue even though you might kill me, and eventually someone will track you down. You have been lucky so far but your time will come and your luck will run out.'

As Matt had gone onto Costain's balcony, two other men had left the lower tub to gain the balcony on the 13th floor. One of them, who was a Marine, had been given particular instructions from Matt. He saw the mechanism Matt had made him aware of and put a wad of Plasticine in the groove a little way along. The other one was from the Financial and Securities Team and, as he was staring at the windows, he did not see this happen or the second piece go in the opposite side.

The Marine was a demolition expert and his job was to affix charges to the window of the balcony. Every endeavour had been made to ascertain if those widows were really blacked out or just one-way but nothing concrete had been decided. All indications were that blackout was used but now came the time to really find out as the charges were laid. Nothing happened, and the two of them went to one side of the windows against a solid wall and hung an anti-blast blanket around themselves.

At ground level, staff for the various offices had already arrived, and from a public utilities vehicle a microwave jamming device was being played into the Reception area as much as possible. Nothing worked until nearly at the end when a larger group of people went in and the door stayed open longer, allowing the pulses to strike home. When the usual last two stragglers arrived, the Security man was busy trying to find out what was going wrong with the various pieces of equipment, and Dave and Tony were able to follow them in without problem.

As far as the latecomers were concerned the two who followed went to the Reception desk, so they went on their way. Security, realising someone was there, turned just as the latecomers disappeared into the lift. It had been decided that, whoever was about the same height as the Security guard would take him out and appear to mimic him.

It fell to Dave, who just vaulted onto the desk, sat there and kicked out with both feet. Security took both in the chest and as he went back against the wall Dave followed, knocked him out, and once at floor level and hidden by the desk, removed the jacket and cap from him and put them on himself.

Tony heard movement on the stairs and dodged by the lifts, hidden from view. A man appeared with earpiece and microphone and started asking what was the matter. Dave kept bent down with his back to the stairs and mumbled something. The man left the stairs, intent on the desk, and the first he knew of anyone else present was the tap on the head which rendered him unconscious. Tony grabbed the headset from him and started monitoring as he went to the door to give the all-clear for the rest of the people to follow. The man must have taken it on himself to come down as there was no chatter on the system during the rest of the operation.

Most of the newcomers took the stairs, two going to each floor. These were all from the Financial and Securities Team. Vanman came in last with a backpack full of explosives. He and three of La Roche's men went into the lift and Vanman lifted the hatch and went topside. One of the others hit the buttons and up it went to the 12th floor, where the doors were secured closed.

On top Vanman was satisfied that where the doorway to the 13th floor should have been was bricked up. Carefully he put the explosives in place and then got the lift to move up. The lift had buttons for all except the 13th floor but beside the one for number 14 there was an aperture for a key. Such had been anticipated, and one of the others, in addition to being an electronics whizz kid, was also knowledgeable about electrics. As the lift was rising to the 12th floor, he had the panel off and, whilst Vanman was fixing the explosives, he had reconfigured the wiring.

Because it was not programmed to stop at that level, the man had to cut the power to it so that it came to rest opposite the charges that had been laid. Back inside, Vanman forced the door sufficiently open to allow one person at a time through and set the fuses. All four now squeezed behind the unopened part of the door and covered themselves with an anti-blast blanket. Now it was time to wait.

All this happened whilst Matt was talking to Costain. Suddenly there was a loud phut and Matt knew his backup had been necessary. He did not look round but heard someone falling behind him. Inside the tub, Dannyboy had been watching for some such activity and was a little relieved when someone armed tried to sneak out onto the balcony. He felt as though he really was helping when he squeezed the sniper's rifle trigger. Sat in the bottom he could not be seen but the tub did not have totally solid sides, which allowed him to see out and take appropriate action if necessary.

Eventually the sound of an approaching helicopter signalled the arrival of the airborne contingent. 'Ah. The rest of my people are arriving. Time to terminate the contract and put your illegal operation out of business.' At that, the words 'All together now' from some long-forgotten song flashed into his mind.

'That's what you might think, but I have not kept going this long without a little backup.' With that he pressed a button on the side of the table where he was sat. The warning light for malfunction did not come on, so he casually made his way to the edge of the balcony.

Matt looked as though he was wondering what was going to happen next, but of course he was not surprised when, without looking, Costain just jumped over the rail. His scream, as he realised the safety net was not there, was drowned out by an explosion. As Matt moved to the rail and looked over he could see Costain's body spreadeagled on top of a car and the safety net awning eventually started moving out again. The Marine had used his gumption.

The arrival of the air support group was the signal for action. Six men abseiled down from the hovering helicopter and their touchdown caused a sequence of events to take place.

It was only Matt who was not in communication with the rest, hence the need for his backup. Had he been wearing an earpiece, Costain might have realised a bigger game was in play. Everyone else was in the loop and at the word 'Go' from the leader of those from the helicopter, Vanman triggered the explosion. Some of the blast came into the lift, but those there were safe, and immediately it was over they went through and into the room.

Outside on the balcony there happened to be a communication blackout, but as soon as he heard the other explosion, the Marine fired his so that it sounded as one long one. Having seen the body fall from the floor above whilst waiting for the dust to clear after the explosion, the Marine went back to remove the two pieces of Plasticine, whereupon the awning started to move out again.

The two of them then moved into the room. Across the room where the wall had been blown in, equipment lay in a mess, and a body was mixed in with it. One man nearby was obviously trying to clear something off the screen in front of him but received a bullet in the arm for his trouble from the Marine as both he and Vanman shouted for everyone to freeze.

On the other side of the room Vanman, being first into the room from that side, saw one of the workers, who had been taken aback by the explosions, try to bring a gun to bear on those entering from the balcony. For that he received a bullet in the shoulder. Seeing three men down, all the workers in the room just raised their hands, and at the next request to move away from the machines, did so and lay on the open expanse of floor at the centre of the room. At the same time the team from the helicopter had found the way in from Costain's 14th-floor apartment and arrived to take control of the situation.

It had all happened in seconds but to those participating each action felt to last minutes and reliving it later, everything was in slow motion.

On the 11 floors below, the Financial and Securities Teams entered all the offices at the sound of the explosion and closed all legal operations for the day until they were able to sort out which were legitimate and which not.

On the lower floor Dave and Tony had secured the outer door to gawkers and sealed the underground garage. Now they just sat looking at the magazines which had been left in the reception area for visitors.

On the top floor Matt watched as the crew from the helicopter came down the external stairway and into Costain's quarters before disappearing down the stairs to the floor below. The crane then swung the tub closer and Dannyboy, who by now was showing over the top, having raised himself up and supporting himself with his hands, was helped by Matt onto the balcony. The helicopter then hovered above, swung down a basket and Dannyboy was whisked away. Matt did not bother following the team to the floor below. Instead he went to the emergency stairs, but as he was crossing the room the telephone rang and he picked it up. Before he could say anything the voice at the other end said, 'Mr Costain.'

Nothing else needed to be said as Matt recognised the voice. 'No, Mr Fontaine, it is Matt Weston.'

'What are you doing there? Aren't you dead yet?'

'I have just terminated the contract on my life. Mr Costain was not very amenable to my request so he took a dive down 14 floors. The relevant authorities are now here and so there will be no-one to pay out on my death. As for anything else, well, you are on your own.' At that the phone was slammed down at the other end and Matt could imagine the consternation there whilst at the same time wondering what Fontaine had to do with Costain.

He then made his way down to the 12th floor, where the door was a panel in the wall, and he left it open. He took the rest of the stairs to the first floor and joined Dave and Tony. All three were soon joined by the rest of the Marines and Rangers who had partaken in the assault. The building was secure and in the hands of the Securities people. Now they had to wait for their transport away.

Dave was looking at one particular colour magazine, with Tony looking over his shoulder. 'Hey Matt. Over here. Can you see anything in these coloured patterns? Supposedly there are pictures hidden in them, but neither Tony nor I can see anything, or at least not what they say is there.'

Matt had come across such things before but had never bothered to check them out. This time, because his attention had been drawn to them, he came over and had a good look. Pictures he did see, but not from the patterns on the pages. Images of what he had seen in the pyramid came to mind and he realised what the colourful montage at the top of the pyramid was meant to do. Without going back and looking closer at it, he had no idea of the outcome. However, he knew that his priority now had to be to get back to the pyramid.

'Nah,' he said. 'Can't make head or tail of them,' which was the truth, but he hoped he had not given away that he had discovered something else. How to get away and get back to the pyramid was the thought uppermost in his mind.

About half an hour after they had all assembled, a truck backed up to the doorway and more men from the Financial and Securities Service, who had been in the back, entered the building and just as secretly, the Assault Team with Matt left in the same vehicle.

Back at the National Guard Base they were reunited with Dannyboy and each had to describe their actions in the presence of La Roche and Wender, who was finding out if his planning of the operation had been correct. The local Commissioner of Police was also present. All stayed together as a group until it was Matt's turn, and then he was alone with the three men. He explained what had happened but leaving out a few minor details such as the deactivation of Costain's safety net.

The Commissioner did not believe certain parts of his statement, which was obvious by the questioning, but Matt never deviated from his story. The Commissioner was doubtful that all had come out but thought it prudent, when he could not catch Matt out, to accept the situation. If he pushed too far a lot of things might come out which he did not want. He had to look to his future political career and here had been a big illegal operation he had not even been aware of, right on his doorstep.

The bodies, together with the injured and those who had been working on the 13th floor, were secretly taken away. That evening the local radio and TV stations were carrying the news that a crooked organisation had been closed down and by morning it was on national newscasts and all the daily papers. The latter even carried a statement that all illegal contracts taken out by Costain or the Cavalcade Corporation would not be honoured. This was a deliberate attempt to stop anyone trying to continue to kill Matt.

By next day all the Marines and Rangers who had stayed on the Base overnight, had been sent back to their particular units, but when Matt was called to see La Roche late in the morning he was surprised to see Tony and Dave waiting for him. All went into the meeting, where Appian and Wilberforce were also present.

Appian was the first to speak. 'You might be wondering why your two minders are still here. Well until we know you are safe, or at least of no further use to us,' which was said with a laugh, 'we want them with you just as they have been in the past.'

Matt noted the attempt at jocularity but could tell there was no mirth there. Get them the goods and he was on his own. Hopefully he still had a couple of aces up his sleeve. They would find out that they should not trifle with him. He also had a feeling that his job was not yet done but felt he had to object. 'It is common knowledge now that there will be no payout, so why?'

'No-one can be sure all those who might wish to collect the bounty are aware. Your job is still not concluded.' At what was going to be a query of that statement from Matt, Appian held up his hand and then continued: 'Identifying the places where these power lances are supposed to be, has shown that we, as Americans, will not be able to get to some of them. It is hoped that you will have better luck, and Wilberforce here has agreed to try to set up B-GEE expeditions as cover. For the moment your minders stay.'

'Just as I thought it was all over and I had done my bit, you find me more. I have had enough. Can't someone else take it from here? You Americans have teams that go into strange territories to carry out tasks incognito; why not use them?'

'Political and international ramifications if things go wrong,' interjected Wilberforce.

'So I am the dispensable one that can end up in some hostile country's prison. Forget it.'

'That is why we are building them all around some sort of expedition or exploration project,' Appian continued. 'B-GEE will organise but we will fund.'

Before he could say more Matt exploded. 'So you have sold out, have you, Wilberforce, just to keep your Organisation intact? I had thought better of you.'

'It is nothing of the sort, but I will admit pressure has been put on the British Government by our friends here and they are forcing my hand if the Executive is to continue. Short-term I have to accept the situation and, as someone paid by the Executive, you will have to accept it as well.'

'I'll resign first.'

'Don't be that rash. Think it over. You will see it makes sense, and all operations under this agreement will include you in their planning.'

Matt knew what he had to do and in so doing might eliminate the need for such expeditions, so seemingly reluctantly he said, 'Give me a little time to think it over, OK?' To this he received an affirmative nod.

La Roche then spoke: 'The initial analysis of the information picked up yesterday goes far beyond what we had hoped. We paid a heavy price for it though. The entire team that went to the dock were drowned when it was sent out to sea and sunk. The bodies have been retrieved and the apparatus that did the deed has been traced to Costain's quarters. Pity we could not have been able to make him pay for that.'

'Maybe I did. Between these four walls, it was no accident that he took that fall. I knew that he would go over the edge and caused the safety net to malfunction. Admittedly it was personal at that time but he did go down knowing that he was going to his death.'

'So Chiefie was right yesterday to think there was more than you were saying.' To which Matt just smiled.

Wender then said, 'We did lose some good men yesterday at his hand and it is no more than he deserves. However, on a brighter note, it seems our Mr Costain has been dabbling in a number of ventures, including an international one to ruin the economy, which could have allowed him, with outside money, to pick up the pieces.'

'The thwarted hijack. Did that delay the scheme?'

'Indeed it did. For that we must be forever in your debt.' La Roche was coming to the fore again.

'No wonder I had such a high price on my head. It must have given him and his backers a nasty financial headache.'

'He was also the Pacific entry for Vassilev's little capers, as well as other little schemes. In fact he was setting up a deal with someone you are acquainted with to try to muscle in on the east of the country.'

'Mr Fontaine. Hilary's other stepson.'

'How did you know?'

'Spoke to him on the phone yesterday as the raid was taking place.'

'That is why he was trying to scarper but we got to him first.' Appian started talking.

'Talking of Hilary's stepsons; any news of Berringer?'

'No, but his departure was deliberate. He had given up his apartment, sold the car and cleaned out his bank account. The only thing he did not do was resign, although he had cleared out his desk. Unfortunately no-one thought to ex-communicate him from the system and since your encounter down there he has been accessing our systems whilst on the move.'

'So he knows exactly what has been going on and what we are doing?' Matt raised the unhappy spectre and shook his head at the failures now mentioned.

'Not quite. Some reports which have been filed have been seen by him but not those appertaining to any action we were going to take or might in the future. And, of course, we have now made sure he cannot access the information any more.'

Appian was doing the talking but Matt could see he was up to his old tricks of limiting the information he was giving out, so Matt asked, 'So where is he now? What is he doing and why? If I am going out there, it would be helpful if I knew what he was up to and if it affected our state of play.'

'Yes, he is a factor to contend with. Where he is we know not. What exactly he is doing we are not aware of but I think we can guess that he is after the power lances, or at least one. His background had not shown any Irish ancestry but when we have looked more closely his great-great-grandfather was an O'Farrell. He died, or should I say was killed, shortly after his grandfather was born. Why, no-one knows, but it was thought to be related to clan rivalry. Anyway his great-grandmother remarried a Berringer and at the same time emigrated here to America. The whole family registered under the name of Berringer, hence the dead-end we had for a start.'

'So did he find something out from his foray into Vassilev's quarters? Was there something we missed by having to get out fast?'

Appian raised his hands to show he had no idea, so Matt continued: 'Ah well, we will just have to expect him to turn up at some time and hope it is not the wrong time.' He had a gut feeling that he would be turning up to try to put a spanner in the works.

CHAPTER 18
OVER SEA AND LAND

THINGS DID NOT GO according to plan once Oleg and Gregor had finished outlining their proposals to Vassilev. For a start, as soon as they launched the adapted mini-sub it became apparent that the balance was all wrong: the stern was nearly under the water, which meant that once it was submerged there would be a tendency for it to try and sink in reverse.

A redistribution of the weight took a couple of days, and when it was launched again there still had to be some juggling of equipment to get the right equilibrium. Submerging and surfacing in the cave provided no problem, and they went out of the tunnel for sea trials without a hitch. Once in the open sea, running submerged was satisfactory but trying to get things right for surface running to recharge batteries etc. showed that the system developed by Gregor was not working how they would like.

Return to Base and the layout was varied, but sea trials were problematic again. It took two further attempts to get things right, or as much as they could with their limited resources, before they were satisfied. Then the weather closed in and they had to sit it out for a few days before the forecast and actual sea conditions were favourable.

All the time Oleg had been in touch with his brother to keep him appraised of the situation, but when they were ready to leave he contacted HQ again and a voice answered that he had heard before but could not place. 'Is Piotr there?' he asked.

'Sorry. This is Pegleg; how can I help you?' was Matt's retort.

There was a spluttering from Oleg before he could speak further and then he asked, 'Where is my brother and what are you doing still alive?'

'There is a lot going on here at the moment,' commented Matt. 'Vassilev is dead and luck has so far been on my side.'

'How did he die?'

'Not by my hand. Another of his enforced guests took umbrage at the treatment he had received and tried to take matters into his own hands. Unfortunately others were involved, and in the shootout, aviation fuel exploded and all were incinerated.'

'What do you mean "others"?'

'Well, a troop of US Rangers first appeared on the scene and went down below. Then two of them, who it turned out, were not Rangers, re-emerged and started doing their own thing. But now a host of mercenaries have arrived and are throwing grenades into every building. I am waiting here for their leader, as I need things clarifying as well.'

'It does not make sense,' muttered Oleg, more to himself than to Matt, and then started speaking fast in Russian.

That was when he heard Matt say, 'If you are going to talk to me like that I am hanging up,' and the line went dead.

Oleg just sat there trying to understand the meaning of what he had heard. Four hours later he tried again and knew it had all gone down the tubes when someone answered in Spanish.

He was years younger than his brother but just looked like him when he had been first put in charge of the new type of submarine. He was three inches shorter than his brother, which was a more suitable height for a submariner. Once in the Service, he had stayed and risen through the ranks, unlike his brother, who had been seconded into the Intelligence Service. He had eventually made Captain and been put in charge of a fleet of mothballed submarines. That had been the cause of his disillusionment and the catalyst to side with his brother.

How much did anyone know about the setup? What part of the

Organisation had been put out of action? There was a need to find out and see if anything could be salvaged. It was now up to him, and the need for Gregor and himself to leave was becoming more urgent by the minute.

They left the next day after making sure that the two British scientists were certain not to get out, or not for a considerable period of time. In addition they made sure there was only a limited amount of food left. The submarine had actually been on its way to collect supplies when it had been sunk, and by the time they were ready to leave all four there were living on reserve rations. Not knowing how long it would take for them to reach safety, if they ever did, they took most of the food with them on the basis that their need was greater. Although Gregor had argued for an even distribution, Oleg had become ruthless and flatly refused, to the extent of loading it himself. If the scientists wanted food they would be able to go fishing for it.

Progress was good for the first two days as the sea was calm; well, relatively so for those waters. Then the swell increased and whilst it did not affect them when submerged they had problems on the surface. Every so often a wave would wash over the outboards and they would cough and stop. This meant someone had to go outside the sub and precariously take one off, and then the other had to pass it inside to be cleaned. As this was happening they were at the mercy of the wind and tide which took them anywhere but the direction they were supposed to be going.

Each of them took it in turn to rescue the engines and they were glad they had kept their Arctic gear, but even with that and waterproofs, whoever was on the outside came in wet through and had to strip off to dry out and warm up. The motor they had fixed inside to charge the batteries for the electric motors that propelled the sub underwater kept going, and that gave them the heat to dry out. They were able to make steady progress submerged until they had to surface again and the sea started playing with the outboard engines again.

On the sixth day they had to surface again to recharge the batteries and found the sea was really angry. They knew that meant they were getting close to the shore. Realising they would not be able to do anything on the surface, they made only a short charge of the batteries and then retraced their journey for a couple of miles before surfacing in better seas. Here they made a full recharge of the batteries whilst using the outboards as a means of keeping them on station.

Then it was one last push under water to the coast. They only just made it before the batteries died and they were forced to surface. When they did they found themselves in a large bay in which the sea was almost calm, the only surface swell coming from the few waves that entered. Most passed by as the contours of the land hereabouts was such that the sea's direction was parallel to the land.

The bay was deserted, with no life to be seen on land. That suited them nicely as they had no wish to be observed or have to answer what could be nasty questions about their arrival. The beach was sandy but of the gritty type and they had no trouble in driving the sub partly onto the sandy shelf, which stretched 50 feet out into the bay. There was another 100 feet of sand above sea level before it ended in a near-vertical cliff. It was into this they fixed a stake and tied a mooring line to it. The first thing they did after standing on the beach was to dance around like excited schoolchildren. They had made it. They were safe. Their makeshift craft had not let them down.

It had been early morning when they had entered the bay, submerged for as long as they could, and mid-morning before the sub was moored. There was plenty of driftwood and soon they had a fire going and cooked a proper meal from their supplies, the first warm one since they had set off. All previous ones had been rather al-fresco and cold. Just walking along the sand felt good after so many days of having no chance for exercise.

Afternoon was exploration time. They split up, with Gregor going left and Oleg walking off to the right. They had tossed a small flat stone to see who would have the choice of direction and as Oleg flipped the stone Gregor had the choice. Gregor had won, as the stone, which had a fossil showing on the side used as the definitive one, landed that way up on the sand. For no reason in particular had he chosen left, but something told him that was the way to go.

He was short and stocky, with his appearance showing his Polish ancestry on his mother's side. Thick black hair which, as it had not been cut recently, was starting to go curly. A walrus-type moustache covered the upper lip and hid part of the mouth. He had been around boats all his life as his father had been responsible for a small river boatyard, which he had ended up owning. However, as he was not the eldest, there had been no chance of Gregor taking it over, so he had studied marine engineering and joined the Navy. Both parents were now dead and he did not get on with his brother's wife. Accordingly, he never went back and had become an ideal candidate for Vassilev's employment.

Oleg's way ended at the edge of the bay, with cliffs seeming to go on forever. Because the arms of the bay reached out to the sea, he had started climbing the cliffs that enclosed the bay as soon as he reached them. Difficult in places, but he got to the top and then saw the rocky land spreading out before him for about two miles before another rocky escarpment rose up with clouds shrouding the tops. When he looked back across the bay he could not see any sign of Gregor.

Gregor had more luck. As he reached the part where the rocky outcrop at his side of the bay turned towards the sea he found a narrow fissure through the cliff and followed it. It twisted and turned and on a number of occasions he thought he heard voices, but when he stopped to listen there was nothing. Each time the fissure turned, he carefully peered round the corner before proceeding to the next one. It took him 10 minutes to negotiate its length and found that it opened out onto another bay.

This one had rocks right down to the sea, but moored against these were small fishing boats, and a little above the water level the ground levelled out, which allowed a village to have been built. Civilisation, but how safe would it be to approach the occupants? As he stood in the shadows watching, he saw a vehicle that looked like an old Land Rover drive down a track into the village. There was a way out by both land and sea. That could be the answer to their predicament.

He watched for about a half hour before retracing his steps. This time the traverse of the fissure only took five minutes and he emerged into the bay where they had landed to find Oleg running his way. Was something amiss? A glance all around revealed nothing. In case there was a problem, Gregor stayed inside the entrance to the fissure until Oleg arrived, and then asked, 'What is the matter?'

'Nothing now that you have returned. You took so long that I thought something had happened to you.'

'I am alright and bear good news. In the next bay is a fishing village, but there also appears to be a way out of it for vehicles.'

'Take me and show me. It may be the answer but we will have to tread carefully as we are here, wherever that is, without having declared ourselves. We are going to have to think up a covering story. But let us see the lie of the land first.'

Both went along the pathway that had been created by the fissure, and Oleg kept stopping, thinking he heard voices, but they both realised that it was only the echo from village life. Keeping to the shadows, the two men peered out across the bay. There appeared to be no continuation of their path to the village; it just seemed to peter out 10 feet above the water.

'I think I know where we are,' whispered Oleg. 'Somewhere along the Chilean coast, but exactly where, I am not too sure. Are we safe to make landfall and declare ourselves? That, as they say, is the 64,000 dollar question and we will ponder on that overnight. We are safe for the moment and haste could be our downfall.'

With that they returned to their bay and after another cooked meal settled down for the night in the submarine. Gregor dropped off as soon as his head hit the pillow, but Oleg was restless and could not get to sleep, as things were turning over in his mind.

Suddenly he sat up and said out loud, 'That's what we'll do.'

Gregor awoke with a start. 'What's wrong?'

'Nothing. I think I have found out our way from here but it involves a little piracy.' As Gregor looked at him quizzically he added, 'We will steal one of those fishing boats and sail away.'

'But they are ancient and it looked as though the engines would be as well.'

'True. But you are the genius. Actually there was one boat that interested me. It was powered by an outboard and I was thinking that if we replaced it with one of our powerful ones we could be long gone and far away before anyone knew anything.'

'Fair enough, I can go along with that, but which way do we go?'

'I have been giving that some thought myself. My preference would be to go up the Pacific coast, as I would like to cross that ocean before starting the next part of my search.'

'Search for what? You keep referring to the search for something but you never tell me what it is. I know you keep looking at the book you brought with you. Maybe if you shared the difficulty with me we could solve the problem between us.'

'I prefer to keep it on a need-to-know basis. Fear not, though. If we are successful and I need you with me to help eventually, we will both be made for the rest of our lives.'

'How do you propose to cross the ocean? I would not like to try in an old fishing boat. Pity we could not link up with the supply vessel.'

'That's it! I knew I needed you. I wonder where Captain Abramovich is at present?' With that he reached for the satellite phone and selected the appropriate number.

A rather sleepy voice answered. 'What is it? You woke me up.'

'Better than being broken off in the middle of making love,' Oleg said.

'Who is that? Come on, be quick or I will put the phone down.'

'It's Oleg Vassilev. I need your help. Where are you?'

'Stuck in Puerto Montt, halfway down Chile, thanks to your brother.'

'How do you mean? What has happened out there? I have not been able to get hold of him.' Oleg did not let on that he was aware the whole shebang had gone down the tubes.

'You must know that the Organisation has been smashed. Your brother is dead and I have not been paid for that abortive journey to supply your submarine.'

'That explains a lot, but I have only just managed to get away from

Antarctica myself, thanks to the submarine being sunk.'

'Well, I cannot do anything as I cannot afford to refuel this tub.' Oleg knew he did not mean it as he loved that ship. 'Me and my crew are stuck here until some means of rescue appears.'

'It is here,' said Oleg. 'I am able to pay for your vessel to be refuelled providing they will take gold.'

'One of the re-fuellers here will take anything, including your mother. I even thought about letting him have the supplies I still have aboard, but I know that I will get a better price in the Philippines.'

'Fantastic. I am on my way to join you but it will have to be surreptitiously. When I am nearer I will contact you again. Might take three or four days, but just be ready to go when I do get there.'

'Just make it fast as the crew is getting a little jittery.'

'Await the call and everything is going to be alright. Out.' With that he cut the communication and turning to Gregor said, 'Tomorrow at nightfall we are going into the next bay and taking one of those fishing boats, and if everything goes our way we will be on our way before midnight. Tomorrow I want you to take one of these outboards and prepare it. Also we need to offload some of the fuel as well.' With that, he lay down and fell asleep; things were falling into place for him. Now it was Gregor left awake, wondering how it was going to be done.

The following morning Gregor took what he thought to be the better outboard engine and stripped it down, cleaning every part before reassembling it. At the same time Oleg went to observe the next bay and saw the fishing boats depart. Later in the day, after helping with the transfer of the fuel required and a charging of the sub's batteries, he went to watch as the fishing boats returned, noting the location of the one he favoured stealing.

As dusk arrived, they set out in the submarine, submerging as soon as they could, and made their way to the next bay, where they waited under the water in the darkness of a cliff face until it was dark. Once satisfied everyone was in the village they slowly made their way to the location of the boat Oleg had selected and surfaced at the side of it. Nothing was moving on board and in no time the mooring had been slipped and it was being towed by the sub out of the bay. If anyone had seen it, they would have believed the boat was moving under its own power, as the sub had once again dipped under the surface.

Back in the bay where they had been hiding, it took less than half an hour to fit the new outboard and load the fuel before they resumed their journey. Gregor took the fishing boat and Oleg manned the sub. Straight out to sea and at the appropriate time the sub was scuttled in deep water and Oleg came aboard the boat. With the new outboard they made good progress northward and had about 100 miles under their belts before the first traces of dawn appeared and they had to find a bolt-hole for the day.

Another cove, but this time lush vegetation right down to the water's edge provided their cover. One slept whilst the other kept watch, and when it was Oleg's turn to be the watcher he had a wander but found no trace of human existence there. On one occasion a powerful boat crossed the end of the bay and a little while later it retraced its journey. A couple of times a helicopter could be heard overhead but whether either was to do with them, they did not know.

At dusk they set off again, but come morning the coastline gave nowhere to hide so they continued on their way but at a reduced speed in line with what a fishing boat would be expected to be doing. They kept out at sea but just sufficient to be able to see the land, hoping that they were far enough away from the bay where they had stolen the boat for it to be of no consequence.

By nightfall they had seen no other boat, and after increasing their speed they saw a glow in the distance in the early hours. By their reckoning that should be Puerto Montt, which then gave the problem of how to get to the ship without the authorities being aware. It was one thing that had been taxing Oleg's mind for some time and he thought he had an answer, but it depended on the terrain around the harbour.

As luck would have it, there were a few rocky outlets to one side of the estuary mouth, and before pulling into one, Oleg contacted the Captain again and gave his instructions. Half an hour later an inflatable with outboard pushed off from the ship, apparently with four people on board, and made its way to the rendezvous.

The Captain was one of them, as he needed to be sure he was collecting who he thought. The other was an armed seaman just in case there was trouble. The other two were dummies dressed as though working seamen. At the rendezvous they approached the fishing boat with caution, but Oleg and Gregor stood there unarmed. Close enough to have checked, the Captain then greeted them and nudged alongside.

The two dummies were stripped of their clothes and Oleg and Gregor took their place. The Captain and three seamen had gone out and the Captain and three seamen would return. Anyone watching would not be any the wiser. Gregor realised the outboard on the Captain's inflatable was rather old, so they swapped it for the one that had been taken from the sub. Once everything was transferred over, the fishing boat was set on a course for the wide sea, powered by the old outboard. Once it was sufficiently distant, the inflatable returned to the ship.

On board, the Captain asked, 'Have you got the gold you promised? The sooner we are away from this place the better.' Captain Abramovich looked like a pirate, with long white hair and a dark, full set of whiskers. The rolling gait of someone who had spent many years at sea showed. Relatively tall, but although he looked wasted, there was a strength about him as well as muscles. When he had joined Vassilev's empire, he had been clean cut, but a long time at sea had left him not bothering too much about his appearance. No family; the ship was the only love of his life. Vassilev had bought the ship, but in the Captain's name, and now that the Organisation was no more, the ship was his by default.

Oleg reached into the meagre belongings he had been able to bring along and handed a few bars over. 'That should suffice, I would have thought, but how are you going to arrange it?'

'There is one rogue around here who would sell fuel in exchange for your mother. No problem there, although we will need to go with emphasis.'

'No problem. First thing in the morning. Just let us get a good night's sleep. That is something we have missed over the last week or so.'

'Right, I have made a couple of spare crew cabins over to you. Let me show you the way. Admitted they are not that luxurious, but should be sufficiently comfortable for your needs.' With that he led them away and the two weary travellers were able to get their first full night's sleep since leaving Antarctica.

The following morning they awoke to the sounds of activity. Washed and dressed, they went on deck to find the fuel being loaded from a small coastal tanker. Seeing how the rest of the crew appeared to be scruffy, they did not shave and wore the clothes that they had worn the night before.

They went to find the Captain and saw he was entertaining a stranger, which one of the crew said was the fuel man. Because the Captain had said there would be the need to be hard with him, Oleg and Gregor returned to their cabins and armed themselves with a revolver each, which they just tucked loosely into their belts. Then they went to see the Captain, eliciting a few stares from the crew as they passed apparently armed. Once on the Bridge, the Captain saw them and their weapons and said, 'This is Mr Swenson, who has kindly agreed to give us full value of fuel for the gold. Mr Swenson, these are the two principals who have now taken control of the ship.' All three nodded to each other and Swenson noted the arms and the hard look in the eyes of the younger one.

He was in his late 30s but going to seed. Wispy hair on top of the head with unkempt beard below. The eyes told of the over-indulgence in alcohol the night before. Clothes were scruffy and looked as though he had dribbled vomit down them as well as having traces in the beard. When he left the ship he walked with a waddle.

After the refuelling was complete and Swenson had left with the gold on the fuel tanker, the Captain said, 'We are now clear for departure. The Port authorities are glad to see the last of us and have not asked a lot of questions. I do not know what your intentions are but I know I can get rid of the stores that you should have taken in the Philippines and that is what I have told them I intend to do.'

'I have no problem with that. My initial target is to get across the Pacific and as far as I am concerned the stores are yours to do with as you wish. All I ask is that when I am sure of our final destination, you will take us there.'

'Agreed. It is the least I could do. But why did you come in armed?'

'I picked up on your saying last night that there would be a need to possibly come on heavy towards the fuel supplier, so we thought we had better play the part. Anyway, why the change of plan?'

'Each night I allow two seamen to go into town and the two last night were my engineer and another. They found Mr Swenson the worse for wear, and knowing we were going to be dealing with him, brought him back here. Incidentally, my engineer has been checking the quality of the fuel supplied and is happy. Anyway, we struck a deal after I threatened to take him out to sea and dump him if he did not play ball, especially when he was still a little hung over. Everything was nearly over when you two ruffians appeared and it probably made him realise how good a deal he had got. Yes, I have paid a premium but not as much as he would have liked.'

Two hours later the harbour pilot was guiding them seawards. Most of the crew had been involved with fuelling and so afterwards a good breakfast was had by all. The Captain had enough funds to keep the crew fed with some raiding of the supplies not transferred in Antarctica. Once the pilot had left, the Captain set course westward for the Philippines.

Although the ship was old, a new engine had been fitted some years ago at Vassilev's expense, just to make sure there were no breakdowns when it was operating for him. This gave it a top speed of 12 knots, but by the time they reached their first destination it had been increased to 13. This was because Gregor spent most of the time with the ship's engineer and used his expertise to make adaptations to the engines. However, he also made them more fuel-efficient so that they were getting nearly 20 percent more.

Most of the time Oleg stayed in his cabin, poring over papers he had brought with him, although after a couple of days he did allow himself to become the cook for the crew. They were nearly at the Philippines when he had the breakthrough he had been looking for. Now he knew where he was finally heading, but the ship could not take him all the way.

The Captain did very well out of the sale of the supplies, and travelling without cargo, the ship made steady progress northwards. Their speed increased after further bits had been fitted to the engine. Gregor had told him what was required and he had been able to get all with the aid of just one gold bar. The Captain was a happy man. He would soon be rid of the two passengers; he had a fantastic ship under him and, already casting about for trade, had found a need on the Pacific coast of Central America. Two weeks or so and he should be back in business for himself.

As the ship entered the Sea of Japan, Oleg and Gregor parted company with the Captain and crew. It had cost Oleg another gold bar but the Captain had been able to come up with the local currency so that when they were on land they would be able to survive. They were about to enter Mother Russia at its most easterly part. At Vassilev's instruction, all his personnel had been told to keep their Russian identity papers and such. Oleg and Gregor therefore would have no problems once they were inside the country.

Getting in could be problematic. They left in an inflatable with an old outboard and hit the coast just short of a naval base. They sunk the boat and walked into town and caught the first train out; it did not matter where to; only a need to get away from that area before someone could start asking questions. It was only a local train, and three stops down the line they were able to alight, and with the help of a timetable picked up in the first station, catch another going in a different direction with only half an hour to wait in between.

The terminus for this train was a station on the line that stretched right across Russia, and with that many people milling around they were able to get tickets and eat in the café without any problem. Although not going all the way, they nevertheless bought through-tickets as that was what would be expected. Oleg produced his Captain's certificate, which immediately gave respect from minor officials.

Gregor, ever the pragmatic one, had obtained a map and one day into their journey, they left the train. It would not be until nightfall that they would be missed and by then they intended to have lost themselves.

Others had left the train at the same time and, by following the crowd, they found themselves on a bus going northwards, the general direction they were wanting. Gregor still did not know where they were bound, or why, but a trust had grown between them and he was happy to go along.

The end of the line for the bus was a mining town and those on it were mostly heading there, which meant they got a few strange looks. However, Oleg had no intention of going that far, and two villages before it they got off. Here they found a dealer who was prepared to sell them, for gold, two yaks and necessary trekking supplies, no questions asked. He even fed them and allowed them to sleep in the barn.

They did not feel able to trust him, so that night they slept and kept watch time and time about. Nothing happened and after the dealer had provided a breakfast of sorts they set off. Oleg had indicated the direction of intended travel and they kept to this route throughout the day. That was westwards into the wasteland, on the basis that they were from the naval base trying to find a new way of testing officers under extreme circumstances.

To the north, Oleg could see his goal. It looked like a range of mountains but he knew it was the edge of an extinct volcano, and it was in that direction they set off on the second day. If one had seen it from the air the centre of the volcano had only part of its perimeter, and that was what was visible to them. In fact there was only a semi-circle of rock around it, and the north side dropped off where over the centuries the land had become eroded.

The yaks were being used to carry both themselves and the supplies, but on the third day the one carrying Gregor gashed its hind leg as it climbed a narrow path. Gregor ministered to it for the rest of that day and when they set off again he walked and took some of the load. When he was near he would put his nose to that of the yak and caress the side of its face, under the chin and behind the ears. That made the yak, as they progressed a little slower than intended, become attached to Gregor as he continued to dress the wound. It followed him wherever he went, even if it was only to relieve himself.

Legacy of the Ancients

Instead of five days it took seven, but by that time the yak had recovered enough to carry the full weight of stores, although Gregor still walked at the side of it. If Oleg was concerned at the delay he did not show it. Instead of going round to approach the easy way, they went over the top on the crater edge through a pass that he had spotted when they were close.

Once they had gained the centre of the volcano they could see for miles northwards as there was no rim in that direction. They decided to make camp at one side of the edge of the crater so that behind them they had a cliff face protecting them from the wind and at the side there was a drop of 100 feet, but if the sun were to get up on the following day they would have some shining on the camp.

An hour after arriving they had the camp sorted and the yaks had been ankle-tethered to stop them wandering too far. It would stop them either climbing to go back out or finding a way down the other side. Oleg and Gregor were looking out across the country when suddenly a shot sounded and a bullet whined off the rock behind them.

Both dived for the ground, and looking over the edge they could just make out in the dusk a person pointing a gun their way and shouting in a language they did not understand. When they did not answer, another shot clipped the edge of the rim. The shots had made the yaks move more towards the cliff at the back, and they were the ones who first became aware of the other person.

The first Oleg and Gregor knew about his presence was when two bullets were fired straight after one another, nearly sounding like one shot, but a bullet gouged into the earth at the side of each of them. They rolled over to face their new adversary, who started shouting in the same language as the other. As no further shots came their way, they stood up and raised their hands in the air.

The man who had appeared behind them walked towards them, never letting the rifle waver from their direction. All the time he was talking loudly, but they could not understand as it was Gaelic. Oleg answered in Russian for a start but the gun waved him quiet.

Gregor's fear was palpable. He was an engineer and not used to active service. Oleg, on the other hand, was weighing up the chances of tackling the newcomer, and tried talking to him again, only to be waved into silence again.

Gregor's friendly yak could sense the fear in what it thought of as its friend, and as the newcomer, still covering the two men with the rifle, started talking to his colleague below, it charged. Too late the man realised something was happening, but as he turned and tried to bring the rifle to bear, he slightly lost his balance on a pebble. It only gave the yak an extra couple of seconds, but that was all that was needed as it hit the man head-on.

The rifle seemed to jump out of his hands and Oleg, who was the nearest, dived forward and managed to catch it. The man was just launched over the edge to fall the 100 feet to the bottom, but before he had landed, Oleg had taken out the man at the bottom with a single shot. When it was over, Oleg just stood there whilst Gregor went to the yak and started blowing nose to nose and caressing the head. 'That was brave, my friend,' he said.

Meanwhile Oleg was looking around and asking no-one in particular, 'Where did he come from?'

Gregor heard him and answered, 'I have no idea, but let it wait until morning. I have had enough excitement for one day.'

'You are right, my friend. We are a good team and you keep me from going headlong into things. Watching you over the past few days has shown me that haste is not always best. Better to be sure of the ground and your equipment before setting off.'

Neither could see where the man who had gone over the edge had landed because night had come, but they decided he could pose no risk in the dark, even if he had survived the fall. Just to be on the safe side and to ensure there were no others around, they took it in turns to keep watch.

Come the sunrise it was possible to see the body of the man below. The strange shape of the body showed it had not landed well. They started to look around their environment and it was Gregor who found the fissure in the rocks that led inside the wall of the crater. After 20 feet it turned, and darkness enveloped him, so he made his way back out and called Oleg over.

Gregor went to make breakfast whilst Oleg went inside with a torch. When breakfast was ready and Oleg had not returned, he went to the entrance and shouted, 'Breakfast is ready.'

There was silence for a start and so Gregor shouted again. Once more he was met with silence, but just as he was starting to get worried Oleg's voice came from a distance. 'Come and see what we have here. All our troubles are over and we have the Power.'

CHAPTER 19
ENDGAME

Having slept on things overnight, Matt was aware of how he could work things to his advantage, and rang Wilberforce, who was still in the States. 'Morning, Boss.'

Before he could say any more, Wilberforce asked, 'Have you decided if you are going to help us?' The question was given curtly.

'Yes, I have, and you can count me in. At the debriefing, it felt as though it was going to be me, me and more me without any US input. I realise that pressure is being put on you, but no-one yesterday seemed to give a toss about me. It nearly sounded like an instruction and not a request. The more I come across Appian the more I realise he is a cold fish and does not care a fig what happens to me as long as I come up with the goods. To him I am dispensable. On that basis, I will leave it to you to give him the good news.'

'Well, you are not dispensable to me. I am sure it would be difficult to find someone of your calibre to replace you. Definitely glad you have come round to our way of thinking, although from the tone of your voice I take it this is a rather reluctant decision.'

'To a certain extent, yes, but I think that is more because I have been on the go for goodness knows how long.' He was stretching a point, hoping it would be to his advantage. 'It will take a little time for you to set up any expedition, and so I am going to take some of the leave you owe me. How much am I owed?'

'If you are going to come on board wholeheartedly then you can have as long as you need to recharge your batteries.'

'How soon do you think I will be needed?'

'Probably about a month to have some semblance of a general strategy. Does that give you long enough?'

'Right. See you four weeks today in your office. In the meantime I intend to take Hilary on a bit of an adventure; back to where the pyramid is and do a bit of jungle trekking and such. Something she has said she would like to do. No doubt I will have to have the minders in tow.'

'Fraid so. Until Uncle Sam is satisfied about your safety from the contract, they are your shadows. You seem to get on with them alright, don't you?'

'Oh yes, they are great buddies but … well, you know.' Matt had nearly given the game away as to what he was about.

'Why do I have the impression that you are up to something?' Had Wilberforce sussed him out?

'Moi?'

'Yes, you. I can almost hear the cogs in your brain whirring round from here. Perhaps I do not want to know, but I take it that you have seen something down there that has a bearing on this caper.'

'Better you don't know, but I think there could be shortcuts to achieving what we want if, as I think, the information is at the pyramid. Let us just keep it on the basis that for the present I am going on R&R. That should keep Appian happy, especially if I am out of the way.'

'I know you well enough to believe you will not do anything to compromise the situation. So agreed. Just keep in touch if you find anything, and also if you don't. I will keep Appian off your back but suggest you make your departure quick.'

Wilberforce was going to be disappointed with him this time if he had interpreted the pictures at the pyramid correctly, but he said nothing about it as he signed off by saying, 'Right. I'll get onto it immediately. Speak to you later,' and with that he hung up.

The next call he made was to Hilary saying, in a happy mood, 'Grab your medication and some clothes for a bit of a jungle adventure. I have been given some leave and we are going down to Panama. Trouble is, we will not be alone as I still have two minders. Speak of the devil and he will appear. Are you up for it?'

'Wonderful. That is something I have always wanted to do. When do we set off?'

'As soon as I can arrange transport.'

Before he could say any more he was interrupted by Tony asking, 'Where are we going now and what have you got lined up for us?'

'A trip to Panama. Back to see the people outside the Pyramid. I have been given some leave before we get back into power lance expeditions and am taking Hilary down there. It is something she has always wanted to do. Just let me arrange the flights and we will be off. If I stay around here any longer I will feel as though I have to be on call, and for the moment I have had enough.'

'I got that feeling yesterday, when you came out of that meeting,' commented Dave. 'We all held back because none of us wanted to say something to cause you to explode, as someone could have ended up getting hurt.'

'Was it that obvious?'

'Yes, but we understood when Wilberforce put us in the picture. Mind you, we nearly had to twist his arm off before he would say anything.'

'We are here to guard you and needed to know what the problem was.' Tony now spoke. 'I hope you will look on us as friends as well as minders, and if we can help in any way, then please, please let us know. Remember the saying, "a problem shared". You take too much on yourself, no wonder it is starting to tell on you.'

'Thanks, lads. I may just take you up on that if things get sticky.'

'You are up to something, aren't you? Come on, spill the beans.' Dave was getting on the same wavelength as Wilberforce. Maybe it was the same type of education they both had.

'That might depend on who you are reporting to and why.' Matt could not really deny it.

'To all intents and purposes, Appian is now our boss.' Tony made the statement. 'Our remit is to keep you alive, but if something comes up pertinent to the current project then we will have to report that.'

Matt knew then he could be a little judicious with the truth. 'That pyramid intrigues me. It does not seem right in relation to others I have been in. There is just something about it; a secret waiting to be revealed. I can feel it in my water. I have been on the periphery of a few good finds and, whilst I am not a an archaeologist or anything of that nature, it would be wonderful to find something that I could call my own discovery.'

'Treasure?' asked Tony.

'History,' suggested Dave.

'I don't really know. Every time I have been inside, there have been other things to think about. It is only on reflection that there appear to be idiosyncrasies within the place. I just feel that if I can give it some time, I will find something of importance.'

'What are we waiting for?' Tony sounded enthusiastic. 'Sounds fun, and to be there at the discovery of something significant would be good. I'll go collect Hilary. Dave, you stay with Matt, and you, Matt, get it organised.'

By the end of the day, the four of them had landed in Costa Rica, as it was uncertain how they would be welcomed by the authorities in Panama. After over-nighting there they went on their way to the border, where they surreptitiously crossed into Panama and made their way to the Pyramid. On their arrival late on the next day, they were welcomed by those gathered there as if they were the Gods themselves.

The Shaman could tell immediately there was something wrong with Hilary and, on being told what, went away and came back later with a potion. He told her to throw away the other medicine and take what he had prepared, but she was a little dubious, so he allowed her to take both. In the morning it was as though she was a different person. The tiredness she had felt in the previous few days had gone and she was alert; ready for anything. After a few more doses of the Shaman's 'magic potion' she threw her prescribed medicine away. All knew that the potion would not cure her but it gave her a new zest for living and over the next few days she threw herself into the life of the village that was nearby.

Matt was glad of this as it allowed him time to explore the pyramid on his own, albeit with either Dave or Tony in close proximity, although once on the first day when he was alone he was stopped by a woman holding a small child by the hand, who pointedly asked, 'Did you kill my husband?'

Matt was a little nonplussed for a start but then saw the child had some European blood and memory of Vassilev's words came back to him. 'Vassilev?' he asked.

'Piotr. Did you kill him?'

'No, and the European man who came with me can confirm that.' Matt looked directly at her as he replied. 'We both saw what happened on camera.'

'I believe you, but how did he die?' Matt inclined his head towards the child, wondering if he should tell in front of one so young, but she continued: 'We want to know.' At that, Matt explained what he had seen.

At those times in the morning when the sun shone on the mural, Matt would study it. As the sun altered its angle of light onto the coloured montage, Matt was able to discern different images. In effect it was like a run of negatives on three levels and each one showed a separate piece of the action. After a couple of days Matt had some from each both in his head and in a small notebook he kept with him.

Once the sun had left the mural, he would go and explore the various levels of the pyramid, carefully noting if one of the pictures had shown something in particular. Also he climbed all around the outside, always making it appear he was seeking answers. In fact all his findings confirmed the information he had gleaned from the pictures.

The pyramid was strange. All internal walls were smooth, as though they had been made in the same method as the caves. Outside was completely different. Here it looked as though it had been built from rocks, which had no doubt been placed against an internal framework. All the rocks were of the same size, and from a distance the sides appeared smooth. The surface, though, had allowed Matt to clamber all over it, but there had been no hindrance when the boxes of gold had been slid down previously. There were stairs on one side and these had obviously been made in the same way as the interior. They were, as he had discovered earlier, steep, and the indigenous population at that time, being smaller than today, would have had difficulty in surmounting them. The steps led about four fifths of the way up, ending at the platform and entrance before the rest of the structure continued up to the apex. This was not a temple but had been created for a deliberate purpose, and Matt now knew why.

On the third morning Dave, who was with him, asked, 'Have you been able to discern anything from it?'

'Little bits, but none of them seem to make sense.' Matt made his voice sound unsure, although he had made a couple of startling discoveries. Then, to make sure he had not given anything away, he said, 'See if you can see anything.'

'All I really get is a blur of colours. When I focus on a particular area there appears to be something forming but I don't know if I lose concentration or blink. I seem to then lose it and cannot bring it back. I have looked at it from all angles but the main images that stick in my brain are all to do with a bright light.'

'That is a recurring theme I get. It must be something to do with the power lances, but how or what is beyond me at present.' Matt was lying. From the ones he had been able to decipher it was obvious that here was the key to destroying them, but there was also another strong message coming through which seemed to affect the Earth.

It took another three days before he had most of the story. Not all the so-called negatives had revealed themselves to him but in the main he knew he had been right about the mural and what he had to do. During that time he had been all over the pyramid from top to bottom, inside and out. Now it all depended on the sun being in the right place for it all to happen.

The top line of hidden pictures revealed the making of the pyramid by the likes of those whose body he had seen in Nevada and the pictographs in Greenland. The second line showed how to destroy the power lances and the last row proved that those who had created these wonders were also aware that the Earth would one day start to destroy itself, or at least civilisation would cause it to happen. Here they had also given an antidote, but both actions could only happen together.

For two days he did not revisit the pyramid, on the stated grounds that he had done enough staring at the picture and wanted to give his eyes a rest. These two days he spent with Hilary as she went about the village talking to the people and showing them how to better their living conditions. All this with the blessing of the Shaman. This was the centre from which a new Mayan civilisation would spread out at the appropriate time. The Shaman knew it would not be long before the way was revealed, but he too had been seeking the inspiration from the pyramid and had failed to find it.

After the sabbatical from his research of the mural, Matt returned to it and saw that the sun was in the right position. It had to be within certain parameters on the mural. Today was the day to act. 'Bloody hell, it has been staring me in the face all this time,' he lied, but put so much enthusiasm into that statement that Dave, who was with him, called Tony.

When he arrived he asked, 'What is it?'

'I have found the answer,' Matt continued the lie. 'Come on, let's go. It is down underneath this thing, although I am not too sure of what it is that we will find.'

With that he led the way down the inside of the pyramid until they reached the access to the tunnel. As he looked down he thought he saw a shadow move at the edge of one of the tunnel exits onto the place where the base stone lay. A second glance revealed nothing and he thought in the excitement of the moment it had been a mirage.

The ladder was still down and he had both the others go down first, saying, 'I am that excited if the ladder is not steady I might not step right. I need you to hold it for me.' They fell for it as he managed to inflect more excitement in his voice.

Once they were both down, Matt again thought he saw movement and drew their attention to it. At the same time he became aware that one of the railcars was standing there. Strange, and the hairs on the back of his neck started to stand on end. Someone really was there and he had an idea who, but without the ladder they would have difficulty accessing the inside of the pyramid. What was also strange was that the second car was not in sight.

As Dave and Tony both took their eyes and hands off the ladder, Matt raised it up and smashed the system for lowering and lifting it.

'What the hell do you think you are doing?' Tony was the first to turn back and see the ladder disappearing.

'I am going to destroy all the lances and then there is no chance of them falling into the wrong hands. Then I am going to save the Earth from its eventual destruction. The actual countdown will start when I reach the top of this pyramid and remove its cap.' Matt had originally intended to give them 24 hours to get well away, but the sight of the railcar made him decide to take immediate action. 'It will then destroy itself along with all those lances. Now, if you want to stay alive, get moving. You have time to reach the underground lake and escape that way. The dinghy should still be waiting for you. Now get in the car and go.'

'What is going to happen to you?' questioned Tony.

'That is in the lap of the gods, but I do not want the blood of friends, which I consider both of you to be, on my hands whether I survive or not. So go!' Matt almost shouted the last two words.

With that, Matt went into one of the side chambers on that level and removed a stone which revealed a hidden chamber. Once things started happening he would have only minutes to reach its safety before the aperture closed.

Being off to one side, Matt did not hear the discharge of guns below. Whilst Tony had been remonstrating with Matt, Dave had been watching where Matt had suggested and had seen a movement but nothing more. The other railcar then arrived and so the two of them got in it, but the controls did not work. The power had gone and that was why it had arrived after the other.

As the two men crossed to the other car, Dave looked to one side and saw someone dressed in black move as if to go under the pyramid.

Realising that one of those leaving had observed him, the person took out an automatic and fired a shot in their direction. Dave pushed Tony out of the way and, side-stepping, drew his own gun and had chance to get off one shot before the figure disappeared.

Tony had also caught sight of the disappearing figure and said, 'Who was that?'

'No idea, but if what Matt says is going to happen does, I am not about to find out. Come on. Get in that contraption and hope it works.' It did and they were on their way.

Matt by this time was climbing the stairs and had reached the platform when the figure re-appeared, having satisfied itself that the others were long gone. From one of the many pockets of the one-piece coverall it was wearing, a grappling hook was produced and at the second attempt it caught the end of the ladder, which Matt had carelessly left hanging there. A line was attached to the hook and, after pulling it down, the person made short work of climbing into the pyramid.

On the platform, Matt attracted everyone's attention by beating the drum. When the Shaman and a few others were present he announced, 'I am now going to destroy this pyramid and in so doing save the world. Get everyone away from here behind that hill over there or else they will be destroyed, and when it is all over look at your refuge hill from this side. Your dream is about to become a reality. Now go. There is no time to spare.' With that he turned his back on them and, with difficulty because of the false leg, climbed up to the top, singing all the time 'Climb Every Mountain'. Once there, it was with a great effort that he slid the capstone off and sent it clattering down the outside of the pyramid. Beneath the capstone, in a recess, was a large crystal, and as soon as sunlight fell on it the core began to glow and soon it could be seen from below, which gave the impetus for everyone to do as Matt had said.

The Shaman was in no doubt that here was the start of a new beginning. All the portents had been there and the signs had been increasing of late. Without making a speech, he ushered the people away to where Matt had indicated.

The countdown was on. Matt, who had climbed there with difficulty, then slid back down to the platform and went inside. It was now too late to halt whatever was about to happen and Matt had to make it to the hidden room and hope that, as promised by the mural, it would provide the refuge he would need. Including the platform area there were four levels in all and he had got down to number three when he was caught from behind.

'What have you done?' the person who held him screamed. 'The greatest power on Earth and you are destroying it.'

'So that people like you, Mr Berringer, and the Chieftains cannot have it. Nor anyone else for that matter who would use it for power and not good.'

'And just how do propose that this will save the world from its own destruction?'

Matt was not about to get into a discussion. His means of escape on the floor below he knew would be getting smaller by the minute. Pinioned as he was from behind, his assailant was taking all his weight. He swung his false leg forward and then brought it sharply back, cracking into the other's shin and then, for good measure, stamped down on the foot. Berringer cried out with pain as the weight of the leg caught him, and released his grip somewhat. Matt, using one hand to give additional pressure to the other, jabbed his elbow into Berringer. At the same time he was turning and, when facing his opponent, grabbed him by the arm and swung him into one of the side chambers. Because he was off balance he had no option but to go flying, and fell on the floor. Matt did not wait to see the outcome and immediately fled down the last flight of stairs and headed for his refuge. As the crystal increased its power from the sun, so it needed more energy, and this it took from the interior of the pyramid, whose core was plasma. It did not take long for the plasma to become incandescent and the heat started to permeate throughout the centre of the pyramid as the walls began to crumble. This action also caused a second stone to start dropping into place on the entrance to Matt's would-be refuge.

Matt could feel the heat intensifying by the second, and as he shot along the short corridor to his escape he could see the aperture becoming smaller. Taking a chance he dived head-first through it and had almost made it when his progress was arrested. The entrance was four feet long and the stone that was lowering was the exact dimensions of the gap. A second earlier and he would have made it, but the stone trapped his false leg, which he always trailed behind him.

He quickly undid the leg and crawled the last little bit into the refuge. If the stone did not close the room off completely, he would be fried. He was hoping the false leg would be crushed, but it was the foot that was caught. However, as it was not fully horizontal, the weight of the stone started to crush it and then the leg part moved upwards. That was sufficient for the foot to skid out from under the stone and be launched, hitting Matt on the head. For a few moments he was dazed.

As the crystal took its energy and the centre of the pyramid became hollow, the sides started to cave in as the construction collapsed. All, that is, except the four corners, which were reinforced and stayed intact. It was in one of these corners that Matt's refuge had been created. When he came back fully to his senses, he realised that it was bathed in a strange glow, and checked to see the entry was fully closed, not letting light in from the furnace which was now raging within the pyramid itself.

By the glow, which came from a small slit letting in light from outside that was then reflected from the surface of the walls, he could see that the room, if such it could be called, was four feet square and six feet in height, but totally empty. All around him there was a creaking and a groaning but his place stayed secure, although he could feel the build-up of heat. He first sat down with his back to the inside wall, but soon moved as it became hotter and hotter. How long he would be in that place he had no idea, nor even how to get out of it, so he sat with his back to one of the outside walls, replaced the false leg with the now-deformed foot and closed his eyes.

On the stairway, Berringer regained his balance and, when he dropped down a flight of stairs, he was just in time to see Matt disappear into his refuge. He raced after him, but too late. Looking up he could see the fire gradually getting closer and jumped down to the passageway below. The railcar was dead and as he got out to start running everything above him became consumed by fire, as the more it ate into the pyramid, the more intense it became. Eventually the pressure became too much for the crystal to give out and the rest just came into the tunnel. Berringer had not even reached the tunnel entrance from there when, like everything else in the vicinity, he was vaporised.

The railcar got Tony and Dave to the end, but for the last few yards it was shaking as the earth itself moved and rocks dropped out of the roof. The airlock still worked and they were through it, not bothering to close it behind them. They took the quick way down by jumping into the lake and hoping the dinghy was there. In fact, when they surfaced, there were two there.

They took the nearest one and started rowing as fast as they could, knowing their lives depended on it. The surface of the lake was agitated and more rocks fell around them, one or two actually bouncing of the edge of the boat. They could hear the earth trying to break itself up, and then, when they were about a quarter of the way across, the sound hit them. It was as if all the ghouls from Hades had been released: a high-pitched screaming magnified a thousand or more times.

Then, looking back, they saw it. It was as if the entrance of a furnace had been opened and the fire was coming at them along the tunnel. They realised they would not be able to get out in time, but before they could do anything the pressure wave in front of the fire came into the cavern, assailing their eardrums, making them unable to think straight. They watched, fascinated, as the fire stayed in the tunnel as the pressure built up in the cavern.

From somewhere in the recesses of Tony's brain, an idea emerged, and without realising what he was doing, he tipped them both out, overturned the boat and pushed Dave under it, himself following. having created a breathing space to let them think as the sound and pressure were muffled a little. Suddenly the surface of the water became calm. Tony knew something was about to happen and he outlined what they needed to do.

Along the top of the inflatable was a rope, which was now under the water with them. They both intertwined their arms into this rope, one at each side, and then hooked their legs together. No sooner had they done this than they felt themselves moving. If the assumptions were right, they were in for a bumpy ride.

The pressure inside the cave built up so much that it started to push the water out through the entrance. Once it started to increase, it did so at an alarming rate, and the two of them found themselves in a maelstrom as they were spiralled around and shot out of the entrance like a cork from a shaken fizzy drink bottle. Banged and bruised from bouncing against the sides of the entrance, they shot to the surface. Neither realised they had been holding their breath until they surfaced, but in reality they need not have as the water never came inside the boat.

Once the water had been expelled, the pressure still kept on building to such an extent that it could not get out of the entrance fast enough and the cap from the cave blew off. Even the weight of the walled compound which had been built on top could not keep it in place. Dave and Tony had only just surfaced, thinking they were out of the woods, when stone, concrete and other rubble started raining down on them. Glancing up, they could see the cap in its entirety cart-wheeling in the air. Because of its weight it did not move far away and eventually slipped down the side of the cliff. Neither of them saw it, as once again at Tony's insistence, they went under the upturned boat to protect themselves from all the other material which was showering down, only emerging when there was no longer the sound of debris hitting the upturned hull.

The crystal at the top of the pyramid changed colours by the minute and then it sent out a pillar of power. There was no colour to it, but to anyone watching it was nevertheless a visible entity. Most people on the outside had retreated behind the nearby hill, but two had stayed to watch. They were fascinated by the phenomenon but realised too late that they could not escape. The power surge upwards caused a wind of hurricane proportions to follow it and anything loose on the ground for a mile radius was sucked up into the vortex it had created, including the two, who became instantly vaporised. As it continued, bushes, trees and

Legacy of the Ancients

any other foliage were uprooted and taken up.

As the power hit the stratosphere, it started to spread out and the sky changed through various colours to end up with a grey-pink tinge which spread itself swiftly around the globe. As it passed over any place where the power lances had been secreted, it seemed to send out some signal and they started glowing and rapidly went through a change of colour until they eventually exploded, but none of the eggs situated with them were damaged.

EPILOGUE

IN THE NORTHEAST OF Russia, Oleg had just called Gregor to come and see what he had found when Gregor looked back at the entrance and saw the outside changing colour. Instead of going to Oleg, his curiosity was aroused by what was happening on the outside and he started back to the entrance. He had not retraced his steps far when there came a whooshing sound from behind him, quickly getting ever closer.

Inside the cave, Oleg was mesmerised. He had found the source of power his brother had been seeking, and there was also an egg-shaped article. No sooner had he approached the lance than it started glowing and went through a colour-change sequence. It then dissolved as a massive burst of power came from it. Oleg was thrown against the wall and the pressure continued to grow, squeezing the breath from him before squashing his body to the wall, flattening it like a pancake.

The pressure also found its way out to the entrance, overtaking Gregor, who had started running. It ejected him roughly and deposited him on the plateau outside, whereupon it started to dissipate as it was no longer in a restricted space. As suddenly as it started, so it stopped, but all Gregor could do was lie there, catching his breath, staring up at the sky with its ever-changing colour, and forgetting all about the breakfast he had prepared earlier. He was bashed, bruised and unsure which part of his body hurt most, but he was alive. Whatever had happened inside meant that no-one could have survived and he was in no fit state to prove the point.

His friend, the yak, had run away scared at the first indication of the sound from inside the hill, but when all was quiet, it returned to find the injured Gregor. It started licking his face and the stench from its breath made him decide he had to do something. Somehow he found the strength to get up and lie across the animal's back. In this manner he was carried down to the nearest village, where his wounds were tended, and he continued to live in the area, using his engineering skills to help the community. Although still in the vicinity he never returned to the cave, not having any wish to do so.

When all was quiet, the people who had been living around the pyramid came to look at what remained, but were astonished on looking back at the hill that had protected them. Stripped of all vegetation, there now stood another pyramid, but this time there was no mistaking that it was a temple, which had been raised to the Ancients who had created the other, as there, in front of the entrance, stood effigies of them. The Shaman did all that was necessary to give allegiance to the new-found sacred place and then, leaving the others celebrating, found himself drawn to the remains of the old pyramid.

Inside his refuge, Matt had eventually explored a little further and found that there was a small antechamber leading off from it and the roof of this was obviously meant to be raised. The space was cramped and he could only squat inside it. Matt could not move the slab and then realised that there must be earth piled on top. Looking out through the aperture that gave him light he saw the Shaman approaching and called out to him.

The Shaman looked apprehensive as he could hear this disembodied voice, a voice of someone who should obviously be dead, as Matt kept calling out, 'Over here. Not that way, follow my voice.'

Eventually he found the aperture, which allowed Matt to explain the predicament he was in and the way out. 'We need to dig the loose earth from above the trapdoor, but do not let anyone know what you are about. I want to disappear from here until the furore, for be in no doubt that is what will happen, dies down. Do not even tell Hilary.'

The Shaman went away a little perturbed by the instruction not to tell

Hilary, someone he had come to respect. However, he did as instructed, returning a little later alone and with a spade. He dug where Matt had suggested and found the slab of stone covering the antechamber, which allowed Matt to exert pressure from underneath and lift it. Once outside, he replaced the stone and backfilled with earth, scrawled a few marks on the soil as though something had been dragged across it so that it resembled the rest of the immediate adjoining land.

Matt's exit was on the side of the old pyramid away from public gaze, and when he emerged he was amazed to see that only the base from one side was still standing. At the side, where flat land had been before, there was now a rubble-strewn valley stretching both ways as far as the eye could see. Matt took this in at a glance and then was escorted away by the Shaman to a safe place from where he could watch everything going on without being seen. When eventually he found out how much damage he had caused, he was amazed. He had only thought the pyramid itself would be destroyed, and not anything like the large-scale destruction which had occurred.

On the Pacific side, the cave had been similarly affected as the one in the Caribbean. Both had been totally obliterated and the sea had re-entered, creating lagoons. The pressure travelling along the connecting passage had been so great that it had weakened the roof and, as soon as it had gone, the roof collapsed, creating the valley which now stretched across the isthmus. Over the next few days, all sorts of people turned up to see what had happened. Matt stayed hidden, being fed by the Shaman and being reminded whenever he looked down from his hiding place on the new landscape of the Sinatra song, 'I did it my way'. When all the hoo-ha had died down, he made his appearance and was reunited with Hilary, staying with her until her death.

Before they could be dragged back into the newly created lagoon, Tony and Dave managed to paddle the boat, using their hands, to the cliff face and climbed onto a small promontory. This was where they stayed for the next few hours until a Royal Navy frigate came into the bay to see what help they could give to anyone. Tony and Dave had no room to stand and could only wave from a sitting position but eventually they were spotted and rescued.

Once on board the frigate they were met by the Captain and Dave said, 'Corporal Paragem, US Rangers, at your service, and this is Sergeant Panchetti of the Marines. It is important we speak to Wilberforce of the B-GEE.'

'Never heard of him or it,' was the Captain's retort. 'Stop acting silly and tell me what has happened over there.'

'We are who we say!' This was Tony, saying it with emphasis. 'Now find out where he is so we can report to him. Time is of the essence.' The last part was nearly screamed and the Captain went away, leaving the two of them surrounded by curious sailors.

A shout from further down the deck a short while later called them to where the Captain was. 'I have learnt something today. The man and the Organisation do exist and he is waiting to hear your report. Come this way.'

As they entered the Radio Room they could hear Wilberforce talking to the operator. 'We are here,' intoned Tony.

The response was, 'Where is Matt? What has happened down there?'

'Sorry,' said Dave. 'We have no idea of Matt's status. He kicked us out of the pyramid before setting about destroying it. He said that it would destroy all the power lances and then re-balance the Earth.'

'The first part he could have done, as we are getting reports of seismic occurrences from all parts of the Globe, more particularly the areas where explorations were to be mounted. Not sure what he expects from the other part, as this cloud formation covering the Earth does not look benevolent. Satellite pictures from your area are just coming through, although fuzzy because of the cloud formation. Digital enhancing is being undertaken at present, but the initial images show that the pyramid has all but disappeared and been replaced with a valley.'

'Not surprised,' was Dave's comment. 'The power that we experienced was on a colossal scale and capable of anything.'

Wilberforce then continued: 'Strangely, though, a new pyramid has appeared nearby and there is a lot of interest in what has happened there.

Stay where you are. Do not, I repeat, do not go back on land. Mr Appian is arranging to recover you so we can have a full debriefing. Thanks for letting me know the position. All we can do now is hope that he managed to escape somehow.'

The Captain and Radio Officer stood there gobsmacked at what they had heard. As they awaited instructions, Dave and Tony were given food and a change of clothing.

It took two days before the discoloration of the sky faded and normal sunlight could return, but when it did the experts found out that the hole in the Ozone Layer had been repaired. Gradually over the year, the ice stopped melting at its alarming rate and the sea level actually dropped by a couple of millimetres. All but one of the lances had been destroyed. One remained intact. This was the one Matt had seen in Nevada. Working on his suggestion, it had been crated up and sent up to the Space Station on a Shuttle that had been launched a few days earlier. It had been marked as equipment for future use and put in storage there to await the opportunity of the Army getting their man up to the Space Station.

A few days later the US submarine *Michigan* came to the Antarctic and made its way into the cave there. It was a smaller one to the Bradenton and time had been taken to fit it out with various sensors so that it could better negotiate the way in. When they surfaced they were astonished to find it already a working base.

Following the return of McPherson and Colton to the Base, they had persuaded Bill Morgan to look at the possibility of moving into the cave, and had shown him the way in from the surface. This was the way they had been taken on being captured by the Russians, when they had been caught in the open tampering with the British equipment. A flurry of encoded messages had resulted in the go-ahead, and those at the Base made a start on opening up the entrance. A group of men from the RAF Regiment had been on a winter training exercise in New Zealand. Having the appropriate Arctic clothing, their orders had been changed. A Hercules in that area had been diverted to pick them up and then disappeared off the radar as it took them to the Antarctic Base and landed them before returning to its original duties.

With the additional manpower it had proved easy to get into the cave and get it working as a Base, without giving the game away. When the submarine surfaced they found themselves welcomed, but at each side there were armed men. This was going to stay a British Base, although through time it became an international one because of its size, but still remained under British control.

MELROSE BOOKS

If you enjoyed this book you may also like:

An Ordinary Signalman
John Dawson

John Raymond Dawson joined the Royal Navy in Leeds, his home town, in December 1940 aged 19, with his best friend Norman Brooks. He served until early 1946, which was when he wrote up his "diary" setting out his experiences during the War.

His son promised him in 1985 that one day he would write this up for publication. John agreed but only if this was after his death. Sadly this came too soon in the following year when he was aged just 64. In 1999, letters John had written during the War to his elder sister Eileen were found in her attic when she was moving. This provided more valuable material to work on. He has written *An Ordinary Signalman* since he retired in 2006.

Being a signalman in the Navy led John to see parts of the world he would not otherwise have seen. He saw danger even in his training at Devonport from severe German bombing in the week of his arrival. He visited the USA and Canada before a relatively quiet time based in Scotland on HMS Forth, a submarine depot ship. John had to swim for his life in January 1944 when after being involved at Minturno and Anzio, HMS *Spartan* was sunk. He and most survivors then joined one of the most famous ships of the Second World War the light cruiser HMS *Aurora*. He saw action at the invasion of the South of France at Toulon, at the liberation of Greek islands and Greece itself, before playing a lot of cricket in Malta.

The diary and letters provide an insight into the adventures of a young man from Leeds, progressing from Ordinary Signalman to Yeoman of Signals, seeing action from the bridge in his signalman's role. They also provide an insight into the effects on him being far from home and what was a very close family, with his strong beliefs and views often expressed.

Size: 234 mm x 156 mm
Binding: Royal Octavo Hardback
Pages: 160
ISBN: 978-1-906561-04-8
13.99

St Thomas' Place, Ely, Cambridgeshire CB7 4GG, UK
www.melrosebooks.com sales@melrosebooks.com

MELROSE BOOKS

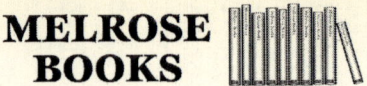

If you enjoyed this book you may also like:

Solomon Quest
Andrew Whitehead

Underwater adventurer Jim Lawrie is lured to the Solomon Islands by an offer to explore a newly discovered wreck. Diving from the M.V. Solomon Explorer, Jim identifies the wreck as a Japanese submarine from World War Two. Rumours of smuggled treasure are a regular occurrence in the Solomons, and a story quickly spreads that the wreck contains a large shipment of gold.

The beautiful, feisty and independent Rene Armstrong is also on board ship for a diving holiday. The two soon join forces to explore the deep, mysterious wreck, ward off the Japanese dive team who are keen to recover the gold, and the deadly local gangsters eager to steal the bullion for themselves.

Jim's quest takes him to the very limits of normal scuba diving and into life-threatening danger as he struggles to uncover a secret that has rested on the sea floor since WWII.

Size: 198 mm x 129 mm	Pages: 336	
Binding: B Format Paperback	ISBN: 978-1-905226-65-8	£12.99

The Inheritance
George Timmons

John More, a 36 year old Englishman takes a space ship flight, won on a TV game show, to the moon and back but on his return journey somehow manages to travel through time to the year 4058, two thousand years into the future.

Here he learns of the 'Dark Times' when chaos gripped the world and discovers how humankind descended into a maelstrom of war and oppression, of famine and disease, of exploitation and suffering, before, after centuries of misery, they formed the utopian society in which he finds himself. But can he live with the knowledge he has gained? Can he return to his own time to warn of what is to come or must he come to terms with the new world?

The Inheritance is in turn a romantic love story, an exciting sci-fi adventure and a theological and philosophical meditation on the ills of modern society and on what life could be like if we followed the original teachings of Christ.

Size: 234 mm x 156 mm	Pages: 224	
Binding: Hardback	ISBN: 978-1-906050-05-4	£13.99

St Thomas' Place, Ely, Cambridgeshire CB7 4GG, UK
www.melrosebooks.com   sales@melrosebooks.com